Marya Hornbacher's first non-fiction was published to critical acclaim in 1998. She is now Senior Editor at *Minneapolis-St. Paul Magazine* as well as Adjunct Professor of creative writing at the University of Minnesota. *The Centre of Winter* is her first novel. She lives in Minneapolis, Minnesota.

By the same author

Wasted: A Memoir of Anorexia and Bulimia

MARYA HORNBACHER

The Centre of Winter

HARPER PERENNIAL
London, New York, Toronto and Sydney

Harper Perennial
An imprint of HarperCollins*Publishers*
77–85 Fulham Palace Road
Hammersmith
London w6 8jb

www.harperperennial.co.uk

This edition published by Harper Perennial 2006
1

First published in Great Britain by Fourth Estate 2005

A catalogue record for this book is available from the British Library

This novel is entirely a work of fiction. The names,
characters and incidents portrayed in it are the work of the
author's imagination. Any resemblance to actual persons,
living or dead, events or localities is entirely coincidental.

ISBN-13 978-0-00-655205-5
ISBN-10 0-00-655205-6

Typeset in New Baskerville with Van Dijck MT display

Printed and bound in Great Britain by Clays Ltd, St Ives plc

For Officer Christie Nelson, M.P.D.

ACKNOWLEDGMENTS

This book is a love letter to the people who surrounded me while I wrote it, waiting patiently, encouraging, supporting, and believing in what would ultimately become.

I thank the readers who read and critiqued this novel in countless drafts, including Ruth Berger, David Batcher, Lora Kolodny, Marlee MacLeod, Patrick Whalen, Megan Rye, William Swanson, and many others. There is no way to either name them all or thank them enough for their intelligence and insight.

I thank Joy Johanessonn for her invaluable editorial insight and work on the book in its latter drafts. The book would not have come to completion without her, and I am indebted to her astonishing gifts in coaxing the story to light.

To say I thank Sydelle Kramer, my agent, and the Frances Goldin Literary Agency, is an understatement. Your absurd faith in me and in this book made it possible. There is too much for which to thank you, so I shall leave it at that.

Thanks to Terry Karten for her astonishing loyalty, kindness, and faith during this process. I have finally written the book I wanted to write for you, and I am deeply grateful for your patience as I learned to write a novel we both could love.

Finally, thanks beyond words to my family and my friends. As for Jeff, my husband, closest editor, and most faithful fan, all my love.

But where was I to start? The world is so vast, I shall start with the country I know best, my own. But my country is so very large. I had better start with my town. But my town, too, is too large. I had best start with my street. No, my home. No, my family. Never mind, I shall start with myself.

—*Elie Wiesel*

 KATE

It begins with a small town, far north.

Motley, Minnesota, Pop. 442. Near the headwaters of the muddy Mississippi, past the blue glass of the cities and the stained red brick of the warehouse districts, past the long-abandoned train stations and the Grain Belt sign and the Pillsbury Flour building on the riverbanks, past the smokestacks and hulking wrecks of the industrial section, the town lies past all this, in the centre of the prairie that creeps north and west of the river, into the Dakotas.

Seen from above, this prairie, its yellow grasses, is dotted sparsely with towns too small for mapmakers' concern.

Just south of Staples, on the county road that runs through the centre of town, passing the school at the south edge, Norby's Department Store, Morey's Fish Co., the market with the scarred front porch, the old brick storefronts with small wooden signs on hinges, the painted names of businesses faded and flaked. Morrison's Meats, the Cardinal Cafe. By the time you've noticed that you're passing through, County Road 10 swerves sharply to the left, past Y-Knot Liquors, and all semblance of town disappears, leaving you to wonder if there was a town after all. All you see are acres and acres of field.

On the corner of Madison Street is a pale eggshell-blue house with three steps leading up from the walk and a postage stamp of yard in the back where my mother, when the spirit moved her, gardened feverishly and then let the garden go sprawling untended in the tropical wet of July.

My father would sit on the back porch watching her, sitting the way men here sit: leaned back, feet planted far apart, arms on the arms of the chair, a beer in his right hand. The beer would be sweating.

They met in New York, at a club. They met and got married at city hall, and when I had my mother alone, I demanded she tell me again about the dress she made from curtains, and the red shoes, and the garnet necklace she got for a song. They had a party with cheap wine back at the apartment. I picture it all in rich colors. I remember the club for them, with red walls and small, spattered candles on the tables. Whether it had these things or not is of no concern to me, because it's my story, not theirs.

The garnet necklace is mine now. I keep thinking I ought to get the clasp repaired.

"What were you wearing?"

My mother was soaping my head.

"Sweetheart, I don't remember. Dunk," she said. I dunked and spluttered.

"You have to remember," I insisted. She laughed. "All right," she said, and I could tell she was going to make it up, and I didn't care. "Black. A black coat. And a hat."

"What kind of hat?"

"Katie, for heaven's—hold still—what? A hat with a feather." She scrubbed my ears. In the hall my father was yelling for her, and the door opened. She turned to look at him.

"There you are!" he said. "When's dinner?"

"I'm bathing Katie."

"I can see that."

"When I'm done."

He stood there. "Esau's sulking," he said.

My mother turned back to me and started scrubbing my neck ferociously. "What am I supposed to do about it?"

"Hi, Daddy," I said.

"Hiya, kiddo," he said. "I see your mother's in one of her moods again."

I nodded. My mother rolled her eyes.

"Well, all I can say," my father said, and then paused as if thinking. "Yep," he noted with finality, and closed the door.

In the summer I wore a white nightgown and the sun didn't quite set, the sky turning a faint purple that lingered late. We ate dinner out on the back porch. My father was watching the sky.

"We ought to go down to the city," he said.

My mother snorted.

"What, we shouldn't go down to the city?" my father asked. "You don't want to go down to the city? There was something wrong with the suggestion?"

I sucked on my tomato wedge. My mother said nothing.

"Claire?" my father said. "Answer me. Do you or do you not want to go down to the city?"

"Mom, just answer him," Esau muttered.

We waited.

"Yes," my mother said carefully, "I would love to go down to the city."

My father grinned. "Good!" he said. "We'll have dinner. See a show." He looked around the garden, pleased, and took a swallow of his drink. He leaned over and kissed my mother on the cheek. "Good," he said again.

My mother smiled faintly at her plate.

We would never go down to the city.

The light was fading, the way light fades in a memory, objects losing their definition, faces falling into shadow. My mother was clearing the table and telling me to get ready for bed.

And the house settled into obscurity for the night. My father watched night fall over his small square of the world while his wife did the dishes and his children did whatever it is that children do before bed.

What was he thinking about?

Perhaps my mother startled slightly when he came up behind her at the sink and placed his hand on her arm.

Perhaps she relaxed, and turned her face a little toward him.

Perhaps they danced then in the living room, to old records, while I stood in my white nightgown and watched through my cracked-open door.

I went to bed to the muffled sound of Count Basie, and the hot night, and imagined my brother on the other side of the bedroom wall.

It was 1969. America had gone all to hell, but that was far away.

Nothing could happen to us because it was June and my brother was sleeping and my mother was the most beautiful woman in the world. Soon my father would dip her, kiss her, go to the bar for another drink.

Esau and I squatted by the lake, using sticks to overturn the dead fish that washed ashore from time to time, poking holes in their staring eyes, and took turns telling ourselves stories.

"Mother comes from Georgia. Down south," he said.

"Where's that?"

He nodded his head in a direction.

"Are there snakes?"

"Yes. Don't eat that," he said, and slapped my hand.

"Is she rich?"

"Who, Mother? She was."

"Till when?"

"Till she went to New York."

"Then they were bohemians."

Esau nodded.

"If I poke it in its belly, will its guts spill out?"

Esau shrugged. "I don't know. Try it," he said.

I did. A spray of water, then a spiral of wet guts. "And she got knocked up," I said, prompting him. "With you."

He nodded.

"And you slept in a drawer. In the apartment in New York."

He smiled.

"They took you to the parties and you slept in the coats."

He nodded, still smiling.

"Do you remember?"

"No." He stirred his stick around in the split belly of the fish. "I don't know," he said, shrugging. "Maybe."

I was jealous of this. I narrowed my eyes. "Liar," I said, and wandered off down the shore, looking for a new fish.

He crouched next to me again because we were by the water and he was twelve and in charge and you can drown in two inches of water, even, whether you thought so or not. I thought about lying down on my front and putting my face in the water to test the truth of this. I tapped my stick on the fragile shells of sea snails and scraped the shatterings back into the slow lick of the lake tide.

"Were they happy?" I asked.

"No."

I looked at him sharply.

"They were never happy." He pressed his lips together like he did when he was thinking, digging a hole in the fish-smelling mud.

"They said they were happy," I accused. He had his facts wrong.

"They lied."

He stabbed his stick in the centre of the hole he'd dug. He grabbed my hand. "C'mon," he said.

I pulled my hand away and walked a few feet behind him, kicking mud at the back of his legs.

"They were happy," I called up to him.

"Okay, they were happy," he called back. "Suit yourself."

"They said they danced," I called. "They still do, sometimes. In the living room. I see them."

He stopped and waited for me, looking over his shoulder.

We walked along in silence for a good while, looking out at the lake.

"I want an Icee," I said, feeling as if I had lost.

We were at another funeral party. I wasn't sure who had died this time, but it was a suicide, and upsetting because it was completely out of season. No one killed themselves in summertime. It was rude.

Suicides start at the centre of winter, and fall like dominoes all the way down the square row of days, until the weight of snow lifts off and lets us breathe again in spring.

There were the gathered loved ones. The gathered loved ones hovered around the edges of my childhood like heavy ghosts, faceless, vaguely disapproving, square and wearing wool. They said *make do. We make do.* My grandmother saved the ham bone and the scraps of soap, making a new soup, boiling the soap into a new bar. Nothing wasted.

When someone killed themselves, it was a waste. No one ever said so, but we knew.

My father will kill himself. It will be a waste. We will have to make do, and hold our chins up when we walk down the street.

But we were still back at the funeral party. My father was still alive, he was standing with the rest of the men by the table, eating off a paper plate, stabbing meatballs with a toothpick as if he was popping balloons. I was six; this was the year before the year that collapsed on us like a roof caving in from the weight of snow. My father was intoning. I was tracing the pattern of blue flowers on the couch that had a scratchy nap, like Uncle Lincoln's stubble on his chin when he kissed me on the mouth with pursed lips. I wiped the kiss off with the hem of my dress and my mother whacked the back of my head.

The older women did not approve of my mother. She was, they whispered, a little different.

My mother was God.

The gathered loved ones sat stiff in their wooden pews in the chapel that afternoon, expressionless. They were stuffed into their second-best suits and dresses (first best were saved for going to the city once a year to the theater to see Shakespeare), which itched at the armpits and high collars. They sat through the warbling ancient soprano's keyless meander through "Amazing Grace," through the emotive (and really, they said afterward, at the reception, a little excessive, didn't you think? I mean, considering everything) eulogy by the weeping son. They lifted their eyes to the heavens so as not to see the pallbearers' embarrassing inability to lift the casket, nor hear their impromptu muttered recruitment of their wives. They filed slowly out of the chapel behind the precariously tilted casket, squinted in the sudden Saturday-afternoon sun, gloved hands lifted to shade the eyes. They endured the pastor's heartfelt two-handed hand-clasping as the mourners shuffled by, his excess of eye contact as he gave his condolences to each and every person. I sat in the backseat of the car, pulling at the collar of my dress and breathing on the window, writing my name backward on the glass: ETAK.

At the funeral party I sat wedged between my mother and someone's aunt Eunice, looking out the window at the lake, watching the sun set orange and pink on the last few boats. I wanted to go outside, but my mother was holding my wrist, gently, just forefinger to thumb, under the folds of her skirt. I leaned against her and watched Aunt

Ethel's head shake as she spoke. Everyone forgot themselves and started slipping into German, their voices dropping into warm growly sounds. Because it was a funeral party, the ladies allowed themselves a drink. My mother drank water and stared into space.

I fixed my eyes on my brother, across the room. He had his hands in his pockets and was standing in the doorway to the porch, looking out. He hated funeral parties. Uncle Ted sat in an armchair staring at the TV, which wasn't on.

"The boy isn't right," said Cousin Bernie, and I turned to look at her. She was ugly, including a wart. She meant Esau was crazy. That was the talk. I didn't believe it, and I stared at him as if to fix him correctly in place. Set him right.

"Takes after his father," sniffed Mrs. Johannesson. My cheeks got red. My mother's hand tightened around my wrist. They were talking as if we weren't there, knowing we couldn't talk back. We couldn't talk back because we weren't like them. We weren't as good. My mother's nostrils flared, her collarbone rising and falling in measured breaths.

The Schillers, people said. *You know about them.*

I was *that Schiller girl.* My name made a sort of spit-hiss sound when they said it. *That poor Schiller girl,* they said, and I turned and stared.

"Remember the aunt? Arnold's sister. Mad as a hatter. Frail as china. Always fluttering around. You remember," the women said to each other, shaking their heads.

"Jabbering about God knows what, writing things down on little bits of paper and putting them in her pockets. Taking to her bed," the woman said, and the others snorted and said hmph.

Arnold's sister was my aunt Rose. She died before I was born, when my father was young, before the war. They said she was beautiful. I pictured beautiful Aunt Rose taking to her bed, tossing among the silky pillows, looking frail. The door closed, the heavy curtains drawn.

No good woman would take to her bed. I knew that. A good woman didn't even sit, except at funeral parties, let alone take to her bed. A good woman stood in the kitchen, or dusted.

My mother was not a good woman. She worked. She caused a rustle of whispers when we walked down the street. I copied the almost-a-smile she gave the other women, and her not-really-a-nod.

"And what happened?" asked a stupid fat woman who didn't know about my dead aunt Rose, her hand at her throat.

"Hung herself," crowed Aunt Ethel, who was not really an aunt anyway. "In the drawing room on Christmas Eve. There she was, dangling from the chandelier in her best dress." She gestured toward the ceiling and we all looked up, as if expecting to see the chandelier.

They all shook their heads. Three times. Hmm, hmm, hmm. The End.

They always told this story at funeral parties. It was the best dead-person story they had, so they told it again and again. I liked it myself. The Story of Dead Aunt Rose. I liked it the same way I liked The Story of Teddy's Last Ride—the time Uncle Ted got so schnockered he suddenly stood up from his chair and went rumbling out to his new Studebaker, waved to Aunt Agnes who stood white haired and whimpering on the porch, and peeled backward out of the drive, yelling, "Here he goes! Teddy's going for his last ride!"

It wasn't really his last ride. He just ran the car into a tree. But Aunt Rose went and did it. I had a certain admiration for Aunt Rose. I pictured the drawing room—having never seen a drawing room, having never even been out of Motley except once, but nevertheless I pictured it all rose colored, the walls and the fabric on the couches and chairs, and paintings of roses. A Christmas tree, obviously. And Aunt Rose in her best dress, swaying slightly from the chandelier.

I always pictured her with a little smile on her face. And tiny buttonhook boots peeping out from under the best dress.

"Well, and you know," piped up the small-voiced, tiny Mrs. Knickerbocker. "Arnold was the one found her. Mmm-hm. Never got over it. And now just look."

We all looked over at my father. They sighed and looked content.

My brother walked out the back door, across the yard, down to the dock.

It was dark and the men were drunk, bent over their elbows on the table, gesturing and spitting as they spoke. My father had undone his tie. When he lifted his glass, he leaned his head back and tossed the drink down his throat, then chewed the ice furiously. Someone suggested they go for a spin in someone's new car, and then we were leaving. My mother stood up from the couch, and I watched her unfold like a letter, stiff and thin in her long skirt, her hand on the back of my head. The women watched her too, heads lifting in unison, hands folded in their laps, the fingers swollen and chapped, the wedding bands a brassy dull gold, pinching the flesh below the knuckle. I studied their hands, their feet stuffed into navy blue shoes, thick pantyhosed feet set apart to keep them square on the ground. The women watched my mother and murmured, disapproving, that she was very tall, wasn't she? Yes, quite tall, and heavens, how thin. Nothing to hold on to, one woman said, in German, and they laughed. I wrapped my arm around my mother's leg.

The hand on the back of my head pressed me forward. My father veered into view, complaining, saying, "Aw, Claire," and she smiled the flat smile and said very softly, "Now we are leaving, find your jacket, Arnold, get your jacket right this minute, we are going home, say good-bye."

I watched my father's feet do the soft-shoe four-step they did when he drank, a little square of spit-polished shoes stepping back and forth and side to side. My mother said, "Kate, run fetch your brother." I slid my feet slowly across the thick carpet to make patterns and went out onto the back porch. It smelled of wet leaves and heat.

"Esau," I called. My voice echoed, skipping like a smooth stone across the still lake. I could see him down on the wooden dock, the outline of his shoulders black against the water. The moon was very white, the way it gets when the sky is clear. I ran across the yard and stood a few steps short of where the dock began. I called his name again and said, "We're going now." He turned and came creaking up the planks.

He reminded me of an old man.

I put my hand in his jacket pocket and he wound his fingers through mine.

"Do you see the man in the moon?" he asked me. I turned to look at the moon. Esau bent down so his head was level with mine. He pointed.

"Right there," he said. "Do you see him? He's sitting on the edge of that big crater. They left him there when they landed, by accident. They forgot him. Now he just sits there and thinks."

I squinted hard and said, "I see him!" We stared at the moon awhile. "What does he eat?" I asked.

"Moonflowers."

"Is he lonely?"

Esau said, "Oh, yes. He's very lonely."

"That's sad."

"But see where the light comes down from the moon and hits the lake?"

I nodded.

I would see anything my brother wanted me to see.

"Sometimes he slides down the moonbeam and goes swimming and talks to the fish."

"Then why can't he just go home?"

Esau straightened up, and we turned toward the house. "He doesn't remember home anymore," Esau said. "Moonflowers make you forget things like that." We stood stalling on the porch, watching the party through the window, listening to the roar, the screen door banging in the wind.

We went in. We said good-bye and were kissed. We followed our parents out to the car. Our father was singing.

In the backseat, riding down County Road 10, I tilted my head to look out the window. I watched the man on the moon swinging his legs over the edge of the crater. I wondered if he was whistling.

"Esau," I said. I turned to look at him. He was half asleep, with his head on the window, his cheek squished against the glass. I pulled on his sleeve.

"What?" he mumbled.

"Does the man whistle?" I asked.

"Of course he does," Esau said, smiling. "He whistles all the time."

I turned back to the window to watch the moonbeams. They cut through the sky, cold and white, hitting field after field of corn, the perfect rows like an army of narrow men. The fields were lit up by the high, white moon, glistening like an eyeball in the sky.

"Katie, wake up." My brother was shaking me. I sat up in bed.

"What? Can't you sleep?" It was dark out. He stood there in his pajamas, excited.

"Put on your shoes. We're going out."

"Out where?"

"I don't know," he said, exasperated. "Out."

I looked at him suspiciously. "Are you sick?"

"No! I'm fine. Hurry up." He hopped from foot to foot.

I climbed out of bed and put on my shoes. "Are we going out the window?" I asked.

"Good idea. Yes. If we go out the door, they'll hear." He punched a hole in the screen. I looked at it.

"Maybe you shouldn't have done that," I said. "Tie my shoes."

"Doesn't matter. We'll fix it later." He knotted my laces and lowered me out the window and into the flower bed, then dropped next to me with a small thud. I looked at him for direction. In the white light of the moon, his cheeks were shadowed with a hot flush.

We walked along the dry creek bed. The crickets were wild with the heat. He said nothing, but moved quickly, his feet sure on the flat rocks, his striped pajamas flapping around his thin legs. I stumbled along behind him, sometimes jogging to keep up, my hair starting to get damp.

He was talking to himself. It wasn't the kind of talking you listen to, so I didn't.

I heard the train that ran along the edge of town. I didn't know how far away from the house the train was, but we were getting close to it. The high weeds scratched my legs, and my shoe had come untied. He was speeding up. "Wait!" I yelled.

He turned but didn't stop walking. "Hurry up!" he said. "We're almost there."

"Where?"

He reached the bridge and stopped to wait for me. When I caught up with him, I hit him in the stomach.

"Don't walk so fast," I said. "I'll get lost. And then you'll be in trouble."

He glanced down at me, distracted. "We should have brought provisions," he said severely.

"How long are we staying gone?"

He shrugged. "Come on."

And he ran. I watched as his body got smaller ahead of me, though I struggled to keep up. I fell, hit my knee on a rock, got up and kept going. The moon was straight ahead; it looked as if it dangled heavily over some nearby point, a smooth stream of moonlight sliding along the creek bed. The sound of Esau's sneakers faded and the bobbing figure ahead of me narrowed to a point, and disappeared.

I found him at the train tracks.

He was *on* the train tracks. He leaped along them in long strides, looking like a white bird.

"Katie!" he called.

"Get down from there!" I yelled as I trudged up the hill.

"Come on!"

"No! Get down!"

"Do you know how to tell if a train's coming?"

"How?"

"You stand . . . here"—he came to a stop on the iron trestle farthest from me, his arms out, balancing—"and it shakes."

He started laughing.

If I turned around and went straight back down the creek bed, I would get home.

His body trembled where it stood. He laughed and laughed.

The train turned some unseen corner and flashed its single light on him.

My knee was bleeding where I fell on it.

He balanced there, lit by the moon and the beam of the train, his arms out like a marionette, his body dancing as if in a strong wind.

I stumbled backward as the train rushed by. Out of habit, in the roar and clatter, I counted the cars.

In the ringing silence that followed the last car of the train, I heard my brother laughing. I walked up the hill and stood next to the tracks. He was lying in a ditch.

"Esau," I yelled.

He scrambled to his feet and ran off into the dark like a frightened deer.

Into the dark. That's what I called it then: I said that he had gone "into a dark." It was a confusion of what my mother told me, that he "got very dark." Doc Parker called them "episodes," and when Esau had them, he sometimes went into his room, and sometimes went Away, and then it was much too quiet, and my parents didn't look at me, but fought in the night.

It was only later that I knew I was right, only when I had my own, much lesser darks and realized that it felt very much as if you had entered, by accident, a separate place; as if you had been feeling your way along a dimly lit hallway, turned a corner, and found yourself in absolute dark.

We were sitting in the living room. We were listening to the shape of silence. The shape of silence was in his bedroom, pulling on the rest of the house. Everything tipped toward him in the force of our listening to his total lack of sound. My mother fussed with the corners of a book, shifting where she sat. Her stockings shushed as she recrossed her legs. My father was in his La-Z-Boy, not leaned back but rather looking as if he might pounce out of it at any moment. He was watching the television, which murmured almost inaudibly, like voices in a hospital hall. Quietly, conspiratorially, and with respect for our silence, Walter Cronkite told us about the war in Vietnam. My father swished the drink in his glass.

I was coloring everything red.

"You know what kind of bird that is?" my father said to me.

I didn't look up from my coloring book. "Cardinal."

"State bird," my father said absently.

"No it isn't," I muttered.

"What's that?"

"No it isn't," I said louder. "It isn't the state bird."

"Shhh," my mother said.

"Shh yourself," I snapped.

"Katie," she warned.

"What do you mean, it isn't the state bird?"

"It's not," I almost yelled, scribbling hard.

"Okay, Miss Smarty-pants." My father stopped swishing his drink. "What is the state bird, then?"

"Oh, for God's sake, Arnold," said my mother. "Don't encourage her."

"Loon!" I yelled, and my red crayon snapped.

"What?"

"It's the loon!" I threw the pieces of my crayon at my father, who looked startled. I sat quietly, looking at my cardinal. I turned the page, selected a green crayon, and carefully outlined a finch.

My father went to the bar and got another drink. He sat down again.

"Quite so," he said, rocking his La-Z-Boy slightly back and forth. "Quite so."

Silence settled back in around us, tucking its corners under our toes.

Summer was ending. My brother had been in his room for days. During the day, when my mother went to work at the department store downtown, smelling of the lilac hand lotion she kept in a jar by the kitchen sink, my father sat reading the paper, lowering it when I came out of my bedroom.

"Morning, kiddo."

I climbed up onto the couch and lay my head on its arm, looking at him. He was drinking grapefruit juice and vodka from a tumbler. His hair was rumpled, and he wore the blue robe my mother had given him last Christmas because she said it was unseemly for him to go gallivanting about in his pajamas, even if he was just getting the paper out of the driveway.

"You hungry?" my father asked.

I shrugged.

"Cat got your tongue?"

I stuck it out.

I listened to the silence. Esau was still sleeping. I didn't know how I could tell, but I could. The silence was quieter, somehow. The silence was probably laid out cold on his bed, exhausted from a night of night fears.

When I think of my father now, I remember him smiling. Which seems, in light of things, incongruous, maybe even entirely invented. I can hardly remember him. Maybe I've pasted a smile on his face because I want something to remember and I want to think that we sat, summer mornings, in peaceable silence and my father smiled at me and I was enough.

My father wasn't a happy man. I suppose I knew that, though when you're six, you don't call someone happy, unhappy, bitter, cruel. When you're six, those are transient feelings, as changeable as clouds, not states of being that define you.

He wasn't a happy man. I know that because of what happened, because of what my mother told me later, because of what I have pieced together and what I have made up.

You say of a man, when he's gone, simple things, as if to try to sum him up: He loved his children. He loved his wife.

Often, you say: He did his best. Or, with more hesitation: He did what he could.

You do not say that he hated himself.

He must have worked at one time, possibly in insurance. He no longer did by the time I was old enough to notice such things. Such things as the unmentionable fact that your father watches soap operas while his wife goes to work.

You say of such men, without further comment: He drank.

Such men gathered at Frank's around three in the afternoon to play pool with cracked cues and watch the game. They wore plaid flannel shirts, and caps with logos of feed stores perched on top of their heads. Their wives worked. It may have been strange for a woman to work in the suburbs back then, but not in a town that was in a depression and had been as long as anybody could remember.

In Motley, everything was *a long time ago.* That's what people said: They told a story, then let it trail off into the twilight and wet heat of August, fanning themselves with paper cocktail napkins. But that was all a long time ago, they said, and watched the fireflies beating their bodies against the damp blue dark. They never finished the story. The story disappeared, wavering up in front of them like heat, just slightly contorting their faces as they wiped the sides of their hands against their foreheads and shook off the sweat. Their mouths clamped up like small trapdoors.

It was a long time ago. The trains and the red iron ore. The town was gone before my time. We lived in its skeleton like a pack of hermit crabs. A solitary train went past every night. Its whistle blew once while we lay there in our separate beds, waiting for the sound. When I was older, we lit bonfires and drank down by the tracks, digging small holes with sharp stones and passing the bottle around. The iron mines were stripped, rusted husks of equipment left to rot in the ditches' faint red dirt.

Everything the town knew was a long time ago. All that was left were the stories. The seasons. The dull, familiar rage of men without work for their heavy hands.

The men did not complain because to complain implied a hope that things could change.

The women complained about the men, and dragged them to bed when they passed out on the couch, and took their shoes off. Hesitating, kissing their cheeks. People love in strange ways.

My father tapped me lightly on the head with his newspaper, getting up from his chair. "Want to go fishing?"

We sat on the side of the bridge with our fishing hats on. I caught a perch, and we put it in the cooler with the ham sandwiches and beer. Cattails crowded the banks of the river, humming with bugs. The air had that late-summer feeling of everyone having left.

"Is Esau going to be all right?" I asked.

My father sat quietly, looking out at the water.

"Not for a while," he said.

I considered this. "Is he going to die?"

"We're all going to die someday."

"Soon, I mean."

"No."

I looked at my father.

In the memory of my imagination, he looks tired, the brim of his hat and his crooked nose and bushy eyebrows jutting out in relief against the sharp blue of the water. His back was hunched.

He took a swig of beer and turned his smile on me. "No one's going to die, Katie."

I never forgave him for the lie. I ought to forgive him, I suppose. You should let the dead lie.

The man did what he could.

There was a little thump on my window on the first day of school. I went over and moved the curtain. Davey was standing in the flower bed.

"Are you ready?" he asked.

"It's not time to go yet," I said, pulling the screen out and reaching down. He grabbed my hand and I hoisted him in. He straightened his sweater and smoothed his hair.

"What's your mom making for breakfast?" he asked.

"Biscuits. Nice haircut."

"Thanks."

"You still got the tag on your shirt."

He felt the back of his neck. "Well, pull it off already," he said. I did.

Davey and I had been best friends for my whole life. His birthday was in September and mine was in June, so he was almost a whole year older than me, and bigger. He could rest his chin on the top of my head. But we were both starting first grade that day. We didn't really want to go to school, but we couldn't figure a way out of it so we were going.

"Morning, Davey," my father said. He was reading the paper in his chair.

"Morning, Mr. Schiller." Davey liked my dad.

"You're looking sharp this morning."

"Thank you, sir."

"That's a good-looking pair of pants."

Davey hiked them up by the belt loops. "They're new," he said.

My mother came into the room, carrying a plate of biscuits. "Didn't like what your mother was making for breakfast, hmm?" she asked Davey as he sat down at the table.

"Oatmeal," he said.

"I see. Did you throw your lunch away?"

"Yes, ma'am." He looked apologetic.

"Uh-huh." She bent over him, pouring his juice, and ruffled his hair on her way back to the kitchen. He smoothed it down with both hands. He didn't like to be messy.

"Hi, squirt," Esau said, sitting down.

"Davey, do you want ham or bologna?" my mother called.

"Ham," he called back, eating his biscuits. He liked it at our house.

Esau walked us as far as the middle school, then we continued along Main Street alone. "You scared?" Davey asked me. We were kicking a pinecone back and forth ahead of us. "Nah," I said.

"Mrs. Johnson's nice, my mom said."

"Yeah. Erick Janiskowski's in our class." I made a face.

He shrugged. The pinecone went into the street and he retrieved it. "I won't let him bug you. My mom's sad," he said.

"How come?"

"'Cause. My dad. I dunno. Hey, look," he said, pointing up. There was a nest in the eaves of a house. "They had a fight," he said, putting his hands in his pockets.

"Maybe it was just a discussion," I offered.

He shook his head. "Even my mom called it a fight. I asked her."

"Did she say it was a big fight? Or just a little fight?"

"She said it was little, but it was big. Now they're not talking."

"How long have they not been talking?"

He shrugged. "Couple days. My dad's in the basement all the time. I think he's making something."

Their house was spooky. It was always quiet, except when baby Sarah cried. It was like nobody lived there, or only ghosts. Every now and then Davey's dad would come up from the basement and look at us as if he didn't know how we got there. We'd look at him. "Hi, Dad," Davey would say. And his dad would nod at us and go back down the narrow, creaky stairs.

"I saw my mom cry," he said sullenly.

I stopped walking. "Your mom cried?"

"Sort of. She didn't make any noise or nothing. She was just sitting with the baby in her rocking chair and sort of crying. Come on, we're gonna be late."

We started walking again. I couldn't picture his mom crying. She always knew what to do. She was pretty.

We got to the school. "Ready?" Davey asked. He grabbed my hand and shoved through the door.

After school let out, Davey came over. We were playing explorers in the yard when my mom came out on the back porch. "Davey, honey, do you want to stay for supper? I already called your mother. She said it was okay."

"Yes, ma'am. Thank you."

She laughed and went back in the house. Then she stuck her head back out. "You guys want to walk down and get your dad? He's at Frank's."

We decided we did and headed off down the road. We liked

Frank's. Everybody was nice to us there. We went there sometimes to get my dad, and Frank gave us a Coke. Sometimes fries, if we were lucky.

"Well, look what the cat drug in," Frank said when we came in the door. We blinked in the hazy dark, getting our bearings. The pool tables were busy, and men stood leaning on their sticks, squinting at the green felt. They tapped their hats at us and slugged their beer.

My dad was sitting at the bar with a couple of other guys. He turned his head and grinned. He said, "Well, Frank, you know what that is."

"What's that?" Frank popped the tops off our Cokes and put straws in them.

"That there is a couple of first-graders."

"Naw," Frank said, slapping the counter.

"Yes, sir, it certainly is."

"Well, tarnation."

Davey gave me a push up onto a stool and sat down next to me. "Hi, Frank," he said.

"How's by you, little man?"

"Oh, not bad, I guess." He put his face close to a giant jar of pickled pigs' feet and studied it.

My dad kissed my head and slapped Davey on the back. "Well, I tell you. This is an occasion. This calls for a treat. What'll you have?"

"We want fries," I said. "Please."

"Fries it is," Frank said. He called back to the kitchen, then leaned his hands on the bar. "So tell us. How's it, being first-graders?"

Davey and I looked at each other. "S'all right," Davey said.

They laughed. "So you think you'll go back, then?" Frank asked.

"We got crayons," I said, pulling them out of my bag. "Mrs. Johnson brought crayons for everybody."

"Damnation!" my father said. "Will you have a look at that, Frank." He whistled through his teeth.

"Kate did better than anybody on letters," Davey bragged. "She won the big box of crayons."

I hit him in the arm and drank my Coke, elated. My dad picked me up and put me on his lap. Davey scooted one stool closer.

"Well, you know why?" my dad said. "'Cause you two are about as smart as they come. You two and your brother, I tell ya. Make the rest of us look like we ain't got the brains God gave a goose, is what it is," he said, winking at Frank and raising his empty glass.

We wiggled happily and ate our greasy fries. Frank poured my dad another drink. "Last one," he said.

"Aw, hell," my dad said, joking. "Why you want to make a fella beg?"

Frank turned his back and started polishing the long row of sparkly bottles. My dad picked up his drink. "You want the olive?" he asked me, and I stuck my fingers in and ate it. "How's your dad, then?" he asked Davey. "Ain't seen him around in how long."

Davey ate the ends off his fry and handed the rest to me. He only liked the crispy parts. He shrugged. "I dunno."

"Whaddaya mean, you don't know? You saw him just this morning."

Davey slid off the stool and walked to the bathroom. I twisted around on my dad's lap. "He doesn't want to talk about it," I said.

"Hup. Why's that?" My dad licked his thumb and rubbed something off my cheek.

"'Cause they got in a fight. His mom and dad."

"That so?"

I nodded. "His dad's mean."

"Hey, now, Katie," he said, frowning. "Don't be talking about folks."

"Well, he *is*," I said, and moved to my own stool again.

"Naw, he ain't mean." My dad stared into his glass and turned it in circles. "Man's got all kinds of reasons. You don't know."

"I do know." I sulked.

My dad shook his head and smiled at Frank, who was popping open two more Cokes. "Thanks," he said. "Ain't that so, Frank?"

Frank leaned his hip against the bar and smiled at me. "Carrottop, tell us what's so." He glanced at my dad, sighed, reached back on the bar, and poured him another drink. "Drink it slow, 'cause that's all you're getting," he said, and my dad raised his glass at him. I think Frank was my dad's best friend. I turned to look at the bathroom door, wondering what the heck was taking Davey so long anyway.

"Kate here and I were just discussing that it's best not to talk about folks."

Frank nodded wisely. "That's so."

"A'cause you can't say, really, what's what. You just don't know. They got all kinds of reasons, and you just don't know."

My dad was getting boring, so I slid off the stool and banged on the bathroom door. "Davey!" I yelled.

"What?" he yelled back, so I knew he was okay.

"You fall in?" That was one of my favorite jokes. I cracked up.

"No, dangit!" he yelled. He sounded mad. I stopped laughing.

"Well, come out already, then." I picked at a crack in the wood door, and then it swung open and Davey walked right past me. I scrambled after him. He got on the stool next to my dad.

"My dad's a *big jerk*," he said loudly. "That's how he is." He grabbed his Coke, took a deep breath, and blew bubbles furiously through the straw.

We all stared at him. My dad picked him up and put him on his lap. Davey leaned back into his chest, holding his Coke with both hands. His nose was running and he wiped it with his sleeve. He glanced at me and then away. His eyes got super blue when he cried. They were cornflower. I had a cornflower crayon. I didn't like it when Davey cried. I shredded a little napkin.

"Say, now," my dad said, smoothing Davey's hair for him. "Had a long day, I think."

Frank stood there with his arms crossed, looking sadly at Davey. "Well, little man," he said. "You know what this calls for?"

Davey shook his head. There was so much snot on his face I finally wiped it off with my own sleeve.

"Cheeseburgers," Frank said seriously. "That's what. Wouldn't you say?" he asked my dad.

"Damn straight," my dad said. He set his chin on Davey's head and rocked him a little. "Damn straight."

I hopped down and went to call my mom to say we'd be late.

In September, Esau went Away. I know it was September because on the first day of school, he was there, and then he was not. He came home, but Away hung over the house like the threat of war: We waited. The waiting gave us something to do. There was some quiet agreement among us that we would not proceed without Esau, and this agreement killed my father.

I am getting ahead of myself.

Every time Esau went Away, it was only for a Little While, until he was Feeling Better.

"How long is a little while?"

"A few weeks."

"And then he can walk us to school."

"Of course he can."

"Does he go to school at Away?"

"No. He's not feeling well enough."

"How is he feeling?"

My mother was standing at the window with her hands on her hips. My father and I were playing gin rummy.

"He's delusional."

"Arnold," said my mother, her voice heavy with sarcasm. "That's very helpful."

My father was drunk.

"What? I'm not going to lie to her."

Somehow my mother was able to convey, with her back, disdain.

"Gin," my father said.

"What's delusional?" I watched the cards arch under his rough thumbs.

"Cut," he said, smacking the deck on the table between us.

"See?" said my mother. "Now you've got her started."

"It means he doesn't know who he is," said my father, and dealt. He looked once at his cards, laid them down, and went over to the bar. "Want an olive?" he asked me. I nodded, trying to organize my cards without dropping them.

My mother turned. "I'm going out," she said.

"Out where?" my father asked.

"I don't know," she yelled, startling us both. "Just out, if you don't mind." She walked over to my father, furious, and yelled in his ear, "Out!"

And left.

I didn't want to look at my father. I studied my cards and carefully laid down the queen of spades.

We sat there for a very long time.

"Is she coming back?" I asked.

My father nodded slowly. "I would assume so," he said. "One never knows."

He picked up my queen.

After a while, I asked, "Do you know how to cook?"

He looked up at me. "What?" he said. "Yeah, I know how to cook. Why?"

I shrugged. "What do you know how to cook? Eggs?"

"Sure, I can cook eggs. I can cook all sorts of things, Katie, why?" He laughed.

"In case she doesn't come back," I said. "Gin."

My father tossed his cards down on the table, threw his head back, and roared. "Oh, my," he said. "Katie, what would I do without you?" He sighed and giggled and got up for another drink. Passing me, he ruffled my hair and said, "Well, we won't starve. I'll tell you that for sure."

"So she might not come back," I crowed, triumphant.

"Naw, she'll come back. She'd never go anywhere without you," he said, and looked out the window, and remembered his drink. He drank the whole thing and set the glass down hard on the table. "Let's go get ice cream."

We stumbled to the store in the thick September night.

My brother was standing on the sidewalk outside the grade school staring up at the sky, his thumbs hooked through the straps of his blue bag.

"You're home," I said as we started walking.

"Looks that way," he replied.

It was a cold day, and his cheeks and nose were red. I stopped and dug my gloves out of my bag. We hunched forward against the wind.

"Didja see it snow?" I asked. "We were at recess. It melted, though."

He nodded. The buses passed us in a streak of yellow. He glanced down at me. "What happened to your face?" he asked mildly.

"Nothing." I put my hand to my cheek where the wind stung it, just under my left eye.

"Looks like someone scratched you."

"So?" I scowled. Sara Mortinson had a bump on her head where I whacked her with my reading book when she said, loud, that my brother was crazy. I wasn't really sure what order things happened in, whether I hit her or she scratched me first, but we both sulked in the nurse's office with ice while the nurse whisked papers.

"So nothing. Just asking."

"Are you better now?" I asked after a while.

He shrugged. "Guess so," he said. He nudged me with his elbow. "Let's go down to the creek."

We rustled through the thick trees and dropped our bags in a pile of pine needles. We crouched by the creek. The September rains had come and gone, and the water was clean and high.

"What was it like?"

He picked up a long, narrow branch and snapped it into tiny bits.

"Slow," he finally said. "Everything was slow."

"Is everyone crazy?"

He shook his head. "Not really."

"Why are they there?"

He wrinkled his nose. "Just sad, I guess."

"Are you crazy?"

"I don't think so."

"You don't seem crazy."

"I know," he said. "I don't feel crazy."

"What's wrong with you, then?"

He swept his bits of pine branch into a careful pile with his hands. "I feel too fast," he said, sounding confused. "And I have dreams that I can't tell whether I'm sleeping or not." He scratched his nose. "And I get scared."

"What did you do there?"

He was silent for a minute. "I don't remember," he finally said. He made a shape with his hands, a sort of oval he seemed to be holding gently, like an egg. "Your dreams got better there. It's like you're dreaming all the time." He considered the oval he was holding. "It's nice."

I had collected a handful of pine needles and was sorting through them. "Are you going back?"

"I dunno," he said.

"Were you homesick?" I wanted to know if he missed me.

He shrugged.

I got to my feet, angry, and said I was going home.

* * *

Later that evening, Esau and I were playing Monopoly. From the kitchen came my father's voice: "Esau, come take your medicine."

Esau stayed where he was, organizing his properties into tidy piles. My father took a few steps around the corner. "Esau?" he said. "Kiddo, come take your medicine."

I rolled the dice. Esau continued, unnecessarily now, to tap the edges of his piles on the table. I moved the dog onto Park Place and sighed; Esau owned it and had covered it with hotels.

My father set a glass of water and two large pink tablets next to Esau's elbow.

"I don't want it," Esau said flatly.

"Well, I don't know what to tell you," said my father. "You gotta take it."

Esau picked up the water, stood to get some leverage, crushed the tablets with the base of the glass, and brushed the powder onto the floor. I hesitated, counting out what I owed Esau, then kept counting.

"There's plenty more where those came from," my father said, "but if you do it again, it's coming out of your allowance." He leaned against the bar with one hand and dropped ice into his glass with the other.

"I don't care," Esau said.

"Let me explain something to you," my father said patiently, taking a drink. "Every time you stop taking your medicine, you get sick. And every time you get sick, you wind up in the hospital. And every time you wind up in the hospital, I wind up further in debt." He walked back into the kitchen and came out with two more pills, holding on to them this time. "Eventually I will run out of money," he said, his voice rising. "Do you follow? And there won't be any left for hospitals or medicine or your mother or your sister or your sorry ass, for that matter. So you're going to goddamn take your medicine if I have to force it down your throat."

Unexpectedly, his voice broke. He leaned down and awkwardly touched his forehead to Esau's hair, his drink resting on Esau's shoulder. Esau, who was holding the dice, waited until my father straightened up and then put his hand out for the pills. He sat looking a little sick after he swallowed them.

"Can I have some milk?" he asked.

My father brought him a glass of milk. He drank it, then got up from the table and sat down on the couch. My father sat down next to him. From the back they looked like the same person, only different heights. Esau's head dropped onto my father's shoulder and I knew he'd fallen asleep.

I stood up and went over to them. My father was looking out the window, but there wasn't anything to see. It was too dark.

Maybe it was the same night, maybe another. It didn't matter. I woke to the sound of voices in the living room. I cracked open the door.

My mother's legs were crossed and she held a glass of wine. My father's elbows were on his knees, his drink dangling between them, catching the light. He was crunching ice. In the silence it sounded like he was chewing on glass.

"He's not any better," he said.

My mother didn't answer for a moment. "He is. He's a little better."

My father shook his head. "Claire," he said, "we're just biding time."

She said nothing. My father sat back in his chair.

"So what, then?" she said. "So we're just biding time. Do you have a better idea of what we should do?"

It was hard to tell sometimes whether my mother was being mean, what with the smooth southern drawl that rolled along under her words like a low tide. Her words came out soft and slow when she was telling me stories, and they came out soft and slow when she said to my father, *Oh, honey. Go on to hell.*

"You think it's my fault," my father said.

I wondered what my mother was looking at. She was staring steadily ahead. She sat with her back straight, her fingers playing around the stem of her glass.

"No," she said eventually, her voice neutral. "Not your fault, exactly."

My father looked at her. "What's that supposed to mean? Exactly?"

She sipped her wine.

"It's sort of my fault, then? A little bit my fault?"

"Arnold," she sighed. "It's not your fault. Is that what you want to hear? It's no one's fault. That's what the doctors said."

"But that's not what you think."

"I don't think anything."

"Of course you think something. You think that whatever I touch turns to shit. You think whatever's wrong with the world is somehow the direct effect of me."

"Arnold, don't be dramatic."

"Claire, you are a true bitch, you know that? You really are."

"Yes, you've told me."

My mother took a sip of wine, and my father stood up to freshen his drink.

The night fights were as familiar and expected as breakfast in the morning and church on Easter. They fought almost companionably, as if it were as good a way as any to converse. But later I would riffle through the fights in my head, trying to find the one fight that set it all off, the one where they turned a corner, the one where it was no longer a quiet, ever present cruelty but something more. For years I was sure my mother's slow, cruel words made my father do what he did; and then for other years I was sure my father had done something to make my mother say what she said. Now I think that certain things just tend toward their own centre, and implode.

It's interesting that two people can sit in a room, doing nothing more than being precisely themselves, and, in each other's eyes, utterly, generally fail.

"I'm going to bed," said my mother, not moving. "Are you coming?"

It would occur to me, older, that this was an invitation.

"Not right yet," said my father, picking up a deck of cards and dealing himself a hand of solitaire.

And it would occur to me, older, that this was a kindness of sorts, not flatly saying *no*. Letting a woman get into her nightgown, lotion her hands, fall asleep with a book and the bedside light still on, having forgotten to hope.

My mother was angry. I stood on a chair by the stove, waiting for a pot of water to boil and listening to her bang.

"Where's Dad?" I finally asked. It was getting dark out. No one had been home when Esau and I came in from school. Last I checked, Esau was sitting at the writing desk with his head in his hands, trying to do his homework.

"How should I know?" she snapped. I got off the chair and walked out of the kitchen in a huff.

"Katie?" she called.

I sat down on the couch. Esau was looking out the window and didn't notice. My mother's head appeared around the corner.

"Katie, come help?"

I didn't look at her. She sighed and went back into the kitchen.

"Dammit!" she yelled, and something got thrown. She came out of the kitchen, pulling her apron over her head and throwing it on the floor. She went over to the bar, poured wine into a flowered juice glass, and lit a cigarette. Esau turned half around in his chair. He and I watched her pace back and forth in front of the windows.

"I'm sorry?" I said.

"Oh, it's not you. It's that rat-bastard father of yours. It's nothing. Never mind." She sat down in a heap next to me on the couch.

Esau started to giggle. I could see him biting the insides of his cheeks. He turned around again and put his head down on the desk. His shoulders shook.

"What's so funny, may I ask, mister?" asks my mother, starting to smile. He put his hands over his ears, which were turning red.

"Did you take your medicine today?" I asked, feeling important.

"Yes," he said, giggling. "Rat bastard!" he finally shrieked.

I looked at my mother, shocked. She laughed.

Esau apologized, and said, "Don't tell Dad I swore."

"I won't tell him if you don't tell him I called him a rat bastard," she said, setting Esau off again. I giggled and picked at the soles of my shoes, looking sideways at my pretty mother.

The front door opened. "Claire!" my father called. Esau stopped laughing abruptly and looked at his books. My father came into the room and surveyed us.

"Are you growing a beard?" I asked. He put his hand up to his stubbled face and looked as if he was considering it.

"Sure," he said, and turned to the bar. "What's for dinner?"

"Nothing," said my mother, and took a sip of wine.

My father nodded. "Okay," he said, and headed into the kitchen. "There's water boiling over in here," he called. "Were you planning to cook something in it?"

"No," called my mother. "I just wanted to boil some water." She went over to the bar and brought the bottle of wine back to the couch, wedging it between the cushions.

"Well, then," my father said, coming back into the room and sitting down. "We'll starve, then."

"Most likely," she agreed.

"Claire."

"Yes, Arnold."

"Go make dinner."

"Make it yourself."

My father stood and looked out the window, then turned and pitched his highball glass against the north wall.

"Claire."

"Go to hell."

"Claire."

"You're drunk."

"I'm drunk and hungry. And I'm getting annoyed."

"That's a shame. Go sweep up the glass."

My mother poured more wine for herself. I realized they were both drunk. I was hungry too. It seemed like a bad time to move, though, so I stayed still.

"Claire," my father said, turning on the television, "I'm going to watch the news. When it's over, I want dinner." He sat down.

"Well, you'll have to make do, then." She stood up, steadying herself on the arm of the couch. "I'm going out."

"No you're not," my father said calmly. "You'll stay right here."

She didn't stop, and suddenly my father was standing in front of her, blocking her way. She moved left, and so did he. Right. They stood still.

"I can't make dinner if you don't move," she said.

He moved, and she walked out of the house.

My father stood there for a second, then followed her out. We heard them yelling in the driveway. Esau and I both bolted for the front door just as my father shoved my mother back through it and into the hall, where she sprawled on the floor.

My father's face was red.

"Rat bastard! Rat bastard! Rat bastard!" Esau screamed, his legs flying at my father's knees. He seemed to be dancing around my father like a weird little elf, flapping his hands, but his feet were connecting. My mother scrambled away and got up as my father lunged after Esau's impossible, electric feet. Esau turned and ran, and his bedroom door slammed.

My father turned and smacked my mother. She barely flinched.

"Nicely done," he said, breathing hard. He looked at the door as if noticing that it was open, then went through it, shutting it with strange care on his way out.

My mother was looking at nothing.

"Does it hurt?" I finally asked.

"What?" she said, looking down at me as if surprised to find me there. "Oh. No."

We stood there for a moment more. She reached for my hand and we went into the kitchen. She set the chair by the stove again and lowered the heat under the empty pot where the water had all boiled off.

"It needs more water," I said, pointing. She looked. She turned the heat off.

"I'm not very hungry," she said. "Are you?"

I shook my head even though I was so hungry I wanted to chew my fingers. She looked relieved. We sat on the couch and I watched her light cigarette after cigarette, the smoke blue in the glow of the television. She petted my hair as if I was a dog, and ashes fell on her skirt. We watched the news.

We sat in the thrumming space between my father and my brother. I wanted time to move slowly, to linger here, where my mother was not my own but almost.

"You're tired," she said. Her breath was dry and smooth on my cheek. "Go to bed."

I could feel her eyes on my back as I went down the hall to my room.

I took off my shoes and got into bed in my clothes. I listened to the rustle and murmur of her in Esau's room, giving him his medicine. She sang softly until his crying slowed.

I dozed and woke sometime later to the thumping, whimpering sound of Esau having a nightmare.

I stood outside his door. The house was silent except for the muffled sound of tears in a pillow. I whispered, "Esau." I knocked hesitantly. I tried the door, but it was locked. I knocked and knocked. I sat down cross-legged in front of his door, knocking. He stopped crying after a while, his breath shivering. I lay down on my side on the floor and kept knocking. I heard him get up, cross the room, lie down on his side of the door. I whispered, "Esau." He didn't answer. I heard him breathing; we were only a few inches apart. I held my arm up with my other hand because it was getting tired, and knocked as I fell asleep, feeling the knocks grow further and further apart, rousing myself to keep knocking, drifting off.

And then I was half awake, my father picking me up from the floor. It was dark, I was cold. I snuggled into my father's chest, and he brushed my hair away from my face with big, clumsy hands and put me into my bed and sat beside it, breathing whiskey breath in the dark.

My father was huge and irretrievable, like an era.

He was inseparable from the size of his hands and his belly laugh, and the worried wood of the bar at Frank's where he sat for hours and days, shouting with the men; he was the sound of the front door slamming and the shuffle of slippers on the floor on mornings white and blinding with winter light. He was the same as his profound, useless, oppressive love of his wife, and his desperate love for his son. He was the amorphous shape of need, a need that grasped at whatever was left: a small girl, easily picked up, of manageable size and always at hand.

My mother loved us in a way that was both fierce and abstracted, like an animal. We were something that had happened to her, and she lived with it, loving each according to our need and without frills. My father couldn't forgive her for it and called her cold. He meant it as an insult, of course. I think she may have taken it as a simple statement of fact.

I sometimes think I see my mother. She is always disappearing around a corner ahead of me, her long camel-hair coat swinging behind her like a door swinging closed.

I say, when asked, that I hardly remember my father. I remember that sometime that year, he started to fade. And then without warning he was gone, leaving me to wonder if he'd ever been there at all.

It was late October. No snow that stayed yet, only frost that bit the tips of the tall grass by the lake. I snapped them off as if they were heads. Winter was coming. I could feel it around the corner, lurking like a thing in the closet. Esau only sometimes went to school. Most days I left the house alone in the blue early light and walked to Davey's house, and together we headed down Main Street, crushing patches of frost-covered grass with our shoes. My father didn't come home sometimes, or he was always home, heavily home, holding down his La-Z-Boy and breathing through his mouth.

One evening, I went down to Frank's with my mother after dinner to pay the bill. She pushed open the door of the bar and I blinked in the smoky haze. The bar was full of men whose heads swung up and nodded slightly to us. I followed her to the bar and climbed up on a stool.

My mother slapped her gloves down on the counter and pulled out her pocketbook. "How much do I owe you?" she asked.

Frank shook his head. "Let's call it good," he said. He smiled at her.

"Frank, no."

"I mean it." He gave my mother a look and she sighed. He tapped my nose and asked me if I wanted a soda. He glanced at my mother. "On me."

I drank a bottle of orange soda through a straw, studying the gleaming rows and rows of bottles behind the bar.

"What time did he come in here?" my mother asked.

"Opening." Frank poured her a drink.

She looked at it. "How long did he stay?"

"Mosta the day. Ate something."

My mother nodded. I leaned against her shoulder, and she sipped her drink.

"How you been, carrottop?" he asked me.

I shrugged, suddenly shy. It felt funny to be here with my mother.

"Getting prettier all the time. Look just like your momma."

I smiled and blew bubbles in my orange soda and got them up my nose. They laughed, and my mother cleaned me up with a napkin.

We walked home together slowly, looking up at a yellow moon.

I sat in the La-Z-Boy after school, keeping my father company while he lay on the couch, poking my toe through the hole in my sock. My father's face was darkened around the jowls. He smelled like the bar and the brown cigarettes he smoked. At night, he stayed up, so that under my door there was a fan of yellow light on the carpet. I could hear him shuffle the cards, slap them down. Then silence. Then the thunk of his drink on the table, his hard sigh.

He didn't yell anymore, almost never. But he cried. At night, when he was up, listening for Esau. It sounded like a broken bird.

I liked it when he was out there, awake. Keeping watch. Nothing could happen to Esau or me so long as he sat guard. It was like God in his pajamas, playing cards. And when he cried, it was as horrible as if God cried.

My father pulled himself up on the couch and slapped his hands down on his knees. "Well," he said. "Better get going."

There was nowhere to go.

He looked out the window that faced onto the yard as if just preparing to leave. Night fell earlier now, and we watched it inch lower in the sky. He leaned back into the cushions and looked at me.

"How's school, Little Bit?" he asked cheerfully.

I shrugged. "S'all right."

"Keeping your grades up?"

"I don't get grades."

He looked at me in confusion.

"I don't get grades until later," I explained. "Fourth grade, I think."

"Well," he said, bewildered. "Whaddaya know. That's a damn shame."

I nodded. He took a drink and gestured with his glass. "I mean, how are you supposed to know what's what, then?"

"Progress reports." I had carefully shredded my own all year so far, their steady row of bad marks in red pen fluttering into the creek, the water lifting the ink away like red threads. Last year in kindergarten, I had gold stars and Es for excellent, except in penmanship, where I had a solitary S for satisfactory. I studied my father, trying to tell how drunk he was, and whether I could disclose this tidbit of information in secrecy.

"I'm unsatisfactory," I blurted out, feeling brave.

"No," he said, looking concerned. I nodded.

"How do you figure?" he asked.

"In 'Stays on Task.'"

"Really."

"And 'Listens Well.'" My cheeks blazed, and I watched him closely. He looked as if he was mulling this over.

"And I hit Sara Mortinson."

"Hup. What for?"

"Said Esau was crazy."

"Ach. No good telling stories." He nodded.

"See."

"Course, hitting's a problem."

"She scratched me."

He rubbed his stubble with the palm of his hand and squinched his mouth, considering. "Who hit who first?"

"I forget."

"Well then."

We sat a moment.

"I'm going to be a nurse," I offered.

He grinned. "Admirable, admirable." He huffed to his feet and went to the bar. Sitting again, he said, "A regular Florence Nightingale. Lotta blood, you know. Person's got to be prepared."

"I don't mind blood. I don't like the hats, though," I said.

"No."

"I wanted to be a doctor."

"So be a doctor."

"Can't."

"Why not?"

I sighed and rolled my eyes at him. "Daddy, girls aren't doctors."

"Hep! See here now. Oh, say now." He looked at me in alarm. "Who told you that?"

"Erick Janiskowski." I pulled the lever on the La-Z-Boy and

lurched backward suddenly. Erick Janiskowski was the smartest, ugliest boy in first grade and my personal nemesis.

"What's he mean? Well, that's a bunch of crap, I mean to say! Ha! That boy's an embarrassment to his family, and I'll tell you what's more, missy." My father sat up, waving his drink. "Just because his father's the doctor in Staples and they've got enough money to choke a horse doesn't mean a damn thing, is what. Peter Janiskowski's been asking for it all these years, and his wife thinks she's all sorts of special and now that ugly little boy serves them right, is what. I tell you what," he said in a warning tone, leaning toward me. "You tell that boy you can be a goddamn doctor if you goddamn want to be a goddamn doctor. You tell him that."

He harrumphed back into the couch, pleased with himself.

"A woman can do what she likes, these days," he announced.

I nodded, a little overwhelmed.

"Take your mother, for example." He swallowed his drink and sighed with satisfaction. "Now, there's a great lady." He looked out the window. "Day I met her, I'll tell you, I thought to myself, Now, this one's smart as a whip. *This* one's a keeper. Heh," he said, smiling at the thought. "A lady who knew what she wanted and wouldn't nobody stop her. You meet that kind of lady, you think, I made her up in my head. You know the dumbest thing your mother ever did?" he asked suddenly.

I shook my head.

"Married me," he said, chuckling and getting to his feet. As he shuffled out of the room, I heard him say, bewildered, "Never know what got into that woman."

I sat there awhile, then got up and knocked on Esau's door.

"What?" he yelled.

"It's me."

"So?"

"So let me in."

"What for?"

"Come out, then."

"What for?"

I thought about that. "Let's make dinner for them."

There was a silence, then a shuffling of sheets, and Esau opened the door, looking rumpled. "Okay," he said, and we went to the kitchen.

He set a pot of water on the stove and got out a box of macaroni and cheese. I asked, "Were you in bed?"

"What do you care?"

"I don't care. I was just wondering." I yanked open the refrigerator to get butter and milk. "You're so mean lately. You can stay in bed all the time, for all I care."

He dumped the macaroni into the water and fished out the packet of cheese. "I'm not mean," he said.

I snorted.

"I'm not," he said, sitting down on the floor and putting his head on his knees. "I'm sad."

I looked down at him. "Why?"

He shrugged. Uselessly, I watched the macaroni boil.

"Do you want to watch TV?" I asked. "I could bring you some when it's done."

He went and lay down on the couch. I followed him. "Do you want the blanket?"

"Okay."

I put the blanket over him and turned on the TV. "Mom will be home soon," I said.

He nodded.

I hesitated, then went back to the kitchen. As I was stirring in the cheese, my mother came in. I didn't look up.

"Esau's sad," I said. "He's on the couch."

She went past me and into the living room, and I heard her murmuring.

I was tired of everyone except Davey.

The four of us ate quietly in front of the TV that night. My father sat next to Esau with his arm around him and Esau folded into his side. My mother brought him his medicine, and he fell asleep with his head in my father's lap. My father carried him into his room as if he was dead.

My mother looked around at the dishes and said, "Well." She gathered them up and went into the kitchen.

My father closed Esau's door carefully, went over to the bar, and sat down at the dining-room table with his drink.

"Claire," he called. My mother came to the kitchen doorway, her hands in rubber gloves.

"Sit down with me a minute?" my father asked. My mother hesitated, her mouth opening. She crossed the room. She sat across from him, perched on her chair.

"What, Arnold," she said finally.

He shook his head, as if to shake himself awake. "I just thought we might talk this over."

"What's to say?" My mother rubbed the bridge of her nose.

"Claire, I want—" He stopped. He rubbed his cheek.

"What do you want, Arnold," she said, shifting in her chair.

Esau back, I thought. He wants Esau back.

He smiled at her and shook his head. "Nothing." He cleared his throat. "The medicine should help soon," he said, gently. She nodded, looking away.

She rose and took his empty glass. She turned to go back into the kitchen. My father said, "Wait."

She paused. She stood there.

He reached one arm out and wrapped it around her waist.

He put his face against her belly.

Her arms hung down at her sides. Slowly, she lifted one hand and laid it on his head. They stayed like that for a long time.

I watched them. Froze them that way in my head. Stay there, I almost said aloud. Like that.

But they broke apart. They always did.

I think these things are true. I think it happened like this.

I don't know what day it was. I know the snow had fallen, had been falling heavily for days, blanketing the fields overnight, softening and silencing the world. I know winter had come.

At breakfast, my father and I were eating eggs when Esau walked out of his room naked as a jaybird and sat down in the wrong chair. My mother came out of the kitchen in her robe (she called it a dressing gown) with the bamboos and hummingbirds on it, holding her cup of coffee, her hair all a mess, her face sunken in the cheeks but puffed up under the eyes.

She stopped when she saw Esau, sitting with his back to her, his bare behind on the chair. She opened her mouth. She shut it again. My father popped his egg yolks and sopped his toast in them, folded the toast in half with one hand, and bit in. Esau was pale, and the circles under his eyes were crayon purple. I looked at him and scraped the jam off my toast with my teeth. Esau smiled at me, and I was so startled I choked on the jam, then looked over at my father to see if he was going to tell me to eat my toast like a normal person. My father picked up the *Motley-Staples Gazette* again, and kept reading the obituaries. My mother turned around, went into the kitchen, came back out, and looked at Esau as if she wasn't sure she'd seen him in the first place.

"Would you like some coffee?" she asked Esau.

Then I understood that everyone had gone crazy but me.

"Oh, for Chrissakes, Claire," my father said, slapping the paper down on the table, which had little squiggly things that looked like threads under the clear surface. "Of course he doesn't want any coffee."

"Well, I don't know," my mother said, looking from my father to the back of Esau's head. "I thought he might like some coffee."

"What the hell are you talking about, he'd like some coffee?" my father bellowed, patting his toast in the yolks without looking at them. "He's twelve years old, for God's sake."

"Well, what am I supposed to ask him?" she said. I looked up at her. She was supposed to be in charge. Besides, Esau looked perfectly fine, except that he was in the wrong chair. I scowled at him, cranky that they were making such a fuss. He smiled at me again and I stuck out my tongue.

My mother stood there, her robe knotted tightly at her waist, holding her coffee cup close to her chest, fingers flickering, her dark-red hair spilling over her shoulders, lit up by the light that hung over the dining-room table. Esau scratched his head and wrinkled his nose and fiddled with the fringe on his place mat.

"Ask him if he's hungry, dammit!" my father shouted.

"Are you hungry, honey?"

"Yes," Esau said, his voice creaking.

"You see?" said my father, slapping the table with his hand. "He's hungry." He picked up his paper and said to it, "Make the kid some breakfast, Claire."

"Of course he's hungry," she said on her way to the kitchen. "Poor thing hasn't eaten in two days."

Three days, I thought. He's been in his room for three days.

"Poor thing my ass," my father muttered. "Sitting there in the damn dark."

Esau squinted up at the light fixture, a wagon wheel laid flat, the spokes holding fake candles with bulbs in the shape of flames. It looked sort of like a birthday cake. I drank my juice, watching Esau over the rim of my glass. My father turned a page. My mother came back with eggs and toast and bacon.

"The bacon's cold, honey," she said to Esau as she set the plate down in front of him. "I'll make some new if you want. I can make more eggs, you must be starving." She lay her hand on his shoulder and touched his hair, pulling bits of lint from the curls.

"Can I have a fork?" Esau said.

"Oh, Lord," she laughed, "a fork! Of course, I'm sorry." I heard her jangle through the silverware drawer. Her hands trembled as she put a fork, knife, and spoon by Esau's plate. She went back into the kitchen. I wondered what he needed with a knife and a spoon. It was just eggs.

"Mom?" I called. "Can I have more toast?"

There was no answer save the sizzle of bacon and the crack of eggs at the edge of the pan.

"Mom?"

"Claire!" my father hollered. Something clattered in the kitchen and she said, "Dammit," and came in and said to Esau, "What is it?" Esau looked up at me.

My father said, "Katie wants more toast."

"No, honey, you haven't finished your eggs," she said over her shoulder.

My father shoved his chair back and stormed into the kitchen and started popping toast in the toaster.

I looked at Esau and asked, "Are you out of your dark?"

He nodded and smiled. He was smiling a lot. His eyes were a little funny.

"Are you coming to school, then?"

He smiled at his plate and said, "Yes."

"Why were you in a dark?"

"I wanted to die," he said, smiling and starting to giggle.

"You were in there for three days," I said reproachfully.

"Did you miss me?"

"No." I looked at my plate, blinking hard. I all of a sudden wanted to cry, but I would rather have eaten a raw toad than let Esau see.

"Would you miss me if I died?"

"No!" I shouted, and threw my napkin at him. I put my face in my hands and bawled.

My father walked back in and put two pieces of toast on my plate. "Now you've made your sister cry," he said to Esau. "Nice to have you back."

"I'm not crying," I said from inside my hands.

My mother came out and slid more eggs onto Esau's plate.

"He's made Katie cry," my father informed her.

"I'm not crying!" I shouted, wiping my face and snuffling. I picked up my toast and nibbled at the crusts. I could feel Esau looking at me. I looked past him, out the window. There were frost patterns on the glass.

My mother sat down and watched Esau.

"Well, he's going to school, anyhow," my father said. "It's just making it worse that he's in there all the time. He needs to get out."

"Oh, no, I don't think so," said my mother, shaking her head. She reached a hand out and put it on Esau's forehead, then his cheek. "I think he should stay home today."

"Hell, no," my father said. "Dammit, Claire, what did I just say?"

"Arnold, he needs to rest. He's been sick."

"What's he been doing in there for two days besides resting?"

"Three days," Esau said.

"He should stay home," my mother said.

"If he's staying home, I'm staying home," I piped up.

"And he hasn't been sick, dammit, he's been feeling sorry for himself," my father snapped, taking a swallow of coffee.

"Three days," Esau said, louder now.

"Oh, and you're any better?" my mother retorted, her voice rising.

"I don't feel good," I said.

"I didn't say I was better, I said he needed to get out of the house!"

"Arnold, he's staying home," my mother shouted, her hands shaking, one on her place mat and one on Esau's bare shoulder. The one on his shoulder tightened, fingertips pressing into the thin skin and imprinting it with the white shadow of a hand.

"Goddammit, he's going to school if I have to drag him there myself," my father said. He looked at Esau. "What the hell are you doing showing up for breakfast without any goddamn pants on?"

"I'm sick," I said, feeling my forehead. "I'm staying home from school today."

"It was *three days!*" Esau shrieked, staring at his hands. His head was trembling as if it was about to blow straight off his shoulders.

"Now what the hell is he talking about?" my father said. "Claire, I need more coffee."

Esau stood up and threw his plate onto the linoleum floor, breaking it to pieces.

"Goddammit!" my father roared.

"Honey, do you want to stay home today?"

Esau picked up his juice glass and shattered it on the floor. Then he saw my glass and dropped it too. He was smiling and his hands were shaking. His head began to duck oddly to the left, just slightly, as if he was trying to scratch his shoulder with his ear. His left hand flew up and started to rub his cheek, slowly, softly, and his eyes darted over the table, then up to the ceiling, then from side to side. He started speaking very quietly to himself. His eyes were glassy and too blue, as if he'd been crying, but he was laughing. His right hand fluttered near his hip, then at the edge of the table, then across the place mat, his long fingers trembling and flinching back from everything they touched.

"Esau, now." My father leaned his elbows on the table. He wasn't mad anymore. His voice was low, like when he was up with our nightmares, when he came running in and pulled us out of bed, walking in circles through the house, talking quietly. This was an episode. A bad one. They were going to make him go Away.

"Esau, now," my father said again. Esau glanced at him wildly, then away, rubbing his cheek harder. "Son, can you sit down? Sit down, Esau. Let's just all sit here and have breakfast, ah?" My father rose slowly from his chair, his hands on the table, his eyes on Esau's hands. Esau's sunken chest began to fill and fall quickly. His nostrils flared, his mouth was busy forming words nobody could hear.

My mother stood up to reach for him, but her chair scraped behind her and hit the wall. We all flinched. Esau screamed, batted at her with his hands, his eyes racing over the room, his body straining away from her, a horrible braying sound climbing out of his throat and into the air. My father went to stand next to him, tried to put an arm around his shoulder, but Esau wrapped his arms around his own body and leaned forward and rocked, singing: "No, no, no-no-no-no-no-bad-bad," shaking his head. Then he took the coffeepot and poured coffee down the front of our father's pajamas, hurled the pot to the floor, and stumbled into the glass. "Sorry-daddy-sorry-daddy-sorry," he said, shaking his head back and forth as if to shake it off completely. He put his hands against his ears and shook. My father's face twisted, for an instant, in pain, and he backhanded Esau, his arm shooting out as if it was on a spring. My mother screamed as Esau's head snapped sideways, taking his thin body with him as he fell to the floor. My father held his arm to his chest, his eyes wide, and said, "Oh my God."

My mother, barefoot, screamed, "The glass, the glass, Arnold, you bastard, the glass, he's bleeding all over the floor!" I stood up in my chair and looked down at Esau. "I don't feel good," I said, and threw up all over the table.

My mother bent over Esau and tried to pick him up, but Esau twisted away from her grip. He raised himself to sitting and cringed and started laughing. He sat hunched over, naked, picking glass out of his feet. I wiped my mouth on my napkin, got down from my chair, and went around the table. I glanced up at my father, who was still standing at his place, not moving. I looked down at the blood pooling on the linoleum. The blood looked so smooth, the pool's edges round as it moved over the floor. I watched my mother trying to sweep the glass away from his body with her hands. Esau rocked and laughed.

"Honey, I want you to stop laughing, can you do that?" my mother said softly. "Can you just breathe in and out a few times, deep breaths, like at Doc Parker's? Just a few deep breaths now, sweet pea. Stop laughing." Her long hands moved quickly over Esau's skin, plucking bits of glass and laying them aside. I suddenly wanted to go to sleep.

"It's funny," Esau whispered, grimacing, his hands together, thumbs rubbing methodically over each other, right over left, left over right.

"You're bleeding," she said. "We're going to clean you up, all right?"

"It doesn't hurt."

"I know it doesn't, but we don't want it to hurt later, okay?"

"It just tickles." Esau pulled a piece of glass from the arch of his bare foot and laughed when a gash appeared and blood poured out. He ran the sharp sliver of glass down his leg and a thin red thread appeared on his thigh.

"Esau, now stop," she said, grabbing his wrist firmly, like she did when I pitched a fit. I wondered if they could hear my heart pounding. It thundered in my head. I put my hands over my ears.

Esau did it again, harder this time. A wide red line welled up on his leg and spilled over.

"Esau, stop!" she shouted, grabbing at his hand. He shook her off and started slicing quickly all over his legs.

"Mom!" I yelled. Her hands chased Esau's as if his were fast bugs.

"Dad!" I screamed, looking up at him. He was just standing there, staring at Esau.

You don't know, when you're six, how a person's face will stay in your brain forever. How, as you get older and you get more words, you will remember that face and apply those words. Terrible words. *Helpless. Useless.* When you think of your brother, screaming and bleeding on the floor, you will think of your useless father's face. And you will cringe and hate yourself for thinking of him that way, especially when he's dead.

My mother picked Esau up by the armpits and ran with him to the bathroom. Esau screamed and kicked and wriggled and started sobbing. I ran after them and stood in the bathroom doorway, watching my mother pin Esau's body to the edge of the sink, hold his head down with one hand, and pick glass out of his back, his legs and bottom, his sides. Esau muttered and cried and gasped when my mother turned him around and set him on the edge of the sink, facing her. His face was red and tight with tears, but his eyes were glassy and wild. He was looking around for something, but there was nothing to see. I felt like I was going to throw up again. Esau was talking about *the numbers, the answers,* one arm gesturing as he talked, shaking his head and then nodding, slowing down, laughing softly, closing his eyes.

"Mom?" I whispered.

"What, Katie?" she said, irritated, taking a wet cloth and wiping at the blood on Esau's legs, leaning down hard on the cuts.

"Are you going to take him to Away?"

My mother didn't answer for a minute. "He's sick, Katie. We'll do what's best."

She dabbed iodine on Esau's cuts. The screaming and wiggling started again and Esau called out for her and she pinned his arms down with one hand and said, "I'm here, I'm right here," but Esau didn't believe her and kept screaming and my mother was losing her grip. I couldn't see how Esau was suddenly so strong, his skinny limbs full of a furious force, wrists slipping through my mother's hands like snakes. She said, "Katie, tell your father I need his help," her voice rising on *help,* as if she was yelling for him herself. Esau wriggled off the sink and fell to the floor. I looked down at him, his face unrecognizable, not my brother, laughing but not laughing and crying at the same time, and talking, talking, talking, his mouth moving in words that didn't make any sense. I watched my mother's hands, white at the knuckles, circle Esau's wrists and hold them above his head on the floor. She said, "Katie, *now.*"

I ran back out to the dining room. My father was standing at the head of the table, looking at the glass and blood on the floor. The room was smelly with my barf, still dripping off the edges of the table. My stomach heaved and I was embarrassed.

"Dad, Mom says she needs you to help."

"Not now, Katie." My father's voice was calm. He turned and walked to the living room and poured himself a drink the color of iodine. "Daddy's just having a little pick-me-up." As he passed me, he laid his hand on my head and kept going.

I went back to the bathroom. Esau mumbled, then let out a raspy scream. I thought his throat must be hurting by now, but if the glass didn't hurt then maybe his voice wouldn't either. My mother struggled to hold him, one hand around his wrists and one on his ankles, Esau's naked body stretched and arched in the middle like a bow, trembling violently. My mother looked up and said, "Where in the hell is your father?"

"He said he's having a pick-me-up."

She laughed. "Oh, Jesus," she said, shaking her head. "All right. I need you to get something out of the medicine cabinet."

I stepped over Esau, stood on the edge of the bathtub, climbed onto the sink, and opened the cabinet.

"Top shelf," she said. "Back behind the other bottles. Brown bottle. No, the one next to it. That's it. Get me four of those and a glass of water."

I climbed down. Esau opened his eyes and looked straight at me.

"Three days, I was dreaming the numbers, all of the numbers, *I had the answers,* are you listening?"

I nodded, paralyzed, holding the pills and the water.

He talked to me when he had his episodes because he knew I would listen. My parents said he didn't know who I was, but that was a horrible lie. Your brother always knows who you are.

My mother took the pills. "Katie, come hold his wrists." I knelt on his wrists, but they pulled away. I tried to be heavier, to hold myself steady as Esau's arms shook and yanked under my knees. My mother put an elbow on Esau's chest and pried open his mouth with one hand, pushing the pills to the back of his throat with the other. Esau gagged and spit, wrinkling his forehead. Tears ran down the sides of his face and into his ears. She poured water into his mouth. Esau coughed and gagged, but he swallowed.

We sat in silence for what seemed like hours while he screamed, then sobbed, his cries gradually slowing down.

"Now what?" I whispered. Esau's body jerked awkwardly.

"Now we wait," my mother replied. Her face was drawn.

I slumped where I sat on Esau's arms. "Why does this happen?" I asked.

"What do you mean?"

"I mean, why does he get sick like this?"

She sighed. "He has a sad-sickness."

"Why?"

"Because it runs in the family." She looked at me. "You know how you have red hair like mine and Esau has black hair like Dad's?" I nodded. "Well, that's what it means when something runs in the family."

"Did he get it from Dad?" I asked.

"No," she said. "Why do you think that?"

I studied her face and decided she was lying. I only asked because she had told my father to his face that this was All His Damned Fault.

"Was it Aunt Rose?" I asked doubtfully.

"Maybe. We don't know."

"Am I going to get it?" I panicked a little and looked down at

Esau. He was breathing more deeply, his eyes low lidded like a frog's.

"No, you're not going to get it. You're born with it. It's not like catching the flu."

"I have the flu."

She laughed a little. "I know."

"I don't want to go to school today."

"No, you don't have to."

"I want to stay here with Esau."

She didn't say anything.

"Esau's staying home today," I told her. "Esau," I said, watching his face. His eyes didn't move.

"He can't hear you, baby," my mother said.

"He can so. Esau," I said again, shaking him. His chest was narrow and caved in, the ribs moving under the skin when I shook him. He looked like the drawing of Jesus that hung on my grandmother's wall. Skinny and dead. "Esau, you're staying home with me to play Monopoly and have SpaghettiOs and take a nap. We're not going to school. We have the flu. We have a sad-sickness. Dad has a pick-me-up. He's not mad about the coffee. Right?" I looked at my mother. She nodded.

"Esau," I said. His mouth moved slightly.

"He wants to talk to me," I said, louder. I felt my chin start to wrinkle and pursed my mouth to stop it. "He has something to tell me."

My mother reached out to touch my head. I jerked away.

"He's not here, honey," she said.

"Yes he *is* here, he is *so* here," I cried, shaking him some more. "He has something to *say,* he said we should *listen,* you're not *listening* to him." I put my head down by Esau's mouth to listen. I felt his breath on my ear, the hissing sound of words that wouldn't come out.

"Katie, he's sleeping."

"Liar!" I yelled. I stood up and went to the door and turned to face my mother. "You're going to send him to Away, aren't you?"

"Katie, we—"

"You are. You're going to send him to Away and then I can't sleep and we eat fish sticks and Dad goes for a drive for forever and everyone *leaves* me and and and—," I wailed, and started crying too hard to talk, so I gasped and hiccupped and sat down on the floor and put my head on the bathroom tile and watched it get all wet from tears.

She picked me up and carried me to my room. We walked down the hall, through the dining room, past my father in his chair. I bawled, "He hates Away, he told me the food is awful and the beds are hard and everyone's sad there and he hates the white room," and my mother said, "Shhhh, you're tired," and I yelled, "I'm not tired, what about Esau, he hates the white room." I was falling asleep as we walked, as my mother set me down on the bed and pulled the pink quilt over me. She leaned down and put her hand on my forehead and said, "You're giving yourself a fever, honey. Just try to sleep. I'll be back in a little while and bring you Seven-Up," and I said, "Everybody just leaves me," and my mother said, "I'm not leaving," and I nodded and closed my eyes. My mother began to move away and I said, "Mom," and I had something to ask her, but I forgot what. The morning light came through the curtains, a cold winter white. She leaned down and kissed my forehead.

"I'm not going to go away," she said. And shut the door.

I could hear my parents talking in the living room. I slid off the bed and opened my door.

"Arnold, we have to take him in." My mother stood with her back to my father, looking out the window with her arms crossed. My father let out a long breath.

"I know," he said.

"How long do you think it'll be this time?" my mother asked.

"I don't know, Claire. How would I know?"

In September, it had seemed like a very long time. The longer it was, the quieter they were, until they were almost whispering when they sat at the table. As if the words were so heavy they couldn't be said out loud, they would be too hard to lift. I had heard them talking about the doctors. My father had spat out the word *institution*. He had spat out *facility*.

Institution, facility, episode. Also, *medicine, court order,* and *They*.

You could arrange the words to mean different things. I arranged them in my head, filling in the blanks like I did in my vocabulary workbook. The way they went, if I had it figured out correctly, was: The *episodes* are occurring with *increasing frequency and severity*. (Sometimes there were long phrases or whole sections of the conversation that I didn't get.) The *facility* where Esau usually went was *low security*. *They* said that the *patient* might soon require a *high-security facility*. Otherwise known as an *institution*. Or simply *State*.

My *brother*, in other words, would be *institutionalized* and, my father spat out, turned into a *zombie*, handed over to the *experts* who could take care of his *son, goddammit*, better than he could himself.

On the other hand, you could arrange it this way: *They were having increasingly frequent episodes and the patient would institutionalize the zombie experts himself. Goddammit.*

It was good to have a word.

There was a pause. My mother asked, "Do you think they'll put him into State?"

My father shook his head. "Could be. I almost hope so. We can't keep paying for this." He put his head in his hands. "Do you know what this means?" he said quietly. "I will have failed. Do you understand that? Failed."

My mother turned from the window then and looked at my father. "No," she said. She touched his shoulder, and went down the hall to the bathroom.

I went out to my father where he sat and waited at his elbow until he picked me up and put me on his lap. Together, we looked at the place where my mother had been.

Somehow the day disappeared. My father's voice rumbled on the phone, and then he went into the bathroom and wrapped Esau in a quilt. He carried him, looking like a quilted cocoon, to his bedroom. I listened to my mother in the kitchen and went down the hall to sit where I could watch her. I heard my father close Esau's door and watched him go to the bar.

His voice sounded like someone talking underwater.

"I've put him down," he said.

"What time are we taking him in?" asked my mother, accepting the drink he handed her as he entered the kitchen.

"They said early afternoon. Need to leave around ten." He leaned back against the counter, set his glass down, and put the heels of his hands to his eyes. "Do you know what he said to me?" he asked.

My mother shook her head, staring down at the pan on the stove.

"He said—he looked right at me, you know how he does? How he gets clear for a minute, like the fog just lifts for a second? He looked at me and said, 'Dad, it's better in here.' Like to reassure me."

My father laughed as if he couldn't believe what he was saying. "And I didn't know what he meant. Better where? In the blankets? In the hospital? He doesn't know where he is, Claire. In his mind, maybe? He said, 'It's quiet now.' Before he fell asleep. 'It's quiet.'"

He fumbled behind him for his drink, his mouth moving.

My mother turned and offered him a plate of mac and cheese, and he knocked it out of her hand. A splat of yellow hit the wall by the new avocado-colored phone that matched the fridge.

Then he cried.

My mother's hand hovered in midair. She put it on his arm. He jerked away, bumping into his drink, the glass skidding on the counter, sloshing a little. He leaned against the hallway wall and bent over, his fists against his stomach.

"What have I done?" he said.

Then he walked into the living room and put his fist through the window.

Cold wind exploded into the room as if it had been pressing up against the glass, a dark animal rubbing its skin against the house, looking for a way to get in.

He stared at his arm, distracted. What little blood there was, what with the cold, froze to his skin in black dribbles of ice.

He walked down the hall. The front door shut and the car started, its wheels crunching through the snow.

My mother came into the living room and rested her hands on the back of the couch, looking at the black hole where the window had been. The oak tree behind the house seemed to have come inside to stand between the La-Z-Boy and the TV, its boughs sagging with snow, blue in the moonlight that poured into the room. Wind picked up the dry snow and sent it hissing over the windowsill, small drifts piling against the furniture, settling into the corners of chairs.

I went to my mom. We looked at the window together.

"We can't leave it like that," I said. "Can we?"

She shook her head.

"Should I get a blanket?"

She pushed herself off the back of the couch, and we got blankets from the linen closet. I held them while my mother threw them over the curtain rod. My hands got cold.

My mother dropped her arms when she was done, and said, "Go to bed now, Kate." She turned and went to her room.

I stood there, looking around. The dark living room was like a winter field, shadows of furniture gradually disappearing under blown snow. There's glass under there, I thought to myself. Carefully, I walked through the snow, skidding my toes first. I decided to wait until my father came home. I would keep him company while he played cards. I sat down on the snow-covered couch and looked at the blankets, blowing softly, letting in snow.

My face was frozen. Esau was sleeping in the other room. Tomorrow he would be gone. He was going away for a long time. They were taking him and it was their fault and now there wasn't even a window.

I stood up, yanked down all the blankets, and sat back down on the couch.

I watched the wind whisk a pile of snow from a branch of the oak and blow it toward me. I flinched and closed my eyes as the spray of ice hit my face.

On Christmas morning, I woke up and lay in bed, not wanting to leave the tunnel of my own warmth. Out in the living room, my mother put on a Christmas record. I smelled bacon and coffee. My father's voice came down the hall, booming along with the carols.

Everything was fake. They were only doing it because I said I was quitting Christmas. Last night I had refused to trim the tree. It was Esau's and my job. Both my parents were drunk and nearly set the house on fire, getting tangled in the lights and laughing until they sat down in the middle of the boxes of tissue-wrapped ornaments and cried.

We were going to visit him at State.

I got up and dressed in all red. I knew my mother wouldn't tell me not to wear red, what with my orange hair, because it was Christmas and I could do anything I liked. I got my sleeves confused and went out the door and my father set me straight.

"Santa came, Katie," my mother called. "Why don't you see what he brought you?"

"Your mother's making pancakes," my father added, sitting down on the couch and rubbing his hands together. He nodded toward the tree, lit up like Las Vegas. "Go on and look in your stocking."

I shook my head, but my parents looked so crestfallen I couldn't keep it up. I sat down among the piles of presents and started fishing treasures out of the stocking my grandmother had knit for me when I was born.

There were dozens of presents from Oma and Opa, the cousins and uncles we never saw, my parents, who always were broke after Christmas. My father spiked his eggnog with brandy and my mother put used bows in her hair. They sang. They laughed when I liked things. The pancakes were from scratch. They gave me candy and oranges and new red boots. They gave me everything on my list.

They gave me the orange boy's bike. The one Davey had. My heart's desire.

I said thank you and began to cry, for reasons of which I was not aware.

"Oh, now. Say now," said my father. He came over and sat next to me on the floor, rubbing my back with his hand. "See here."

"It's not the bike," I said, wiping my face with the heels of my hands. "I love the bike."

"No, of course not. It's everything," he said.

"It's just *everything*."

"I know. Of course it is."

"The bike is the best present ever."

"It's not bad, is it? No. It's all yours. We'll teach you to ride in the spring."

"With Esau. I want Esau to teach me to ride."

The record had stopped. My mother got up and moved the needle to the edge. The Mormon Tabernacle Choir exploded into the room like a drunk uncle, screaming, "Joy to the World."

"Well now," said my father. "We'll just see what's what when the time comes."

I was done crying. "I want to go see Esau," I said.

"Well, we're going to," said my father, surprised.

"Now."

He looked up at my mother. She raised her eyebrows and shrugged.

"Hup, then," my father said, getting to his feet. "I guess that settles it. I think I'll get my shoes on first, if that's all right?"

I nodded.

We slid through the winter landscape as if the car was on skates. Whiteness. White ground, white sky, neat piles of snow on the thin wooden fences at property lines. Bare black branches of windbreaks here and there. My father babbled excitedly for a while, then lapsed into a silence that lasted until we arrived.

The building wasn't ugly, exactly. It looked like a mansion, brick and five floors high. I trailed behind my parents, who straightened themselves and walked toward the double front doors. My father pushed me slightly before him as we stood waiting at the reception desk, as if he'd brought me there as a gift. My mother carried a shopping bag of presents for Esau and looked hopeful.

I began to regret having asked to come.

"Visiting?" asked the square woman at the desk. Glasses dangled on a cord off the shelf of her bosoms.

"No, we're checking in," my father said, and laughed loudly at himself. She looked up at him with her chin tucked in. He cleared his throat.

"Name?" she said.

"Schiller."

She fussed and shuffled. "Hmm," she said, as if she had discovered something on the piece of paper she held. "Fifth floor," she said with finality, and put her glasses on her nose and started typing.

We got in the elevator. As the door closed, my father muttered, "Merry Christmas to you too." I giggled.

The elevator opened and we stood outside a Plexiglas door, through which I could see a desk and then another door. A buzzer sounded, and my father pulled open the first door.

A pretty nurse looked up at us and smiled. She wasn't wearing the silly hat. "Merry Christmas," she said. "Nice to see you again, Mr. Schiller, Mrs. Schiller." She looked at me and said, "And you must be Kate."

I nodded, feeling put on the spot.

"Your brother talks about you a lot," she said, coming around the desk with a huge key ring. She paused in front of the door and turned to face us. "Now, I should tell you, Esau's not doing so well today." She studied the reactions on our faces. "He had a long night last night, and we had to put him down with a pretty powerful medication. You know how it comes and goes. He's done just great this week, really. But today he's not very clear."

My father nodded, as if taking this lightly. "So, he's a little foggy?"

"He might not know who you are." She looked at him steadily.

"Does he know it's Christmas?" my father asked. He sounded so sad I winced.

"Hard to say," she replied as she turned and unlocked the door. She held it open for us and we filed in.

The wide, carpeted hallway smelled of medicine, Lysol, and pee. We went into a large room where people were clustered at tables and on couches, or sat alone in chairs. The room was decorated like a classroom, with glittered cutouts of paper stars, Christmas trees, and angels pasted to the windows. A little plastic tree sat crooked on a side table and an old woman in a hat knitted a long thing.

"Esau," the nurse called, going over to a shrouded figure in a chair by the window, its back to the room. We followed her and stood stiffly a few feet away as she bent over what I realized was my brother, shrunken. "Your family's here to celebrate Christmas with you."

Esau turned around and looked at us, his eyes moving slowly from one to the next, taking each of us in. "Hello," he said formally, as if it took him that long to think up the right word. "Why don't you sit down," the nurse suggested, dragging chairs up in a semicircle around him, as if he was going to give a speech. To my father she said, "Let me know if you need anything." She left.

"Merry Christmas, son," my father burst out, leaning down over Esau and giving him a hug. My mother kissed him on the cheek. "See, we brought your presents," she said. I sat down in a chair and tugged my skirt over my knees.

"Hello," Esau said again. "Thank you." He paused. "Hello."

"Do you know who we are?" I asked.

"Yes," he said, looking right at me, and I believed him.

"It's Christmas," I said.

"Okay. Thank you for the presents," he said slowly, as if his mouth was sticky.

I helped him open them because his hands shook from the medicine. He thanked us for the magazines. He thanked us for the new games. He thanked us for a book on bugs, thick, elaborately illustrated, that I wanted myself. He unwrapped the last package, looking bewildered by the sudden largesse of his world, and held the ink-blue corduroy shirt in his hands.

"A blanket," he said softly, pleased with it. He ran his hands over its nap.

"That'd be your good old-fashioned shirt, son," said my father. "For wearing."

My brother nodded. "To sleep with." He bunched it carefully and held it up to his face.

We sat silently, trying to decide what to do with this.

"Well, I don't see why the hell not," my father said finally, and reached out to pat Esau's knee. It startled Esau, and he pulled himself into the corner of his chair. I saw the hurt cross my father's face as he took his hand back and showed it to Esau, palm out, the way you'd show your hand to a skittish dog.

The smells of cafeteria food seeped into the room, and the garbled murmurs of the other residents grew louder.

"I have to go now," Esau said, his voice heavy with regret. He stood, holding his new shirt, abandoning his blankets in the chair. "Thank you." He walked stiffly to the doorway. Our heads craned to watch him explaining something excitedly to the nurse. He showed her the shirt and gestured. She helped him get his arms into the sleeves, pulling the corduroy over the shirt he already wore. She led him back, and he sat down again. He looked pleased.

"She says—" He looked up at her and suddenly went blank. "Oh! She says do you want lunch."

"Would you like to stay for lunch?" the nurse echoed. "Esau would like it if you stayed."

"It's a special thing," he added.

"It's a special Christmas dinner," she translated. "The residents planned their favorites. What did you pick, Esau?"

"Peaches!" he crowed, rocking in his chair.

"I think he picked pizza, but that's all right," she said. "I'm sure there will be peaches too. There always are."

We ate pizza, French toast, corn, and peaches for Christmas dinner. Esau ate with unexpected daintiness, a napkin tucked in his collar. After lunch there was medicine in paper cups and Christmas carols.

Esau didn't go over to the group that gathered around the ancient record player. He hung back, with us, standing next to my father, every now and then reaching out to touch my father's face. My father sat very still as Esau's pale, translucent hands fluttered near his eyelids, tapped his brow, his earlobes, his chin. My father began silently to cry.

Esau edged closer to him, a look of concern on his face. He pressed his thumb into each slow tear as it appeared, then walked his strange stiff walk across the room and returned with a tissue. He handed it to my father, and my father blew his nose.

"Thank you," he said.

"You're welcome," Esau replied. He waited until he saw that my father had finished crying. He sat down in my father's lap, his thin side against my father's chest, his arm over my father's shoulders. Carefully, my father wrapped his arms around my brother. They rocked.

"I have to go now," Esau said peacefully. He pulled up the hem of his new shirt and laid it against his face. His head fell heavily against my father's neck.

I sat in the backseat of the car, watching night fall on the white prairie, unaware that in the front seat my parents' marriage had cracked down the centre the way a frozen lake will crack: deeply, invisibly, without explanation, the eerie noise a muffled clap of thunder that rolls from the south side to the north.

My mother drove. Both of them smoked. Nothing was said.

We drove through the night in a narrow tunnel of headlights. I felt safe and hot, zipped into my jacket, buckled into my seat.

I kicked the back of my father's seat steadily and he didn't tell me to stop, but I grew bored with it and I stopped.

As soon as we pulled up to the house, I ran in to survey my new riches. My mother made toast from Christmas bread for supper and called us. We'd been sitting there only a minute when my father pushed himself away from the table. But instead of getting a drink and sitting down again, he just picked up a bottle. Then he went out to the porch and sat down in a chair full of snow.

My mother turned to me. "I can't do it," she said, as if she and I had been discussing something. "I just can't." After a minute I nodded, because she seemed to be waiting for a response. She nodded once in return, stood up, and went into the kitchen to make coffee.

I sat there awhile. Since no one was looking, I ate all the toast. Eventually my father came back inside and sat down in his chair. I got up from the table and passed by him, feeling invisible. I wondered if this was what it was like to be a ghost. I sat down on the floor of my bedroom with my blanket and watched him in the living room and wondered if Esau could do this. If he was a sort of ghost, and could float through space, watching. The idea comforted me, and I thought I felt him settle down next to me on the floor. I laid part of my blanket over his invisible knees.

My mother came out of the kitchen with two cups of coffee and handed one to my father. She sat down on the couch. She looked out the window, the way I had noticed her doing more and more—as if she was looking toward a particular place, a place she wanted to go. I thought of what lay in the direction she was looking: first, the Andersons' yard, then Main Street. If she was looking at Main Street, she might be thinking about turning left. To get to the city, you turn left on Main Street. If you turn right, you wind up in Canada and then the North Pole.

I figured that if I needed to find my mother, I would have to take a left on Main Street.

But they were sitting there, my mother and father, peacefully enough. I pulled my blanket up to my nose and smelled it and thought maybe things were all right now that they were having coffee and it was Christmas night.

When you're six, you don't know about what happens at the end. Because the world revolves around you when you're six, you assume the end must be catastrophic, because it would be catastrophic to you. The end would be dramatic and loud.

But what really happens at the end is that you sit down and have coffee without looking at each other. There is a sort of strange relief: The thing that was hanging in the air like a gas leak, invisible and toxic, has happened. It's out. It's a relief. It is a solid, tangible. When you're six, you can't possibly imagine that your parents—who are blowing carefully on their coffee—are only being peaceful because they know what you don't: that there is no stopping whatever comes next, and so they might as well have coffee while they wait.

Four little Indians. Three little Indians. Two little Indians, sitting on the couch.

I watched my mother cross one nyloned knee over the other, and I thought that the best thing about night, in wintertime, was how cold it is outside and how inside the lights are yellow and safe.

"I'm in love with you, you know," my father said.

"That doesn't seem," my mother said gently, "very relevant."

"Well put," he said. He took a sip. "You're thinking of leaving me, aren't you?"

After a minute, my mother said, "Yes."

There was a long, calm pause in the living room.

My father said: "Claire, I want to die."

Carefully, my mother replied, "You're aware that you've said that before?"

"Jesus, Claire," he said. I flinched at the rising voice. "I mean, my God, you won't let me near you, not that I blame you, I don't have the energy to do a damn thing with myself. Christ, I'm *useless,* I sit here all day thinking about you, about Esau, what I could have done, anything I could have done—" He put his forehead in his hands. "I don't blame you for wanting to leave. I don't have anything *left,* Claire."

"You do have something left," she said, her voice low and angry. "You have us. You have a family. You selfish, selfish man. What more do you want?" She turned her face away from him and I watched her wipe a finger quickly under her eyes.

"So do you!" he cried. "And what, you're planning to walk away yourself! What the hell business have you got telling me to stay for the sake of my family?"

She turned on him. "I need to *leave* for the sake of my family! I cannot have them watch you sit here and *rot*! I *will not* let my children watch their father die!" She put her face in her hands. "Darling," she said, her voice fragile. "Darling, darling man. They love you so much."

"They do," he said flatly. "Not you."

She looked up, resting her chin on her fingertips. She said, "I do. I wish I didn't. But I do." She turned her face to him.

"You've left already," he said slowly. "Haven't you?"

She didn't speak for a moment. Then, angry, she said, "Why should I stay when you're already gone?"

He looked at her, then slumped forward in his chair. His face showed a fury I had never seen. He spoke slowly. "You don't have to wake up every morning and think of one reason, just one good fucking reason, to go on."

My mother was quiet for a minute. Then she said, "Are you waiting for me to feel sorry for you?"

He didn't answer.

"Because I don't," she said, setting her coffee down. "I just don't."

I watched her walk down the hall.

My father's face crumpled like a paper napkin.

Sometimes you are very young when you learn how important it can be to lie. How you can sometimes shatter an entire tiny universe by telling one horrible truth.

I watched my father sit there in his chair with tears running down his cheeks. Not making any noise. I wanted to stand up and go over to him and tell him it would be all right.

But I was glued to the floor, and it wouldn't be all right.

You don't know until you're older how many times you will go over one night in your head—replay each exchange, remember each look, each gesture. You will remember how you sat glued to a dark corner. You will remember how you did nothing.

You did not go to your father.

You did not say it would be all right.

You did not say the magic words.

You did not say, I love you. It's not your fault. It will be all right.

You did not lie.

You did not say good-bye.

My father wiped his face and stood. I heard him out in the garage. I went to stand at the living-room window, pressing my face against the glass.

Out in the dark, I watched a tree split down the centre from cold.

 CLAIRE

I heard the shot.

In memory, I knew before I heard. It goes like this:

I know. My head snaps left.

I hear the shot.

I run. Kate is coming down the hall. In one motion, I grab her, turn, *fold over* on her completely, in slow motion, as if actually *tucking her into* my rib cage.

I remind myself of an animal.

We sat in the back of the sheriff's car, heading north, toward Nimrod.

I might have bitten the officer, which would take some explaining. I wiped Kate's nose with my hand. Her head was damp. She was hysterical, which calmed me.

She fell asleep in my lap. We crunched into their drive. The door flew open. Oma trudged through the high snow in her nightdress and a coat and yanked open the car door. Opa peeled Kate off me, tucked her under his arm, and plodded back into the house while she screamed and flailed.

Oma wrapped a blanket over my shoulders. "Inside. Right now," she said. She watched me for a moment, then slapped my left cheek, whipped out a flask, poured whiskey into my mouth, and snapped my jaw shut with her gnarled hand. *"Ja, ja.* Okay. Here we go, dear." I swallowed it and gasped, and she pulled me out of the car.

I was almost two feet taller than she and I trailed her like a gigantic child.

Inside, Oma poured me another whiskey. Kate was under the dining-room table, playing with two spoons.

She showed no intention of coming out anytime soon. Her spoons whispered happily to one another and danced. Her lips were purple with grape juice. Her skin was the color of paste, her eyes sunken and blue. She looked dead. Tubercular. Drowned. I took a swallow of my drink.

"Katie," I said.

"What." She fitted the spoons into each other. Turned to look at me with her horrible eyes. "What," she repeated.

I couldn't think of what, so I left her alone and she forgot me. *Are you dead, Katie?* I was not feeling myself.

Around three in the morning, she emerged from under the table and crossed to the centre of the room. She lay down on the floor, tucked her arms and legs tightly under herself, and shut her eyes, her rump in the air, like an infant.

Oma sat in the chair across from me, knitting. *"Kleine,"* Oma said. Her twisted fingers did not stop. *"Kleine,"* she said again, more firmly. She sighed, set down her knitting, pushed herself out of her chair. "Bed now," she said. "To bed." She bent down and took hold of Kate's shoulder, whereupon Kate, without opening her eyes, let out a shriek that could have shattered glass.

"Go away," Kate said calmly. "I'm sleeping."

Oma sat back down in her chair and resumed her knitting.

It was still dark when Opa's bedroom door opened. His aftershave preceded him down the hall. His white hair was combed and slick. He had a little piece of bloody tissue stuck to his Adam's apple. He stopped when he saw Kate.

"What the hell," he said, shaking his head. He hooked his thumbs through his suspenders and gave them a snap. "What in the damn-blasted hell."

He looked at me. "'Bout time for coffee, you think?" He turned and went into the kitchen. The percolator began to spit and hiss like a cornered cat. When he came out, he crouched over Kate, his hands on his knees. He eased and grunted his way down to one knee.

"Say there," he said. "Say there, Salamander." She pretended to sleep.

"Salamander Suzy," he sang. She fought a smile.

He put his arms around her and wrestled himself upright. He walked out of the room with her, whispering, "Slippery slimy Salamander Suzie."

It was silent for a moment. Then, in the guest room behind us, I heard the gruff rumble of his made-up salamander song.

At breakfast we told her he was dead.

She was eating a soft-boiled egg in an egg cup. It was her favorite thing, and I couldn't make it for her. Only Oma. At home, she'd sit at the table and squawk, "Three minutes!" like a tiny queen. But I never cooked it right. "Three minutes, Mom," she'd call, and despite my vigilance at the kitchen clock, despite knowing how she wanted it, a liquid yellow yolk without any watery white, despite the fact that I *could* for God's sake boil an egg, I always lifted it from the slow-boiling water with a sinking heart. At my silence, she got nervous. I'd hear her chair push back, her feet squeak across the floor. She'd step over to the egg and the two of us would look at it. "Take his hat off," she'd suggest, as if this time I might have done it right. I'd get a sharp knife from the drawer, tap the shell once, and slice off the pointed end, holding the egg upright. I knew before I lowered it for her to look. "Too done," I'd say. A gold yolk, not hard-boiled but not liquid either—four minutes, easily. She'd give it a long look, deciding if she could pretend. She wasn't a good liar, though, and she'd say, "That's all right."

It wasn't as if the child starved.

Oma dropped an egg into boiling water when Kate came into the kitchen, herded by her grandfather, who had braided her hair with lopsided good intent. One braid by her ear, one near the nape of her neck. Kate settled into the chair he pulled out, making minute adjustments to her place setting: grapefruit spoon laid out below the grapefruit bowl, fork switched to the right of the plate, where it could more easily commune with knife and spoon.

"Napkin in your lap, Katie," I heard myself say. My voice startled me, and I watched Katie place her napkin over her knees. She looked up at me, waiting. For approval? Greeting?

Helpless for the correct reaction, I said, "Oma's making your egg." Kate smiled and turned to look at Oma. I went into the bathroom and threw up my coffee. I ran cold water on my wrists and looked at myself in the mirror. This will be the face I have now, I thought, though it made no sense, the face was no different than it had been twelve hours before. This will be my face.

I went out and sat down across from Kate again. She was eating the crusts off her toast, saving the buttered centre bites to dip in her egg yolk. One piece of her toast was smeared with raspberry preserves, and this she ate in delicate spirals from the outside edges in. Opa set another cup of Folgers in front of me and put his hand on my shoulder. Oma lifted the three-minute egg from the water with a spoon, put it in the cup, tapped and chopped the hat off neatly, set both cup and hat on Kate's plate. Kate put her toast down and scootched up to sit on her feet so she could peer directly down into the egg as she salted and peppered it carefully, adding a tiny dab of butter, never once chipping the shell.

"Well, somebody tell her, then," Oma said quietly, her back to us. She scrubbed out a pot and set it in the rack to dry.

Opa was leaning up against the rust-colored refrigerator. He took a swallow of coffee and sighed. "Salamander Suzie, now, you know your dad's gone and died."

Arnold's absence stepped into the kitchen, a fifth body, and pulled up a chair.

I watched my daughter's face. She put her spoon down and wiped egg from the corners of her mouth. She sat back in her chair and played with the white cotton lace that hemmed her dress. She was wearing a yellow-checked dress that Oma had made for her, a summer dress, one of her favorites. Carefully, she turned the hem over, picked at it a moment, then took her fork and ripped it. She stood up and twisted herself around slowly, pulling the hem completely off, and then she sat back down with a fistful of lace. Using her fork, she tore the hem into inch-long bits and set them in a pile by her plate.

The three of us watched her pick up her spoon, peer into the egg, begin eating again.

I looked at Oma, who shook her head and shrugged.

"Well, okay, then," Opa said, turning to the coffeepot.

"Do you want more juice, *kleine*?" Oma asked.

"No!" Kate shouted.

"Katie," I said. "Don't yell at your grandmother."

"It's all right," Oma said, pouring Kate more juice.

"I don't *want* any more juice!" Kate shrieked.

"Katie!" I said, shocked.

"Fine," Oma said, whisking the juice away and pouring it back into the pitcher. Kate looked sadly at the place where her juice had been.

"Say you're sorry," I said.

"You're sorry," she muttered.

"Very clever," I snapped.

Kate dipped her toast in the egg repeatedly, and wiped her eyes with her fist. She hunched over her egg and wouldn't look up at anyone.

Opa went over to her and tugged one of her braids. "Life's no fun sometimes, hmm?" he asked. Kate shook her head and nibbled her toast. "No fun," he repeated.

I watched a couple of tears roll off the tip of her nose and into the egg. She stirred them in with a spoon.

We were quiet while she finished eating. She didn't seem to mind the three of us staring at her. She sat back in her chair to survey the tidy wreckage of her breakfast: the unbroken eggshell, the grapefruit rind, a few crumbs and a smear of red preserves on her plate. She stood up and took all her silverware to the sink, then returned for each dish. Each dish, both hands. Each dish up to the sink, then over the side.

I found her smallness oppressive.

She climbed onto Oma's step stool and leaned in to wash her hands. The threads of her lace hem dangled down; I noticed that her white tights were on backward, bagging at the back of her knees.

Climbing down, she said with weird formality, "I am having a nap," and walked out of the kitchen. Down the hall, the door closed.

At least there are rules.

There are rules for what you do when someone dies, and better ways to die, and better times of day to die. It is better when someone dies at night, like this. When my mother died, it was one o'clock in the afternoon on a bright spring day. A southern spring day. There were lilacs, a sprig I'd cut from the bush outside the front door and put in a glass by her bed. I was alone with her. She was sleeping. She woke up, called for me, and I went in with her lunch on a tray, but she was dead. I looked at the clock, and it was only one. A whole day with the lilacs, the uneaten lunch, the spring sunshine coming at me like a wall falling down, a wall she had been holding up with her breath. I set the lunch down by her legs and pulled a chair up next to her and brushed her hair, and then I read a book all day until I could see through the drawn blinds that it was getting dark, and then I called a funeral parlor from the phone book.

But this was better, since he died at night. This way we could just refer to him as *he,* as in *he died yesterday.* This way it was *yesterday.* As in, it took place in the past. It is something that happened. It is no longer happening.

Now it was time for *arrangements.*

Oma washed the dishes and Opa dried. Then Oma pulled off her blue rubber gloves and said, "Get dressed, dear. We need to make arrangements."

You do not make arrangements in your bathrobe.

Arrangements are what you make when someone dies or goes mad. Arrangements are orderly. They are the answer to chaos. I have myself made many arrangements, I am good at it. I got dressed.

I went into the guest bedroom. It took me a moment to remember what I was doing there. I remembered that I was getting dressed to make arrangements for the burial of my husband, who had died the night before. Had killed himself the night before. Because of what I said. Because of me. The remembering of this caused a wave of profound exhaustion, and I faltered at the side of the bed, suddenly able to taste the coolness of the sheets, as you can when you have the flu. Instead I opened the dresser, where we kept spare clothes for long weekends, and put on underwear, a brassiere, and stockings.

Then I stood looking at myself in the mirror, thinking, I am only thirty-eight.

I smoothed my hair and went to the closet for a suitable dress.

Oma sat in her chair under her fold-out leather lap desk, which contained seven separate compartments for paper (everyday paper, list-making paper, formal letter paper, liner papers, note cards, calling cards, and *etvas* paper for jotting), three compartments for envelopes, one for her stack of return-address stamps, one for postage stamps, pen compartments on the left and right, an inkwell, a pencil sharpener, a blotter, a diary, an address book, a calendar, and hanging from the lid so that it faced her, a daily Scripture passage and attendant prayer. At the top of each sheet of paper was printed:

> Mrs. Elton Schiller
> 14571 County Road 19 Nimrod, Minnesota, 94782
> *Job 1:21–2: The LORD giveth and the LORD taketh away.*
> *Blessed be the name of the LORD. In all this Job sinned not, nor charged God foolishly.*

The lap desk had been a wedding present from her mother-in-law forty years before. She polished the leather and brass locks every time she used it, and she used it every day, when she wrote her letters. She'd get comfortable in her chair and Opa would carry it over and set it on her lap; when she was done, he'd fold it up and take it off her again.

She sat there looking efficient and licked the tip of her ink pen. "Sit down, dear," she said, and I did.

"What first, mmm? Flowers," she said. "Flowers. Nothing showy, but nothing cheap either, no. We're not going to hide our heads under our arms in shame, no," she went on, her pen scratching against the heavy paper. "So then. We'll have Dot do the flowers then, *ja?*"

"That sounds fine."

"*Ja.* Okay. And what colors? White, some. But some color too. Too showy, all white." She lifted her pen and looked at me.

"Roses?" I ventured, sitting up straighter, wanting to be part of the arrangements.

"You know, and I have gotten so *sick* of the lilies," she announced. "At Easter, with the lilies, and then again they sell the lilies for the young people's mission, and then more lilies at Christmas and Epiphany, all year the lilies." She motioned with her pen. "Nowhere in the Bible does it say the lilies."

"'Consider the lilies,'" Opa said. He was sitting with his back to us at the dining-room table, reading the paper.

"'Consider the lilies,'" Oma conceded, after a pause.

"No carnations," Opa said, taking advantage of his opening.

"Why not?"

"Hated 'em."

"No."

"Yes he did. The man hated carnations."

Both Oma and I stared at his back.

"Swore he was never going to one more baptism, wedding, confirmation, graduation, or funeral if it meant he'd have to wear another damned carnation in his buttonhole." Opa set down his paper and turned in his chair. "No carnation in his buttonhole, neither."

He looked at Oma until he was pretty sure she wouldn't go and stick one there when he wasn't looking. Then he turned back and picked the paper up, shook it out, and started reading again.

"You knew this? Your husband hated carnations?" Oma asked me. I shook my head no.

"Well, what in the Pete's sake are we going to do, then? We'll ask Dot, she'll know. But then, I don't want her doing all showy and flashy. What colors. Maybe some nice blue? He liked a good blue suit."

"Name me a blue flower, Oma," Opa said.

"Iris."

"Which one's that?"

"Looks like a—" She stopped, scribbled, and ripped off a paper. "Show him," she said to me, and I took him the drawing. He studied it.

"Hmph," he said. "Besides that."

"Hydrangea," she said proudly, already waiting to hand me the next sheet of paper.

"Looks like a damn fluffy bowling ball. Okay, blue. Blue, fine."

"What about some roses?" I asked. "For some—extra color?"

It was very important right then that I be allowed to have some roses.

Oma was making a list of blue flowers.

Opa read his paper.

Finally he turned his page. "No roses," he said. "Can't do roses."

"People would talk," Oma added.

Opa closed his paper and stood. "Making a little coffee, I think," he said, and went out of the room.

Oma looked up at me brightly. "Now!" she said. "The casket."

"Yes," I said, feeling dizzy. "The casket."

That night, after we had made the arrangements and were sitting all together in the living room watching the news, a shot went off on TV.

I screamed and covered my mouth. Oma patted my arm. Opa got me a brandy.

Kate, who was sitting on her knees two inches from the screen, did not move or appear to blink, either when the shot went off or when I screamed.

Opa turned off the television. Oma went to fetch our lists, so we could review the arrangements, so I could get to sleep.

Pioter Gustofson ran the funeral home. "A good man, he is," Oma said from the passenger seat in front of me as we drove toward Staples. She wore her good blue coat and gripped her black leather pocketbook in her lap. Kate gazed out the window, craning her neck to look at a herd of cattle that stood knee deep in snow.

She turned to me. "Do their feet get cold?"

"I don't think so."

"Why not?"

We drove. She gave up on me, leaned forward, and patted Opa on the shoulder. "Opa, why not?"

"Why not what, snickerdoodle?"

"Why don't cows' feet get cold?"

"They ain't got toes."

"They don't?"

"Nope. No toes. Can't get cold feet without toes."

She settled back to think this one over for a while.

"Pioter Gustofson has been very good to us, hasn't he." Oma looked out into the blowing snow that went skidding across the county highway.

"Yes, he has." Opa put his hand on Oma's gloved hands and squeezed.

Kate tipped over and put her head on my leg.

"What else doesn't got toes?" she asked.

"Snakes," said her grandfather. "Spiders. Creepy crawlers." Kate giggled and wiped her nose on my knee.

I looked down at her. My snotty little beast. I picked her up and settled her into my lap and she put her arms around my neck. She smelled of milk. She gazed out the rear window and I counted the tiny white bones of her spine that showed above the collar of her dress, each an imperfect pearl pressing up through her thin skin.

She shifted and sang under her breath, "Snakes, spiders, creepy crawlers, creepy crawlers, snakes and spiders, snakes and spiders." She took a deep breath, and sighed.

Out in the middle of nowhere, a green sign said WELCOME TO NIMROD—POP. 561.

The circular drive in front of the funeral parlor and the wide steps up to the double doors were shoveled with precision. The two-story sandstone building sat with a sort of modest grandeur at a corner in the centre of town, as if presiding over the redbrick town hall, the library, and the steepled Methodist church, none of whose walks were shoveled nearly as well.

We were expected.

Pioter Gustofson met us at the door and ushered us into the dark, silent, heavily carpeted foyer. The smell of lilies was overwhelming.

"Madge," he said, holding Oma's elbows and looking at her intently. She bowed her head as if she were being blessed. "And Elton." He gripped Opa's shoulder. Opa shook his head slowly and made a sound, as if to say, Damned if I know.

"And you're Mrs. Schiller," he said, reaching for my hand, which he clasped with both of his. "I am very, very sorry for your loss."

"My dad died," Kate announced loudly.

We all looked at her. She stared at him suspiciously. She didn't like men she didn't know. "Kate," I said, "This is Mr. Gustofson."

"Hello, Kate."

"Hello."

"How old are you?"

"Eleven."

"She isn't," I said to him, startled.

"Yes I am. I want to go now," she said, and turned for the door.

"*Kleine,*" Oma said very gently. Kate turned around and hid behind Opa's leg.

"Let's go down to my office, shall we?" Mr. Gustofson said.

I sat in a chair by the window with Kate around my neck like a monkey. She was heavy, seemed to be making herself heavy on purpose. She needed a nap. I squinted. The glare off the snow through the leaded-glass windows made it impossible to tell where Nimrod left off and the sky began. All flat white. The dingy clapboard Methodist church seemed suspended in midair, a black iron cross above the black iron bell dangling somewhere against sky or snow.

"Cardinal," Kate said into my ear. "Two cardinals."

I took the cup of coffee Gustofson offered me. Oma and Opa sat very straight in their chairs, and Gustofson sat down at his desk. He shuffled papers for a moment, then pushed them aside and leaned back.

"Well, damnation," he said.

"Darn right," Opa concurred.

Oma and I sipped our coffee.

"Known you folks, what, forty-odd years?"

"'Bout that."

"Tough times, these are."

"Hard times."

Gustofson studied the silver pen in his hand, his mouth turned down at the corners in concentration.

"Good man, Arnold," he said.

Opa nodded slowly, stretched his fingers out in front of him, studied his nails. "That he was. That he was."

"Loved his family."

"Yes he did."

Kate shifted in my lap. "Can I take my shoes off?" she whispered. I pulled her Mary Janes off her feet, and she curled up completely, her head against my chest.

"How's the little girl, then?" Gustofson asked, nodding toward Kate.

"Not so good, I don't think. Taking it pretty hard," Opa said.

"She'll be all right," Oma said.

"Of course she will," Gustofson assured her. "Give her a little time, of course she'll be just fine. This young, may not even remember it."

Oma nodded. "Maybe not."

I stared out the window and went over it again to be sure. I heard a sound: It was the shot. I ran. I caught Kate running down the hall, her arms lifted up. I doubled over, tucked her into my rib cage. I pushed her skull into my right shoulder as I turned. She did not see. Her skull fit perfectly into the palm of my hand.

"Blue jay," she said, and I turned to look. She giggled. "Silly. There's no blue jays yet."

I was fairly sure she did not see.

A small figure in a black coat walked out of the Methodist church, pulled its collar around its neck, and tucked its nose into its scarf. Slowly, with a cane, it made its way down the steps and out of view.

Arrangements were made. My coffee cup was filled. The flowers would be white and blue. There would be no lilies (the scent of them was making me dizzy even now), and there would be no carnations. The senior pastor at Grace Lutheran would speak, not the strange new one from out east, but the old one who knew them.

"Baptized Arnold, he did," Opa said.

"'Ashes to ashes,'" Oma said, nodding in agreement. "It's fitting."

"Yes it is," Gustofson said.

The pastor would speak of hope, and would not speak of sin or Hell, which would cause talk. In lieu of flowers, donations should be sent to the Shriners' Children's Hospital, which also seemed fitting. The reception would be held at Oma's house directly following. The obituary would say he was a good man who loved his family and lived in the faith of Christ. It would not mention that he would be missed, which would seem to belabor a point. He was preceded in death by his sister, Rosalina Schiller, and survived by his mother and father, Mr. and Mrs. Elton Schiller, his loving wife, Claire Jacobs Schiller, and his two children, Esau age twelve and Kate age six.

An open casket would not do.

Readings with references to death would not do.

Roses would not do.

They were looking at me expectantly. I looked back at them.

"Dear, what do you think about music? 'Amazing Grace'?" Oma asked.

"No," I said, louder than I meant to.

Kate petted my ear. "Mom-mom-mom-mom," she sang softly.

"He was fond," I said, trying to look friendly and sane, "of Mozart."

They looked at me sadly, worried. "Anything else?"

Suddenly I saw him, just a few years younger, leaned back in his La-Z-Boy, his undershirt torn and sweaty from work in the garage, a beer on the TV table to his left. Leaned back like that, eyes closed, conducting an invisible orchestra to the rising swell of Mozart's *Requiem*.

Hearing my skirt shirr. Opening his eyes midphrase, smiling at me. Glancing around for the kids, reaching out his arms. Wrapping his arms around my hips, kissing my belly, looking up at me and whispering, *"Listen! Listen!"* He closed his eyes again and pointed to a place I couldn't see.

That terrifying rapture.

Mozart would not do.

Oma, making dinner, leaned her hands on the counter next to the stove, bent her head, and said, as if startled, "Oh."

Kate, who was helping, stood on the footstool. She paused in her stirring of cake batter in kind, as if to wait for Oma. A raw roast sat in the roasting rack amid a naked-looking pile of peeled carrots and potatoes, quartered onions. Kosher salt and pepper, rosemary, red wine.

Oma slapped her hand on the counter once, as if to try the gesture on for size. She did it again, harder. She straightened, placed her hands over her face, and did not move.

Kate set her mixing bowl carefully on the counter and looked steadily into it, licking batter off the wooden spoon in small catlike licks.

Now he was definitely dead.

Now the arrangements were made, and the funeral would be on Friday, and tomorrow the casseroles and pies and bars and salads would begin to arrive, because due time had passed. Tomorrow the women would descend, and say very little, and not mention death, and tape notes to the plastic wrap and aluminum foil that would read, in perfect, identical handwriting, "Heat 20 min. at 325. Freezes well 4 wks." Now Oma would have to reheat everything, and serve it on Friday, at the reception, so the women would see that it didn't go to waste, like her son, and that she appreciated, even in her grief, a kindess done, and Oma would have to bake all day as soon as they arrived, to make something to return in the handmade towels in which the women would wrap and knot their pies and cakes and casseroles and bars, the hand-stitched heirloom towels passed down through generations, given at weddings for brides to use when they went to another woman's house, whether for a meal or for a death, fragile towels that never broke with the weight of what they carried, no matter how heavy the gift.

Kate dipped into the bowl again and ate a whole spoonful of batter.

Opa's chair broke the silence as he stood and led Oma down the hall.

Kate looked at me. "Can we still have cake?"

"Did you butter the pan?"

She nodded and held it up.

"Is the oven on?"

She pointed at it. We poured the batter into two pans and put them in. I got her a glass of milk. The roast sat exposed on the counter. I stood, covered it, and put it in the fridge.

I loved watching Kate drink milk.

She set down her glass and gasped. "I miss Esau," she said, milk at the corners of her mouth.

"Me too."

"Can we go on Sunday?"

I nodded, wondering how I would tell my son that his father was dead.

Kate stared at the oven with amazing concentration, as if willing the cake to be done. I studied the side of her face. She looked horrible. She started counting down the minutes. "Seven." Pause. "Six." Pause. She sat down cross-legged in front of the oven and stared in at the cake. "Five. It's rising."

The buzzer went off and I jumped, choked on my drink. She looked at me, got up, and turned the buzzer off. "It's done," she said.

She stood there, head level with the stove top.

I realized that now it was time to stand, to check the cake with a clean knife, to blow on it because she wanted it to cool down faster, to turn it, to frost it, to give her a piece on a small plate, with ice cream so the cake wouldn't be lonely, and a small spoon, and get some for myself so she wouldn't be lonely, and some milk because you give children milk at least three times a day, with every meal and whenever else possible. She stood there, near my legs, turning as I turned, waiting to lift up her open hands as children are always doing.

So I did that.

And she lifted her hands, and while we ate she made me list all the animals with teeth I knew.

"Is there a shark in the lake?"

"No. Definitely no sharks. Only in the ocean."

"Are we going to the ocean?"

"It's a long ways away."

"Can we go?"

"Sometime."

"Can I see a shark?"

"In a zoo."

"Will it eat me?"

"No."

"You'll make sure it doesn't eat me?"

"I'll make absolutely sure."

"Can I have more cake?"

Opa came in, opened his mouth to talk to me.

"Want some cake?" Kate asked. Opa looked at her as if startled to find her there. "No thanks, Little Bit."

"Too bad for you," she said affably.

"Claire, could you give the doc a call?"

I stepped into the hallway with him. He held up his hand. "She's just fine, now. She's just a little worn out, you know, with everything. Little trouble breathing, good if she could get some sleep. Just ring him, ask him to come by if he's in the neighborhood."

He turned, then turned back. "And now, you tell him he doesn't need to be talking."

I dialed the phone and cut another piece of cake for Kate while the phone rang. She had dismantled the table clock and was lining its parts up in a row.

"Doc Peterson? It's Claire Schiller."

"Well, shoot! If I'm not glad to hear from you. How're you doing, Claire? Really, now."

I suddenly wanted to collapse on the floor and scream, but it passed. "Actually, it's Madge. I'm over there right now."

"Well, hell. Sure makes sense. I'll be right on over."

I hung up and watched Kate eat her cake. Past her, out the kitchen window, it began snowing again. What was left of the winter-evening light was a soft blue-gray, like cotton batting, and it looked as if you could reach out and touch it, but for the stark calligraphy of trees etched onto the sky.

At a certain point in winter, there is a slow-growing feeling that it has just begun and it will never end and there is no way to escape it. The feeling seeps out from the centre of your body, somewhere in the heart, and you become aware of the fact that you are nothing but warm flesh wrapped in wool, protected only by wool. It is an almost calm feeling. It is like despair, but it is not pure despair; there remains the quiet, insane hope that if you cannot escape winter, you can befriend it, give it due respect. It is like God. Insofar as you hold out the foolish, childish hope that you can dodge its wrath if not its omnipotent force.

All the seasons here in the north move toward their own end, except winter, which moves toward its centre and sits there to see how long you can take it. Spring twitches impatiently in its seat like a child wanting to go outside, straining toward summer, and summer, all lush and showy, tumbles headlong toward the decay of fall. Fall comes and goes so fast it takes the breath away, arriving in brocades of red and gold and whipping them off in only a few weeks, leaving a landscape ascetic, stunned with loss.

Outside, in the soft blue-gray dark, the snow fell. A child sat at a kitchen table and pretended her father had not died, because you were there. As long as you were there, she did not need to be afraid, or go outside, and so she was not afraid, of cold or anything else. Death did not kill her off but merely left her maimed, like a shot animal that startles at the noise more than the pain and scrambles even faster through the underbrush, wide-eyed and sweating at the flanks, not pausing for the ripped and useless leg it now drags behind it as it runs. The animal has three legs left. Terror makes that enough.

She ate her cake.

"Do I have to go to bed?" she asked.

I thought about this. "I guess not."

"Ever?"

"Eventually."

"When?"

I was overwhelmed by the idea of time. By the notion that there were days after that one. That there was a tomorrow, and another one after that, and eventually we would have to go home, back to that house, and Kate would have to have baths and go to bed and be fed breakfast and handed lunches in brown paper sacks, and that groceries for these lunches would have to be bought, and the trash taken out, and leaks fixed, and that I would have to go to work, and talk to the women there, and eat my lunch with them and smoke my cigarettes with them, and sell cosmetics and brassieres and slips and sweaters and china, and then there would have to be dinner, I would have to make dinner, and it would be just me and Kate at that enormous table until Esau came home, and I would spend the long evenings with her looking at me for something to do, or think, or a way to spend the hours of an evening, which I didn't know how to spend, and then I would have to go to bed after she had gone to bed because what else was I supposed to do in an empty house with a sleeping child, and I would have to lie in bed not listening—and that was when the grief set in, the sound of nothing to listen for, and I realized I had spent twelve years of my life listening, tracking the sounds of him around the house, lying still in bed, so still I would not disrupt the distance between him and me with the noise of sheets, waiting for him to get his last drink, shuffle his cards, tap his deck against the table and leave it there until the next night, grunt as he stood, creak down the hall, open the door and click it shut with painful care, not waking me up, undress to his shorts and shirt, and, in the slow-motion of drunks who do not want to fall, ease himself into bed and fit himself into my side. Where he would hold his breath until I turned toward him— yes—or did not.

And then he'd tumble into me or into sleep.

"It's snowing," Kate said. "Can we go outside?"

I looked at her and nodded. "Get your things," I said, and she returned wearing her hat, dragging her scarf, snow pants, gloves, jacket.

I held her snow pants out for her to step into. She steadied herself on my knee. I watched my hands stuff her skirt into the snow pants and zip her in. She watched my face.

Children, I remembered, mirror the expression of their mother. We stared at each other seriously and without fear.

Opa turned his back to me so I would not see him toss back a shot of whiskey before pouring himself a double in a lowball glass.

He crossed the room and handed me one as well. It was a sign of respect, not pouring me a ladies' single, a nod to the fact that it was night and there was a death and we were all men here, or something to that effect. He settled into his chair and looked into his glass.

"Is she all right?" I asked him. He nodded and took a swallow.

"She's a tough old bird," he said. "She just needs to sleep it off."

He adored her. Loved her to distraction. The first time I saw them, when Arnold and I stepped off the plane in Fargo, I knew who they were. They were the handsome older couple who stood close together, she clutching her white leatherette handbag that matched her shoes, he with his hands on her shoulders, their faces bald with expectation. On seeing us, she burst forward with her arms out and he clucked behind her, pleased with everything, his hands hovering at her back.

We had just gotten married. I was six months pregnant. She grabbed my wrist and said, in a rush, "Oh, it's all right. It's all right now, you're home. We'll take care of everything. And look!" she said, throwing her arms up, whacking Opa on the shoulder with her bag. "Look at your, what's the word, belly! Oh!" And she burst into tears and kissed me all over my face.

Opa stood grinning down at his tiny wife.

"Yep," he said now, looking out the window. "Katie down for the night?"

I nodded. "I told her she didn't have to go to bed, but she fell asleep anyway. Tried not to."

Opa smiled. "I bet she did."

We'd walked through the snow, down to Main Street. She showed me a shortcut through an abandoned lot where a metal FOR SALE sign was obscured and bent by the snow. We walked down the street, the muffled sound of a jukebox and voices coming from the Hi-Top Bar. Otherwise, the street was silent.

"It's sleeping," Kate said, looking up at the empty windows of the butcher and the general store.

We crossed the street, and she lay down in the snow in front of the church and made a busy-armed snow angel, then got up to make another one by its side. Her arms and legs splayed, she lay there looking up at the sky. It was too dark to see her face.

"Is Esau coming to the funeral?" she asked.

I was startled. I didn't realize she understood about the funeral, though we'd been talking about it in her presence all day, of course, and had gone to the funeral home. What did I think she'd think?

"No," I said.

"Does he know?"

I wondered if she was getting cold down there, lying in the snow. But suddenly the snow looked so soft, and we were exhausted, and it was so tempting that I gingerly stepped toward her and lay down in the snow myself.

Together we stared into the sky.

The correct thing to say, I thought to myself, is—Does he know what?

But that would be an insult, and Kate, it seemed to me, was a perfectly intelligent person who did not deserve to be treated like a child. Under the circumstances.

And I did not want to make her say it. Or I did not want to hear her say it.

"No," I said.

Kate and I lay in our row of snow angels, thinking our thoughts.

We took a hot bath when we got home, and polished off the cake. She dozed off, one eye first and then the other, struggling to stay awake as we sat on the couch in our flannel nightgowns, looking at the TV with the sound turned off.

Long after she fell asleep, I held her there on my lap because she was small and warm, like a cat.

"You want I should freshen that up?" Opa asked, standing over me, and I held out my glass, embarrassed that I had finished the drink without noticing.

"Good heavens," I said, laughing a little. "Guess I was thirsty."

"I should think so," he said, and handed me another. Sitting down, he said, "Me too."

We studied each other.

"Well, I'll tell you one thing." He took a sizable swallow of his whiskey. "You deserve better than this."

I didn't know what to say. He narrowed his eyes at me. His carefully combed white hair had come free of its Brylcreem rows and was looking a little roosterish.

"That's the damned truth," he went on. "That sonofabitch, no offense to my beautiful wife, had no business going and getting himself dead when he had a good wife and two good kids, is what I think." He shook his head. "I tell you, Claire, I don't know what in the hell."

He looked at me as if I did. I burrowed farther into the corner of the flowered couch and pulled my feet under the hem of my flannel nightgown.

"He was sad," I said. I had difficulty getting the words out of my mouth. I wanted to tell him. I wanted to tell him what had happened, what I had said. Why his son had gone and gotten himself dead. But when I opened my mouth to say it, my tongue was dry. I took a swallow of my drink.

Opa nodded. "I know that," he said slowly. "I know he was." He spun the ice in his glass. "I just don't know why."

He fixed his gaze on me. "Now then, I want to tell you something. Right in there," he said, gesturing at the guest room, "is a little girl so sad she doesn't even know how sad she *is* yet. She's so sad she can't even *be* sad yet, that's how sad she is. Sad ain't even a big enough word for what that baby girl is right now"—I looked away as he spoke, realizing that he must have had quite a bit to drink and was breaking a little, and it was good to give a man his privacy and not stare at him when he cried—"because her daddy's gone and shot his head off. That's sad." His voice lost its waver. "Now, his mother." He pointed toward Oma's room. "That woman has lost two children—*two children*—because they didn't want the life she gave 'em. She's down the hall in there, and I can tell you, and I confess, Claire, that I am not a godly man, though I am a God-fearing man, I can tell you, she is having a dark night of the soul. That is what she is having."

He stood up and looked out the window at the white hill that led down to the wide white lake, all pale blue under the indigo sky.

"Now all those old biddies are going to come here tomorrow with their damn casseroles, looking to see how she's holding up. So she'll have to hold up and she shouldn't have to, it's not right. What's right is for her to be how she is. And they'll all be looking at you too, don't think they won't."

He turned to me. "It ain't fair, that's all. And I know life ain't fair, but a man can't rightly just go an quit it because he's sad, and leave it for everyone else to clean up."

I wondered for the first time if I would have to clean up the bedroom, or if someone else had done it for me. It seemed simultaneously sickening that I might have to face it, and worse still that someone else might have to face what was, in truth, my mess. My husband. My fault.

I felt my head getting heavy and rubbed my eyes.

"Now, you know you're going to be all right." Opa studied me. I looked back at him, uncertain. "Financially, you're all right," he said, and it seemed to give him some comfort to move into this topic, where he was capable of doing something, of making things all right. He was a successful man, and a proud man, and he liked to pay for things and keep his affairs in order, that was his way. That, and his wife, and my children, that was his life.

He sat down and leaned forward with his elbows on his knees. "Arnold had his life insurance, you know, and that'll be plenty in itself. But then, if you want to keep working, I would understand that, and I know you make good money at the store." He drank the last of his drink and looked at the glass. "And a'course, you know I'm here to help out any way I can."

I was mortified. "Oh, now. You don't have to—"

"Now, dammit, Claire!" He stood up and I snapped my mouth shut. He held his hand out for my glass and I gave it to him, thinking wildly, What the hell, we'll be sober by breakfast, when the biddies come. Pouring two more drinks, he said, "Don't you start any of that ladylike bullshit, excuse me, right now. It's not the time for it and it's not like you anyhow."

I was tipsy enough to take a certain amount of pride in that.

He took a swallow and sighed hard. "What do you think, I'm blind? I haven't been planning for this for a while? Now, that's not to say I wished the man ill or I didn't love him, because Lord knows I did, but at the end of the day, I'll tell you something, Claire. You've got to cut your losses and plan for what lasts, not just what you love."

We both held still, hearing a thump from Katie's bedroom.

"She fall out of bed?"

I nodded. "She likes to sleep right at the edge. With the sheet tucked in, you know, tight under the mattress." I gestured with my hands to indicate the elaborate tucking ritual I went through with her nightly, listening to her complain, "It's not tight enough yet!" until she finally snuggled in, leaning her whole small weight against the tense sheets.

"She all right?"

"Happens every night."

"Heh." Opa smiled, which was good to see. He shook his head as if clearing his thoughts and moved back to the subject at hand.

"All I mean is, while I didn't plan for the man to die, this family is what lasts, so I planned for that. Those kids, they've got a nice savings for them set aside, and that'll grow. They can go to college, they want to, or buy a house when the time comes. And you, there's plenty of money for the house and Esau's medical and whatnot. Summer camp for Katie, whatnot like that. And everything that would've gone to Arnold when his mother and I pass, that goes to you, even when you marry again."

I stared at him. I meant to say something, but nothing came. He took my silence as insult and gentled his voice.

"You're a young woman yet, Claire, and those kids'll need a father in their lives. Don't get yourself all tied in a knot about it, and I don't mean to disrespect the dead. I don't mean tomorrow. But for God's sake. We're your family now. You're our daughter and that's that, we're not going to let anything happen."

Horribly, I laughed. It startled him, but he laughed his heh-heh-heh laugh.

"I don't mean to laugh," I said.

"I know you don't. I gone and got you a little tipsy, is all. Oma'd have my head, she saw either of us right now."

"I wasn't laughing. I mean, I was. Just the idea of nothing happening. Well, what else is going to happen?" I waved my hand vaguely about. "Hell, my husband's dead and my son doesn't even know it. What's next?" I started to cry.

Opa nodded. "You have yourself a point there. Oh," he sighed. "Hell and damn, Claire. I'm sorry he's gone."

Somehow, the light of day was coming up. In winter, it looks less like there's a rising sun and more like the snow itself begins to glow, a surreal, icy light.

"He's gone," I repeated after Opa. I'd meant to say, *Me too.*

Opa looked steadily at me. "Yes he is." He watched me while the light came up, making sure I knew.

We were still sitting like that, drinking extremely strong coffee, when down the hall the door opened and out came Kate.

"Is today the funeral?" she called from the kitchen. There was a clatter of plates and the sound of one hitting the floor. "Oh, *shit*," she said. "Mom!"

"Katie! Watch your mouth!"

"You all right in there, Little Bit?" Opa called, grinning. "You wearing shoes?"

"No."

"Hold still, then. Is the plate broke?"

"Yes." She sounded so plaintive I almost laughed. I set my coffee cup on the end table and went in. She looked up at me sorrowfully.

"It's only in two pieces," she said.

"I see that. It's all right."

"I'm sorry I broke it."

"We can glue it. There's plenty of plates."

"I only wanted a toast."

"I'll make you some toast."

She wandered out to the living room. I made toast for the three of us, listening to her and Opa talk.

"How'd you sleep?"

"Okay." She laughed. "You didn't shave."

"Nope. I didn't yet."

"Scritchy kisses!" she shrieked. I could see them without even looking, rubbing their cheeks together, lips pursed, like a pair of fish. "Sandpaper kisses!" she shrieked again.

"They're the best," Opa concurred.

"Except for butterfly kisses," Kate said. This was their routine. Now they were putting their long lashes together, Kate's pale blond, the same color as mine, Opa's thick and black, like Esau's and Arnold's.

I put the toast on plates and just made it to the bathroom to throw up a night's worth of booze in a slosh. Unladylike, I thought. My mother would never approve.

Washing my hands, I was relieved that my mother was dead and did not need to see me this way, whatever way this was, or know Arnold was dead, or say anything awful about who my husband was or why he was dead and what would become of me now.

I buttered the toast.

The three of us settled into our chairs to eat. Kate wiped her fingers on the upholstery, and I didn't have the energy to tell her not to. Opa pretended not to see.

"Can I go visit Davey today?"

"We're a ways away," I said.

"Can Davey come here?"

"Same story," I said. "He's a ways away too."

"Oh, I don't know," Opa said, looking at me thoughtfully, his mouth full of toast. "Little Bit might be getting a little squirrelly today, what with all the people coming in and out."

"Who's coming in and out?" Kate demanded.

"Oh, folks."

"Which folks?"

"Just folks coming to say hello."

"What for?"

Yes, I thought. What for? I looked at my daughter, who had a rat's nest in her hair the size of her head. A busy night of dreams.

"To be neighborly."

"But why?"

"Well, buster, because your dad died."

Kate looked at her plate and sighed. She asked Opa, "You want my crusts?"

"Sure." He leaned over and took them off her plate.

"So are we having a funeral party?"

"A what?"

"A funeral party. With ham sandwiches."

"Oh," Opa said, not missing a beat, "and Lutheran buns."

"Yes! And pickled beets."

"We are, but not until tomorrow. Today people are just coming to bring food and pay their respects."

"Are they going to bury him in the ground?"

We looked at her. She licked jam off her fingers slowly. When we didn't answer, she looked from one of us to the other. "Are they?"

"Well, yes, ma'am, they are."

She nodded and scootched to the edge of her large armchair, hopped down, and took her plate into the kitchen. She returned and climbed into her chair again.

"I was just wondering," she said.

"Well, all right, then." Opa looked at me. "All right."

Down the hall, Oma's bedroom door opened, and then we heard her pour a cup of coffee in the kitchen. She crossed in front of us and sat down in her chair, her knees together, blowing on her coffee. She wore a smart navy blue suit with square white buttons and had tied on an apron printed with blowsy blue flowers.

"Katerina, you have not dressed," she observed.

"It's early."

"Yes, but we are all awake."

"Mom isn't dressed."

"Your mother can get dressed when she likes."

"Why?"

"Because she is a grown-up and doesn't need any help."

Actually, I do, I thought.

"Neither do I," Kate protested.

"Then go get dressed." Oma sipped her coffee. Kate, realizing she'd been tricked, shrieked and stalked off into the bedroom.

Opa and I stared at Oma.

"Well, Mr. Schiller, what for you're staring at me? You have no manners, is what?" She raised her eyebrow at him and he looked away. "Your paper is sitting there on the step, heavens only knows how sogged by now."

Opa heaved himself out of his chair and went off down the hall.

Oma stood up and looked out the window. "For Christmas sakes, more snow." She sighed. "How did you sleep, dear?"

I hesitated, mouth open.

"Never mind," she said mildly, and went on without raising her voice or turning her head, "Katerina, you get back in there right now and put on a suitable dress."

I swiveled around to look and saw the back of Kate's red sweater disappearing through the door. Opa came in, shaking the paper out, and offered me a section.

"Mr. Schiller, you smell disgraceful."

Opa froze mid-sit, then eased himself the rest of the way into his chair, hoping she'd leave it at that.

"I hope you didn't get poor Claire drunk too."

"No, Mother, I most certainly did not," Opa boomed, snapping open the paper.

"I am *extremely* glad to hear that. It is *quite* enough without, I should say. Though I suppose you kept her up all night."

"I am ashamed to say I did." He met her ferocious gaze with the most pathetic hangdog look I have ever seen, and she promptly forgave him. A tiny bow-shaped smile lifted her lips, almost flirtatious. "Well, then," she said, and smoothed her apron, and held out her hand for his coffee cup. He lifted it, his head still bent in apology, and she went out of the room. "Claire? More coffee?"

"Yes, thank you," I called, idly wondering if I was still drunk or perhaps my head was now spinning from an overdose of Folgers.

She returned with the pot and put her hand over mine to steady the cup as she poured. Her sharp blue eyes met mine, as if she were looking for something. Without warning, my eyes welled up, though I wouldn't call it crying, more like morning sickness, just as she turned her back. I hurried out of the room.

Shutting the bathroom door, I saw Kate lying on the shag in the guest room, trying to wriggle into a pair of white tights with both feet in the legs and her shoes already on.

"Mom?" she said.

"I'll be right there."

I tilted my face over the sink, feeling oddly as if I needed to drain my head of saltwater. I watched myself drip. There was a knock. I reached behind my back and turned the doorknob. Kate came in and saw me like that, and seemed to think it called for an elaborate quiet. She shut the door very slowly and stood next to me at the sink.

"Are you crying?" she whispered loudly.

"No," I whispered back.

"It sort of looks like you're crying."

"I know. It's weird, isn't it?"

She nodded. "Do your eyes hurt?"

"No." I grabbed a tissue and soaked up the last of the tears in the wells of my eyes. "See?" I said. "It's fine."

She looked wildly relieved. "I can't get into my tights."

I looked down and started to laugh. She giggled uncertainly. I joined her on the floor and pulled off her shoes and tights. "There," I said, once they were back on, and smacked her lightly on the butt. "Run out and have Oma brush your hair."

When she left, I reached up and locked the door. I sat there with my back against it, tracing the pattern of the porcelain tile with a finger until my eyes burned and spilled over again.

Kate was suspiciously good all day. It turned out that Opa had promised her that if she was, he would go get Davey so she could have a friend for the funeral party. Thus, she sat in an unnatural state of absolute stillness in the centre of the couch with her white patent-leather shoes sticking off the edge, her hands folded, for what seemed like hours at a time. Periodically she'd get a desperate look on her face and I'd tell her to go to the bathroom. The hours trolled over the house in rolls of excruciating white sunlight through the southern windows. The women came and went, trailing the occasional husband. The husbands immediately shook Opa's hand and stepped into the living room to stand shoulder to shoulder at the window, hands in their pockets, looking out at the utter lack of movement on the frozen lake, while Oma and the women stood in the kitchen, discussing anything but death. Everyone who was pregnant, in or out of wedlock, was discussed, as was everyone whose house, ranch, or farm was threatened with foreclosure, and the weather, and the incessant snow, and God help us, what was February going to be like if it was already this deep in December, and how the children and grandchildren were doing in school, and wasn't Kate turning into a beautiful girl, but did she get enough to eat?, which made me quietly, insanely rageful, as if I was *denying* her enough to eat, why did they have to say it that way? Did she *get* enough to eat? Why not, Did she eat enough? Why not that instead? No, she did not *get* enough to eat, and I did not *take good care* of my husband! I wanted to scream, or my son, because now that Arnold was dead, there was no one but me to blame for all this, was there? Because troubles couldn't just come, could they? It couldn't just all *fall apart completely,* could it? It couldn't just *happen to anyone,* no, that would be too awful, wouldn't it? It had to be the strange woman, from *somewhere else,* who wasn't like us, who brought this on herself. Did something to bring this on herself.

At some point between visits, Oma sat down at the kitchen table. "Sit, Claire," she said. I did. She surveyed her crowded kitchen, the refrigerator and freezer having long since run out of space and spilled over with covered dishes that took up every inch of counter space. "Oh," she sighed. "How are we ever going to eat all this? Funeral food for weeks to remind us, *ja?*" She laughed. "Oh, they mean well," she said, still looking at the casseroles. "They do, the ladies. You do well to say nothing. A smart woman knows when to keep her mouth shut. I tell you, I would not have the patience. But they don't mean anything by it, you know." She looked at me. I nodded.

"I know," I said. "They're being very kind."

"No they're not," she snapped. "They gossip. Old bunch of magpies. Come in here and kiss your cheek, no business doing that. They haven't said a thing to you in what, all these years? No business. Whether Kate's a skinny little bird or what."

She stared at me with her sharp little eyes. I had always loved Oma, but now I loved her hopelessly. I felt as if I could just stay here in the kitchen forever while she said all the right things. She patted my hand.

"She just came that way, is all," Oma assured me, standing up and busying herself with a dish towel. "She'll be a tall, lovely thing, just like you. All in good time. Some of those ladies would do well to be a little not-so-plump themselves, no? Now," she proclaimed, skimming over the compliment. "You need to eat something." She made me a sandwich and perched on the edge of her chair to watch me eat it. She had cut the crusts off.

"Thank you," I said.

"I have to do something."

She looked at me, her back very straight. "I have to, yes, like you have to take care of Kate? That is who I am. And you will have to get Esau now, and bring him home."

"When he's well enough," I said, nodding.

"He was always well enough. It was Arnold made it hard to care for him. Too many sad men," she said. "You cannot love everybody at once."

Horrified, I pressed the pads of my fingers into the crumbs on my plate. I wanted another sandwich. I wanted to eat all the casseroles.

"You think I'm unkind?" she asked. "He was my son. I know who he was."

The percolator sighed with relief, having at last finished a new pot. She stood up to pour us a cup. "He was a man who wanted all your love and did not want any of your love. He would give you all of himself and then could not give you any. You cannot dance like that always and forever. There are other dances to be doing."

She sat. "Esau is not his father," she said abruptly. "He is all love." She sipped her coffee. Thoughtful, she added, "He does not want to die."

"Sometimes he thinks he does."

"No, but he doesn't. That is his biggest word for a thing. He doesn't have a big enough word. When he has a word, it will be better. He will say, I don't know, *awful* or *horrible* or something. He will say— what is it—*desperate.* But it will be all right, because he will have you. He will have us. It is like when I was learning English, yes?" She laughed suddenly. "Opa was making us speak only just English in the house. I hated him. For two years I hated him. He would pick fights, just to make me practice fast English. Because I have a temper and he has no temper. So he would pick my temper. And I would get so mad." She laughed and sighed, putting her hand on mine. "Oh, Claire, you can't think how silly. I would be yelling, but I would run out of words and start yelling in Deutsch, and the children laughing because they didn't know what I was saying and Elton holding his hands over his ears, saying, '*Ohne Deutsch!* English only, Mrs. Schiller!' And with such a grin on his face, I can't tell you. Oh, it was awful, I would just burst into tears."

The doorbell rang. "Oh, for Christmas sakes," she said, taking one last swipe at the table with her dish towel. She stood and pointed a finger at me. "Now, no more laughing for us. It won't do." She pursed her lips, turned on her heel, and went down the hall.

* * *

I was standing on the front porch in the late afternoon when Opa pulled up in the driveway. Donna Knutson stepped out of the passenger side. We waved to each other, and I tucked my hand back into my armpit to warm it. I realized I was standing there without my coat and it was snowing. I reached up. My hair was wet, so were my cheeks. I watched Davey plod up the long driveway in boots that were clearly not his own. From behind me, a shriek, and Kate exploded out the door, down the steps, and launched herself at her best friend, screaming, "Davey!" They toppled into a heap of snow and had to be extracted.

Donna joined me on the steps, and we watched them meander their way up the driveway, waving their hands in animated conversation.

"I wonder what they talk about," I said. "Times like this."

Donna shook her head. "Lord only knows. How are you, Claire?"

She didn't turn her face to look at me. I liked Donna. She was a person I very much liked. She always made me think of the word *solid,* in her men's flannel shirts with her hair pulled back into a braid. Until today, I'd never seen her wear a dress, and even now she stood with her feet planted apart, her arms crossed over an enviable bosom in a shirtwaist the color of melted chocolate. She was beautiful in some strange way. She wore no coat and a pair of fleece-lined mukluks.

"To tell you the truth, honey, I haven't the faintest idea," I said.

From the corner of my eye, I saw her nod. "Least you're sane, then. I would've worried if you'd said you were fine."

"I'm glad you're here," I said, surprising myself and her. She looked at me.

"Well, damnation, Claire. Of course we're here."

Kate and Davey approached, Kate tugging at Davey's hand with the unspent hysteria of a child who has held still for an entire day.

"Kate, wait," Davey commanded. He was the most serious child I had ever seen. He addressed Kate almost always as "Kate," using the informal "Katie" only rarely. He took her very seriously. When they played, he listened carefully to Kate's plans and then hunkered down on his miniature cowboy boots and said, "Okay. What we'll do is this."

"Hello, Mrs. Schiller," he began, then seemed to get stuck. Worried, he glanced at his mother. She nodded.

"I'm sorry for your loss," he said, very formal, very slow. He then walked up the steps and wrapped his arms around my knees for what seemed to him an appropriate period of time. He tilted his face up to me and added, impulsively, "Really really."

I bent down and hugged him. "Thanks," I said.

He let go. Kate, who had been very patient, said, "Okay."

"Okay," I replied.

"We're going in now."

"Okay."

They tumbled in the door.

Opa came up the steps. "You coming inside? I wouldn't, I were you."

"In a while," Donna said. "Awful nice of you to give us a ride."

"Pleasure."

He hadn't been gone but a minute when he returned with two drinks and my coat.

"Almost five." He smiled at me and hung my coat over my shoulders. "Now, you keep her out of that goddamned kitchen, is what," he said to Donna.

"Will do."

"We'll have supper shortly, when all these fool people leave."

"Davey gives you any trouble, you send them on out here."

"Nah. We'll play 'em some poker, keep 'em busy."

Donna laughed. "Have your head, you do."

The door swung shut and slammed behind Opa, echoing into the empty street. The sun was down. Night hovered just over the horizon, the thick dark hesitating at the edge of town.

We sat down on the porch swing, and the frozen iron links creaked under our weight.

"You know what it feels like?" I finally said. "Feels like I'm waiting."

Donna said nothing. She took a swallow of her drink and pushed us gently with her toe.

"That's what it feels like," I said. "Like I'm waiting for something to happen. What for? The funeral? The man's already gone and died. So then what?"

Donna nodded. "That's a bitch," she said.

"And what now, you know?"

She nodded again. "More life."

"Right. Nothing but more life."

She understood perfectly. We sat and drank. Night snuck closer, slid down a little farther over the rooftops, then held itself still, like a child trying to creep out of a room unseen.

"You know what it reminds me of?" I stopped, half afraid of what I was about to say. "It reminds me of getting married."

She let out a short bark of surprised laughter. "Yep. I hear that."

"That day you suddenly realize it. Not the day you do it, you don't know what you've done right then."

"Lord knows."

"But later. What, a year later?"

"'Bout that."

"You realize, Oh my Lord, what have I gone and done."

"And there you are," she said.

"There you are."

"And now what."

"Exactly. Exactly."

"And now more life."

We laughed for a long time. Night tripped over the telephone wires and fell heavily into the streets as we laughed.

"Oh, Jesus," she said, catching her breath and squeezing my knee. "And then you look at them, sitting there."

"Sitting there."

"And that's all they're gonna do, then. You got babies crawling up your legs and they're sitting there. They want dinner, and what, that's it, forever. Dinner and babies."

We crowed.

"Hell, I'll tell you," she said, shaking her head. "Start to think they *are* dead, just sitting there dead with the television on, and then you start to wish they *were* dead, just so something would happen. Not really, but it crosses your mind, from time to time. My mind, at least, can't speak for yours. But then, shit. Whaddaya do then, right?"

I tipped my head back, trying to get some air. I felt as if I'd gotten the wind knocked out of me. "Right," I finally breathed. "What then."

"Leave a big hole in your life, no matter how you cut it. No matter what we say."

I pictured all of us sitting in the living room, a hole cut out where Arnold was.

"Holes," I said. "There's holes all over the house. Where he sat down. Where he played cards, at the table."

She took a swallow. My drink was gone. I wanted another one.

"Hole in the bedroom," I said, staring out across the street.

"Yep," she said after a pause. "One there, for sure."

In the dark I felt her glance at me. I stared steadily ahead. The neighbors across the way were sitting down to supper. The yellow light shone on the snow, a long square. A squirrel skittered across it, weightless, and disappeared into shadow again.

"I was thinking about that this morning," I said. "Last night. Whenever."

"Slept much?"

I shook my head. "I was up last night talking with Elton. Listening. I'd rather listen to him talk than me, Lord knows. And I can't—" I gestured toward my mouth. "I can't find the words."

I laughed lightly and winced. In the laugh I heard my mother's laugh, the fragile southern bell of her pained laugh. I straightened on the porch swing.

"So I was thinking," I said, feeling a little off centre, as if I had to remind myself what I was thinking even though it was the only thing I could think about. "The bedroom. In my head. It looks like a hole, in my head. It's like I'm picturing it"—I held my hands up, cupped at the sides of my face, feeling my voice rise—"like a tunnel, down the hallway, and it ends in this *hole.* This nothing. This *stupid, empty space.*"

Silence hung, and then was swept away by a small cold breeze. Embarrassed, I wiped the spit from my mouth. "I'm sorry," I said.

"Oh, shit, Claire," Donna said in disgust. "You got a hole in your life. Say what you need to say."

I didn't need to say anything for a minute, I guess. I watched the woman across the street push back from the table and go into the kitchen. I watched her lean her hands against the sink and look out the window, her face tired, and it seemed for a second as if we were face to face. Maybe she'd gone to the kitchen to get something and paused because she wanted to be alone for a minute. Maybe she was tired of him talking to hear himself talk. Maybe she was tired of his silence.

"But see, look," I said, gesturing at the woman with my glass. "He's not dead, is he? She'll turn around, and there he is, holding her place. He'll be in bed, holding her *place*, her *place* there, all heavy and breathing." I broke off, not knowing what I meant.

Donna looked at me. She took my glass, stood up, went in, and came back out with two more drinks.

"Oh, honey," she sighed. She sat down carefully, making sure I had a grip on my glass before she let go. "Let's get drunk."

We watched the woman pull herself up to the table and put her napkin on her lap.

The next day they buried my husband.

I say they buried my husband because I did not. I may have killed him, but I did not bury him in the ground.

There is something about a coffin. It is a big, long box.

It is the first thing you see when you walk into the church. It is the only thing you see, the only thing you are aware of, besides the lilies. You are sickened by the scent of lilies, which, despite specific instructions, are everywhere. Everywhere.

Each of you present loses awareness of the other. There is no time now, there are only a few minutes left, and each of you must go inside your own grief alone. First you begin your walk down the aisle. Then you disperse like a shattered atom.

There is the coffin, a long, dark box, and inside the box is your broken husband, and the lilies are crawling down your throat, closing in as you go, gagging you with their sticky pollen, their fake spring, their cheap dime-store perfume.

Your child clings to your hand and begins to whimper like an infant. You are viscerally aware of her, or more, of it. She is not a person, but a thing that is yours, ferociously yours, another part of your body, resisting forward motion, a damp and whimpering limb. This is reassuring. As you walk down the aisle, she clings to your leg like ivy, like a curled fetus, and you drag her along, she is trying to climb up you, back inside you, and this too is reassuring, as if it should be this way, has always been this way, the disgusting wet fertile rot smell of the lilies and the child pawing at your skirt, your crotch, as you slog up the aisle toward the box wherein your husband lies, dead and ever present, rotting and growing, and the thick air of the church makes it an effort to walk, and faces with eyes in their heads turn toward you in some vaguely bridal ritual until you reach the front pew, where you sit and watch the edges of the lilies' petals brown and curl in the human heat.

In a box, under a sagging pile of lilies, lies your husband. He stares straight up at carefully, pointlessly quilted satin and a pile of lilies.

No. He cannot stare. He has no head.

I bent my own and pressed my lips onto the top of Kate's skull.

I wanted to leave, but it seemed the minutes were passing without my permission, and they only went in one direction, and you could only walk into the church once, and then out only once, and Kate was on my lap, and Oma and Opa were blocking my way out of the pew, so no matter what I did, this was going to happen, like when I was giving birth, that first contraction when suddenly it's not an idea anymore, it's going to happen, like that, exactly like that, they were going to bury him.

And I felt that if I moved at all, I would become detached from Kate, and then I would die.

Kate turned toward me, her face twisted into a knot, and refused to watch. There was nothing to watch. She pressed her body against mine, wrapped her legs around my waist, laid her face between my breasts, whimpering. She pressed her small skull bones into the soft flesh hard enough to hurt, nudging and shifting, trying to find a place she liked.

She found it, the spot she'd always used when she was falling asleep, milk drunk, after I'd nursed her. She settled in and tucked a curled fist under the breast she faced. Her breathing slowed slightly. The light through the stained-glass windows shone on her cheek so that she looked like a painted harlequin doll. I closed my eyes.

The service began. I realized at some point that I was looking out a stained-glass window on which St. Christopher held up his hand in blessing—*safe journeys,* was that him?—and turned my head forward so as to seem to be paying attention. My attention was on Kate's breath. She breathed into my neck, shallow breaths, tiny, as she had when she was a baby, dreaming. I remembered watching her, in this kind of stillness, wondering what she dreamed. Looking up at Esau, then just six and still as cheerful a child as they come, gloating in my luck, terrified by the fragility of their bones.

There is no protecting a child, my mother told me once, waving her hand at me as if to wave me away. She'd leaned back, I remember the purple velvet settee, the tattered luxury I'd grown up with, the kind that seems to say, "We are above new things." I'd brought only a few dresses for my visit, all carefully chosen, all wrong. I could see it in her face, they were all wrong, the fabric cheap and small town.

I was trying to repair something with her. I was telling her about the children; I'd brought pictures. See, I wanted to say, look at how perfect and strange they are. Look at what strange, perfect things I have made. Impulsively, I told her about the terror, the terror that took hold of me when I woke in the morning and as I sat up late at night, unable to sleep. I can't even remember the last time I wasn't afraid, I said, laughing, sounding afraid even then, even to myself, half hysterical in her presence, as I always was. Embarrassed by myself, tall and excitable and lacking in grace, nothing like her. Like your father, she always said, with disgust so thinly disguised it was barely a sheen on the surface. The children came, I said, laughing inappropriately, and I've been afraid ever since.

"Oh, God, Claire," she drawled. She looked me over. "There's no protecting a child."

I realized the funeral was nearing its end. Kate seemed to sense it too, and, as if in protest, repositioned her head against my breast and tucked herself into me as far as she could. I winced, breathed deep to make a hollow of my rib cage, and drew her in.

They picked up my husband and carried him down the aisle.

It was a warm day, icicles dripping from the eaves of the church as we stepped out into the blinding sunlight, thick piles of wet snow falling from slick branches. From the steps I watched them put the coffin in a gun-colored hearse. The minister stopped and said something to me. I stared at him over Kate's body. I wanted the sun to go away. I wanted a thunderstorm to roll in and crack open the sky and cause a flood. I blinked at the minister, who took his hand off my shoulder at last.

I put on a pair of sunglasses as we rode over in the car, and felt hidden. I wanted Kate to say something.

"Katie," I whispered into her neck. She made no response. I

squeezed her so tightly she pushed at my arm with one hand, very nicely, and tucked her hand back into my chest. I felt better. I could feel Opa in the front seat trying to think of something to say. He opened his mouth and took a deep breath several times, glancing at us in the rearview mirror, and then stopped. Finally he let out a slow sigh and drove.

Fields and more white fields. Sugar beet and corn, soybean, sunflower, cattle land, roiling under the frozen ground beneath feet of snow. I loved the split-wood fences at property lines and the telephone poles that stayed up God knows how, a procession of tilted crosses that ran north-south along the county roads.

The first time we drove this way, I was in charge of the radio, and country music played on every station except one, on which a Lutheran minister droned. It was summer and the sunflowers craned their necks to face south.

"Is it all this flat?"

"Yep," he'd said with a satisfied smile. "Here to the Rockies, not counting the Black Hills."

I whistled through my teeth, impressed.

Another field rolled by. "What's that?" I asked.

"Sugar beet."

"What's that?"

"What it sounds like."

I grinned out the open window.

I felt him look at me. "You like it?"

I nodded.

"Think you could stay here awhile?"

I laughed and held up my hand. "Where'm I going?"

That is a graveyard, I thought.

We were parked.

Cemetery was a nicer word. But there were gravestones, gray ones, others black with age, the names so old they'd worn off. Some had lichen, moss. Esau had learned about lichen. Do not pull up lichen; it takes them a hundred years to grow. Also, bears like lichen, so leave them for the bears. No, there are no bears in town. There were graves with flowers and graves with dead flowers and graves with nothing at all.

Time did not pass for a little while as the four of us sat there listening to the car tick. Then Opa said, "All right now."

Still no one moved. At the edge of the graveyard, there was a gathering of people in dark coats and hats, looking toward the car, the men with their hats removed. There was a minister. There was a grave, and a box. All of it meant for us. Like a birthday party, I thought.

I looked down at Kate. She was gazing steadily out the window at the very same place.

"All right," Opa said, quite certain this time, and he got out of the car. He came around the other side and helped Oma out, making sure her shoes were steady on the ice, and then opened my door. It was good that he did, because I found I couldn't move.

He went to take Kate, whose whole body seized as she let out a chilling scream. I closed my eyes. Please don't let it be like this, I thought. Opa lifted his hands away as if burned. "It's all right," he said in a low voice, to her, me, himself. "All right."

Stop saying that, I wanted to yell. We will stay here in the car, I wanted to say. It isn't all right right now. We are all right where we are. We are not all right.

In my confusion I suddenly got out of the car and found myself walking up the hill. Faces came into focus and I wanted to spit at them. I stared at people. They looked away in sympathy, which was worse. Kate's body was clenched so tightly around me that my eyes widened in pain and my whole body shook. I kept going, unable to stop, my legs pumping with blood. I wanted to carry Kate home. Donna caught my arm and pulled me to her side, and that was all right. That was all right. I stopped. Then I was standing there staring at a hole in the ground.

Before I could stop myself, I cried, "Oh, Jesus Christ."

It was gauche. It was wrong. People stared and tried not to stare, but it was either stare at us or stare at the hole, wasn't it? Donna wrapped her arm around my shoulder and held me up. We were falling. Kate and I were falling and there was a hole and I needed to keep my child away from the hole.

I backed away from the edge of the grave, turning to look at Donna. "It's sunny," I whispered, panicked.

"You have your sunglasses on, honey. It's almost over." She squeezed my arms, staring straight into my face. "Almost done."

I nodded at her because she was nodding at me.

The minister started talking. I kept an eye on the clouds that had gathered themselves up, thick clouds, snow clouds. Snow tonight, I thought.

The minister stopped talking. In the void his voice left, there was only the deep breathing of the pallbearers as they bent—*on three?*— and lifted the casket. Kate's head swiveled slowly.

"Are they putting him in the ground?" she whispered.

I nodded against her neck.

"He's in the box."

I nodded again. "He's in heaven."

She turned suddenly, a wild look in her eyes.

"Is he in the box?"

"Yes, and his spirit is in heaven." I needed her to stop asking. I was trembling and wanted to run and get her away from the hole.

"But what's in the box?" Her tiny, shrill voice soared above the silence. The pallbearers paused.

"Sweetheart, Daddy's in the box." I forced the words out and heard the hysteria in them. "Stop, now."

She pushed away from me violently, scrambled down as if I was a tree she had climbed that was bending under her weight. She took my skirt in her fists and twisted it, yanking with all her strength. Her head thrown back to look up at me, she screamed, "Where is he? Is he going in the ground? *You said they would put him in the ground!*"

"Darling, stop," I pleaded. I bent, reaching for her, but she flung herself away, kicking. I lurched toward her where she lay sobbing in the snow, her hair dangling into the grave. I leaned toward her, reaching, sick at the thought of all those eyes on our rawest parts. I felt the furor behind us, Oma and Opa and Donna, voices rising, and I wanted to turn and lash out, but I could not take my eyes off Kate, who choked and howled, her small hands reaching for something to cling to, finding only the edge of the hole. *Look away,* I wanted to scream at all of them, *look away, let us alone.*

I grabbed Kate's foot. She kicked and sobbed herself out. When she spoke, it was another voice, not hers, an old and angry voice, betrayed.

"What's in the box?" she said, her eyes closed.

"Daddy's body."

"Where's the Daddy of him?" She lay there in the snow, utterly still.

"Sweetheart, he's gone." I took my hand off her foot and put my palm to her wet face. A flood of heat.

She stared up at me, lost.

I bathed Kate slowly, with scented bubbles. She was very serious as she played with the soap. She held still and did not complain. She stood shivering in her giant bath towel while I helped her get dry. I put her into her flannel nightgown. She wanted to wear socks to bed, so I put socks on her feet. For a minute I sat on the bed next to her. Then I got up, put on my own flannel nightgown and socks, got into bed, and turned out the light.

Together we lay there in the dark, listening to the funeral party.

Suddenly she said, "Do you ever think about what if the roof flew off?"

We stared at the ceiling.

"Of course," I said. "Everybody thinks about that, don't they?"

She giggled. "Yeah. I bet."

She put her socked foot on my knee and rubbed it. "I like socks on in bed, don't you?"

"Very warm."

"Yeah. Safe."

"Yes."

"Sometimes I feel like my feet are flying away."

This took me a minute. "How do you figure?"

"I don't know. Like they're escaping."

"What do you do then?"

"Sit on 'em." She giggled again. "What do you see when the roof flies off?"

"A thunderstorm. A big one, with lots of lightning. And trees waving their arms." I stretched my arms toward the ceiling to show her.

"Oooh, yeah! Except we don't get wet."

"Right."

She was quiet. I turned my head on the pillow to look at her. "What do you see?"

"Daddy," she said tentatively, almost asking the question.

"Yes."

"Up in heaven." More certain this time.

I realized I was holding my breath, and let it out slowly. Out in the living room, the funeral party was in full swing; something broke and there was a roar of laughter and a bluster of men.

"What's he doing?" I asked, not sure I wanted to know.

"Not telling." In the dark I saw her grin.

"Pretty please?"

"Sneaking a nip."

"What?"

"Sneaking a nip before dinner. He's looking to make sure you can't see. He's making funny faces at me."

I laughed so hard I worried the funeral party would hear. "Oh, lordy. You're right. That's exactly what he's up to, isn't it?"

"Yes!" she crowed, rubbing her feet madly on my knees.

I tickled her until she begged me to stop.

"He likes heaven," she said.

"Really?"

"Doesn't he?" Her voice was anxious.

"Well, sure. What's not to like? It's heaven!"

"Right!" She sighed with relief. "And he can go fishing."

Okay. "All kinds of fish in heaven."

"That's what Esau says."

I looked at her. "Is that so?"

She nodded. Apparently they'd discussed it between themselves.

She took my hand. I squeezed. We took a long breath. I said, "We're going to be fine."

She shook her head. "No," she said solemnly. "Me and Davey think we're going to be sad for a long time." She looked at me.

I nodded. "Yeah."

She looked back up at the ceiling. "Yeah."

I stood in the kitchen with the light from the refrigerator shining on my socked feet. It seemed necessary to eat. I couldn't tell whether I was hungry or about to throw up again, but I couldn't remember the last time I'd eaten. I peeled the aluminum foil back from a casserole dish and found sweet potatoes.

Then Oma was prying my fingers off a spoon. I was sitting on the front porch. The sweet potatoes were mostly gone. I felt as if I'd swallowed something warm and huge, like a child. I was starving and freezing. My teeth were chattering, and I had a hard time getting the words out.

I looked up into her face, partly hidden in shadow. "I'm hungry," I said.

"I know. Give me the dish."

I let it go.

"Come inside."

I followed her in and sat at the table. She stood before me, a curious look on her face. "What are you hungry for? Salty? Sweet?"

I stared at her. "I don't know. Food."

She shook her head. "Answer my question. Salty or sweet?"

"Salty, I suppose."

"One or the other. Yes or no. Salty? Yes? Now, do you want smooth like silk or do you want to break a glass?"

I thought about it, my head pounding with sugar and lack of sleep. "Oh, I don't know," I said, putting my head in my hands.

"Answer me!" She clapped her hands twice.

"A glass."

"What? Which is it?"

My head snapped up. "A glass!" I yelled. "A fucking glass! I want to break a glass!"

I clapped my hand over my mouth, unable to believe what I'd just said.

We stared at each other in the dark.

"Very good."

She turned her back to me. I sat slumped in my chair, looking confusedly at the wall. I wanted to break a glass with my *teeth*.

I listened to her washing something at the sink.

"There," she said, setting an overflowing bowl of radishes and a salt shaker in front of me. "Eat!"

I picked up a radish and was about to bite into it.

"Salt," she commanded.

I salted and ate it.

I don't know when she went to bed. I sat crunching in the dark, licking the salt off my fingers, eating the radishes, chewing with my molars, staring down into the bowl to see where the next one would come from, until suddenly I was full, and I got up and fell asleep on the guest-room floor next to Kate, who had fallen off the bed.

"I want to go home."

Kate was bouncing up and down in her red boots, looking out the back door at the lake. She'd spoken casually, as if it mattered very little to her when, specifically, we went home, as long as we did.

"You will," Oma assured her, not looking up from her letter desk.

"Quick as you please," Opa seconded idly from behind the paper.

"Now," Kate said, still bouncing on her toes.

Oma raised her head slightly. "Not good enough for you here, ah? You're tired of me and Opa?"

"Opa and I," Opa said.

"No, Mr. Schiller, it is 'me and Opa,' thank you and good night." She licked her pen and wrote.

Kate turned to me. "Can we go?"

I opened my mouth as if I expected words to form themselves. "Okay," I said.

She and I looked at each other.

"I can go get my stuff?" she asked.

I nodded, stunned.

She left the room. Oma and Opa stared at me. I avoided their eyes.

"We have to leave sometime," I said, sounding like a sullen teenager. "Don't we?"

"Claire, now. Stop and think this through." Opa leaned forward, his elbows on his knees.

"There's nothing to think through," I said. Kate walked back into the room, staggering under a pile of clothes.

"What should I do with them?"

"Leave them," Oma snapped. "You're not going anywhere."

"Yes we are. Mom said." She shifted her arms, and a tiny sock fell on the floor. She looked at it, trying to decide whether she should attempt its retrieval.

"Katerina, your mother is tired and she needs to stay here and rest."

"No she doesn't. No you don't, Mom." She looked at me, pleading. "You can rest at home. Right?"

I nodded.

"I'll take care of you," she said firmly, and bent down to get the sock, and dropped the entire pile of clothes. Scowling, she set about picking them all back up.

"No!" Oma nearly shouted. "You are not to go home and that is all."

"Now, Oma," Opa said, soothing.

"No, no, no." She shook her head. "I won't have it. First one thing, and then another thing." She slammed her pen down on the desk. "Up last night dying of starvation, she is. Crazy she is with lonely. No sleeping for days. Sitting there with the radishes."

She took her reading glasses off and put her hands to her eyes. Kate sank down slowly, a head above a pile of clothes.

Opa said, "Now, Oma. It isn't so bad. We'll see them in a few days."

"Oh, that is it? No, that is *not* it! Not us, *them*! How are they going to *do* with it? I think they will starve to death!"

"Well, dammit, Mother, I guess they'll muddle through." Opa was irritated now. "They'll just do what they do and none of our business, is it?"

"Yeah," said Kate sullenly.

"Katerina, you mind," Opa snapped.

Kate put her face in the clothes and started to bawl. Oma sniffled, furious. Opa gave me a look, stood up, and said grimly, "Well, get your things."

I felt like I was falling backward. Opa went out to start the car.

Opa and I stared over the dash at the black ribbon of road that spooled toward us from the south. Kate sat by herself in the backseat, bouncing from one side of the car to the other, quietly singing, "Home again, home again, higglety pig."

She burst in the door and ran through the house, calling gleefully, "We're home! We're home!"

I stood in the hall, watching her, listening to the hysteria rise in her voice. Opa carried our things inside. He came back to where I was, frozen, put his arm around me, and squeezed. He led me into the living room, past the closed bedroom door. I could have sworn I smelled bleach.

Together we watched Kate run, her voice strangled and hoarse.

Eventually she stopped yelling. A claustrophobic quiet settled in. Dust motes floated down the sunbeams. The stale air bore the scent of us, the unmistakable smell of our bodies and meals.

My face was suddenly clammy. It felt like there were hands around my throat.

Kate was standing in the middle of the room, still wearing her coat. She looked very small. She glanced up at me with no sign of life in her face. Then she crossed over to his chair, curled her entire body into its wide seat, and fell instantly asleep. Opa hugged me and left.

I sat down on the couch and looked out the window at the split tree. Have to get that sucker removed, I heard a voice say.

You son of a bitch, I replied. Don't talk to me.

Kate's coat rose and fell. Blessedly, the sun began to set. I looked up at the clock and watched the hand tick toward five.

"You hungry?"

I screamed, dropped my glass on the floor, and stood paralyzed among the shards.

"For *Chris*sakes," I said. "You scared the bejeezus out of me."

"Sorry," Donna said from behind me. "Stay still."

"I'll do that, thanks."

I was standing in the living room in my stocking feet, staring down the tunnel of the hallway at the closed bedroom door. I swept the glass out of my way with my toe and went over to the table.

"Thought I told you to stay still," Donna said, emerging with a broom and a towel. The sight of her comforted me. She wore a plaid flannel shirt, purple and red. I wanted to sit on her lap. I was drunk.

"I'm drunk," I said.

"You don't say." She crouched and cleaned up the mess.

"Is it late?"

"Round ten." She stood up, pulled out a chair at the table. "Siddown."

I did, and she went into the kitchen. "You want a beer?" she called.

"No. I want the drink you made me drop."

"Suit yourself. I'm having one."

"All right."

She came in with a beer and sat down.

"Thanks a lot," I said.

"What?"

"You could have brought one for me."

"You said you didn't want one!"

"But then I said I did."

"Oh, for—" She heaved herself up, disappeared, reappeared, and set a beer down in front of me. "May I get herself anything else?"

"No thanks."

"You sure?"

I laughed and waved my hand. "New house? New life?"

She sat down. "No can do. I was thinking more along the lines of a sandwich."

"Ugh."

"You got enough food in that fridge, you could feed the whole town for a week."

"Why then, let's call 'em up, honey!" I said grandly. "Invite 'em all over! I got nothing better to do, now do I? We can have a little church-basement social."

"Your accent always get this thick when you're drunk?" she said, smiling.

"Why, it sure *does*," I drawled, and glared at her, and took a swallow of beer.

"Yep. Claire, how long you been drinking?"

I waved away the thought. "Not long. A couple of hours?"

She nodded and sipped her beer. "Well, no point getting you sober now."

"No, I don't think so," I agreed.

"Kate asleep?"

"The minute we walked in the door." I nodded over at the chair. "Sat her little self down and fell asleep right there."

We stared at the chair for a while.

"What the hell you doing home this soon, anyhow?" Donna asked.

"Well," I said, plunking my empty bottle down on the table and picking at the Grain Belt label. "I'll tell you, honey. I don't have the faintest *fucking* idea, pardon me." I giggled, shocked at my own audacity. *"What* I'm doing home."

She nodded. "Right. Well, how'd you *get* home?"

"Elton drove us. Kate said she wanted to come home, so we came home."

"What's she want to come home for? I never seen a child so spoiled."

"Oh, tell me. Don't I know. And now she's stuck with me." I laughed. "Poor thing."

"Well, you're stuck with her too."

"True enough." I shredded the label, feeling guilty. "She's no trouble."

"Hell, you say. She's a child. Course she's trouble. Even *Davey's* trouble."

"No."

"Yes he is. If I wanted to sit around, get a proper drunk on, feel sorry for myself, sure."

I considered that. "All right."

"You want another beer?"

I nodded.

We clicked the necks of the bottles and drank. "To Arnold," I said. "May we drink all his beer."

"This his beer?"

"Not anymore, it isn't. He's dead, ain't you heard?"

"Oughtta get your own beer."

"I'll do that."

She stood up, untucked her shirttails, and unbuttoned her shirt, revealing the men's white undershirt she wore beneath. She fanned herself with the side of the shirt.

"Claire, honey," she said, sounding apologetic, "it's a goddamned oven in here."

I was surprised. "I'm cold."

"Well, hon, you're only wearing your slip."

I looked down. My arms were goose pimpled and purple, and my nipples stood out through the nylon. I laughed.

"Well, what do you know," I said.

She raised an eyebrow. "You want a robe?"

I stopped laughing. "No," I said flatly. I took a drink of beer and ran my thumbnail over the textured surface of the table. She was looking at me.

"You been in there yet?"

"No."

We sat in silence.

"I could go in for you. Get you a robe."

I shook my head. "S'all right."

She took her shirt off and passed it across to me, wadded up. I put it on the table and lay my face on it. It smelled good. Wood smoke, cologne, and beer. It smelled like her hair too, which smelled somehow smooth. Like water, or the earthy, clean smell of mud.

I wrapped my arms around it and heaved a sigh.

"You see that?" I gestured toward the hall. "Down there? The door?" I was facing the window, actually, but I would have sworn I could *feel* the door, and behind it a hole, a darkness pulling at the top of my head. "That's it," I said. "That's where he shot himself."

She said nothing. That was fine. I lifted my head to drink, as clumsy as a patient in a hospital bed, almost missing my mouth. I wiped my lips with the back of my hand.

"He shot himself," I said again, to hear myself say it. It sounded like someone else talking. I liked the sound of the word *shot.*

"That's enough," she said, and I felt her hand on my arm, briefly, as if she were pressing a stop button.

"Smells like bleach in here, doesn't it?" I said idly.

"Not really."

I put my chin on the pillow of her shirt. "Yes it does. Don't bull-shit me."

"All right, it does. As you're going past it, it does."

"Thank you." I laid my head back down. It was a perfectly clear night, and the heavy midwinter moon hung high in the wide windowpane, almost full. "Smelled like gunpowder when he did it," I said, suddenly remembering. "Is that possible?"

"I suppose so."

I flared my nostrils, remembering the sulfur burn.

"When I was growing up, we kept a box by the door," I said. I lifted my head finally and sat up, pulling the flannel over my shoulders. "My mother kept a box there, of all her treasures, she said. Heirloom jewelry, pictures, things like that. I think she had a baby shoe of mine."

Donna sat splayed in her chair, her clear skin covered with a sheen of sweat. Tiny hairs at her temples curled. She took a swallow and nodded for me to go on.

"I never knew what it was for. I'd wait until she was out and go dig through it. Try on all the jewelry, look at the pictures to see if I looked like anybody. I didn't look much like her, God knows." I laughed.

"What'd she look like?"

"She was gorgeous. Oh, she was just beautiful. One of those women you hate, you can't help it. Little tiny thing. Little southern belle, round in all the right places."

Donna laughed. "Woulda killed her."

"You would too. She was terrible. But Lord, was she pretty. Scarlett O'Hara pretty, with the black Irish hair."

"Always wondered if you were Irish."

I nodded. "I got the red hair. She hated it. But what she hated worse were my eyes. Didn't like my eyes."

"What's wrong with 'em?"

"Honey, I don't know. They must've looked familiar. Quit looking at me, she'd always say. Can't stand it when you look at me. Always looking at me like you hate me. Can't you put a smile on your face. Hide your teeth."

"Hoo-ee." Donna shook her head. "I tell you."

"So I'd look through her treasures. Pictures of her all dolled up, old pictures. I never did figure out which one was my father."

Donna sucked her teeth. "One of those. Ever meet him?"

I shook my head. "Not that I remember. That's what the box was for, it turned out. It was by the door so if he ever showed up again, we could get out of there and she'd still have some pretty memories, she said."

"He free with his fists?"

"I guess so."

She smacked both hands on the table, pushed herself back, and looked at me. "I'm sleeping here tonight, you know."

"All right."

She stood up and came back with an armful of beers. She lined them up on the table, two by two. She passed her empties to me so I could peel the labels off. My side of the table looked like a down pillow had exploded. She went through the house turning off lights. Moonlight spilled into the room.

She sat down, put her feet on the table, and said, "Arnold ever hit you?"

"Oh, no."

We sat there in the pale dark. I could see her face clearly, faintly lit from below by her husband's undershirt.

"Couple times, he did," I said.

It felt strange to have said it. It had been so long since I'd even thought of it that it felt almost like a lie. "Once, not too long back. Then once, ages ago. Back before the kids." I shook my head, trying to empty the details from my brain onto the table where I could examine them. "He was drunk. We were fighting about something. A man, a friend of his. We'd been out that night, I guess he thought the guy was getting a little too friendly with me," I said.

"Not your problem."

"That's what I said."

"They're crazy."

"I know they are. Anyway, it happened so fast I don't even remember what it felt like. I just remember staring at him, right after."

"It's like that. You forget the pain."

I looked at her. "Dale hit you?"

"Not anymore. Tries to, time to time. Doesn't get too far, the sorry little shit." I saw her teeth in a grin. I laughed. I could picture her snapping her nasty beanpole husband in half. Dale Knutson was a mean man. No other word for him. He was just flat mean.

"So what'd you do?" she asked.

I tried to remember. And suddenly I did. "I slept with him. The guy. I walked out of the apartment and went back to the club. I did. I'd completely forgotten it." I stared at her in disbelief and we laughed.

"Well, then. How'd that work out for you?"

"Oh, God, it was terrible. I went right straight back to the bar and snuck him into the ladies' room. And what for? He was drunker than Arnold, even. I remember," I cackled, "wondering if there was one guy in town who could get it up. You know, you go all those years being good."

"Ain't that the way."

"And then when you finally go and *do* something, nobody there to do it with."

She popped two more beers. "The damn truth," she said, shaking her head and laughing. "Peter Anderson," she said, raising her eyebrows, pointing her bottle at me and throwing her head back to take a swallow. She grinned.

"No," I breathed.

"Yes, ma'am. Two years ago. And!" She held up her hand. "Dennis Knickerbocker."

"You can't be serious."

"Oh, but I am." She chortled.

"Dennis? *Dennis* Dennis?"

"The very same."

I was floored. "He's the ugliest thing I ever saw," I blurted out.

"Don't I know it," she said, shaking her head. "And you ain't even seen his willie."

I screamed with laughter and hung on to the table to remain upright.

"Poor little thing," she said. "Guy'd been after me with this hangdog look so long I thought I'd give the poor sucker a break, you know? I mean, what have I got to lose? Get myself laid. And Dennis, well, he looks like he'd have a big one, don't he?"

"You know, he does."

"My point. Wrong. Negative. Nada." She held her forefinger and thumb out. "Yea big, give or take. Rumply as a baby's face. And I swear to God they shrink, you look at 'em long enough."

"Honey, I think they do."

"Him I regret. He got himself all up in a bundle about it, crying and whatnot. Lord, but there's nothing worse than a naked man blubbering on your tits."

"You don't regret Peter, though?"

"Nah. Least he knew what to do if his parts weren't working. Got busy downstairs in a hurry, turned out just fine for me."

I nearly spat my beer out. I had never before in my life heard a woman refer to this, and now here sat Donna, acting like it was nothing.

"What? You look like you never heard of such a thing. Uh-uh." She smiled at me. "You're not so prim."

I fanned myself with my hand. "I suppose not," I said.

She snorted. "Ha! You put on a good show, though, I'll give you that." She toasted me with her beer and drank the dregs.

"Shit, Claire," she said thoughtfully. She was drunk and it pleased me. We were both stupid now, not just me, but she was stupid and sane, so I would be all right. I wrapped her shirt around me and crossed my legs on the chair.

"We've known each other all these years and never once sat down to talk," she said. "Why in the hell not?"

I rolled my bottle between my hands. "I don't know." I shrugged. It had never occurred to me. "No one ever talked to me."

"Ha! That's a good one, sweetheart." She put her hands behind her head, laughing. "Oh, that's rich. No one ever talked to *you*? Miss High-and-Mighty? Little Miss—" She waved her hand. "Did it ever occur to you to talk to them?"

She looked at me with her mouth cocked in a smile. "Guess not," she said.

"What do they think?" I said, and immediately wanted to grab the words up and stuff them back into my mouth.

"Of you? Shit, what do you think they think? Think you're a snob, is what. Too good for them. Too good for this town and everything in it."

I felt as if I'd fallen onto my back, hard. "What did they think of Arnold?"

Donna looked at me. "Now, that's a tough one."

"Well, too bad," I suddenly snapped. "You're the one started talking. Don't stop now. What did they think?"

"They thought he was crazy." I could see that it hurt her to say it, and I was glad.

"Well, he wasn't crazy," I spat out, furious. "He wasn't."

"Dammit, Claire, I know that!" she shouted.

"And I suppose they think it's my fault he's dead," I shouted back.

"No!" She leaned forward over the table. "No, they don't! For Chrissakes, Claire, they're not stupid! They're not *cruel*!"

She sat back and opened two more bottles of beer. She handed one to me and we drank, staring past each other.

"Loved him to death, Claire. They did. They really did. Long before you ever got here. Long as they could. He was a good man, and everyone knew it." She took a deep breath and a swallow. From the corner of my eye, I saw her watching me. I was looking at the moon, which had sunk a few inches in the windowpane. The room was flooded with pale light. The corners were buried in snowdrifts of dark.

"And everyone knew it was hard for you. Nobody thought you were doing any less than you could do. Everyone knew."

I felt their eyes on me for all these years, watching my family, my husband, my babies. "No one knew," I said.

"No," she replied. "That's true too. No one really knew."

I woke to find Kate sitting in her father's chair, legs stuck out in front of her, watching me sleep.

"Hey, Little Bit," I said, screwing up my eyes and holding a hand over them. From the kitchen I smelled biscuits frying in fat, a yeast-and-salt smell that made my tongue swell in my mouth. I was starving.

"I heard you last night."

"Heard me what?"

"Sleeping."

"Oh yeah? Did I snore?"

"No. You yelled."

"Huh. Must've been a bad dream." I lifted myself up on one arm and looked around the room. Belatedly, the day hit me in the face. I fell back and put my hands over my eyes, my mouth open. Oh, I thought. Oh, hell and damn.

"Donna's making breakfast," Kate said. "She slept over."

"That's nice."

"How do you feel?"

"What do you mean?" I sat up, trying to be fine. "I feel fine. How do you feel?"

"Fine."

She sat there in her clothes from the day before. Blue pants and a green turtleneck with blue whales swimming across the chest, blowing white streams of spray. Her hair was stuck to one side of her face. I tried to remember when she'd last bathed.

"I'm not going to school today," she announced.

"All right."

"Donna said."

"Well, then. What Donna says goes."

"I haven't been to school since last year," she said.

"I know," I said, though I didn't. I realized it was January. I couldn't remember the last time she'd gone to school. I supposed it was before her Christmas break. Before Christmas Day. I didn't care if she ever went to school again. Why would a six-year-old have to go to school?

"Breakfast!" Donna yelled from the kitchen. "Katie, is your mother up?"

"Yes," Kate yelled, still looking at me, as if by staring she would keep me upright on the couch.

"Morning, sunshine! Kate, come wash your hands."

Kate slid off the La-Z-Boy and galloped into the kitchen. She returned, holding her wet hands out as if they were covered with something filthy. "We're having fatback biscuits," she said happily, shifting from foot to foot.

"Yum."

"We're supposed to sit at the table, though."

"Okay." I followed her and sat down.

Donna came in, her black hair still wet from a shower. She set a plate down in front of me and smiled. I studied my plate, feeling naked, as if I was waking up with a lover for the first time. Kate mashed her biscuits with a fork and stabbed the egg yolks.

"I'm going over to Davey's to play," she said.

"Did you ask Donna?"

Kate sighed at me. "Mom," she said, annoyed. "Donna *said* I was supposed to. She says you need your rest."

I looked at Donna.

"Eat your breakfast before it gets cold," she said, and drank her coffee.

"You're taking her home with you?"

Donna nodded. "Think you could use a day to yourself."

"What for?"

"I'll have her back by supper."

Kate glanced back and forth between us. "Is it okay?" she asked, anxious. "I can go?"

"Of course," Donna said.

"Oh, *phew*," Kate yelled. Donna and I winced. Kate shoveled down her food and dashed off to her room. Donna stood up to get the coffeepot and poured us another cup.

"We're what, four blocks away, you need us," Donna said, sitting down.

I nodded into my coffee.

"Kid needs to burn off some energy," Donna said. "Last thing you need to deal with's a pent-up kid."

"I guess that's right."

Kate appeared, fully suited up. "Okay," she said, as if we'd been waiting only for her. "We can go."

I had to use the bathroom.

If I got up, I would have to walk down the hall. If I walked down the hall, I would see the door to the bedroom. I might open the door. I might fall in.

Surely I had gone to the bathroom since I'd been home? Maybe I was drunk and it was dark and I didn't see.

I had to pee so bad my teeth hurt. It was another sunny day, and I wanted to kill it. It was making me have to pee worse.

I got up, shut my eyes, and felt my way through the house to the bathroom door. I sat on the john, peeing like a racehorse, my face in my hands, and began to cry.

The humiliation of crying on the toilet with my underwear around my knees was too much. I stopped, got up, splashed water on my face, shut my eyes, and opened the door. I felt my way back to the living room, got my coffee cup, and went into the kitchen. Donna had left it spotless, the pans set neatly in the rack to dry.

I put the pans away and poured myself more coffee. I looked up at the clock and my heart dropped. It was only seven.

If I went into the bedroom right now, I thought, I could get ready and be at work with time to spare. But that would entail going into the bedroom.

I stood there paralyzed, a statue of myself with a cup of coffee. Woman in kitchen in slip. Smelly hungover woman with coffee. I picked up the phone and dialed Donna.

"Hello?"

"Should I go to work?" I asked.

"Claire, no. It's a holiday."

I held the phone so tightly against my head my ear hurt. "What holiday?"

"Honey, it's the first. What are you doing? Hang on. Davey," she called, "go get Kate for a second." I heard a baby wailing, a stampede of small feet, and the high whisper of Kate's voice. My heart began to beat harder.

"Hi, Mom!"

"Hi, sweetheart!" I leaned my forehead against the wall, my eyes closed, her face filling my vision. "Are you having a good time?"

"Yeah. We're, um—" She whispered and Davey whispered back. "We're gonna build a snow fort and play explorers," she said.

"That's wonderful. That's so great."

"Yeah."

"I love that," I said, overcome.

"Yeah. Mom? I have to go."

I opened my eyes. "Of course you do, honey. Have fun, okay? I'll see you tonight."

"Claire, it's me." Donna's voice.

"Hi."

"Hi. What are you doing?"

"Calling you."

"Right. Well, don't go to work."

"Right. It's the first? Like, New Year's?"

"Yeah. January first, 1970. Hard to believe, huh?"

"Sheesh. What are you up to?"

"Not much. Have you showered yet?"

"No."

"Whyn't you do that."

"Can't you come over?"

"No can do. Houseful of kids, the baby's teething, and Dale's hiding in the basement. I laid some clean clothes out for you. Why don't you take a shower and get dressed. You'll feel better."

"All right."

"I mean it."

"I will."

"Right now. Okay? I'm going to go now."

I held on to the phone.

"Claire? Here I go. I'm going to hang up now. You can call in a few hours and talk to Kate again."

I nodded.

"All right. 'Bye, now, hon. You're gonna want to hang up that phone."

The sound of the dial tone filled my head all morning.

I sat on the couch, facing the window. The light came from the left, inching its way across the yard until it stared me full in the face. I stared back.

Arnold's chair and I sat in silence.

You see, now, he said gently. How hard it is to get through a day.

The sunlight crossed to the right.

I'm sorry, I said. But he was gone.

"Hi, Mom," Kate whispered, and crawled onto the couch with me. Without thinking, I pulled her onto my lap, and we stared out at the dark.

It was snowing. It had started snowing sometime after dusk.

Eventually I smelled food. I turned my head. Donna was setting the table. She looked up at me, crossed the room, and put her hands on my shoulders. She squeezed. "Come on. Haven't eaten a bite all day."

The three of us ate hot dish from the funeral party. There was nothing to say. Kate was sleepy, and Donna put her to bed.

She sat down next to me on the couch. "You didn't go in," she said.

I shook my head.

"Well," she finally said. "How about a shower?"

I bent over and put my arms around my knees. "How am I going to tell Esau?"

She rubbed my back. I started to shake.

"Yep," she said. "About time."

My body flooded with pain so extreme I opened my mouth but couldn't make a sound. I looked up at her for help, my hands gesturing at my chest.

"I know it," she said. "Let's go." She took me by the waist and walked me down the hall.

There was the door. I turned my face away and groaned.

"Come on," she said firmly, and we went into the bathroom. She turned on the water and pulled my slip over my head, as efficient as a mother whose child has peed herself and is bawling in shame. She held my hand as I stepped in, soaped a washcloth, and scrubbed me till my skin was raw.

I stood there naked in the boiling spray and cried.

She handed me the washcloth. "Wash yourself," she commanded. I shook my head, choking. "I can't."

"Yes you can."

"No."

"Yes. Gonna have to happen sometime, Claire."

I took the washcloth and turned away from her. I washed a part of me that I was hoping never to hear from again. My belly contracted and my legs buckled and I lay down in the porcelain tub, my knees pulled up to my chest, and dug my nails into my skin.

I heard Donna kneel by the tub. She grabbed my wrists then threaded her fingers through mine. "Okay," she said. "Okay. See? You're still here."

She left me wrapped in a towel and came back with a nightgown. She tugged it over my head. "Bedtime," she said.

"I'm sleeping on the couch."

"No you're not. You're sleeping in your own bed."

"I'm not ready."

"You ain't ever gonna be. Now's as good a time as any."

She opened the door. There on the wall that faced us was a wide spot, unnaturally white, whiter than the paint. The room was cold. I noticed the window was cracked open. It still smelled like bleach.

Donna crossed and closed the window.

Now that she had gone in, the room was a room. Not a hole. A room.

There was my vanity, just as I'd left it. A tangle of jewelry, an open pot of blusher, a brush. The old oval mirror above it reflected the shadow of us in the doorway against the hallway light. There was Arnold's highboy. There was his reading chair, under the window, through which shone a dusky snow-filled light. His good pants hung over the shoulder of the chair, the belt still through the loops, and his good hat perched on the lamp. And there was the bed, bigger than I remembered it, neatly made. On Arnold's bedside table, a book and a near-empty bottle of beer.

Donna reached down and turned on the bedside light. She folded down the comforter and kicked off her shoes.

"He didn't get to finish the book," I said, still standing by the door. I could see the bookmark sticking out, two-thirds of the way to the end.

Donna looked at me. "Hop in," she said. I crossed the room and sat down on the edge of the bed.

I could smell him in the sheets.

Donna went to the linen closet and made herself a bed on the floor, next to me. She straightened. "Lie down, hon. Can't sleep sitting up."

She pulled the covers over me, turned out the light, and settled herself on the floor.

I lay there listening to her breathe until she fell asleep.

I turned my face to look at his pillow. I rolled over and put my face in it and breathed in his whiskey-sweat-soap smell, deep, gulping breaths. I pulled the pillow over my face, breathing so hard I got dizzy. I could not breathe him deep enough.

Sometime in the night, I woke myself crying. I felt the bed sink under another body's weight. Through a haze of half sleep, I felt Donna's hand on my back. It was warm and heavy, and it seemed to hold me down.

It was February. He might have waited till February to do himself in, the sonofabitch.

My son did not know his father was dead, because I had not told him. We visited him on Sundays, as faithful as churchgoers. Kate appeared, silent, in her best dress and shoes, ready to go at nine A.M.

Kate had stopped talking.

I thought I ought to object in some way, tell her, "Go play, Katie," or "Katie, come talk to me," something like that. But I knew why she was silent. She knew. I knew she knew what I had done.

And in the face of that, I too had nothing to say.

I had not gone back to work. Every night, I meant to. Every night, I stayed up nursing memories until I passed out on the couch. Every morning, I woke up sick, kneeling in front of the toilet, my face cold and my body burning hot. I threw up so often I worried I was pregnant.

And every day, all day, I tried to untangle in my mind the words I'd use to tell Esau what I'd done.

No. What his father had done.

No.

What I'd tell Esau about the hole in our lives.

Around one in the morning, I was working on my foxtrot in the living room, holding a glass of wine out in front of me, conducting Sinatra with a cigarette. Kate opened her bedroom door and stood there with her hand on the knob.

My tiny ghoul. My little nightgown ghoul.

I hesitated, but Frank did not, and so my feet began again. *Your fabulous face* . . .

Everything reminded me of everything. Nothing was the *genuine article,* as he would say. This song was not a song now but a song ten years ago. He danced well enough, in that way of large men: What they lack in grace, they make up for in effort and affable grin.

Now he'd poisoned everything. Mornings, bent over the toilet, I imagined I was throwing him up.

I stopped my drunk stumble, sobbed, sighed. Kate stared, impassive. I turned my back on her and poured a drink. I wanted her to go to sleep, let me keep dancing and watching the movie in my mind.

When I turned back, she was still there, my baby rat, my blue-veined mute, my little leech.

Winter began to break. I went back to work. Still Esau didn't know, and still Kate would not speak.

She and Davey played in companionable silence. Sometimes he

talked, but mostly only to point something out: more snow, less snow, wet snow for snowballs, a frozen bird. She would look up, nod, and take his hand. They could not be pried apart.

At home, she sat in her father's chair and listened to me intently —in the kitchen, on the phone, talking to her, getting a glass and pouring a drink, opening a door and closing it again.

Gradually we stopped eating anything except tomato soup, creamed corn, and bacon.

The click of the can opener, the hiss of air from the can, and the spitting sound of a piece of bacon hitting the pan. The clang of a pot to the stove. I began making noise so she would have something to fill her hungry ears.

The snow began to melt, sliding off the eaves with huge wet thuds.

In April she got up and put a record on the record player and sat back down. After that, she went straight to the record player every day when she got home from school, without taking off her coat. She got up when the record finished, and put the needle at the edge again. She sat down, bit her fingernails to the quick, and looked out the window. I put Band-Aids on her bloodied fingertips and kissed them, kneeling at her feet.

And then one day, she smiled shyly, and took my hands, kissing each fingertip in turn.

The record she liked was Simon and Garfunkel, *Parsley, Sage, Rosemary and Thyme.* It had a black cover with flowery writing on it, and she studied it while she listened. One Sunday she took the record with her so Esau could see it. She clutched it on her lap for the entire silent ride to State.

She held the record out to him when she saw him coming down the hall. He crouched and hugged her. She continued holding the record out to him with both hands, looking up urgently. He took the record. He said it was beautiful. He looked at me, bewildered.

"She wants you to have it," I said. "I think."

"Oh, Katie, I can't take your record." He looked down at her, half smiling.

Kate went over to the hallway wall, slid her back down it, and tilted over onto her side on the floor, where she lay quietly studying his blue tennis shoes.

"Honey, don't lie on the floor in your nice dress," I said.

Kate stared into Esau's giant eyes when he put his face next to hers on the floor.

"You want to listen to it?" he asked. She moved her head in a semi-nod. "You have to get up, then."

She got up and followed him into the dayroom. An old man waved at her, and she waved back shyly. Esau put the record on the old player and pulled her onto his lap in a chair.

She put her face next to Esau's, and together they looked out the window. He sang along with the songs and rocked her slightly back and forth. Her small hand kept time on his back.

When the record got to her favorite song, she put her mouth next to Esau's ear with a secretive smile on her face. I heard her sing, very softly, "'A-a-a-pril, come she will. When streams are ripe and swelled with rain.'"

Then she was quiet again. I looked through the window to the courtyard below, the people pacing in circles, the apple trees blooming white, moving back and forth with a strong spring wind.

I want to take him home.

It was May. I was sitting in the conference room with Esau's psychiatrist and his primary staff. I put my Styrofoam cup of coffee to my lips again, hoping it would ease the words out of my mouth. The three of them were looking at me, waiting for me to say something. They'd just given me his monthly report, and they were waiting for a response. They wanted to know when I planned to tell him his father was dead.

I wanted to go back out and watch Kate and Esau play in the courtyard. Kate had started talking the day the lilacs sent out shoots. Soon the house would bloom with them, the white lilacs that grew on the tree outside. She had run into the house to find me in my bedroom, reading, and she jumped up on the bed and whispered in my ear, "Mom! The lilacs are coming! There's shoots!" Now they were out in the courtyard garden, and Esau was showing her the pale green tips of his tulip bulbs.

I did not like sitting here in this generic room in these generic uncomfortable chairs with these professionals staring at me, wondering what was wrong with me and why I was refusing their sound advice.

"We really feel it is not in the patient's best interest to remain in the dark, as it were," said the psychiatrist, and coughed. It was a fake cough. He didn't need to cough, I could tell. I didn't like this *we*, this general *we*. And *as it were*, what was that supposed to mean?

"I know that," I said.

"Which is not to say we don't sympathize with your situation. You are having a difficult time yourself, to be sure," said another of the three.

"It's not a *situation*," I snapped. "And kindly refrain from telling me what kind of time I'm having."

I sat there enduring their pitying looks.

"Of course," said Esau's primary nurse, nicely, after much too long a pause. I wanted to hit her.

"I just want to take him home."

They looked at me, and then at each other. "We would probably not recommend that at this time," the psychiatrist finally said.

"Why's that?"

"We feel the patient would benefit from a longer stay."

"Jesus! Longer than what? He's been here for months. You said yourself he's doing remarkably well. That's exactly what you said. 'Remarkably well.' You said he hadn't had an episode in *months*. Every week he's better."

"Well, Mrs. Schiller, that's precisely my point. He would continue to improve under our care."

"And he would deteriorate under mine? That's what you're saying?"

"Not exactly. We feel there is an appropriate time for his release, and we are moving *toward* that time, but that time is not right now."

"Because what? You want me to tell him his father shot his head off and then *leave*? Just say, 'Have a nice week, Esau, good luck with that one'?"

"Yes. And leave him where he can safely interpret that information."

I pitched my coffee cup into the garbage can, furious, and leaned forward. "It's not *information* for him to *interpret*. It's a *death*. His father's death. And I am not, under *any circumstances*, leaving him in this *piss-stinking* place full of *strangers* to deal with it." I stood up.

"Mrs. Schiller, I believe you have the best of intentions. But perhaps your maternal instincts are not, in this case, well placed."

I hid my hands behind my back to hide their violent tremor. "Sign him out," I said.

"I can't do that in good faith."

"I don't give a rat's ass what kind of faith you do it in. Sign him out," I repeated, and walked out of the room.

I ran down the stairs two at a time and flung open the door to the courtyard. I stopped to look at my children, crouched in the garden's mud. Esau turned his face and smiled, then spoke to Kate, who turned and waved. I walked over to them.

"We're going home."

Esau looked stricken.

I bent. "No, no, sweetheart. All of us. We're all going home."

I wrapped my arms around them and closed my eyes. Tonight I would tell him. For now, I breathed in the smell of damp, fertile ground and my children's hair. I felt as if we were a planet, spinning out of any orbit but our own. Terrified, I hung on.

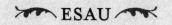 ESAU

When I lived in the place, it was fall and then winter and pretty soon I knew for sure they were not going to take me home.

My father carried me up the stairs. I remember that.

I remember him talking to me in the car, the whole way. Like some kind of music, not stopping. I closed my eyes in the backseat and clung to his voice, feeling like I was spinning, like I was on a carnival carousel, those scary painted horses at the county fair, and it was going too fast and I wanted to get off, and so I pictured my father standing at the edge, spinning past, spinning past, and I tried to get to the edge so I could jump and he could grab me, like when I was little, and we were in the lake and he was trying to teach me to swim. Reaching his arms out: Come on, you'll make it, he said. And because he said so I closed my eyes and jumped and I didn't drown. His hands around my rib cage in the green water, lifting me up and out into the blinding sun, holding me over his head while I spat and laughed and gasped.

So we swam through the dark, in the car, with his voice like his hands, guiding me, keeping me afloat. And he promised me I wouldn't drown and I didn't.

He did.

And he carried me up the stairs and laid me down on a bed in a dark room. Then there were lights everywhere and there were bars on my bed and I liked that. I checked every edge with my fingers and feet, bars all the way around, I wouldn't fall out. My father's hands on my head. I heard him say he would be back.

But I never believed him. Every time he left, they'd tell me again. He'll be back, they said. He's only just gone for a little while.

So I sat on my bed a lot waiting for him to get back. I made my bed superwell and sat on it with my back to the wall. My window looked out on the sky. Every so often I'd get up and stand by it and look down at the parking lot. I'd watch the highway for blue cars. There are a lot of blue cars. So I trained myself not to believe it was him. Because I am a person who likes math and I am good at it, and so I knew the statistical likelihood of it being him in a blue car out of billions and trillions of the blue cars on the planet that could potentially be driving south on County Road 10 was very very small. The statistical likelihood was that it was not him, and never would be him, and in the event that it was him, it was practically a mathematical miracle. I would see a blue car and watch it shoot down the whole thin ribbon of road that cut across my windowpane, north going south, and I wouldn't blink until it had crossed to the southeast corner of the pane and out of sight, not even slowing at the driveway to where I was. Then I'd blink. Then I'd wait for another blue car, and know it wasn't him, and prove it by watching it speed past.

So when he died, I already knew he wasn't coming back.

He left me there, but he didn't want to. I know that. I always knew that. He left me there because I couldn't get better. So I stayed there and tried to get better as fast as I could because I knew he didn't want to leave me there and it broke him all to pieces because he thought it was his fault and it wasn't his fault. At all.

And the only thing I am mad about is that I am better now and he is all dead. When he could have just hung on a little longer. Like he told me to do. And I did what he told me. I hung on. I came home, just like he promised I would.

Now everything is different. Here are the ways things are different.

First my routine. There, I would wake up in the morning and they would unlock the shower room and let me take a shower. After which I would get dressed. Before which, while I was still in bed, I would lie there for a little while in the dark and watch the light turn blue in my room. My sheets, blue. My white walls, blue. Staff had taped up a lot of my drawings on my walls and I would wait until I could make out their shapes.

I was drawing: plants, and bodies, and atoms, and cells. For school, since I was not in school, they had given me some books. Since I was too crazy for the adolescent ward, I lived with the adults, which was fine with me because I didn't want to be around anyone my age anyway. So I was studying hard. I had *National Geographic*s and an *Encyclopedia Britannica* that was missing volume W. My favorite drawings were: a drawing of a foot with all its bones; a drawing of a man-eating plant; a split atom, the best part of which was the shattered cerulean-blue nucleus; and a raptor, which is a bird of prey, such as for example a hawk.

Then after I was showered and dressed I would go sit by the window in the dayroom. Sunrise. Blue clouds, orange and purple sky. It was my special time. My only time. Everyone asleep.

I missed my chair. I would not tell my mother I missed my chair. No one ever sat in my chair. When someone new came, they said, That's Esau's chair, don't sit there. At first, Staff tried to make me turn around my chair to join the group. Then they came over and turned around my chair, but they only did that a few times because I would get up and turn it around facing the window again, so it was a waste of their energy I guess. Someone probably said, That's his chair, why don't you just let him face the window in it? If he wants to. But I don't know that for sure, I never heard anyone say that.

The day did not begin until someone else was up. It didn't count. When everyone else is sleeping, time stops. Nothing moves. Not even me.

Then someone else woke up, and came into the dayroom with their knitting or their talking-to-themselves conversation, and snow started falling past my window, and the day went sucking into its hole.

Here, it is different. Time is different here, it doesn't take so long to get from morning to night. Everything counts whether anyone else is awake or not because even when they aren't, there's my father. Somewhere in the room. There and not there.

He is not a ghost because I am too old and logical a person to believe in that. So he is not a ghost, but he is not gone. Either.

There are so many sounds.

Out in the yard, there's the birds. And in through the window, the light comes up earlier, because it's spring, and the lilac tree outside my window rubs against the screen and sends in smells. I lie in bed and wait for Kate to wake up. She scrabbles around like a rat. She thumps out of bed in the night, and then makes a rustling, just before seven, every day, and then she stops. To hear if she can hear me. We lie there listening for the other one. I hold my breath. She has no patience, because she is a girl and six and Kate, so I know she will give first.

"Esau," she whispers through the wall. Then the day begins.

When a bad thing happens you wake up with it in bed. You wake up and while you're still all foggy and half asleep you feel around because something is in bed with you, making you uncomfortable, crowding you out of your spaceship sheets. You don't even have to open your eyes, because the bad thing is not visible. It is not a visible material object. But it is strange and bulky and you know it is there and you feel around with your hand for it and you find it. And there it is. The bad thing. The bad thought.

And it doesn't even have to be the whole thought. For example, before when I was crazy I didn't have to wake up and think: *I am crazy.* All I had to do was feel the crinkling plastic sheet underneath my hospital sheet and think: *Here.* It was the logical deduction. *Here. Not there.* My father is the same. All I have to do is wake up a little and listen. And I can hear him, not being there. Being gone. It is a loud gone sound. And all I have to think is: *Gone.*

I can turn my head to the left and face the wall. Through the wall is Kate. I can wiggle one arm out from under the blankets and peel the wallpaper. If I look hard enough, she will rustle. If I think, *Cough,* she will cough. I am not crazy. It's true. Or I can turn my head right and look at the homework on my desk, which I stack in alternating directions for different subjects. I am not allowed to do my homework again once it is done. I am not allowed to get up in the morning and work on it all over again, erase all my answers and redo the problems and tear up the book reports and start over once I have done them, because I did them well enough the first time and it's not efficient to do the same thing twice. I made up that rule. Because doing my homework twice is not magic and it will not make me any more right and it will not make my father less dead.

I don't know what the date was when I went to the place. The next thing I remember was a Thursday, because there was Salisbury steak. The next thing I remember, I was sitting at a long rectangular table eating my peas, which came in a small dish on the tray next to the Salisbury steak. Also, there was a carton of milk, a square of orange Jell-O, and rice. It was the best thing I had ever eaten. And all of a sudden I woke up eating it, so at first I thought I was dreaming I was eating peas.

Then I was startled awake.

"Hungry?" asked the man across from me. He was Geronimo, but I didn't know that yet. I looked up at him.

"I guess so," I said, pushing my finger across the plate to get the last bits of sauce.

"Ate like you ain't had a square meal in a year."

"Well, it's good to see," said the grandmother next to him. She wore gloves with lots of rings on her fingers, and a pillbox hat on top of her stiff gray hair. I couldn't imagine what a grandmother had to be crazy about. "He's growing and he needs plenty of protein. I have sons, three sons, and one summer they ate me out of house and home, grew a foot. All I ever saw of them, they wanted something to eat. Swore I'd never cook again, ha! Famous last words. This one, they should send him up two dinners, he won't go hungry." She cut another strip of steak in half and placed it daintily in her mouth. "Doris, this steak," she said, "is really quite satisfactory."

I looked around for Doris, wondering if they could find me another dinner. The only other ladies in the room were a nurse and a woman who sat on the other side of the young, agitated man to my right. His knee bobbed rapidly under the table and his left hand worried the fabric of his gray wool pants. He stared at his plate. Every so often, in a rush, he'd take a bite, looking fierce. Then he'd go back to looking worried. The woman who was maybe Doris wore a pink-flowered housecoat with snaps. Her bosoms rested low on her chest and embarrassed me. She sat slumped over her plate, her gray hair wandering out of the loose bun knotted at the back of her head. She didn't look clean. She looked crazy.

She did not even lift her hand to wipe away a tear that rolled off the tip of her nose.

The nurse sat at the head of the table with a stack of blue folders, one of them open, and she was filling out a form. She laid down her pen and looked at me.

"Esau, would you like to introduce yourself?"

I ate my Jell-O. Maybe if I didn't look at her she would forget me.

"Esau," she said more firmly. I decided to hate her.

The man to my left leaned close and said into my ear, "She's a witch. More or less harmless. The trick is not to say her name. It gives them more power." He glanced over at her, then leaned in again. "Witches. Naming. You know what I mean."

I nodded. She didn't look like a witch, and to be totally honest I was not sure there was such a thing in the first place, but then again, better safe than sorry.

"Darling," said the grandmother, wiping the corners of her mouth, folding her paper napkin neatly, and placing it on her plate. "I'll start. I'm Ellen. I'm up from the city because I tell you my sons are plum out of their mind and they've gone and put me here because all I did was went and fell down. That is *all*. I was wearing my fur coat and getting ready to go out for the evening and wearing a low heel, just a little wedge, and just that afternoon Mavis had come by and she must have waxed the floors a little thick because I tell you, I stepped up to the landing and that little wedge heel went out and I was on the ground, boom, down I went. And for heaven's sake I wasn't down there but a minute when all of a sudden. *All* of a sudden." She threw her hands up and looked around the brightly lit room. "And now, here. Here, of all places!"

"Terrible," said Geronimo, shaking his head.

"Ellen, we've been over this." The nurse at the head of the table had her hands folded in her lap.

"You, missy, can shut your smart little mouth," Ellen said, pointing a finger at her. "You have *no* idea." She sniffed, studying her hand, out in front of her. "Darling, look at this pretty one. It's a topaz."

She stretched her gloved hand across the table to me and I leaned over to look. In among the cluster of gems on her fingers was a fat square yellow one the color of amber.

"Amber happens from the pressure of the earth's plates shifting and squashing the skeletons of dead insects and plant life, which is why you can sometimes find a piece with a whole preserved fly or mosquito for example in a chunk of amber."

She stared at me. "Is that *so*," she said, shaking her head. "I had *no* idea."

I loved her forever.

The man next to me leaned in and said, "Name's Bob Thornton. Paranoid schizophrenic. Nothing to worry about. Shock therapy, meds, just in for a checkup. They put cameras in my shaving mirror, bastards, caught me. By the by, she was drunk."

"Who was?" I whispered.

"Tch, tch, tch. No names!" He tipped his head meaningfully at Ellen. "When she fell."

I looked at Ellen. "Oh," I said. She saw me looking at her and smiled. She held a hand up and waved, although we were only separated by the table.

"So. Now. Geronimo, introduce yourself. Have some manners, for pity's sake," she said, slapping him lightly on the arm.

He stood up, pushed his chair in, tucked in his shirttail, and bowed. "Geronimo," he said. "It is a great pleasure to meet you." He sat back down. Ellen patted his knee.

Bob leaned in. "He's reincarnated. He took over the body of a guy named Charlie. Charlie, wasn't it?" he said, turning to look at Geronimo, who nodded.

"That is correct." He crossed himself. "May the poor sucker rest in peace."

"My name is Jonathan Siebald Peters the Third," said the man to my right, "and I am very, very, very nervous right now and I request permission to be excused from this *fucking* please excuse my French ridiculous farce of a dinner experience." He stood, picked up his tray, and set it on a counter in the corner. His back turned, he shifted from the heels to the balls of his feet like he was exercising. "Which is not to say," he said to the wall, "that I wish to cause any offense to any of the persons present, most especially the ladies, with the exception of the *evil bitch* at the head of the table who is in no way qualified to lock or unlock doors, let alone tell me when I can take a piss."

"You are not well liked," Geronimo said to the nurse sadly.

The nurse opened another folder and wrote something down.

A very small man, as narrow as a bean, sat at the end of the table. He cleared his throat. "If I may remark."

"Go ahead, Captain," said Geronimo grandly.

"Thank you. I would ask," said the little narrow man to me, "after your rank."

"He is a colonel," Geronimo answered.

"Sir, I did not ask you, sir. The question was directed toward the young man, sir."

"Quite so. Continue."

"I have no rank," I said.

"Certainly you have a rank. It is an orderly system. Without order, we would live in a state of chaos, which is no way to run things, making strategy virtually impossible. There would be," he said, "no plan of attack."

Jonathan whacked his head on the wall once, hard. "A sane person might reasonably ask," he shouted, "against whom this *particular offensive* is directed."

"Darling, now, please don't bump your poor little head," Ellen said. "It hurts me terribly."

"My apologies."

"Your rank, young man, is that of lieutenant."

"Here here!" Geronimo cried, raising his milk carton in a toast. "Quite so, sir. With all the decorations, privileges, and rights that are afforded that fine rank."

"Sir, thank you, sir. And he will progress through the ranks according to skill and bravery demonstrated."

"Yes he will. *Yes* he will." Geronimo glowered at me. "What in God's name, Lieutenant, do you mean by showing up at mess in your pajamas?"

"Oh, my stars," Ellen sighed. "The poor thing didn't even know his name until just a minute ago. Let him get his bearings."

Jonathan laughed maniacally. "Yes! He didn't even know his *name*! Let alone his fucking *rank*!"

"Where in God's name is the orderly? Poor Jonathan's in terrible distress," Ellen fretted. She shot a withering look at the nurse. "Someone's going to be sorry if he doesn't get his pills pretty soon, is all I'll say." She pursed her lips. The nurse ignored her.

I leaned over to Bob. "Are we waiting for medicine?"

He nodded. "Also, we can't leave until everyone's talked politely. Part of social skills program, you know how it is."

Jonathan pounded the wall with his fist. "Doris, if you would *please* speak, it would free the *rest of us* to continue our evening, yes? Would it not?"

Doris gazed into her lap.

"Does this happen every time we eat?" I whispered to Bob.

He nodded.

"How long does it take?"

He shook his head slowly.

"My friend, we could be here for days." For the first time, he met my eyes with terrible intensity. "But then," he said, "it hardly matters. In the universal scale of things."

Jonathan gave up. He slid down the wall and lay facedown on the floor.

"Who is the president?"

"President Johnson. Ladybird."

"Ladybird?"

"Ladybird ladybird." I chewed carefully on my right wrist. To stop from talking. The words were getting out today. I knew they were the wrong words. I hated the doctor. The room had two chairs. I was dressed, had gotten dressed before anyone else and sat on the couch in the dayroom so when the doctor arrived I'd be ready for The Assessment. So far not so good.

"You think Ladybird Johnson is the president."

"No."

"All right. We'll move on. How old are you?"

"Twelve." I got up and went to stand by the window, which looked out on the road.

"Are you uncomfortable?"

"No."

"Are you nervous?"

"Nervous. Yes. Very nervous."

"Why's that?"

"Questions." I climbed up onto the radiator and wedged myself onto the windowsill.

"What year is it?"

I paused. "I don't know." I hated that one. Doc Parker never asked me that one. He always skipped that one, even though I know it was on the list of questions, he always skipped it, he knew to skip it because *it didn't matter anyway.*

"It's 1969. Do you know where you are?"

"State."

He laughed.

"Not funny."

"No?"

"No."

"Tell me the names of your family."

"Claire Arnold Kate Oma Opa."

"Very good."

"Very good." He seemed to think I was an idiot. "Not an idiot."

"I know you're not an idiot. I think you're a very intelligent boy, actually."

"Math."

"Really. Math in particular?"

I wrapped myself in a curtain with only my feet sticking out.

"What's the square root of five hundred and thirteen?"

"Isn't. Doesn't. There isn't a have one."

"I see."

I peeked out of my curtain. "Bats hear with their toes."

"I didn't know that."

I nodded, beginning to like him better. "Two hundred and six bones in the body. Approximately. Human body. Not bats. Axial and appendicular skeleton. Mostly toes, fingers. Carpals, metacarpals. Things like that."

"You are absolutely right. You could be a doctor."

"Definitely not."

He laughed. "I'm sorry. That wasn't funny."

"Yes it was." He laughed again. I studied him. He was fifty-four. That was how old he was. I could tell. And he was married and he had two children, daughters, and he was okay. Yes, he was. He would not do anything bad now that he knew about my math.

"So, okay, not a doctor. What do you think you'd like to do?"

"Scientist-inventor."

"Excellent profession. A fine choice. What will you invent?"

"Cures."

"For?"

"Things. Bad things."

"Brain things?"

I nodded. "And fears."

He whistled low through his teeth. "Wow. You'll be much in demand."

"Probably."

"What sort of fears you think you'd like to cure?"

I shrugged. "Darks. Snakes and sharks. Kate my sister's nightmares. People and daytime. Dying." I hopped off the windowsill and walked sideways over to the chair. I sat down and watched him out of the corner of my eye.

"Are you afraid of dying?"

I shook my head.

"Other people dying?"

I chewed my thumb knuckle. Nodded.

"Esau, do you hear voices?"

I thought this over. "Sometimes but not really."

"Do they tell you to do things, ever?"

"No. *My* voices. They're *me*. Parts of me talking. Only at night, falling asleep. All my voices at once, fast."

"Do they have conversations?"

"Yes."

"What does it feel like?"

I ran out of words. I looked at him, helpless.

"That's a hard one, huh?"

I nodded.

"Okay. We'll skip that one, how about. So what about visions. Do you see things, sometimes, and wonder if they're really there?"

"Dreams."

"Yes, like dreams, but when you're awake?"

I sat quietly. I didn't want to tell him. I took a deep breath and looked at him, hoping the words would come out straight.

"They are. My dreams. And you can't have them."

He looked back at me, not writing on his pad. I could tell for sure he heard me.

"Pretty good dreams."

"My dreams." I nodded and studied the coils and spirals of my fingerprints.

"Sometimes, are there bad ones? Where you get confused?"

"Lost."

"You get lost. In the dream?"

"Can't find the door. Horrible trapped."

"I bet it's horrible to be trapped. It is horrible."

I got up and went over to the door.

"Are you ready to be done?"

I made sure the door was unlocked and slid my back down it to sit on the floor and wrapped my arms around my legs and wanted my dad.

"Still with me?"

I nodded into my knees.

"Esau."

I looked up.

"Nobody wants to take your dreams. I don't want to. But what if we could find a way to keep the good ones and make the bad ones go away?"

I watched his shoes. Black shiny shoes on the floor.

"And maybe the voices would slow down. And you could hear them better."

I looked up at his face. I liked his thick bushy overgrown eyebrows. I wanted to touch them, but I stayed where I was. I decided I would say my secret.

"Because they have the answers."

"The voices."

"They tell me the answers."

"To the math."

I nodded and smiled into my knees. I chewed on my jeans. "And the other things. The how things work things, the bats. Wings. A hawk drops two hundred miles an hour. Birds, fish. Bugs have a thorax. Man-eating plants."

I covered my ears with my hands. Shhh.

"Sorry too fast," I said.

"Not a problem."

"Didn't make sense." I peeked out between my knees.

The doctor smiled at me. "Sure it did."

"Crazy crazy." I bonked my head five times with my fist.

"Nah. Just going a little too fast, is all. We'll get you slowed down some, and then we'll see what's going on. Okay. Now, I'm going to get up and come over there."

I scootched my butt out of the way to let him pass. He opened the door.

"I'll see you tomorrow," he said.

The statistical likelihood was good.

"Hello."

I was watching my hands. They were trying to shuffle an old deck of cards, some torn, some crayoned, and I was thinking, slowly, that it would be easy to memorize the cards and cheat, if only I could get my hands to shuffle them. But my hands were pretty uncooperative.

"Hello," the voice said again.

I looked left and studied the person out of the corner of my eye.

These were the things I could figure out right then for sure: 1. It was nighttime. 2. There were three people in the dayroom not counting me. I was sitting back in the corner so I could see them all. We wore the same hospital pajamas, so we were all the Patients and not the Staff. 3. One of these people was standing by the table where I sat. It was him, I figured, who said hello.

He had a bandanna on his head and was big.

I meant to say hello but only wound up jerking my head in a nod. That was going to have to do. I resumed my shuffling attempts and now only my right hand would work; the left lay limp on the table. This frustrated me. "Fuck fuck!" I said. I shook the deck hard.

"Hey! Now. Little buddy. Calm down, there," the big person said. He had a very soothing voice and he was not making fun of me, which was good because otherwise I would have hit him. "Mind if I have a seat?" When I said nothing, he pulled a chair out slowly and sat down.

"Name's Beast," he said, sticking his hand out and startling me.

"Beast!" I shrieked, rearing back in my chair.

"Whoa! Hey now. Sorry about that. Shh. S'all right." He patted the table lightly with his giant hand. The other two in the room glanced up and then went back to their nothing.

He didn't look too upset, but I still felt bad. To make it up to him, I offered him some crayons. I pushed an orange, a periwinkle, and a burnt sienna his way.

"Thanks, buddy." He sounded genuinely pleased, and only took the neat row after I'd removed my own hand. He got up and returned with some paper, sliding a stack across to me. Paralyzed, I stared at it, still gripping my cards.

"You want some help with those?" he asked. I studied the tattoo of a bald eagle on his forearm, fascinated. Underneath his bandanna, his head was shaved. He was a giant. I was in love with him. I nodded. "Happy to shuffle them for you, you want," he said.

"Stuck," I said miserably.

"Say what?"

I held out my hand, wrapped around the worn deck.

"Huh," he said, looking at it. "Well, shit. You want I should unwrap you there, or you gonna sit there holding them all night?"

I shook my head, wanting badly to draw.

"All right, ready? Just like getting a fishing hook out of your finger. One yank and it's over. So gimme your hand."

I screwed my eyes shut and braced myself. He twisted my wrist so fast I dropped the cards. He'd let go of me before I even had a chance to scream.

I looked at the pile of cards on the floor and then at him. He was whistling, a tiny stub of crayon wedged in his huge hand, drawing a field of periwinkle grass.

"Howdja?"

"Old army trick," he said, grinning. "Disarm a fella quick." He picked up the orange crayon and drew in the sun.

I got down on the floor and swept the cards into two piles, red cards and black cards. I would sort and memorize them later. I set them to my right and sat down in my chair.

"Been here long?" he asked.

"I don't know."

He looked at me. "There you go."

I cocked my head.

"Whole sentence," he explained. "You used a whole sentence."

I nodded. "Sometimes, okay. But I think," I said, tapping my head. "All the time."

"You think in whole sentences?"

I nodded again, relieved.

"Well, fuck *me*," he thundered. "That'd piss me *right* off, I couldn't get the words out."

"Fuck *fuck,*" I concurred, happy that finally someone understood. I rocked awhile, watching him from the corner of my eye. I reached across him and tapped his wedding ring. He stopped drawing and looked at it.

"Little Miss Molly. Prettiest girl in town," he said, smiling. "Prettiest girl in the world. See, and I been halfway around the world, and there are all manner of pretty girls, I will admit that, yessir, but there is no one like my Molly, nosiree."

"MollyMolly. MollyandBeast," I said. I liked the name Molly. I decided I would marry me a girl named Molly.

He laughed, throwing his head back. When he lifted it and stopped laughing, his face was wet from tears. I worried.

"Tried to kill myself," he said.

"Oh," I said, horrified. "Oh no oh no."

"Yep. Broke that girl's heart."

"Oh, Beast Beast." My left hand picked that moment to come alive, flying off in no direction until I sat on it. With my right hand, I started going through the cards, organizing them, aces low. "Beast Beast Beast. Can't do that."

"Don't I know it."

"What for'd you did that for?"

"Damned war. Got myself all crazy over there, I guess, that's what the doctor says."

"And then you had a dark."

"Huh. Ain't that the truth. Came home. Never saw such a dark in my life as over there, but when I came home, it was like cobwebs, couldn't shake it. Poor girl, trying to make me happy. Telling me it was all right. Over and over. I swear I started to feel like I was going to have to kill her she told me it was all right one more time."

"Allrightallright."

"And then, I guess, I just couldn't see my way out of the dark."

I nodded. I got up and went to the snacks table and made myself and him some cocoa from packets. I took the Styrofoam cups over one at a time in my right hand.

"Molly Molly," I said, sitting back down.

"Molly Molly," he agreed.

"Out of the dark," I explained. "Molly."

He looked at me.

I picked up a black crayon and drew a long winding black line all over the page, up to the top-right corner. There I put a red X. To clarify, I put an arrow pointing to the X. MOLLY, I wrote. Around that, I put little yellow lines.

"Sunbeams," I said, pleased with my work. "For Molly."

He wiped his nose, nodding his head. "Okay," he said. "That's right. I guess that's about right."

I took a new piece of paper and drew him an apple tree. I drew it so he was looking through a window, with his hands on the window, he could see his hands. And out there the apple tree in spring, with all the white flowers. I drew it so he would have an apple tree to look at while he was here.

He drew me a horrible fire.

I drew him a bed of giant hydrangeas.

He drew me a gun. He labeled all the parts.

I drew him Kate.

"Who's that?"

"Kate my sister Kate."

"Miss her?"

I nodded and drew him the sunrise.

"Snowing," he said, looking past me, out the window. I turned. I got up to stand by the window.

I heard him push back from the table and approach, but he still said, "Right behind you, buddy," which was nice of him, he didn't have to do that but he did and I appreciated it. We watched the snow slant down onto the brick-walled garden below, the buried garden covered in snow.

"Ask you a question?" he said.

"Okay."

"You think I'm crazy?"

I thought it over. I tilted my head and butted his arm with it twice. Then I looked up at him and said, firmly, so he would know for sure, "Definitely definitely not."

His face lit up. I got shy and looked away.

I took his hand and fit mine into it. His hand was rough and he didn't know what to do at first but then he squeezed. We looked out the window.

"All right then," he said. He shook my hand firmly, like we had won a race.

Out in the courtyard, a male cardinal lighted on a snow-heavy branch, shaking it so a small landslide of snow tumbled to the ground. The smells of hospital breakfast seeped down the hall.

Geronimo and I were playing cribbage when the prettiest girl in the world walked into the room.

Geronimo saw her first. He was in the middle of his turn, shuffling and reshuffling his hand, ordering it in some kind of way that made sense to him, and I was waiting to see what he'd put down because I was trying to figure out if there was any mathematical logic to Geronimo's cribbage rules at all, but anyway, he looked up and stared, so I turned to look and there she was, the prettiest girl in the world.

I had so many feelings at once I pulled on my hair a few times and turned my chair a little so I could keep an eye on her.

"Your go," I said.

"Who's that?"

"Molly," I said.

"Who's she belong to?"

"Beast."

"Hell and damn."

The prettiest Molly ever in history smoothed her hands over her red skirt and looked around and sat down on the edge of a couch and picked up a magazine, which she held in her lap awhile.

Since everyone was staring at her, she looked a little uncomfortable.

"Stop it," I said to Geronimo. "It's your go."

He looked at his cards. "I can't go."

"Course you can. Here, let me see."

"No." He pulled his cards close to his chest. He was totally crazy but a nice old guy. His real name was Charlie but he said he was Geronimo in a past life, so he went by that now since no one was stopping him and he wouldn't answer to anything else.

"Well, how're you gonna make a play if you don't let me see?"

"That's cheating."

"For Christmas sakes!" I yelled, pounding my leg. "How can it be cheating if you know I'm doing it, if I already just this second *told* you I was doing it?"

He stared at me. I was doing pretty good today. Staff said so. I made the choice to stop yelling.

"I don't know," he said. "It just is."

"Well, I already know what you have anyway."

"How do you know?"

"I just know."

"Why do you always just *know* shit? How in the *hell's* a man supposed to play cards with you when you already know what's what 'fore he even lays a card down, Je*zus* Mary Joseph! I ask you, where's the *suspense?*"

I sat there arranging my cards. I made the choice to say nothing. Over the top of my cards, I watched Molly, who paged through the magazine but kept her eye on the door.

"He'll be here in a minute," I said.

She looked at me and I looked away.

"Statistically speaking, it won't be more than *six* minutes," I said to my cards.

Her eyes didn't leave me. I turned my chair around so I could see her from the corner of my eye but she couldn't see me. She wore a white blouse with her red skirt and had dark brown hair in a ponytail and bosoms. I wanted to go over and look at her bosoms closer up. They were round. They looked grabbable. I sat on my hand.

"Thank you," she said.

"You are most very welcome," I replied.

"What are you playing?" she asked after a minute.

"This young man," Geronimo boomed, "is cheating at cribbage. He is a spy."

I shook my head. "Not cheating."

"You are a spy. You are a very small spy. That's why they think they can get away with it."

"I am *not* a spy."

"You are a Red and a spy."

"I am not a Red!" I shrieked, and slapped down my hand. "Give me your cards or make a play yourself or I quit."

He laid down an ace and two twos.

I stared at his play. "You're going by sevens and fives," I said, delighted.

"See?" he thundered, smacking his hand on the table.

"And you're collecting the queens!"

"That's it! No more! I'll have nothing more to do with this spy!" He poured a carton of milk all over the table, set the empty carton down, and stormed out of the room, shouting all the way down the hall.

Beast appeared in the doorway and stopped dead at the sight of the prettiest girl in the world. She stood up and the magazine fell off her lap and she didn't even notice, that's how much she loved him right then. And it took him only two giant steps over to her to pick her up and swing her around and sit down on the couch with her in his lap.

He had her smushed so close to his chest I started to worry he would crush her, but his face over her shoulder was smiling and he was talking softer than I could hear so I decided not to say anything. I made myself invisible and watched her pull herself back, look around quickly, and kiss him a million times all over his face.

"Here I am," she said. She said it again and again, like she was teasing him about something, telling him a joke only he knew. Kissing his eyelids and his nose. "Here I am."

He looked like a big dog basking in the sun, his two hands wrapped all the way around her waist.

I snuck off to my bedroom and jerked off in the closet, feeling sort of guilty but not too bad, thinking I would find me a girl named Molly with fat cheeks and soft bosoms and a whisper and a red skirt and when I was in the hospital or in a Dark she would come and kiss me all over my face with her soft bosoms pressed up against my chest.

I came in my sock. Then I curled up and took a nap.

I had a stack of books, and was drawing fish skeletons from memory, and Geronimo and Captain Sir Joe had started calling me Lieutenant Darwin, from the book I was reading. I had several fine rocks from the garden, from when we went on walks around the grounds.

And then one afternoon, when everyone else was having a nap because their meds made them fall asleep, I was lying on my bed staring at the ceiling when I felt someone looking at me. I turned my head on the pillow. Doris was standing in the doorway.

She looked at me, waiting for me to say something, but I didn't know what and my words were all a mess that day anyway. So I just sat up with my feet sticking off the side of the bed. I straightened the covers.

Slowly, as if it was hard to move, she shuffled across the linoleum to the side of the bed. She handed me my new sketch pad. Doc Hammerstein had just given it to me, it was mine, and so far I had used five pages. I was saving them, I didn't want to run out. I used only one page a day, the rest of the time I used regular paper from the stack.

I took it from her, along with the box of brand-new colored pencils, which were very sharp. Every time I used them I sharpened them with the sharpener that had its own compartment in the gray box so that they would be sharp every time I opened it because otherwise it was unlucky.

I sat there holding my things to my chest and looking at Doris from the corner of my eye. She gazed over my head, out the window.

Then she shuffled over to the chair and pushed it so it was facing me. She sat down. She smoothed her housedress over her knees. And then, in the swiftest motion I had ever seen her make, she reached up with both hands and unwound the thick bun of her hair.

It fell, a flood of silver, over her shoulders, over the sides of the chair, all the way to the dirty floor.

She stared directly at the wall behind me and waited, holding perfectly still.

I realized suddenly that she was not an old lady at all. She held her chin up and though I am embarrassed to say this, her bosoms were not old-lady bosoms when she sat up straight, and her feet were just narrow pretty white feet. Her hair was still a little damp, which meant she had taken a shower. I could smell soap.

I blinked, confused, waiting for her to go back to looking like she did before.

She glanced at me once, as if to say, Well?

So since I had not used a page yet today I drew her. I drew her all afternoon.

You start with the structure of the thing. Animal, vegetable, mineral. Same as if you're drawing a machine. The construction of a thing, the underneath, implies the exterior. That is what it says in my book of medical illustrations. "The body's blueprint is of utmost importance in every aspect of accurate representation; the interior will dictate the exterior. To overlook the structure is a grave, if regrettably common, error."

Cheekbone, brow bone, nose: "A single line should suffice. The bones are not a jigsaw puzzle: The body is of a piece."

Doris did not blink, or if she blinked, she did it so fast I did not notice.

Jawbone, line of throat.

Clavicle, shoulder, breast, ribs.

When the structure is completed—waist, hip, thigh, knee, calf, the complexity of ankle, foot—there is time for detail work. The shape of the eye socket, the eye. The line of the lips. Ears and fingers.

"The actuality of the thing will emerge if sufficient attention is given to *each layer* of the object as it is drawn. If done in haste, without consideration for variants and structural integrity, the drawing, far from being an accurate representation, will instead lie lifeless on the page."

Rumple of housedress. Tiny blue flowers. Cornflowers. Petals of cornflowers. Breath beneath the dress, space between the dress and the belly. Slight hills of thighs.

The light faded, so I could only see the left side of her. She didn't move. Her hands curved over the ends of the arms of the chair, cupped because the muscles of the hands, "in their state of full relaxation, do not extend, unlike most muscles, which gives the hand a natural curve, as if about to clench. Drawn without this, the hand will appear stiff. This is the mark of the amateur."

Her hair coiled in thick ropes on the floor. I stood up and went over to the chair, bent in, and studied the color of her eyes. She stared at the wall. My breath ruffled the hairs on her temples. I sat back down and made her eyes the color of fresh mud: brown, green, orange, olive.

"To give the eyeball its natural light, shading will be necessary. The living eye is wet and curved, not dry and flat."

It was dark in the room. From memory, I shaded in the shadows underneath her eyes and cheekbones. She sat there, a shadow in the chair. From the hall, a triangle of light fell on the floor and voices passed the doorway on their way to dinner.

I finished. The whispering of my pencils stopped.

I stood up and turned on the light. She blinked. I tore the page carefully out of the sketch pad, and before I could change my mind I laid it in her lap.

She picked it up with both hands and studied it for a long time. Then she stood up and went over to the small mirror that hung over the dresser. She held it up next to her face and stared at her selves.

The drawing was my best one.

She glanced at me in the mirror and said, like it hurt to talk, "My face."

I shrugged and pulled on my ear.

"It's my face."

"Your face."

She thumbed the edges of the page, still looking at it. "Can I have it?"

I hesitated, feeling my words tangle. "Course. It's for you, I draw, I drew it for you. Of you." I wanted to give her my entire room. I pounded my leg, flopped on my bed in frustration, and curled up in a ball.

I could feel her watching me in the mirror. Then I heard her turn around. She came over and sat down on the bed. She scooched so she sat with her back against the wall.

She patted my head awkwardly. Then her hand went still and she just let it lie there.

I opened one eye. She was staring across the room. It was okay. I rearranged myself, putting my head in her lap. I moved it around until I was comfortable.

"Your face," I said.

She looked down at me. She smiled. I put my hands over my face and nearly died.

Around two o'clock on December 15, they came to get Bob.

We all watched four orderlies in white coats park a rolling bed outside Bob's door. When they didn't find him in there, they came into the dayroom. We all looked down at our cards and pretended they weren't there. They reminded me of Martians. The main Martian looked at his clipboard. "Mr. Thornton?" he called.

Bob stared at his hand of hearts. "Tarnation," he said under his breath. "Knew they'd find me in here."

No one looked up. I noticed Bob's hand was shaking.

"Which one of you is Mr. Thornton?" the Martian asked, looking around.

"There is no such person present," Jonathan said, sounding bored, and passed three cards to the left. Ellen passed three to her left and picked up the ones Jonathan had given her.

"Why, you little rat," she said to him. Her voice was unnaturally high.

"Look, folks, I've got an order to borrow Mr. Robert Thornton for just a few hours. I'm just doing my job. No reason you've got to make it harder for me," the Martian said. "Tell a fellow which one is he and I'll be out of your hair."

Jonathan's leg was going crazy under the table. I passed him three hearts. He looked at them and didn't even blink, just arranged them in his hand, which was a pretty good hand. The muscles in his jaw were working. He was having troubles with his anger management, I could tell.

Bob had started whispering softly to his cards, rocking slightly back and forth.

His voice mild, Jonathan said, "Well, I don't know what to tell you, pal. You are just shit out of luck, aren't you?"

The Martian started to look not so friendly about the whole thing.

Beast had worked his hand over to Bob's side. In a flash, he twisted Bob's hospital bracelet off his wrist and put it in his mouth.

Jonathan was flexing his neck muscles. I didn't think this was good. The Martian approached the table.

"Permission to speak," Captain Joe said. He was ignored. He stood up, saluted the man, and said, "Young pup, I strongly advise you to be on your way. You are on enemy territory."

"That you are," Geronimo concurred in a soft growl.

"We give you fair warning. We may look crazy, sir, but that is relative, and we are extremely organized."

The alien man picked up Beast's wrist. This was dumb. Because Beast grabbed his forearm and twisted it behind his back superfast, laying him out on the floor, at which point Jonathan actually *jumped over* the table and landed on the guy and started pounding on him.

The guy got beat up pretty good before Staff made it into the room and hauled Jonathan and Beast out.

"Crazy motherfuckers," the Martian spat out, standing there with a bloody nose while the nurse patched him up.

Bob stood up abruptly, laid down his hand, and walked stiffly out of the room. Through the Plexiglas windows on to the hall, we could see him climb up and lie down on the rolling bed. He lay there staring at the ceiling until the beat-up Martian was fixed. Then they rolled him down the hall.

"Poor Bob," Doris said softly. She was sitting next to me. She didn't play, but she liked to sit in.

"Poor Bob," Ellen nodded.

"It is truly a pity they didn't take out the entire regiment," Captain Joe said thoughtfully, and tossed down the queen of hearts.

"Damn," Geronimo said, throwing down the king and taking the pile. "Captain, it is. Had we had better intelligence, we might have more successfully braced the camp."

"Sir, we had no way of knowing."

"No, no, I know. But still, it hurts to see your men go down. Hurts terribly."

Ellen patted his arm.

"It does, sir. If I may say, sir, I believe they have demonstrated amply their bravery in the face of adversity."

"Indeed. The purple heart for each."

"Sir, if I may be so bold, I am not certain they sustained injuries in the course of this battle. Seeing as how they so successfully intercepted the surprise attack, and their quickness and sheer physical skill so totally outstripped that of their opponent."

"Heart injuries," Geronimo said, patting his chest. "An inner pain, a *heartache,* for example, is a perfectly worthy cause."

"Sir, I stand corrected, sir." Captain Joe looked at his hand. Then he threw down the queen of spades.

Geronimo stared at it. "Goddammit, soldier."

"Sir, my apologies, sir."

"Well played."

"Thank you, sir."

"I didn't play well tonight."

"Sir, you were distracted by the battle."

"I was. It's true." Geronimo swept the pile into his hand and everyone tossed their cards his way.

"Well," Ellen said. "Tea, Doris?" She stood up and made two cups of lukewarm chamomile, which she swore improved the mood. While it steeped, she looked out the window. Geronimo dealt another hand. "I suppose they're down there zapping his poor little brain," she said.

I looked up. "What what?"

"Zapping him, darling," she said, stirring honey into the tea and setting a cup in front of Doris. She pulled her chair in again, blew on her tea, and picked up her cards. "They came to get him for *electroshock*, why, I couldn't tell you, it's the silliest thing I ever heard."

"Terrible stuff," Geronimo said.

"Perfectly awful. Scares the poor thing half to death. Can you blame him? How would *you* like it if they attached you to a heap of wires and, what is it, *volted* you? Like a *lightbulb*?" She shivered.

"Whole body leaping around like a frog," the Captain said. *"Tzzzt!"*

"Oh, Captain, that's enough," Ellen scolded. "And it makes him so ill."

"Have to strap you down to do it," the Captain muttered. "No dignity."

I sat, horrified. "Bob," I whimpered.

"Honey, he'll be back."

"No respect for a man's dignity *what*soever, that's what it is," the Captain added. "Put those things on his head and try to melt his brains."

I shrieked.

"Captain!" Ellen commanded. "You've simply *got* to stop it. You're being morbid."

"Didn't start it."

"You most certainly did."

"Woman, you're out of line."

"Oh, put it back in your pants, old man!"

"I *will not* be spoken to this way," the Captain said, his face getting red. He stood up and pushed his chair in firmly. "Sir, permission to smack her, sir."

"Denied. Most absolutely denied. Take your seat, Captain."

The Captain and Ellen glowered at each other.

"Captain!" Geronimo bellowed. "I won't tell you twice. *Take your seat!*"

The Captain did so.

"Oughtta tan her hide," the Captain muttered. "Old man indeed."

Ellen waved her hand dismissively in his direction. Doris pushed a tiny piece of paper under my elbow, which rested on the table. *They will be back for dinner,* it said. I turned it over and she handed me the pencil. *Are they in The Room?* I wrote. She nodded. *Will they get zapped?* She shook her head fervently. *They are just Punching some walls.* She shrugged. I tore another corner of paper from the sheet she held on her lap. *Why are they melting Bob's brain?* I wrote.

She laughed out loud. Everyone looked up at her. Her face went back to frozen and she stared into space. She wasn't crazy, she just didn't like being looked at, was all. I could understand that. *Not funny!!!!* I wrote. She shook her head, covering the smile on her mouth. *Not melting it. He will be sick a little but he will feel Better tomorrow.*

I looked at her. She nodded at the table. *Promise,* she wrote.

It was my turn. I put down the four of diamonds and picked up the pencil again. *Are they going to zap me?*

She grabbed the pencil out of my hand. *No!*

She underlined it a few more times, patted my hand, and wandered out of the room.

That night Bob was rolled down the hall in a wheelchair just as we were filing in to dinner. We all stopped, like he was the president or a hearse. He didn't look at us. He didn't look at anything we could see, just stared at the back of his eyes. His head was at a funny angle on his neck, like it was broken. His hands were limp on his thighs. He was dead white and looked like he'd been shrunk.

The nurse pushing the wheelchair turned the corner into his room, jostling his head.

We none of us had anything to say at dinner.

"How are you feeling today?"

"Okay."

"How's the drawing coming?"

I tried to hide a smile. I passed him the sketch pad.

He paged through it and whistled low. "Holy smokes. This is something else."

"For Kate."

"Oh yeah?"

"For Christmas."

"They're coming to visit, aren't they?"

I nodded. "Five days."

"You feeling well enough to see them?"

I shrugged, not wanting to look like I cared.

"Because sometimes when they come, it upsets you. Remember? Esau? Sometimes you don't want to see them."

This is not true.

I always want to see them.

"They leave."

"I know they leave. They have to leave. We make them leave, it's not their fault. Do you know that?"

Sort of.

"Is that why you forget? That they come?"

I don't forget. I just say I forget. From my window, I watch them drive away.

"Because they leave? Does it feel better to forget they were ever here than to see them and then have them leave?"

"Yes."

"That makes sense."

"Yeah." I watch the snow fall. "When can I go home."

"Your affect is much better."

"Yeah."

"And I understand you're doing extremely well, talking to people most days."

"Yeah."

"You seem to have made some good friends. Are you happy here?"

"Yeah."

"Feeling pretty safe?"

"Yeah."

"Still having some night fears, though. I think I'll try a new med to help you sleep, what do you think of that?"

"Make me stupid."

"It won't make you stupid. Knock you out pretty quick, and it might make you a little sedated at first when you wake up."

"Take my dreams."

"Definitely won't do that. Might even give you some pretty wild ones, matter of fact." He smiled.

"Okay."

"Okay. You excited to see your family?"

"Superexcited."

"I bet. What'd you ask for for Christmas?"

I drew a blank. I looked at him.

"You are avoiding the question," I said. I was startled by the intact sentence.

"You're right. I'm avoiding the question because I don't know the answer."

"Approximately when am I going home."

"Approximately a while. It could be a while."

We sat there while that sank in.

"Approximately months or approximately forever."

"Buddy, I'd say you're looking at at least a year."

My head jerked left. "Long time."

"All things considered, it's not long. But it seems long to you, I know."

"Long, long time."

"Makes you pretty anxious, huh."

"Yeah."

"You feel trapped?"

"Yeah, trapped."

"But safe."

"Okay. Yeah. Safe. For a year."

"Well, that's the trick. The idea is to get you safe for longer than a year. For good, so when you leave you're still safe and you still know you're safe."

My head jerked again. "Time to go."

I stood up and walked to the door. I held it open for him. He opened his briefcase and put away my file. Then he pulled out a brand-new sketch pad and set it on my chair. As he walked past, I saluted him. He saluted me back.

"See you Thursday," he said.

"Thursday."

We waited.

We always waited. That was what we did. But today was special because for once we had something to wait for. It was Christmas Eve.

Beast waited for Molly. Doris waited for her daughter, holding in her lap the picture I drew. Bob waited for his mother, and so did Captain Joe. Geronimo didn't wait for anybody, and he didn't care. Jonathan, pacing happily up and down the hall, waited for his wife.

Ellen sat in a chair by the window. Technically it was my chair, but I didn't have the heart to tell her. She had been there all day. She was knitting the world's longest red thing. It stretched out across the room, out the door. Knit purl, knit purl. The spool of red wool wound up her leg and disappeared into the knit-purl pattern of the thing.

"Are her sons coming?" I asked Geronimo.

He didn't answer me. He was doing a crossword. I was helping him with the hard ones. "Seven-letter word for 'redwood'?" he said.

"Sequoia." I watched Ellen lick the blister on her thumb and catch a stitch.

"Spell that."

Captain Joe had his hands in his pockets. He kept looking at his pocket watch. He reminded me of the white rabbit. I laughed.

"What's so funny, Lieutenant?"

"You. Pocket watch."

"Six-letter word for 'songbird.' Starts with a *t.*"

"Thrush."

"Hmph. Sounds like a disease."

"Is one."

"Thought you said it was a songbird."

"That too."

Jonathan flung himself into the doorway. "She's here!" he crowed. "She's here!"

We all stood up and straightened ourselves and tried not to stare when Jonathan's wife, who was just a little tiny tidbit of a lady, came running down the hall toward him and threw herself at his chest and started to laugh and cry. She'd brought presents for everybody. I got a desk encyclopedia, leather bound. I folded the wrapping paper superneatly, not wanting to look up at her. "Thankyouthankyouthankyou," I whispered. Jonathan hopped around behind her like a bird. She kissed my head and I just about died. People have *no idea.*

She took a box over to Ellen and said, "Ellen, here, I brought you something!" and Ellen batted it out of her hand and the box fell on the floor with a thunk and Ellen picked up a dropped stitch and went on knitting.

"Don't need your pity," Ellen sniffed, talking to herself. "Don't need your charity."

Jonathan's wife looked stunned. Jonathan came up behind her and steered her over to the couch. "I didn't mean to insult—"

"No no no no of course not," Captain Joe said, interrupting her, collecting all the pillows in the room and piling them around and on top of her. "Just a hard day. Didn't know."

"I feel terrible—"

"Now, now, now, none of that," Geronimo said, patting her knee with his crossword. "So. Seven-letter word for a perennial flower, starts with *b.*"

"Begonia," she and I said at once, both watching Ellen. "Should I apologize?" she asked Jonathan.

He shook his head, petting her hair with both hands. Gently, she moved his hands. He sat with them in his lap, gazing at her.

"What's the matter with her today, anyway?" I asked.

"Doesn't like the holidays."

"Why?"

The adults looked at me. "Depressing."

"So are her sons coming or not?"

No one answered.

Doris smoothed her hand over the drawing. "Doesn't have any sons," she whispered.

"Course she does," Geronimo said curtly.

"No she doesn't."

"Still her sons."

"They're dead."

I looked over at Ellen, whose hands had stopped moving. She was listening to us.

"Just because they're dead doesn't mean they aren't her sons," Geronimo said.

Ellen stood up, her knitting tumbling out of her lap. She walked out of the room.

"I didn't know they were dead," I said.

"*She* doesn't know they're dead," Doris said. "She just thinks they don't visit."

"Why doesn't someone tell her?"

Doris shook her head. "Doesn't believe it."

Geronimo slapped the table. "And who's to say," he bellowed. "Which would you rather think? You got three good-for-nothing sons who don't bother to visit you in your old age, or you got three *dead* sons? Ah? Which you think it's easier to sleep with at night?"

Doris shook her head to silence him. She whispered to her drawing, "Shhh."

That night I couldn't sleep.

I was too excited. They were coming in the morning and I wanted to be good, I wanted to be clear and alert and in full possession of my faculties, so when the medication cart came around at the nine P.M. snack time, I took my little cup of pills and tossed them back into my mouth and made a big show of swallowing but didn't really swallow. A few minutes later, I spat them out in the toilet and flushed. It took two flushes for them to go down.

I watched them swirl and wondered if that was really a good idea, but it was too late now.

By ten we had to be in our rooms unless we had permission to be elsewhere. By midnight we were supposed to be in bed with lights out, but they weren't too strict about that one because some people just like to sleep with the lights on better, and besides which at midnight it was Christmas and we all had to come out of our rooms and tell each other. Then Staff herded us back to bed. By two A.M. I decided I could not possibly physically lie in bed one more dang-blasted minute.

"Staff," I called when the shadow darkened my doorway on the two A.M. rounds.

She held still like she was caught. "What?" the nurse said.

"I gotta get up."

"You still awake?"

"Yes. Obviously."

"You want something to sleep?"

"No. Definitely not."

"How come?"

"Gotta be clear for tomorrow. Alert."

"Well, how you gonna be alert if you lie here awake all night?"

I sat up in bed. "Please can I get up."

She sighed. I liked her. She was my favorite one, and if she got her charts done and I was still up, she'd play cards with me. She was a mean card player and was teaching me bridge, but we never had a fourth.

"All right, Mr. Up At All Hours," she said. "But if you're still up at five, I'm gonna make you take something. Can't have you all revved up with your family here tomorrow."

"Okay."

I wrapped my blanket around my shoulders and trailed out to the dayroom. She leaned in and said, as I settled into my chair by the window, "You just gonna sit there?"

"Yep."

"Thinking thoughts?"

"My thoughts."

"Okay. Ring the bell, you want anything."

"Turn out the light."

She laughed. "Little bat," she said, and flipped the switch.

Darkness filled the room. I sat there with my feet and hands tucked under the blanket, looking out at the glowing snow.

I felt someone come into the room. I felt the someone pause when they saw me, then cross the room and pull up a chair. Ellen and I stared at the stars.

"I know," she said, defensively. "I do know."

I didn't know what to say so I wiggled a hand out of my bundle and chewed on my nails.

"You remind me of them," she said. "Don't know why. Don't look a thing like them, they're big boys. Big, strapping boys, athletes, all of them. Tommy, he was a smart one, and Dean was pretty. Poor Scott, he was just different. Played ball well enough, but he didn't really want to,

I knew that. Shouldn't have pushed him. Told him he would meet a girl that way, but he didn't want any part of that. Too shy. Funny looking, never knew how to talk to anyone. Such a momma's boy, that's what his father said, but then. What did his father know. Never knew anything." She sniffed her dismissal. "Never mind him anyway, where was he when push came to shove? Ha. Covered for him all those years, *we* took the boys to the lake, *we* had a lovely little gathering. Who, *we*? Me and the mouse in my pocket? I don't fancy so, no indeed." She pulled her robe closer around her. "Do you know what I did?"

She waited a long time, so finally I shook my head.

"I divorced him."

I didn't say anything.

"I did. Knowing full well. My family, that was the end of them, oh, where did they go? When he was gone? And me, a Catholic girl getting a divorce, well, my mother just couldn't take that, no, because that just wasn't *done*, no matter *what*." She sniffed again. "No matter what kind of, what kind of, oh, *awfulness* was afoot, didn't matter to her. And you know what, I didn't even bother to tell her what all. She didn't deserve to know. Wasn't her place to know. To hell with her, that's what I said. I said, 'Well then you go straight to hell, is where you go.'"

I started chewing on my knuckles. She noticed. "Oh, honey, stop that. You know you can't do that." She turned her face back to the window and I stopped.

"So of course the boys are growing up, without even the Church to raise them, let alone a father, so I did what any sensible woman would do, which was to marry the richest man I could find and I tell you, I took that poor son of a bitch for a ride."

I nodded. It did seem sensible.

"And I don't know." She sighed. "Maybe that wasn't right. But I was damned if I was going to let those boys out into the world without a pot to piss in or a college education. They needed those things. They *deserved* those things."

"Yeah."

"And what am I talking about, anyway? *Poor* son of a bitch, indeed. He was mean. He was mean like a *snake*. Ha. There, he was."

She fell silent. We watched the dark.

"So what happened?" I asked.

"Started beating on my boys and got himself killed."

I just sat there. Slowly I turned to look at her.

"Started beating on me too, but that bothered me less. I could use makeup, I could hide it, but my boys, no. I wasn't having them go to school like that. Humiliating. They'd been through enough. Yes they had."

"Did they kill him?"

She laughed her shattered-glass laugh. "Oh, no, darling. I killed him. They'd never have hurt a fly. Don't know what I was thinking, sending them to war."

I looked back out the window. "How'd you do it?" I asked.

"Shot him." She smoothed her hair and tucked her hand into her tightly folded arms again. It was chilly in the room. "There'd been some drinking, I will admit that. He and I were getting ready to go out, you know, for the evening. And Scott, my youngest, the baby, came in the room. Don't know what it was about Scott that made him so mad, but it always did, there was always something. Couldn't stand him. And Scott, well, let's just say there was no love lost on either side. Well, they got into it. When suddenly, I don't even know what happened, but that old man had my baby by the throat and he was throttling him and my baby boy was turning blue and so I tell you, I did. I took a pistol and shot him dead."

She sighed.

"Nice clean shot to the back of his head. Point-blank range. Never saw what hit him, poor old fool. He never did pay attention."

She looked at me. "Sweetheart, your mother must just love you to pieces."

I nodded.

"I bet she does. She should. I'll tell her tomorrow how good you've been since you got here. I've been here for ages, and I've seen just about all there is to see."

"Thanks."

She looked out the window again.

"How did the boys die?" I asked.

She winced. "Killed them too. Not quite so direct, you wouldn't say, but I killed 'em. After that man died, I packed them off to Korea. Toughen them up, they were all so shook from what happened. I worried, I'll tell you. Thought they'd never get anywhere, crazy like they were. I just wanted them to grow up," she said, sounding helpless.

"They used to come visit," she said. "That's why I hate Christmas. They'd take me down the road for supper, then we'd have presents back here."

"You been here *that* long?" I asked.

"Oh, darling, I've been here since 1950." She laughed. "And I'm not going anywhere. Insanity plea. Fact of the matter is, I'll tell you a secret." She smoothed her hands over her knees and examined her rings. "I never been crazy a day in my life. Except one." She held up one finger. "One day. Day I got the news all three had been killed." She looked at me and patted my leg. "Three boys, three units, three battles, and they all went down. When I figured out God had it in for me, then I was crazy. For that one day."

She eased herself off the chair and sighed. "Time for me to go to bed." She leaned down and kissed my head, then turned on her high-heeled mules and left the room.

Around five o'clock, the nurse came in and made me take something to sleep.

The next thing I remember, I was watching my parents' backs go down the hall toward the door. I was feeling kind of foggy but I was happy and I was wearing a soft new blue thing. As they waited for the nurse to unlock the door so they could leave, my father turned to me and smiled.

When I left, it was winter and now it was spring.

It was my first morning home.

My clock with the Mickey Mouse face said it was 5:54. That's five-five-four. Six minutes before six. Neat.

In the place right then I bet they were all getting ready for breakfast.

I looked around my room and wrapped my arms around myself. My room with my Vikings pennant and my Motley-Staples champions pennant and my baseball bat my dad had mounted on the wall.

My dad was dead. My mom told me last night, when she brought me home. I already knew, in a way, but now it was definitely true.

She took me into my room by myself and shut the door, and when she did that I knew what she was going to say, so I sat down on the floor and curled up in a ball. I squinched my eyes closed and decided no I would not go into my closet because who knew how long I'd be in there? As Staff would say. In the dark. And I had the choice to stay where I was on the floor if that was where I was most comfortable. I stayed there all night.

The next morning, I listened to Kate talking to herself. "I'm gonna wear a red dress, red dress, red dress, I'm gonna wear a red dress and Momma can't stop me." I untucked my face from the crook of my elbow and opened an eye. The carpet smelled like dust. From where I lay on the floor I looked up at the tree branches. They had some buds. Kate knocked on the wall.

"Esau," she whispered.

I got up and crawled across my bed. "What."

"Are you up?"

"I'm talking to you, aren't I?"

She giggled. "Can I come over?"

"Okay." I heard her run out of her room and down the hall and to my door. She knocked again. "Come in," I said.

She stood there swinging on the doorknob for a minute and then closed the door behind her. Her face looked like it was about to pop and she stood there pulling at her dress, grinning.

"Do you have something in your mouth?" I asked.

"No." She swallowed something.

"Do you have to pee?"

She looked worried.

"Go pee."

"Okay." She ran off. I got up and made my bed superwell. My left hand got clenchy, so I pounded the mattress for a second but that messed up the comforter with spaceships so I had to remake it. I was too old for a spaceship comforter, I decided. I would tell my mom. Plus which, the plaids on my sheets were worn, so they just looked blue, not green and blue. I sat down carefully on the bed with my back to the wall and my feet sticking out, smoothing the comforter on either side of me. Kate knocked.

"Come in again!" I said. She bounded in and leaped onto the bed. "Wait wait wait wait," I said. "Get off for a second." She did. I tugged the comforter straight and lifted her onto it. "Are you comfortable?" I asked. She nodded. "Okay." I sat down next to her. "Okay." I looked at her and she grinned at me.

"You're back," she said.

"About *finally*," I agreed.

"No *kidding*."

We looked at our feet. She had her shoes on already. Red Keds with a white zig on the side. "Cool shoes," I said.

"Thanks," she said, sounding all casual. "They're new."

"Yeah?"

"Yeah." She grinned at her feet. "I bet mom would get you new shoes too, if you wanted," she offered.

"Huh," I nodded. "My feet have gotten superbig."

"*I'LL* say," she shouted, laughing and pointing.

My right foot started to shake and twist toward me. Dumb foot. I reached down and grabbed it. I pulled it into my lap without touching the covers. Kate looked impressed.

Outside it was sunny. A sunny day is okay, I thought. It doesn't mean anything different. I have the choice to stay inside if I want. I felt better.

"Is Mom going to make breakfast?"

"I'm not telling."

I looked at her. "Fine." That made her mad. Crossing her arms, she said, "No, she's *not* gonna. She's not a housemaid. We make our own breakfast around here, Mister."

"Oh yeah?"

"Yeah."

"Fine. Do we have any cereal?"

"Yeah," she said, reluctantly.

"Do you want some?"

After a minute, she said, "Okay."

We sat there. She looked at me. "Do you know how to make cereal?"

"Yes. Duh." I was embarrassed.

"What's the matter then?"

I sat staring at my feet.

"Do you want your shoes?" she offered.

I nodded, hugely relieved. She hopped off the bed, then remembered and straightened the covers elaborately, smoothing them, the bedposts, my knees. She got my shoes from where they pointed at the window and handed them to me. Looking at the window, she said, "How did you get from there to the bed? Last night?"

"Slept on the floor," I said, holding one shoe under my chin so it wouldn't touch the bed while I tied the other. She nodded.

My shoes were on. I looked at her. "Okay," I said.

"Okay."

We opened the door and charged into the day.

My mother was asleep on the couch with the brown-and-orange knit blanket over her head. Kate walked right past her as if that was perfectly normal. Sometimes I am not the best judge of situations so I followed her into the kitchen.

"We have shredded wheat and Cheerios," she said. "What are we having?"

"Cheerios. Shredded wheat tastes like hay." I looked in the fridge. "You want half an orange?"

"Yes please."

"Quarters or peeled?"

"Quarters."

I got an orange and put it on the cutting board. Now I was stuck.

"Um," I said. She looked at me.

"Where's the knives?"

"In the drawer, stupid. Where they always are." She yanked open a drawer for me. I stared into it.

"What's the matter?" she asked. She'd poured two bowls so full of Cheerios there'd be no room for milk.

"They're moving," I said.

She came over and peered into the drawer. "No they're not," she said.

"Yeah, they are."

She stood there looking at me as if she were putting together a jigsaw puzzle. "Try again," she said. "Maybe they'll stop."

I looked. They didn't. I shaded my eyes with one hand. They were coming at my eyes.

"You want me to cut the orange?" she asked.

I thought about it. "You're not supposed to use the knives, are you?"

"No," she said sadly.

"Could you get one out for me? And then you could shut the drawer and we could see if just the one is moving?"

"A big one or a small one?"

"Small."

She set a paring knife on the cutting board and shut the drawer with a bang. "There," she said.

In this context, the knife looked like a knife. Sharp, but manageable. "Okay," I said.

"I think I put too much cereal in," she said, going back to her station in front of the bowls.

"Put some back in the box." I picked up the knife, testing its weight in my palm. It felt so feathery for such an important thing. So much could happen with such a tiny thing. I wondered how deep in your chest your heart was, then stopped. Knives are for oranges, Esau.

I stabbed the orange. The knife didn't even go halfway through. I sawed it in half, turning it in circles. It looked sort of ragged, but we wound up with two quarters each and a bowl of cereal. We went into the dining room and looked over at the couch.

"Should we wake her up?" Kate whispered.

"I don't know," I whispered back. "You're the one who's been here all the time. Since when doesn't she sleep on her bed?"

"Since when Dad died," she said. "Duh."

I sat down at the table and looked at Dad's place, piled with mail. I pulled out a *Motley-Staples Gazette* from February and paged through it. I had decided I wanted a boat.

"She never sleeps in there?" I asked.

"I don't know." Kate scooted in across from me, getting comfortable. "Maybe she does."

"Look at this," I said, pointing. "There's a pontoon for two twenty-five. With winter storage."

"Is that a lot of money?"

"Tons."

Kate put an orange quarter in her mouth and sucked out its juice. "How much money do we have?"

"I don't know." I turned the page.

"How much money is a house?"

"Why? Are you buying a house?"

"Maybe."

"Kate, you can't buy a house."

"Who says?"

"I say. We have a house."

"What if we lose the house?"

"You don't *lose* a house. How can you lose a house?"

"The people up the street lost their house. I heard Mom say to Donna."

"Who took it?"

"I don't know. I'm just saying."

"Oh."

"But I'm saving my money."

"How much do you have?"

"A lot. I'm not telling."

"Fine."

"Plus, Dad left us money."

I looked up at her. She looked back, gauging my reaction. "How do you know?" I said.

"I know lots of things," she retorted.

"Yeah," I snorted, chasing the last five Cheerios in my bowl one at a time, staring into my milk. Esau, if someone is disturbing your serenity, you have the choice not to engage.

"How do you know that?" I demanded.

"I listen," she said, with her weird little calm. "I read things."

"No you don't. You don't know how to read."

She grabbed the paper away from me. "'The Water Festival in Detroit Lakes was its usual success. The Water Olympics was chilly again this year, but that didn't keep festival-goers away. There were turtle races—'"

I grabbed it back. "Since when can you read?"

She sneezed, and milk came out her nose. She looked at it, fascinated, and wiped it up with her sleeve. "Just because you went to Away doesn't mean I *died*." Suddenly her eyes filled up and she put her fists in them. I watched her chin crinkle up and felt helpless.

"You know," she added, indignant, still looking into her fists.

"I know," I said.

"Good."

"Does Mom know you can read?"

"'Does Mom know you can read?'" she mimicked. "No." She waved a fist at the couch. "Does she look like she knows anything anymore?"

Kate peeked at me and slowly smiled.

"I have so many secrets," she whispered, with huge satisfaction, "you wouldn't even *believe* how many secrets I have."

I pulled my feet onto my chair and wrapped my arms around my legs. She studied me, curious. "Does that make it better?" she asked.

I nodded. "Are you glad I'm home?" I asked.

"I guess." She took a huge bite of cereal. "It's about time," she said through her Cheerios.

"No kidding."

She watched the couch. I watched her temples move as she chewed.

"You're all skinny," I said.

"Shut up," she replied. "I'm growing. Oma said."

"That's cool."

"Can you see the clock?"

I glanced up. "It's seven-thirty."

"Claire!" she shouted.

"What?" Mom sounded completely awake.

"It's time to get up!"

"No need to shout." She sat upright and looked over at us and smiled. "I'm up," she said.

Kate smiled at her. "You have to go to work," she said.

"Right-o." My mother stood up, stretched, and folded the afghan, laying it over the arm of the couch. She came over and put her hand behind Kate's head, kissing her, and then came over to me. She put her nose in my hair. I squirmed in my chair, rubbing my hands together under the table. "How'd you sleep?" she asked. "Okay to be home in your own bed?"

"I need new sheets!" I said, excited, "Mom, and my spaceships are too little for me. On my comforter. And Kate helped me get my shoes. And we had breakfast. I had to use the knife."

"What knife?"

"In the kitchen to cut the orange," Kate said. "It was just a little one. I helped."

My mother looked back and forth from one to the other of us. She shook her head. "Oh, Jesus Christ," she sighed, and turned to go down the hall. "I'm getting ready," she called. "Touch the knife and I'll shoot you both." The bathroom door shut.

Kate looked at me. "She won't really."

"I hate when I get scrambled."

"Why do you?"

"I'm just trying to say what I'm trying to say."

"Oh."

I banged my thigh and rubbed my left temple eleven times. "I have to take my medicine."

"Okay. Where is it?"

"Fuck fuck! In the bathroom. In a brown bag. With a label. With my name. Esau Elton Schiller. On it."

"I'll go get it." She hopped off her chair.

"Hide the knife. Please hide the knife!"

"Okay, hang on!" She ran off.

The doorbell rang. I crawled under the table.

Her feet squeaked at a gallop down the front hall. I heard her yell, "Stay here! Hang on!" I heard her bang on the bathroom door. "Mom!" The water ran.

I closed my eyes and counted by elevenses up to a hundred and back again eleven times. When I opened them there was a small pair of cowboy boots in front of me.

"Hi, Davey," I said.

"Hi. Kate says I'm supposed to tell you she's almost back."

"Thanks."

"Do you want anything?"

"No thanks."

"I could get you a juice. For with your medicine when Kate gets back."

"Okay."

"Or do you want milk?"

"Juice, please. And could you get me that blanket off the couch?"

"Sure thing."

I watched his boots clop off across the room. He bent down and passed the afghan to me, staring at me with his big eyes.

"You want me to come under there with you?"

"That's okay. Just the blanket. Please."

"Ten-four."

I spread the afghan out under the table and lay down on one edge. I took hold of it and rolled myself up. Eighty-nine, seventy-eight (my favorite), sixty-seven, fifty-six.

"Here I am!" Kate shouted, scrambling under the table and dumping a bag of pill bottles out on the floor next to my head.

"I've got the juice!" Davey yelled, clopping and spilling all the way. He crouched on the floor in his little Levi's.

"Two blue, one pink, one white. I think. Wait." My hands felt like pounding and my back arched. "Two pink. One blue. Shit!"

"Wait! Calm down," Kate said, reading a bottle. "Pet his head," she ordered Davey.

He put out his hand and sort of scratched my ears like a dog. I closed my eyes.

"You were right! Two blue, one pink, one white," Kate said. She and Davey wrestled the bottles open and counted the pills out, spilling them all over the place. I rolled back and forth a little to loosen the blanket and stuck my arm out. Kate handed me the pills and Davey passed me the juice.

They watched me as I swallowed. I set down the glass of juice and pulled my other arm out. I set my chin in my hands. It was okay down here. We could stay here all day. My head stopped jerking and I heaved a sigh.

"Cool boots," I said to Davey.

He looked. He nodded slowly at them. "Yeah," he said. "Pretty cool."

"Cool as cats."

He nodded his thoughtful assent. "Are we going to school today?" he asked Kate.

"No. We better stay here and have a sick day. Don't you think?"

"Okay with me."

From the other room came the sound of high heels. They stopped. We all looked out.

"What are you doing under there?" Mom asked, bending over to peer at us.

"Esau needed his medicine," Kate replied.

"He needed it under the dining-room table?"

"I guess so," Kate said shrugging. We stared at her blankly.

"I guess so," I repeated.

"Well, okay. Are you coming out anytime soon?"

"Yeah."

"But apparently not yet."

We didn't move. Exasperated, she gathered her skirt around her knees and crouched. "Well, I need to go to work."

"So go," Kate said.

"Oma and Opa are on their way over. They won't be but a few minutes. Are you going to be all right?"

Kate rolled her eyes and sighed. "Mom," she said.

"We're okay, Mrs. Schiller," Davey said, patting her knee. "Esau can be in charge."

A worried look crossed her face.

She straightened. "There's bologna in the fridge for sandwiches when you get hungry, and tell Oma she doesn't have to make dinner," she called, grabbing her purse. "Call me at the store if you need anything. No more knives!" She clicked down the hall.

I looked at Kate.

"She cries at night," she said abruptly.

"She does?"

Kate nodded. "I hear her."

"I heard her too," Davey piped up. "And she talks."

"Talks to who?"

They shrugged in unison. They were like a two-headed monster.

"I have to take a shower. Right now." I crawled out from under the blanket. "I am completely late!" I yelled, and ran to the bathroom.

In the tub, I washed as fast as possible, in straight lines up and down and then crossways, both, and then I sat with my knees pulled up to my chin, letting the water pour over my face. I washed my feet super extra well, toe by toe.

Esau, I said to myself, just like my mom had last night, your father is dead.

He is just away for a while.

He is dead.

I put my left foot in my mouth and nibbled off my toenails until they were even.

He isn't dead.

"Kate!" I yelled through my toes.

I knew he was dead before she told me.

I picked up my right foot and started working on my big toe. She didn't have to tell me. I knew he was dead.

"Kate!"

"What?" she yelled as she came down the hall.

"I'm stuck!"

"In what?"

"Is Dad dead?"

There was a long silence. Then a loud whispering.

"Are you drownding yourself?" she finally called through the door. The handle was jiggled from the outside. "Can't you come out of the tub until Oma and Opa get here?"

"I mean," I said, lying down completely in the tub and chewing furiously on my left thumb, "he is, right?"

"Can Davey come in?"

"I guess so."

Davey poked his head in. He turned to shut the door behind him and hopped up onto the john. "Hey," he said.

"Hey."

He watched me for a while. "Say, are you sure you're supposed to chew your fingers like that?" he asked.

"No." I put them behind my back so I could stop. It was easier when they were out of sight.

"Kate did that too," he said, swinging his legs.

"She did?"

He nodded. "Yep. Chewed 'em clear off. Band-Aids on her fingers all the time."

"When?"

"Right after your dad died." He looked at the door. "Kate," he called. "He's not drownding hisself."

"Are you sure?"

"Course I'm sure. I'm looking right at him, aren't I?"

"How am I supposed to know?"

"I can hear you perfectly good. You don't have to shout."

"Fine. What's he doing, then?"

Davey looked at me. "He's just lying here thinking."

"What do you mean, lying there?"

"He's lying here."

"Can I come in?"

"No!" we both yelled.

We looked at each other.

"Man, you are a weird little kid," I said.

He nodded. "Ten-four."

He hopped off the toilet and turned off the water. "'Bout done with your shower, then?" he asked.

I sat up. "Sure."

We sat in a row on my bed with Kate in the middle. Oma and Opa were out in the living room, doing the crossword.

"Well, don't *look* at it," she said. "That's only going to make it worse."

"I don't know. Maybe we should open it."

"What for?"

"To see."

"To see what?"

"What's in there."

"There's nothing in there!" She sighed. "It's just a *closet.*"

"Then why can't I look?"

"Because you'll go in and shut the door. Closets are for *clothes.* Not *people.*"

"Dad used to say that."

I stared at it. The door was staying shut. That was good. I still didn't trust it. Before I went away, it used to suck me in.

"Well, he was right," she said.

I turned around and faced the wall. "When did he die?" I scratched at a chipped spot of light-blue wallpaper. It worried me. There was another, darker blue underneath. I chipped a little more.

"Christmas," Davey finally said. "He died at Christmas."

"*On* Christmas," Kate corrected him.

"On Christmas."

"I fell in the snow by the hole."

I looked at her.

"She got all dirty," Davey added. He lay down on his stomach, carefully, and waved his cowboy boots in the air.

"What hole?"

"Where they put him," Kate said. "But he's only partly there." She picked a scab on her knee. She looked up at me. "Do you think he got cold?"

I wanted very much to go in a hole. "I think I would feel better if we could open my closet now."

"Oh, for Pete's sake," she said loudly, and went over to it. Her hand on the doorknob, she turned to me. "If you go in there, I'm getting Opa. I mean it."

"I won't."

"Cross your heart."

I did.

She flung open the door. "See?" she demanded. "Nothing there."

My treasures. On the floor. A flashlight, a blanket, a little beanbag, the size of my hand, that sounded like stars.

"Okay," I said. "Shut it. Quick."

She climbed back on the bed. "Better?"

"Yeah."

The three of us sat there, worrying. I wiggled my thumbnail into the hole in the wallpaper and got a grip and ripped off a big chunk.

"Well," Kate said, looking at it. "Now you're going to have to do the whole room, I guess."

I nodded glumly. It was going to take forever.

No matter how long I stared at the wall, my dad was still dead.

I couldn't sleep that night. That was okay. I didn't mind night nearly as much as day. If I had my way, I'd have it be night all the time, sometimes. But I had a maximum. I was only supposed to have three nights awake and no more or I got pretty wonky.

So I was sitting on my windowsill looking out at the yard when I heard the music.

At first I worried I was inventing things. Which was okay, because imagination is all right, as long as you can tell when you're *imagining* and when you're *inventing*. Imagining is like drawing in your brain. Inventing is really thinking the thing.

I listened intently.

The music was real, and it was coming from outside my room. I got off the windowsill and opened the door slowly.

My mother was dancing barefoot, with a cigarette.

She turned and for a second I thought she saw me. But instead she made a face and sat down suddenly on the couch, as if she was exhausted. From where I stood, it looked like she was staring at my dad's old chair. "Well, what are you waiting for?" she said. "Come on. Join us." She swept her arm at the empty room, put her face in her hands, and started crying.

Her cigarette ash got long and eventually fell on the floor.

I tiptoed through the room and knocked on the couch. She looked up, her eyes all red and wet. She smiled.

"Hi," I said.

"Hi." She patted the couch. I sat down next to her.

"Why are you crying?" I settled into her side, tucking my feet under me.

"Oh, you know. Just stuff. Nothing serious." She rubbed my head.

"You look sad."

"Yeah. Well, you know what, kiddo?" She looked down into my face. "I am sad. I get sad sometimes. But there it is."

I worried.

"Quit looking so worried," she said.

I started plucking lint off her nightgown. She watched me do that for a while. Then she said, "You almost done with that?" so I stopped.

"Dad's dead," I said. I started gnawing on the heel of my hand.

"Yep." She took my hand.

"Since Christmas."

"Yep. Katie tell you that?"

"I asked her."

She nodded. "Did you go in your closet?"

I shook my head, pleased.

"Hot damn," she said, and squeezed my hand happily.

I sat there feeling warm. "Night's almost over."

"How did it go today?" she asked. I could feel her watching me.

"Okay. Scary," I said. "It felt like Dad was around here somewhere. The house is all funny now."

"That's for sure. Do you miss State?"

I flushed. She'd caught me. I shook my head.

"You can, you know."

I glanced at her from the corner of my eye. She understood. "So many things are different," I whispered.

"I bet."

"It was so sunny today," I said. "And I got stuck in the bathtub."

"You did?"

I nodded. "And then we had to look in my closet, and then my afternoon medicines made me stupid and I couldn't draw and I fell asleep on my floor." I sighed.

"Long day." She played with my ears. It made me sleepy. "You know, you can call me at work. Anytime you want, and I'll come home. You know that, right?"

"Yeah." I nodded. I would try to be well, but it was still good to know. The number was easy, and I liked it: 218-9786. "I'm better now, though," I said, looking at her. "Night's better. Safer."

"I have to agree."

"Is that why you don't sleep anymore?" She didn't answer me. She looked so sad.

I reached up and petted her cheek. She smiled.

"You're lonely. I bet," I said, hesitantly. I had a list of feelings that they gave me at State.

She nodded. "Sometimes."

We looked out the window, watching the sky turn a dark red at the horizon, over the Andersons' house and the fields out in back of it.

"Me too. Sometimes," I said. I looked at her. "Dad's not coming back."

"No."

"For always."

"That's right."

I nodded.

"You don't really believe that, do you?" she said.

I thought about lying. I wanted to be all right. I concentrated, but it came out the truth anyway. "No."

She took my face in her hands and put her forehead to mine. "That's okay. Me neither."

"Oh," I said. I put a pillow on her lap and looked up at her. "Okay."

"Okay."

We turned to watch the sky turn purple, then orange.

* * *

My mother was putting lilacs in Ball jars all over the house. Kate thrust her face in the great purple and white bunches and breathed in as deep as she could and bruised the petals and staggered around dizzy. They were her favorite smell.

We were going to school.

Davey and I were sitting at the table, eating pancakes. Sarah was in an old high chair, leftover from when Kate was a baby. Mrs. Donna, Davey's mom, brought out a fresh batch and piled them on our plates. She was over a lot. I liked that. She was comforting.

"Pancakes with your syrup?" she asked Davey. He ignored her and kept mashing the soggy mass on his plate with a fork. "Li'l Miss Kate, git your butt over here and eat something before you pass out," Donna said, and went back into the kitchen. Kate staggered over and collapsed in a chair.

She looked at us dramatically. "I just love spring," she gasped.

"Eatcher breakfast," Davey commanded, and pushed her plate closer.

"Eatcher own breakfast." She picked up her fork and started eating the edges.

"What if they hate me?" I said. I didn't want to go. I wondered if it was too late to back out. Mom had told me a million times I could change my mind. I cut my pancakes into square bites.

"They won't hate you," Davey said. "Why would they?"

"'Cause I was gone." I felt so sick. I put my hand to my forehead.

"So what?"

"So no one else just suddenly disappears because they're crazy or something," I snapped at him. He looked hurt. I felt bad and put my cut-up pancakes on his plate.

"You're not crazy," he said.

"Yeah," Kate said loudly. "And we'll beat 'em up if anyone says different."

"We can't," Davey said. "They're bigger than us." Kate looked crestfallen.

"Does everyone know Dad's dead?" I asked.

Kate shrugged and nodded.

"How does everyone know?"

"'Cause one day he was alive and then one day he wasn't," Donna said. "Claire! That damn bush is gonna be totally bald, you take any more flowers off it. Leave it be."

My mother came in through the screen door, her arms loaded down with flowers. She stood there with the morning light behind her, a fiery halo of red hair.

"Look at you," she said to all of us at the table.

"Esau's going to school today," Kate said.

She smiled. "I know."

I opened my mouth, but I still couldn't think of a reason I shouldn't go. Maybe if I didn't have to talk all day it would be all right. Maybe if I just said absolutely nothing. My words were sometimes not totally organized when they came out of my mouth. They'd think I was an idiot. I wasn't an idiot. I was better than any of them, as long as I didn't have to talk. My dad would know what to do. My dad was dead. I wanted to go to math so bad I could hardly see. I wanted to show everyone how much I knew now, and then they'd be sorry they ever said anything to me, ever.

I decided that if I were my dad, I would tell me to keep my trap shut and show those fools what's what.

"What if someone asks me where I was?" I asked no one in particular.

"You tell 'em," Kate said, pointing her fork at me severely, "to go *straight* to hell."

That was what it was like, once my dad died. Or maybe it was always that way. No one could remember anymore, what with the lilacs everywhere, and my mom so sad and strange, and me trying to stay well so they didn't send me away.

It was very, very important that I not go away. I felt like I was holding still so nothing could bump me and break me apart. It is so easy to get broken. People don't know that, but I knew.

After school, I stood waiting for Kate and Davey on the sidewalk. It had gone okay. Nobody talked to me anyway, really. They just mumbled, "Hi," and left me alone. They were scared of me, I think.

I was feeling kind of sad. So when Kate came busting out of the school and jumped up on me like a monkey, I felt better.

"Git off," I said, happy. She scrambled down.

Davey handed me his satchel to carry. "Did anybody bug you?"

"Nope." We started walking.

"Did they say you were crazy?"

I shook my head. "Nobody said anything."

"See," Kate said importantly. "What did we tell you? You should listen to us more often. We know stuff."

"My mom made a pie," Davey said, so we went to his house.

Davey's dad's truck was parked in the dirt driveway. Their lawn wasn't mowed and the screen door leaned up against the house, off its hinges. We went around to the back door, kicking our way through the dead daylilies, which were keeled over on their faces in the narrow footpath to the backyard.

I peered through the window in the door while Davey dug in his bag for the key. "Where's your mom?" I asked.

"Dunno," he said. "She'll be home eventually." He jimmied the lock and finally it turned. We pushed into the kitchen and stood there, looking around.

It was clean but it looked like it was dirty. There was a plastic tablecloth on the table, wiped down but still sticky. It smelled like shut windows, like people breathing, and old air.

"You have to cut the pie," Davey said, getting a chair and climbing up to a cupboard. He got out three glasses and poured us milk. I dropped our book bags and looked through the drawers for a knife. It was a cherry pie. We sat down and ate without talking.

Davey set down his fork and sighed. He folded his hands on his belly.

"What's the matter with you?" I finally asked him.

"Nothing." He shrugged.

"He gets like this," Kate explained in a whisper.

"No I don't," he said, scowling at her.

She shrugged. "Suit yourself."

"Why are we whispering?" I asked.

"They're sleeping," Davey said.

"Who are?"

He rolled his eyes at me like I was stupid. "The baby and my dad."

"Your dad's here?"

"His truck's here, ain't it?"

"Why isn't he at work?"

"He doesn't have a job anymore. Why isn't *your* dad at work?" Davey yelled, pushing back his chair and going to the counter for the pie.

"My dad's dead," I said, surprised.

Davey shrugged and pushed the pie pan toward me. "I want another piece," he said.

Upstairs, the baby started crying. Davey climbed off his chair and went thumping up the stairs. He staggered back in, carrying baby Sarah. She stared at us with two fingers in her mouth. Kate hopped up and got a bottle out of the fridge.

"You wanna hold her?" Davey asked me. "It's easy," he said, setting her on my lap. "Just don't drop her."

I sat paralyzed. The baby's hair was a thick, soft spray of black. She stared back at me, blinking. We studied each other. She looked like a miniature girl Davey. Even more serious, maybe. She bobbled a little, like she wasn't very good at sitting up yet.

She took her fingers out of her mouth and sighed heavily. Then she stuck them back in and leaned on my chest.

Kate and Davey polished off their pie and went out the back door to play. I said I'd stay and watch Sarah.

It was so quiet in their house that the steady ticking of the kitchen clock above the stove was loud enough to make a person crazy. Sarah breathed in and out. Suddenly, she took off one of her socks and played with her toes. I measured it: Her whole foot was as long as my thumb. Her big toe was smaller than the tip of my pinkie, and the tiny little nail curved up.

I tickled her foot. She giggled and squirmed in my lap.

There was a creaking. I looked up and froze. A man was standing at the top of the basement stairs. He had his hand on the door frame. I'd startled him as much as he'd startled me.

He crossed the kitchen and bent to get a beer out of the refrigerator. His back to me, he popped it open. He looked like a bag of rags. His hair fell over his collar, gray and brown.

"Who're you?" he asked. I almost wasn't sure he was talking to me. I could feel my words scramble. I panicked. My arms tightened around Sarah. He turned and came over to the table. He hadn't shaved in days, and his stubble was white. He reminded me of my dad, but scarier. For a wild second, I wondered if he was my dad's ghost.

He pulled out a chair and sat down. He stared at the pie pan, then took Davey's fork and started picking at the pie.

"Guessing you're Arnold's boy," he finally said. "By the looks of you."

I nodded.

"Ain't seen you in a long while. Didn't recognize you, you got so big."

I watched him finish the pie and wash it down with beer. He studied me. His eyes were watery. They hurt to look at.

"Tell you, you're the spitting image of your old man," he said. "When he was your age. Spooky, is what it is." He shook his head and looked out at the garden where Kate and Davey were playing. I followed his gaze. Davey was standing on a stump, wearing a pith helmet, and Kate was collapsing, shot.

"Damn shame," he said.

I looked at him.

"About your dad," he said gruffly. "Sorry to hear."

"Thanks."

He looked at me. "Well, you can talk, then."

"Yes sir."

"Just don't like to, much."

I shook my head.

He laughed. It was like he was barking. His mouth didn't move when he did it, it was just a noise he made. "Can't say I blame you." He pushed himself to his feet and weaved over to the refrigerator again. I realized he was pretty drunk. "You want a beer?" he asked.

I thought about it. For some reason it seemed like the right thing to do. My dad would have taken a beer, I thought, if he were sitting here in this chair. "Okay."

He set one down in front of me. "We ain't properly met," he said, sticking his hand out. "I'm Dale," he said.

I shook his hand. "Esau," I said.

That settled, he popped the tops off our beers and sat down. "Here's to your old dad," he said, lifting his. I lifted mine back and took a tiny sip. It made me sneeze. Sarah turned around at the noise, delighted.

"We were friends back in school," Dale said, looking out the window. "Arnold and me. He was a smart fella, your old man."

I swished a sip of beer around in my mouth.

"Never thought he'd come back here, you know that? Surprised the hell out of me. He was gonna be an actor." He laughed.

"He was?"

Dale nodded. "We all got our crazy dreams." He took a swig of beer. "Crazy, dumb-ass dreams." He looked at me. "How's your mother, then?"

I shrugged and drank another swallow. I was feeling a little light-headed. I didn't want to talk about my mother.

We sat quietly and drank. I realized after a while that I had drunk a whole beer. My head felt like it weighed about a million tons.

"You miss your dad, I guess," Dale said.

I glanced at him. He was looking at me intensely. "Yeah." My mouth felt like rubber. "I wish he wouldn't have gone and died," I blurted out.

Dale wiped his mouth with the back of his hand. "Well, hell," he said. "Life can hit a fellow pretty hard. You just remember your old man kindly, now." He stood up and pushed in his chair. "He was a good man."

He turned and went back down the stairs.

Right about then, I heard Donna's voice in the backyard. She came up the steps and in the kitchen door and saw me sitting there.

"Well, I swear, what on earth's the matter with your eyes?" she asked, worried. She came over and leaned in to look at me. She sniffed. "Have you been drinking?" she asked, sounding shocked. I figured it was no use to lie.

"I had a beer," I said.

"What in the hell you gone and done that for? Did Dale give you a beer?"

I sat there, feeling woozy.

"Answer me." She grabbed the baby and hiked her up on her hip. The baby cooed with glee.

"No," I said.

"Oh, the hell he didn't. Damnation—Dale!" she yelled, leaning into the stairwell. "I'll have your sorry ass! What in the hell are you doing feeding this poor child booze? He ain't but twelve years old, for Chrissakes!"

She stared into the black hole of the basement stairs. No sound came up at all.

"Well, shit," Donna said. She shook her head and sat down heavily where Dale had been sitting. She studied me and the corners of her mouth started to twitch.

"You got a pretty good drunk on, there, dontcha?" she asked.

I nodded. "I think so."

She laughed. That made the baby laugh, which made me laugh. She got up and set the baby in a high chair and started making supper.

I studied the stairwell, picturing Dale sitting down there with his beer in the dark. Maybe there was a little window, like in our basement, a little tiny window that let in some light. Maybe he was looking up at it. Dizzily, I willed him to look up.

My mom was in the garden and I was lying in the grass looking for bugs. Every so often I'd look up to make sure she was still there, in her white gardening dress with the big blue flowers across the skirt.

"Esau, where's your sister?" she called, bending down and yanking at a weed.

"Don't know." There was a grasshopper perched in front of my nose in the bucket of an aspen leaf, watching me from his sideways eye.

"Can you go find her, please?"

"What for?"

"For I said so, that's what for."

I didn't want to scare the grasshopper. "She's inside."

"Well, bring her outside." My mother had spent the last three days in the garden. All day. It was May. She got like this.

The wind from my breath startled my grasshopper and I got up and went inside. Kate was in her room, lying on her bed.

"Whatcha doin'?" I asked her.

"Nothing much."

"Mom says come outside."

"What for?"

"Don't know. She just said I had to come get you."

Kate sighed heavily and turned onto her side. She flung her arm above her head. "Can't," she said.

"Why not?"

"I've got the sads."

I nodded. "Yeah. Well. Mom's still gardening."

"Sheesh."

Kate had her shoes off and was rubbing her feet, in their socks, together. She did this to make herself feel better. She'd done it since she was a baby.

"What're you so sad for?" I asked.

She shrugged, such as she could lying there on her side. "Don't know. Sunday."

"Oh yeah." She didn't much like Sundays. She said they were depressing. "Well, school's almost out."

"I know."

"Then Sunday won't be any different from any other day."

"Still Sunday."

I peered at her. "You been crying?"

"None of your fat business," she yelled.

"Just asking."

"Well, don't." She rolled onto her other side. She was so short. Her whole self only went halfway down the bed.

"Okay, fine," I said. "What'm I supposed to tell Mom?"

"Tell her," Kate said, sounding mad, "to go straight to hell!"

She kicked the wall, but not very hard, because she wasn't wearing any shoes. Besides, she didn't mean it. I went out of the room and out the back door, the screen slamming behind me. I sat down in a chair on the porch. My mother was crouched in a patch of hostas that were starting to send up shoots. She was clearing out dead leaves so the hostas could breathe. She turned her head and fell back on her heels.

"Where is she?"

"In her room. She's got the sads."

"Oh, for pity's sake," my mother sighed. "If it's not one thing. That is the moodiest child I ever met in my life."

Through the screened window came Kate's voice. "I am *not* moody!" she yelled.

My mother looked startled and began to giggle.

"Quit laughing!"

My mother started laughing so hard she fell on her butt in the dirt. She straightened up and brushed herself off. "Poor little thing," she said. "Esau, come here and help me."

I helped all afternoon. "What are we planting?" I asked.

"I don't know. Whatever looks good to us at the time."

"We don't have a plan?"

"Nope. We go up to Kittie's farm in a few weeks and buy what's pretty, and then we plant it."

I fretted. "We should have a plan," I said. "We should map it."

"A garden map?"

"Well, how are we supposed to know what's where? What if something's already buried and we dig it up by accident?"

"Then we replant it."

"It doesn't like that. I bet. I bet plants don't like getting dug up, once they're all nice and planted."

"Okay."

"Okay, what?"

"Okay, make a map."

"How come he gets to make the map?" came Kate's voice.

"Did you hear something?" my mother asked.

"No."

"I *said,* how come he gets to make the map?" bellowed Kate.

"On the other hand," said my mother, "if your sister ever came out of her room, she'd get to help with this whole garden business."

"I want to make the map," I said, feeling stubborn.

"I want to help!"

"Well, sweetheart," said my mother in exasperation, "you can't very well help from there, can you?"

There was a thump from the corner of the house, a pause, and then the sound of the screen door. We turned around to see Kate, who was standing on the porch in her socks.

"Kate, shoes."

She turned around, ran back in, and came out wearing her shoes. "Help tying!" she yelped.

"For heaven's sake, doesn't she know how to tie her shoes yet?" my mother sighed.

I set down my clippers and stepped through the mud to help. She did know how, she just liked me to tie them. I'd seen her tie them just fine by herself, but who cares?

Kate dashed off in front of me, grabbed the clippers, and said wildly, "What? What?"

"Clip the hedge," my mother said. "Don't make any holes."

Kate clipped the hedge one leaf at a time. "Okay," she said, as if she'd planned the whole thing herself from the beginning. "Esau gets to make the map. But I get to pick what."

"You can pick what we plant."

"Right. Whatever's pretty."

"Within reason," my mother said. "No roses."

"Roses," Kate said.

"*No* roses."

"*Yes* roses. *Specially* roses."

"Honey, roses are really hard to grow."

"So what."

"So we don't know how to grow them."

"We can figure it out," I said. "We'll get a book." I liked this plan.

"No, we won't," my mother snapped. "We won't get a book. We won't get roses. I am done with this conversation."

Kate clipped and clipped. She couldn't even reach the top of the hedge, which was growing wild all over the place. Meanwhile the side of the hedge was getting kind of choppy. "Orange roses," she muttered.

"Dammit!" my mother yelled. She was yanking weeds and flinging them into a pile. She stopped, stood up, and put her hands on her hips. "Now tell me," she said quietly. "Just what would make me buy you a goddamn rosebush when you're sitting here acting like a couple of brats about it. Hmm? Tell me that."

We didn't answer for a minute.

"I want a rose," Kate said, narrowing her eyes, "for my birthday."

My mother tossed a handful of weeds in a garbage bag and went into the house.

Kate looked at me, guilty and triumphant.

I smoothed a patch of dirt with both hands until it was completely level. "We should maybe say sorry," I said.

"No."

"Why are you being so rotten?" I asked.

She snipped what was left of the hedge and sat down with a thump in the dirt. "I don't know." She sighed. "I just wanted her to be happy."

I snorted. "You've got a funny way of showing it."

"She likes roses. They're her favorite."

"They are?"

She nodded. "They had roses at their wedding. She told me."

I scratched my name in the dirt with a pointed rock. "Maybe she doesn't like roses anymore."

"She has to. They remind her of Dad."

"Maybe she doesn't want to be reminded of Dad. Did you ever think of that?" I asked.

Kate looked confused, and her chin started to wrinkle. She shook her head.

I grabbed her hand. "Come on," I said. We went inside.

Mom was lying facedown on her bed. She turned her head to the side when she heard us knock.

"We're sorry," Kate said.

"That's okay," my mom said, flipping over onto her back. "I'm sorry I shouted at you."

Kate took a running start and dove onto the bed. "Are we done being mad?"

"All done."

I climbed on next to my mom. The three of us snuggled up.

"I think a rosebush would be lovely," my mother said.

Mom was going out that night.

This was a new development. It made me nervous. Kate liked it. She knocked on my door and found me drawing in my closet.

"Come on out," she said. "Let's make dinner."

"No." I was busy. I was drawing up plans. It was important that I complete my plans. I was designing a house full of hiding places.

"You have to. I'm hungry, and you're in charge."

"Where's she going?" I was trying to figure out if there was room in the wall I'd drawn to make a trapdoor.

Kate shrugged. "Dunno. Let's have pancakes."

"Is she going to Frank's?" I scowled and drew the trapdoor in. I lifted my hand and studied my work, trying to figure out where the dumbwaiter should go.

She sighed. "Fine. I'll make the pancakes. You can just sit there while I do it. But either way, you have to come out. To make sure I don't burn the house down."

I followed her into the kitchen and hopped up onto the counter. We could hear Mom in the bedroom.

"Who's she talking to?" I asked.

"Herself." Kate pulled the Bisquick from the cupboard and the milk and an egg from the fridge. "She's crazy. Like the whole rest of the world." She snorted.

"I'm not too crazy lately," I said, affronted.

"No. You're all right," she agreed.

Mom came out of her room. "Does this look okay?" she asked. She wore a green dress.

"Yes," I said.

"I don't know," she went on, ignoring me. "Maybe I shouldn't go out."

"Where are you going?"

"Oh, Donna and I are just going for a drink."

"Why can't you have a drink here?" I asked.

"Because they want to have grown-up talk," Kate said.

"Oh."

My mother looked at me apologetically.

"You're wearing an awful lot of makeup," I said just to be mean.

"Too much?"

I shrugged and watched Kate stir the batter furiously.

"Are you getting married?" Kate asked.

"What?" my mother asked, startled. "Kate, for heaven's sake. No, I'm just going to Frank's to have a drink with Donna and that's it. That's *that*."

Kate looked at me pointedly. The screen door slammed in the front hall and here came Donna's voice. "Claire? You ready?" Donna appeared in the kitchen.

"Where's Davey?" Kate demanded.

"I don't know. He's around here somewhere," Donna said.

"Here," said Davey, coming in through the back door, carrying a toad.

"Oh, what in the hell have you got?" his mother groaned.

"Frog."

"That's a toad," I said.

"Is it?" Davey asked. "It's a toad," he said to Donna.

"Yeah, I heard him. Where'd you get it?"

"Puddle."

"For pity's sake," Donna said.

"Maybe we shouldn't go," my mother worried.

"Oh, *go*!" Kate yelled. "Just go and have your grown-up talk if you're going."

"All right," my mother said, kissing Kate's head, then mine, then Davey's for good measure. Davey looked startled, but then he always did.

They left.

"Where should I put him?" Davey said. The toad croaked.

"He needs a relatively damp environment with some rocks and some greenery, possibly some leaves, to feel at home," I said.

"Tub," Kate said. She stood on a chair, pouring a spoonful of batter onto the griddle.

"Tub," Davey said, turning on his boot heel and heading down the hall.

He came back out and said, "Rocks."

"In my room," Kate said, pointing behind herself with the spoon and splattering batter on the linoleum. Davey headed off again, passed by with his hands full of rocks, then disappeared outside, coming back in with a pile of wet leaves and some branches.

When he was done, he leaned against the stove to monitor Kate's progress. She was not so good at flipping pancakes because she always did it too soon, so he got to be the one who flipped. She poured, he flipped. We wound up with a pile of tiny pancakes each and settled onto the floor in the living room to eat around the coffee table.

Kate buttered each of hers individually. "We could go to the graveyard," she said.

I looked at her. She passed her knife to Davey so he could butter his. Down the hall, the toad croaked. "It's not that far," she added. "Specially on bikes."

"Your training wheel's busted," Davey reminded her.

"I could ride in your basket."

"Could do," Davey said.

"You been there before?" I asked.

She nodded.

"She cuts out of school," Davey said, and then, "Ouch!" when Kate hit him in the arm, hard.

I looked at Kate.

"What?" she said. "Mom never takes us. Davey cuts out too."

"Well, you can't very well go by yourself," he said through a mouthful of pancakes. "It's getting dark," he added. "If we're going, we should go pretty soon."

We finished eating in a hurry and washed up. We decided it would be safest to ride back roads and wait until we were outside town before we got on the county road, otherwise we could be spotted. We put oranges in Kate's book bag, and some emergency medicine for me. I zipped Kate and Davey into jackets in case it got cold after dark, and we all tied our shoes in double knots. We decided to bring the toad, who otherwise would be lonely, so we named him Arnold the Toad in honor of our mission and put the rocks and sticks in Kate's book bag with the oranges and then put the toad in, Davey holding his hands over the opening while I zipped and Arnold hopped.

And that was how we came to be riding our bikes, with Kate's feet sticking out of Davey's basket, down County Road 10 toward Nimrod in the purple dusk.

The fields were steaming and black, all damp and tilled for planting. A low ground fog spilled through the property fences, through the dead weeds that bordered the shoulder of the road. To the east, the moon was coming up over a loose string of barns and silos, and to the west, the sky was still orange from the sun burning itself to sleep.

I rode behind Kate and Davey. They were a many-limbed shadow on the road. The air was cold and full of spring smells so I just breathed, dizzy with oxygen. My legs were shaky from not being used much in a while.

"How far is it?" I called.

"A ways," Kate called back.

"A long ways? A medium ways?"

"A medium-long ways," she called. "Are you okay?"

"So far so good."

The dark deepened as we rode north. It seemed almost as if we were riding into the night, leaving the day behind us in Motley. The sign for Nimrod was the only sign for miles, so we saw its shadow against the field long before we turned down the narrow road.

"Here comes the sign!" Kate called, and we turned, our wheels crunching onto the gravel. "Not far now!"

Nimrod had gone inside for the night and closed its curtains. Light seeped out of the houses. We rode down the centre of the main strip, to the east edge of town, past a Tastee-Freez and a one-pump service station and a couple of bars.

The trees thickened around the edges of the road. "We're almost there!" Kate yelled, and Davey wobbled on the bike. "Hold still!" he said, and turned down a driveway I hadn't seen.

I hesitated, adjusting my eyes to the dark. Elms and oaks lined the sloped driveway all along its winding length. As we crested a low hill, the moon spilled over open fields of gravestones that spread out on either side.

The gates of the graveyard were closed and the fence was high. Davey put his foot down, skidding slowly to a halt. I pulled up next to them to find Kate trying to wiggle out of the basket. "Hurry up!" she said. "Help me!"

"I *can't*," Davey said. "If I get off the bike it'll fall over, and then where'll you be?"

"Well, *you* help, then," she said to me, annoyed with his logic. I leaned my bike against the iron fence, pulled her out, and set her on her feet. "Thanks already," she said. "Sheesh." She straightened her book bag on her shoulders. Arnold ribbited.

"Should we check on him?" Davey asked.

"He sounds okay," she said.

"How do you know if a frog sounds okay?"

"How do we get in?" I asked.

"Like this," Kate said, and slipped between the bars of the fence. Standing there with her hands on the bars, she looked like a little prisoner. "Come on."

Davey followed her in, and I squeezed through.

"You're big," Davey said.

"Yeah, but he's skinny," Kate pointed out, and set off across the graveyard.

I found I was frozen, with my back against the fence. I opened my mouth. "Kate!" I called. She stopped and turned around, her thumbs hooked in her book bag straps. She looked so sturdy and sensible.

"What?" she said.

I didn't know what.

"Are you getting weird?" she asked.

"No."

"Are you sure? Do you need medicine? We brought your medicine."

"I don't need it."

"Are you scared?"

I thought about that. "I guess a little," I said.

Kate looked around her as if she was assessing the situation. "That's all right," she said. "Come on. If you don't like it, we can leave."

"You're sure?"

"Yeah. There's no ghosts."

"I know."

"I've been here lots of times, and never once ghosts or anything."

"Okay." She waited for me and stuck her hand out. I took it and we set off. Her hands were supersmall and always hot. Hot, dry, teeny-tiny hands.

Davey came up on the other side of me. Flanked by a two-person guard of midgets, I went down the rows of graves.

"We don't walk *on* the graves," Davey explained. "That would be rude."

"Exactly," Kate confirmed. "Did you know Aunt Rose was buried here?"

"She is?"

Kate nodded in the dark. "Fresh one," she said, pointing to a dirt-covered mound. "So are a bunch of people I think we're related to. They all have messages on their headstones."

"Messages like what?"

"Like how they died," Kate said. "Like in a war, or from a bad sick."

"Plague," Davey piped up.

"There's no such thing as plagues anymore," I said.

"Not *now*," Kate sighed. "A *long-time-ago* plague."

"There aren't any plagues in Minnesota," I said. I was almost sure of this.

"Suit yourself," Kate said mysteriously, as if she knew something I didn't. "Right," she commanded, and our battalion turned right at a crumbling stone cross. "That's the baby one I like," she said, pointing. She stopped and crouched at a headstone on which I could make out a carved cherub face that looked like a monster in the dark. "'Baby Georgina, Beloved Daughter, Gone Home to Jesus Too Soon.' She was four." Kate straightened up and we went along in silence for a while.

"I could die," she announced.

"But you won't," Davey said.

"But I could," she said.

"From what?"

"Dunno," she said. "People die. Everybody dies."

"Yeah, but not right now."

Kate said nothing. "But sometime." She had to have the last word.

"I'm going to die of being an old man," Davey said thoughtfully. "I'll just all of a sudden get tired of being alive, and boom, I'll die."

"No you won't," Kate argued. "You don't get to decide."

Davey muttered something.

"What?" Kate said.

"I said your dad did," Davey replied.

Kate stopped dead in her tracks, staring straight ahead. In a minute she started walking.

"Kate," Davey said.

"Shut up."

"I was just saying."

"Well, don't. Don't say your stupid saying things, then."

"Fine, I won't say anything. Ever. You're so *bossy*."

"I am not."

Davey stuffed his hands in his pockets and dragged his feet in protest, slowing our progress. Kate got a ways ahead of us. She stopped and turned around, her hands on her hips.

"Are you coming or not?"

Davey shrugged.

"Say something."

"Can't," he said. "Not supposed to say my stupid saying things."

Kate shrieked and the graveyard echoed, the sound of her voice bouncing back to us again and again. Then she sat down with a thud and put her forehead on the grass.

Davey and I neared with caution, watching her.

"My dad," came her voice, "did not just *decide* to die."

We stood there. It was not a good time to argue. We waited while she figured out how to explain that one.

"He had," she said carefully, "a *sad-sickness.*"

Arnold ribbited.

"Are you crying?" Davey asked.

"It wasn't his *fault,*" she yelled at the ground. I pictured all the skeletons' eyes snapping open, waking up from their naps. Turning their heads in their coffins, thinking, What's that noise? "He wouldn't have just gone and *done it* for no good *reason,*" Kate yelled.

Davey looked worried and finally tiptoed over to where she sat. He crouched next to her. She hit him in the leg. He sat down, put his hand on her head, and patted it.

"Don't touch me," she said, but she didn't stop him.

"Didn't say he didn't have a reason," Davey said in his most practical grown-up voice.

"Okay," she finally said, her voice full of reproach.

They sat there. Soon enough she lifted her head, grabbed the front of Davey's shirt, and wiped her nose. "Let's go see him," she said, and scrambled to her feet.

I raced to keep up with them as they rounded the corner and headed down a row of graves. They came to a halt in front of one and Kate, alarming me, dove headfirst onto the ground.

"Daddy!" she cried.

"Hi, Mr. Schiller," Davey said, sitting down.

I stared at the gravestone. I walked toward it slowly. Kate rolled onto her back. The moon was just right so that her face caught shadows where her eyes and mouth should have been, a big, grinning empty mouth on her white face as she lay there with her arms flung out across the grave.

The moon caught the gravestone's hollows too, so I could see my father's name. "Arnold Ivan Schiller," it said, black against the blue-white moonlit stone. "1933–1969."

Kate sat up. "Want an orange?" she asked. She set one against the stone, where it gleamed amid a dusky jumble of stuff. I could make out a toy truck. She handed Davey an orange and looked around for me.

"Here," she said, holding one out. "Come sit."

"It's 1970," I said.

She waved the orange at me. "Yeah, so?" she said.

"He died in 1969."

"Yeah."

"He was thirty-six."

She dropped her arm and took the peeled orange Davey passed her. She gave him another to peel.

"Thirty-six," I repeated. I'd meant to say, Six is twice three, but now that I thought of it, that wasn't relevant. Kate sucked on a segment of orange.

"You're slurping," Davey said.

"Sorry." She wiped her chin with her hand.

My left leg started to feel like it was escaping. I sat down next to Davey and twisted myself into a knot so I could hold on to it.

"Coming off?" Kate asked, pointing to my leg.

"Do you—should you be sitting *on* him?" I put my left wrist in my mouth and took a big bite out of it, startling myself. Davey grabbed my wrist, peered at it in the moonlight, and fished a Band-Aid out of the book bag. "For Kate's fingers," he said. Stretching it over my skin, he said, "I wish you two would stop chewing on yourselfs."

"He doesn't mind," Kate said. "He's in a box."

"Coffin," Davey said, patting my wrist. Now I would be crazy for two days trying not to pick at it.

"Coffin's still a box," Kate said. "So I'm not sitting *on* him, but he knows I'm *up* here." She patted the grave and put a huge section of orange in her mouth all at once. Her cheeks full, she said, "Should we give him the frog?"

"I have to say I'm a little anxious," I said. "I think I'll just rock a little, if no one minds."

They looked at each other and shrugged.

"Do you want your medicines?" Davey asked.

"No. Thank you. Not right now. Do you think he can *hear* us?"

"Course he can."

"Oh." I rocked, which helped with the idea that my father was decomposing in a box under where Kate sat cheerfully muttering to the ground and Davey and whoever else might happen to be listening. My father—1969, last year, not 1970, this year. This year, right now, there was a mound of earth with grass starting to send up new shoots on it, the length of a box in which you could put a tall, dead man.

"Maggots," I said.

"What's that?" Davey asked.

"They eat dead stuff."

"Not Dad," Kate said.

"Yeah, Dad," I said.

She shook her head and lay down on her back on the grave, her face lit up by the moon. Davey wiped his hands on his jeans and scooted over. The two of them lay side by side gazing up at the stars, their hands folded on their bellies. The headstone towered over them.

I reached in the bag and grabbed my meds. I choked them down with spit and crawled over to Kate's side. I tried lying on my back but decided fetal position was a better plan.

The grave was soft. We lay there like we were curled up on my dad's wide chest, breathing along with his giant-lunged breath.

"Big Dipper," I said, pointing up. "Little Dipper. Ursa Major. The Clown."

CLAIRE

When we got home that night and found them gone, I thought: I am in hell.

The empty house, all space: That was hell. I wouldn't stop screaming. Donna had to shake me. She called Oma, who said they'd probably run off to the graveyard again. Oma and Opa brought them home.

They sat in a muddy, sullen row on the couch while Oma made them hot milk.

"What in the hell were you thinking, scaring your mother like that?" Donna demanded.

They pretended they hadn't heard. Oma gave me a Valium, and Opa put them all to bed. Oma settled down on the couch.

"I can't lose them," I said stupidly, still crying.

"Of course not," Oma said, reassuringly. "Just being children. They have their reasons."

I did not know children had reasons.

Until that night it was my grief. But then their reasons broke in on my secret and my grief like a wave. When I walked into the house and found them gone, it was no longer merely grief. It was hell, and I could not stay in hell, and it was time to live again.

After that we went to the graveyard on Sundays, like a normal family. We had breakfast with Oma and Opa after. On Sunday and Wednesday nights, Donna and I went to Frank's for Ladies' Nite specials. I paid the bills and fed the kids and bought their shoes and kissed their mangled, scraped, cut, or otherwise damaged bodies as need be. Weekdays, I went to work at the store. And ate my lunch and smoked in the smoky break room with the other smoking women who did not yet have, had, had never had, or had for some reason lost possession of husbands, and were getting on, and were frightened of getting on, and had children or did not have children, but in either case were tormented by their presence or absence, the husbands being primarily occupied with labor, if living. If there was no husband present, having for example been recently killed in Vietnam or having shot himself or having simply *walked off*, their vicious, voracious bitterness was given wide berth.

It was a life.

I have two children. I am a widow. Sometimes I'd find myself thinking things like that. Talking, as if explaining it to someone. Answering a question. Yes, I'd think to myself. I have two children. My husband passed away. Thank you.

In this conversation with an imaginary person, I was very polite. They'd say, *Oh, I'm sorry to hear that.* Thank you. *And how are your children?* They're well.

They were a mysterious, serious, big-eyed thing. They were my life. They were absurd. I had no idea what they wanted. We set out each day as if we knew where we were going. They knew we didn't. They handled me with the polite care with which you treat the fragile or the very old. They humored me. They were in charge now, though they let me pretend.

So here we were. Here I was, with my two children plus Davey, with my Sunday and Wednesday and laundry and meals. Arnold didn't come and talk to me at night. I slept in the bed. It was my bed now, though I still slept on my side of it. I lay there talking to the imaginary person.

The conversation went like this: Forgetting? No. He is always there. He is everywhere. The children, yes, I suppose they're well enough. They stare up at me, wearing his face. They know what I did.

It was the hottest summer anyone could remember. The garden was a riot of color, vines tangled around the fence, plants clambering over each other for space. In June it rained and rained, the steaming world outside the window a crazy tropical green splattered with too bright color and blooms. The rosebush we bought for Kate's birthday grew at the centre of the map taped to the refrigerator, each plant with its Latin name carefully penciled underneath its roots.

By July the sun had moved directly overhead, and beat down without pause from morning until late at night. Kate, Esau, and Davey dangled off the furniture like melted candy. Periodically, they'd whine. Then the room went still again, the only motion, the only sound, a tiny rattling wind created by a dusty box fan.

"Mom, take us to the lake," Kate commanded limply.

"Later."

"When."

"This afternoon. Too hot right now, baby. Heatstroke."

She didn't even have the energy to argue. She sighed, slid off the couch, and lay down in front of the fan. She took a deep breath and said into the chopping blades, "Ah-ah-ah-ah-ah-ah-ah-ah-ah."

Davey was always there, a pleasant, strange little presence. Without him, I would not have had Donna. Without Donna I obviously would have died.

"Darlin'!" she called from the front door.

"In here," I said, too hot to throw my voice very far. I sat on the floor folding a pile of laundry. I'd only gotten through socks and underwear. We'd been sitting there all morning.

Donna walked into the room, carrying Sarah, and saw us. "Well, for pity's sake. What're you three doing lying around like a bunch of good-for-nothings? Go outside."

"Can't," Davey said to his mother. "Too hot."

Donna lay Sarah belly-down on the floor and threw herself into a chair, limbs splayed. "That's the damn truth. They fed?" she asked me. I hadn't gotten around to it yet.

"We had hot dogs," Esau whispered, one eye open. His skinny legs stuck out of his cut-off pants, and his giant feet looked like white flippers.

"For breakfast?"

He shrugged.

Donna heaved herself off the chair and sat down next to me to fold. The summer morning heated up. I pushed the damp hair back from my face.

"All right," Donna said suddenly, throwing down a tiny undershirt of Kate's. "That's it. We're going to the lake."

"Heatstroke!" Davey yelped, but his mother waved a hand at him and called him a worrywart, so that settled everything. Kate and Esau were already off the couch and into their rooms to get ready. Davey wandered down the hall.

"What's with you?" I asked.

She looked at me. "Gonna kill that man."

"Dale?"

"Who do you think? Yes, Dale."

"What'd he do?"

"Borrow me a swimsuit," she said. In the bedroom, while we changed, she said, "Didn't *do* anything. Wish he *would* do something. But I swear, he ain't said a word in two weeks. I tell you, Claire, I'm going crazy in that house."

"Honey, the problem isn't the house."

She laughed. "Sure it is. He's in it. I'm in it. That's a problem."

Kate torpedoed into the room, buried under a pile of beach towels. "Esau's getting a picnic," she shrieked.

"Where's my swim shorts?" came Davey's voice from down the hall.

It took an insanely long time to get everyone in the car all together. Someone kept forgetting something and remembering that they desperately needed it. Kate needed her rocks. Esau needed a book. Kate needed two apples, not one, because she only liked the red parts. Esau needed another book, plus his little beanbag. Kate burned her butt on the metal seat-belt buckle. Donna said she would drive, then decided I should. Davey sat in the middle of the backseat, stoic.

Then we drove the four blocks to the lake.

It was cooler by the water, and Donna and I spread a blanket out under a tree. The kids raced directly from the car into the lake, shedding everything they'd brought in a trail on the sand. We settled in with a thermos of iced tea, put on our hats, and squinted at the water, trying to keep an eye on the bobbing shapes of our kids, which looked exactly the same as the bobbing shapes of all the other kids in the crowded swimming hole.

"You think I oughtta divorce him?" she asked mildly. We waved to Tabatha Hendricks, who was new in town and had four kids. Poor thing wasn't twenty-five and went around looking as harried as hell.

"Jesus," I said. "That bad?" Pete and Edith Anderson, my neighbors, stopped by to say hello, and the four of us shaded our eyes to see each other in the blinding sun. Their kids were around here some-where, they said, waving vaguely. I liked the Andersons. They said we should come by for a drink this evening.

"Yeah, I guess," Donna said when they'd left. "How'm I supposed to know? What's bad enough? When do you cut your losses? There's that what's-his-name," she said, pointing. I turned to look. "And what do you know, there's Frank!" She sat up and waved wildly.

"Oh, quit," I said.

"What?" she asked innocently. "Frank!" she called. I pulled my floppy hat down lower on my head and wished I'd worn the bathing suit with the skirt.

Frank approached with what's-his-name, Jamie Kittridge, who I had to admit was a handsome devil, with a foolish grin and a farm-boy manner and a crush on Donna.

"Afternoon," Frank said, looking pleased with the world. "Claire," he said, nodding, squinting in the sunshine. "Donna."

"Afternoon, ladies," Jamie said, grinning.

"Hello," I mumbled.

"You fellas want something to drink? Have a sit," Donna said cheerfully.

"That'd hit the spot," Frank said, smiling down at me. "Provided it's not any trouble. You sure it's no trouble, Claire?"

I shook my head. He seemed disproportionately concerned with me. He eased himself down by my side and took the bottle of Coke Donna gave him.

"You see Kate?" I asked Donna. She dug in the cooler. Frank peered out at the lake.

"Pink bathing suit?" he asked. "Ruffle on the fanny?"

"That's her."

"She's trying to drown her brother," he said.

"All right, then."

"It's hotter than hell," Frank remarked after a long moment.

"Lord knows." I fanned myself with a magazine.

"Wait all year for summer to roll around, then we complain it's hot."

I laughed. "Too true."

"How's life treating you, Claire?" he asked, taking a sip. From the corner of my eye, I caught the wince on his face when he realized he oughtn't have asked that, quite. It occurred to me that Frank might know more about my life than I did myself. Arnold had sat there on a bar stool telling him God knows what for how many years. I was embarrassed for Arnold. He was a sloppy drunk, and he let his mouth run.

I laughed to lighten things up. "Oh, I suppose it's all right," I said. "You know how it is."

Frank smiled out at the water, immensely relieved. "Sure do." He slowly stretched his legs out and crossed them at the ankles. He had odd, delicate ankles, pearly bones at the end of solid brown legs. His father was Sioux, I remembered, looking up at his dark hair, shot with silver threads. Arnold had told me that.

"My wife, when she left," he said, shaking his head. "Swear, I slept on the couch for six months."

"Oh." I didn't know what to say. I didn't know he'd had a wife.

"Then I knocked out all the walls and rebuilt the house."

"Oh?" I peered at him from under my hat.

He nodded, gazing out at the lake. "That did the trick." He paused. "Esau's getting big."

"I know it. That child is eating me out of house and home."

"'Spect he is," Frank said. He had a funny upside-down smile, the corners of his mouth curling down and his crow's-feet showing. "How's he been?"

The question caught me off guard. "He's—he's doing much better," I said. That was the correct answer. That was the one you gave. Esau was better, and fragile, or maybe a little worse this month, it was hard to say, and in any case he was fragile, would always be terribly fragile. I was afraid I was not, in some way, enough, would fail him, and so I held his wellness close to my chest where no one could see it, breathe on it, discuss it, make it go away.

"Glad to hear it. Great kid. Absolutely great kid."

"How long did you know Arnold?" I asked, feeling suddenly defensive. What did he tell you, anyway? I wanted to yell. How much do you know about my family? What do you know about me? Do you know how hard I tried? My son is fine, thanks. We are all fine.

Frank looked startled. "Hell, Claire. I known Arnold since we were kids. We were the same year at school."

That set me on my heels. "You're joking."

"What, you thought I was older?" He grinned stupidly, and ruffled his silver-streaked hair. "Been like this since I was twenty-some. I tell everybody it's from listening to their sorry tales at the bar."

I laughed, and he looked at the lake, alarmed.

"You want another Coke?" I asked.

"All right. If you're sure you got enough."

I got us two and we watched the kids. "I guess you hear more than your fair share of sorry tales," I said.

"Oh, I don't know," he said. "Somebody's got to listen."

I nodded, not sure why that struck me as unspeakably sad.

"I'll say, though," he confided. "Times, I feel like I know more than's proper about folks." He looked out over the beach. "I can look around, I know something about everybody. Them, them. Bump into somebody at the store, I know something I probably shouldn't. I mean, how's a person get any privacy around here?"

"Small town," I said. For some reason I wondered what he bought at the store. Beans, bananas, milk? Coffee? A little handheld basket.

"Sure," he agreed, nodding. "Sure, but. What'm I supposed to do with all that? All that knowing?"

I lifted my head so I could see out from under my floppy hat. "Why, I don't know," I said.

"Claire," he said, sounding concerned, "that is a fine-looking hat."

"Thank you." It was new. I adjusted the brim, embarrassed.

"Certainly. Nah, I don't mind," he went on. "Only time I mind is when I feel like something oughtta be done. A fella hits his wife, say. Well, next time he comes into the bar, I feel like I ought not to serve him. Ought to give him a piece of my mind."

"What do you do?"

"I serve him and keep my mouth shut. Feel guilty as hell, but what'm I supposed to do? I'm not one to say what's right or what's what."

"I guess not," I said. We sat there. I watched his feet. They were clean, pale from the ankles down. Like most folks around here. Tanned from the ankles to the thighs and from the bottoms of the shirtsleeves down to the hands.

"Heh!" he said suddenly, like something had just occurred to him. "Don't know why I'm bothering you with all this."

I shrugged. "You're not bothering me."

"Sound like one of my own customers," he said, grinning.

"Somebody's got to listen," I said.

From the corner of my eye, I saw him look at me. I felt like we had a secret. I flushed, confused.

"Claire, honey, you two want a sandwich?" Donna leaned over. "It's only bologna," she said to Frank, "but Esau made enough to feed a church social, and somebody's gotta eat 'em." Jamie was munching on one already. I stood up and walked down to the water. "Kate! Esau! Davey! Lunch!" I called.

Kate's tiny red head bobbed like a buoy. She was a good swimmer but had a tendency to sink, she was so skinny. I pictured her little limbs flapping and kicking like hell underwater to stay afloat. "We're busy!" she called. I shaded my eyes and watched a heated discussion take place between her and the two other drowned rats. "All right!" she amended.

I turned back toward the picnic blanket just in time to see Frank watching me. He looked away and busied himself stuffing half a sandwich in his mouth. I trudged up the sand. Somehow, knowing his age made him look younger. He was younger than me. I was suddenly conscious of my bathing suit.

"Apple?" Donna held one out. "Sandwich. Chips. My God, that boy packed your entire kitchen. What in the hell. There's a whole chunk of cheese in here. And no damn knife."

Frank and Jamie simultaneously reached into their pockets and proffered hunting knives. If there was one thing you could count on a man for around here, it was that he'd have a knife and a handkerchief on his person.

The kids arrived and flopped down in a wet heap, covering themselves with sand. "Oh, for heaven's sake," Donna and I both said, shooing them off the blanket and away from the food. They squirreled their way into the basket anyway, and made off with damp sandwiches, settling on their bellies and elbows like three beached seals.

"Hello, Frank," Esau said.

"How's by you, my friend?" Frank asked.

"I'm well, thanks. We have identified three separate types of seaweed on the lake floor."

"And we saw a fish!" Kate yelped, so excited a bite of half-chewed sandwich fell out of her mouth.

"Oh, ish," I said, snatching it from under her head before she had a chance to pick it up.

"A fish," Frank said admiringly. "What sort?"

"It was a northern!" she said.

"No it wasn't," Davey muttered.

"It was a crappie," Esau corrected.

"It was *huge*," Kate crowed.

"It was fairly large for a crappie," Esau concurred. "As fish go, however, it was quite small."

"It had teeth," she said, scowling.

"It did not have teeth," Esau said, stuffing the last bite of his sandwich in his mouth and getting another one out of the basket. "It lives on algae and microscopic life-forms."

"Shut *up!*" Kate said. "You are no fun."

Esau shrugged.

"Anyway," Davey said, delicately nibbling at the crusts of his sandwich, "it touched *my* leg."

None of them had an argument with that.

"Who's he?" Kate said, pointing at Jamie.

"Well, ask him," Donna said, exasperated.

"Who're you?"

"Kate," I chided.

"What?"

"Name's Jamie," he said, touching his baseball cap with his fingers and putting out his hand. Kate shook his hand seriously.

"Who are you and what do you want?" Esau asked.

"Esau!" I said. Frank and Jamie laughed.

"My dad died," Kate said amiably, peeling the top slice of Wonder Bread off her sandwich and licking the mayonnaise off the bologna.

We sat there. Only Davey didn't pause. He reached into the bag of chips and munched loudly.

"Is that so," Jamie said.

Kate nodded. "When I was six."

"She's seven now," Davey explained. "So am I."

"It's good to be seven," Frank said thoughtfully.

"We like it," Davey said. Kate nodded.

"Well, all I can say is, the three of you are burnt to a crisp," Donna said. "More lotion when you're done eating."

"And no swimming for half an hour," I said.

"That," said Esau, sitting up and wiping each of his fingers on a napkin with extreme care, "was a complete non sequitur."

He glowed with the use of his new word. None of us knew what it meant, so we ignored it. At times his vocabulary troubled me.

"And," he said haughtily—he was in fine form today—"there is absolutely positively no scientific basis for the belief that consumption prior to aquatic submersion is in anyway detrimental to one's health."

With that, he turned on his heel and loped across the sand, walking upright into the water until he disappeared.

Kate ate the red parts off her apple and handed Davey the rest. He buried it in the sand.

Abruptly and without speaking, the two of them stood up and departed for the swings.

Jamie looked at me. "Is your kid some kind of genius?"

"I don't know," I said. The idea made me tired.

"He reads the encyclopedia," Donna said. "I think he's trying to memorize it."

"Is he?" I asked. I leaned back on my elbows and buried my toes in the warm sand. "Great. Pretty soon we won't understand a word he says." I pulled my hat down over my eyes and laid back to bask in the sun.

With a little more awkward small talk and an ungraceful scramble to their feet, Frank and Jamie, brushing sand from their rear ends and tapping their hat brims, took off. Donna flopped down next to me. I flipped the brim of my hat up to look at her.

"Why do you always look better in my clothes than I do?" I asked.

She snorted. "Matter of opinion."

"Jamie shares it."

"Yeah, well. I'm not married to Jamie, am I?"

"Shame."

"It is a shame. It's a damn shame. Oh, *Lord,* but that boy is good-looking."

I said nothing.

"Quit with that," she said.

"What?"

"That disapproving."

"I didn't say anything."

"Didn't have to."

I lay there.

"Wasn't like I ran off with him," she said reproachfully.

"What in the hell," I said, sitting up. "I didn't say anything! What do I care?"

She muttered something.

"What?" I asked, not sure I'd heard.

"He tried to hit me." She studied her nails, bright coral pink. "Last night."

I stared at her. She lay on her stomach, her bosom spilling perfectly over the top of my baggy bathing suit. Well, it was baggy on me.

"What for?" I asked.

She glared at me. "What do you mean, what for? What's it matter, what the fuck *for*?" She looked back at her nails and pushed at the cuticle of her thumb.

"Sorry," I said stupidly.

"S'all right. Sorry I yelled."

"You didn't yell."

"Well, not *yelled,* but you know what I mean."

"Did you get in the first punch?" I tried to joke. She tried to laugh.

"Yeah. Bloodied his nose."

"Well, that's something."

"Yeah." She lay down with her face on her arms. I watched the lake. The kids were jumping off a raft over and over and over. How it could still be fun after that many jumps, I didn't know.

"He just got crazy, is all," she said, her voice muffled. "Doesn't say a damn thing for weeks, and just when I think he's gone and died down there in the basement, he comes hauling up, plum crazy. I don't know which of us is crazy. Who starts it. Winds up so we're both crazy and throwing shit and I don't know what all."

A brief, cool breeze skimmed over us and disappeared, rippling the water from south to north, then letting it go still.

"Davey saw," she said, so softly I almost thought she hadn't spoken. She waited for me to answer, but I didn't know what to say.

"That," she said. She tapped her finger in the sand, as if pointing at something, a specific thing. "That's too much."

"Yeah," I said. I opened another Coke. "What'd Davey do?"

She turned her face so that she was looking away from me.

"Didn't see him at first, tell you the truth. That's what gets me. We were so busy screaming we didn't hear him. And I'm trying to think, how'd that happen? I'm trying to think, his bed squeaks, the hallway floor makes all that noise, the stairs, the door, and how come we didn't hear him?"

I didn't know. I remembered that awful moment, though. When you turn and see your child staring at you like you're a monster and you have no idea how long they've been watching or what they saw or how long it'll be till they forget, if they ever do.

"So what'd he do?" I asked again.

She sighed and sat up. She sat slumped, looking out at the lake. "Ran over to his father and hit him with a poker."

"What?"

She nodded grimly. "Grabbed himself the poker from beside the fireplace. Must've been standing there with it awhile. Soon as Dale came after me, Davey pops up from out of nowhere and starts swinging this poker at Dale's knees." Her face shifted and she tried not to smile. "Tell you, it was a sight. This little kid in his pajamas, swinging this thing around"—she started to laugh—"but it's too damn heavy, and pretty soon it's swinging *him,* and he fell over." She sighed. "Got one good crack in, though. Put Dale's left knee right out, and that's his good one too. Serves the sonofabitch right."

"He hit Davey?"

"Tried to. That's when I bloodied his nose."

We watched Tabatha Hendricks leap up from her blanket, hike her skirt up, and stride without stopping hip deep into the water, screaming at all four of her children to get here right this minute before she came to get them her damn self.

"Tell you the truth, wasn't really a fair fight," Donna said. "He was drunk as a deacon on holiday. Didn't see me throw the punch."

"Yeah, well," I snorted.

Tabatha walked out of the water, stripped down to her under-wear, and walked right back in. She emerged with two kids by their hair and went back for the other two.

"You know what's crazy?" Donna said.

"What's that?"

"Mothers."

"Oh honey. Tell me." We laughed. I thought of my mother. *Oh, darling,* she'd said. *You can't protect a child.* Or did she say *save?* You can't save a child? I watched Kate burst through the surface of the water with her face lifted, gasping for air.

"Thought I'd have to kill him," she said calmly. "When he went for Davey."

"Yeah," I finally said. "Yeah, you probably would."

"Wouldn't you?"

"I wouldn't think twice."

She eased herself down onto her elbows. "Shit, Claire. What're we gonna do?"

I nodded slowly. "You could leave him."

She said nothing.

"You're the one who mentioned it," I reminded her.

"Didn't mean it," she said.

"Sure you did."

"No," she said. "I didn't. I don't have the balls. You know that."

"Oh, for Chrissakes."

"No one gets divorced around here. What am I gonna be, the town home wrecker? Walking around like some fancy *divorcée?* No thank you."

I laughed. "It could be worse. You could be me."

She giggled. "Nah, you're the town heathen. When're you gonna go to church, anyway? It looks bad. Give me a cigarette."

I pulled the pack out of my purse and lit hers and my own. For three blissful seconds, we were just ladies sunning ourselves on the beach with not a care in the world.

Then we exhaled.

She looked at me. "Claire, I got two kids. You're outta your mind."

"I've got two kids too," I said, shrugging.

"It's different."

"Yeah?"

"What are you doing this for, Claire? You know it's different."

"Tell me."

"Jesus Mary, you're as dim as they come, I swear to God. You didn't leave your husband, if you'll recall."

"I was going to."

She blinked, gazing at the lake. Then she lifted her cigarette to her mouth again and took a drag. She exhaled through her nose like a lovely dragon.

"Beg pardon?" she said politely.

"I said, I was going to."

"That so."

"Yes."

"You'd thought it through?"

I blew smoke upward and watched it climb toward the lower branches of the tree. "For years. Off and on. Then on. Every time I looked at him, I thought, *Leave.*"

We sat there quietly for a long time.

"Well, he did," she finally said.

That hung in the air between us.

Slowly, I turned to look at her. "Did you just say that to me?"

She didn't return my gaze. "No," she said.

"I didn't think so."

We waited while it blew over.

"Did he know you were gonna go?"

"Yes he did."

The night in the living room. I sat on the couch, he sat at the edge of his chair. Holding our coffee cups. My tongue working in my mouth, trying to form the words. *I don't want you.* No. *I'm leaving.* No. *Go.*

No.

"That's why," I said.

She looked at me, puzzled.

"That's why he did it." I dropped my cigarette. She grabbed it and handed it to me. It had burned a hole through the blanket already. The smoke scribbled weird writing on the still air.

"What are you talking about?" she asked.

"That night," I said. "That's why he killed himself. That night. That's why he killed himself that night," I shouted, and gasped. My hands flew up to my mouth. People turned to stare, then looked away.

"Did they hear?" I asked.

"No," she said, sitting up and taking the cigarette away from my face.

"Did they hear what I said?"

"No, Claire." She put my cigarette out in the sand and took my hands. She squeezed them. "Okay. That's all right."

"They know."

"No, they don't know anything. Bunch of busybodies. Just some noise, turned to look."

"Where are the kids?" I squinted out at the lake.

"There," she said. "And there, and there's Esau. Okay?"

"Okay." I lit another cigarette and took a deep drag and choked. I tried again. "All right, then," I said, calmer.

"Good."

"You know, I drank too much." I smoked so fast I was dizzy. "At first. When he died."

"That's sensible."

"You remember how much I drank at first?" I shook my head. "Poor Katie. Always waking up, seeing me like that."

"She won't remember, honey."

"Won't remember when? When do they forget?"

She rubbed my back. "You're getting burnt," she said. "Let me put some lotion on."

I sat with my arms around my knees while she pointlessly put lotion on my back. "When? Do you think?" I asked.

"Don't know," she said. "That one, I can't answer."

I wanted to tell her Kate saw the bedroom. But I didn't know if she saw. And if I told her Kate saw, then it would be true, and then my life would be over.

When you get married, you think it would kill you to lose him. Because that's the worst thing you can imagine. But then you have children, and you know you were wrong. You find out that the worst thing that could happen is that your children could be hurt.

And then they are hurt, and you are destroyed, over, and over, and over, forever.

"It's true," I said. My voice sounded flat and far away. "That's what did it."

Her hand paused on my back. She snapped the bottle of lotion closed and crawled over to sit next to me.

"I told him I was leaving."

"That night?"

I nodded. "I told him—well, he asked me. I said I was thinking about it. It was Christmas, the damn tree all lit up."

"Christ."

"But it was like—like he knew. Like he just wanted me to say it. Just wanted to make me admit it." I shook my head. "And damned if I didn't do it out of pure spite. I just—" I paused, searching. "I just wanted him to be quiet."

"Well, hell. He wanted you to give him a reason," Donna said.

I laughed shortly. "I did."

"Hell you did. Gave him an excuse, maybe."

I looked at her.

"Not a reason," she said, looking at the lake. "No reason good enough for what he did."

On the way home, the kids fell asleep in a wet, sandy, sunburned pile in the backseat. Sun stunned, they dozed while I hosed them off and Donna unloaded the car, then they staggered into the house, not to be heard from again until the sounds of dinner roused them from their dazed naps. The light wouldn't fall until late. Donna and I sat on the porch with a couple of beers.

"And another thing," she went on, "is the money. I get stuck on the money."

It took me a minute, since we hadn't been talking about anything in particular. She took a swig. "Garden looks good," she said. "I'm jealous."

"Thanks. What money?"

She looked at me. "If I left. Where the hell am I gonna get the money?"

I shrugged. "Get a job?"

She rolled her eyes at me. "Yeah, thanks. I know. That isn't enough. Two kids and a house payment on—what do you make?"

"Enough."

"Enough with Arnold's life insurance, you mean."

I looked at the garden. That rosebush needed pruning. It was so heavy with roses you could have decorated a funeral with it. "No, I mean enough. I haven't touched the insurance money."

"Why not?"

"I haven't needed to yet. If Esau gets sick, I'll need it. I don't want to use it up."

"Still," she said, setting her bottle down on the picnic table and putting her feet up. "That house."

"You owe a lot on it?"

She snorted. "Bank's about to take it back. That a lot?"

"You could say that." I laughed.

She sighed and shook her head. "We been in debt since the day we got married. Always something. Always some damn new thing he had to have. Had to have that big house. Had to have that silly-ass truck."

"That's about the ugliest truck I ever saw."

"Don't talk to me about it. I can't even stand to think about it. And what's he need with a house that size? Who cleans that house? And he's in the basement all the damn time anyway, what's he want it for?"

"Leave him there in the basement, then. If you don't stay in the house, you won't have to pay for the house."

She picked up her beer and took a swallow. "It's my house too," she said, looking sullen. "I been *cleaning* it every damn day since 1959."

"Honey, you been married that long?"

"Since fifty-eight." She smacked her lips.

"How old were you, twelve?"

"A ripe old nineteen, thank you very much. And terribly, *terribly* grown up. Jesus, what a mess. You want another beer?" she asked, standing up and going inside without waiting for me to answer. She came back out with two more bottles and handed one to me. She plunked down, kicked off her flip-flops, and put her feet across my knees.

"Got married in fifty-eight, had Davey in sixty-three. Dale got stationed in September. Came back in sixty-eight." She shook her head. "Married one man, and a few years later another one showed up at my door. Shrapnel in his leg and demons in his brain. He's never been the same." She stared at the ground. "Jesus, those nightmares. I can't even imagine. I can't imagine what he goes through, and the hell of it is," she looked at me, "I don't want to. I don't want to see that ugliness. I keep waiting to see something in his eyes besides hate, besides this huge *need,* and I don't. I don't see anything else, and I don't want to look." She looked out at the garden. "He didn't used to be like this. He didn't. And God, I tell you, Claire, I miss who he was."

The sadness in her eyes made me wince. "I know that feeling," I said, and took a swallow of beer.

"Had Sarah nine months after he came home," she said. "Couldn't get him to hold her for the longest time." She picked at the label on her beer bottle. "Like he didn't want to break her, or ruin her, or something. Shied away from Davey too, poor little thing. Tell me something," she said, looking up. "If you could say one reason you got married, what would you say?"

I smiled, thinking about it. There were a million reasons. Because he was arrogant, and asked me to dance that night even though I was tall and wore daring pants. Because his name was Arnold, of all the damn things: I picked up the letter on his kitchen table while he slept in the other room. Because I was tired of buying one lamb chop from the butcher every night on my way home from work, and tired of eating it alone in my fifth-floor walk-up. Because he touched me right. A million reasons that were nothing and everything and added up now to only the space in my bed.

"Love?" I finally said. "I suppose. That's what I'd say."

She raised her eyebrows at me and wiggled her coral-nailed toes. "You sound pretty sure, there."

"I loved him, for sure. Why I got *married?* To be completely honest," I laughed, "we got married on a whim."

"No kidding. Just thought, what the hell? One day, out of nowhere?"

"Something like that."

"You weren't knocked up or nothing?"

"Sure I was. But I don't think that would've done it if it wasn't Arnold."

She whistled. "What was so special about him?"

I smiled and shook my head. "Oh. What wasn't. He was something else. He was quite the ladies' man, back then. He could talk you into anything. Before I knew what hit me, my last name was Schiller and I lived in Motley, Minnesota. Honey, I thought Minneapolis was the name of a *state*."

Donna threw her head back and roared. "I swear," she said, shaking her head. "City people don't know shit."

"That's the truth."

"Tell 'em to drive north and they ask you is that left or right.

Shoot." She shook her head, still laughing. "You know why I got married?" She lit a cigarette and handed me the pack. She shook her cigarette at me. "I can top your whim. I wanted a *dress*."

"You got married for a dress? You married Dale so you could have a *dress*?"

"Yes, ma'am. Well, I liked him plenty. Like I said, he was different back then. But really I wanted a party. At the Elk's Club."

We hooted. "Yep," she said, pleased with herself, "wanted to show up Little Miss Better-Than-Anybody Patty Swanson. That's Mrs. Joel Lillenthal to you," she said pointedly, and I gasped. "Patty and I had it in for each other ever since she stole my boyfriend in the second grade and I wasn't going to rest until I saw her dead or miserable, and by God"—she smacked the table—"she is *miserable*. And that Joel Lillenthal's a piece of work, let me tell you, so when I went waltzing down the aisle and she was *already* a fat dropout with a snot-nosed kid, it didn't matter one damn bit to me just *who* was at the other end of that aisle. You should have seen the look on her face. The flowers. The dancing. And that *dress*." She busted up laughing. "Eight underskirts of dotted Swiss. Swear to God, I must've looked like a chicken exploded. Still, it was the fanciest wedding anyone around here had seen in a long time. I'll always thank my father for that. Poor guy practically had to sell the farm."

"I always wanted a wedding," I said.

"Everybody does," she said, shrugging. "Yeah. It almost made it worth it."

She looked at me and smiled. "Almost." She set her bottle down and put her hands on her knees. "I'm gonna grab my little man and head home."

"You don't have to go." I didn't want her to.

"I know that. Thanks, though. I told Dale I'd make supper."

"Tell Dale to go to hell."

She stood up and sighed. She ruffled my hair. "Oh, what would I do without you, Claire. You're sweet. Quit talking about it like I'm serious. You know I'm just making noise."

She left.

* * *

It had to happen sometime. It was just too damn hot.

The sky broke open on us like some biblical thing, a flood after weeks of drought. The kids came running in from the yard, drenched and yelling. Faster than we could get the windows closed, the sky went black and the rain slanted in, a hard rain pounding at the panes and the dirt-brown ground. Dust spat up from the parched grass, and the street hissed and steamed.

One day, and the garden had grown over the fence and was heading for the Andersons' house.

Two days, and the lakes had swollen up and overrun their banks.

Three days, and the crops unbent themselves and turned a surreal green. Talk in the bar was of rising ag stocks, low seed prices, pork and beef, soybeans and corn. Sugar-beet farmers bought drinks all around. Salvation came.

The kids baked chocolate-chip cookies and played Monopoly in the endless bottle-green light. I cleaned and cleaned, elated, half wishing I could rip the roof right off and let the rain wash the whole house clean. The world smelled new.

Four days, and the phone lines went down. Donna came over with the baby. The electricity went out. We ate tuna sandwiches and played another round of Monopoly.

"You guys gonna be all right?" Donna asked them, pulling Arnold's old raincoat around her and stepping into his mud shoes. I stood there in my own red raincoat. We'd wind up drenched anyway, it hardly mattered what we wore.

"Of course. Do you want us to feed the baby?" Esau asked. He could not be separated from that child. She sat on his lap, held firmly upright by his left arm, and chewed on Park Avenue.

"Fed her already. She gets fussy, give her the teething ring."

"Where ya goin'?" Davey asked.

"To Frank's. We're getting stir-crazy. Mrs. Anderson's coming from next door to watch you."

"I like Mrs. Anderson," Kate said thoughtfully. She looked at Esau. "She gets to play on our team," she said, and turned to me, adding, "We have to beat Esau." Esau looked up apologetically.

"So far we have figured out a way to handicap me, but I keep winning anyway," he explained.

"Ah," Donna said. "Well, there's food in the cooler and you know where to find us if you want to say good night. Tell Mrs. Anderson and she'll dial for you. We left the number on the counter."

"Phone doesn't work," Davey said.

"Oh, hell. You're right. I forgot. All right, anyway, here comes Mrs. Anderson across the yard. We're going."

We thanked Cookie Anderson as we met at the door, and stepped through the wall of water that poured off the eaves of the house. The sky was army-coat green. We walked in companionable silence for a while, just listening to the rain, and then Donna said, "I love those little guys."

"Hell yeah."

"They make it all worthwhile, don't they."

I nodded. "They sure do."

"Didn't want 'em," she said. "First time I got pregnant, I thought I'd die. Locked myself in the bathroom at the doctor's office and cried for an hour until the nurse came in and talked me into lying down."

"Yeah?"

She nodded. "I thought maybe I'd get lucky and never get pregnant. Hell, I hadn't the first six years. It took me damn near three months to figure out why I was so sick. But now. Man, I wouldn't trade it for nothing." She pushed back the hood of her raincoat and let the water stream down her face. She looked at me. "You want kids?"

I shrugged. "It didn't matter much to me one way or the other. To tell you the truth, I'd gotten pretty used to the idea that I'd never get married. I was getting too old, I thought. And of course," I said, grinning, "you can't have kids if you aren't married."

"Right," she laughed. "Course not."

"But it's funny you mention it. I knew I was pregnant almost right away. I couldn't have known that moment, but I almost had myself convinced I did. And I walked around awhile with that, you know, keeping it to myself. I liked knowing something nobody else knew."

"When did Arnold figure it out?"

"Pretty quick." I smiled. "He was so excited he did a little dance in the doctor's office. All these nurses laughing at him. He picked me up and swung me around and then panicked, like it was going to break me. I think he would've put me on bed rest himself, if he'd had his way." I laughed. "He took me out to dinner that night, and the next day he comes home with a stack of books yea high on pregnancy.

Followed me around the house for the next nine months reading out loud. Snatching my cigarettes away every time I tried to light up. I swear to you, all I wanted when I finally got that baby born was a glass of wine and a cigarette."

She laughed. "See, that's how it ought to be done. Dale was like that the first time, with Davey. But when he came home from the service, it was a whole different thing. Aside from the fact that he'd started sleeping downstairs." She shivered. "He'd come in at night, not say a word. Leave. Then, surprise, I got pregnant. I don't think we even talked about it until I was six months."

"How in the hell?"

"Just never mentioned it. I got bigger and bigger, and then one day me and him and Davey are sitting there at supper, and he says to me, 'Well, what do you plan to do with it?'"

"He did not."

"Oh yes he did. And I was so pissed I didn't say a thing. So he says, like he does, 'Donna. See you got yourself all swole up again.'"

I snorted. "All by yourself, I guess."

"Guess so. Neat trick, huh? So I said, 'Looks that way, don't it?' And he says, 'Well, how you plan to feed another mouth?'"

"Good Lord. That man has a way with words."

"Doesn't he? Mr. Romance. After that was when I moved into the spare room for good."

"He say anything?"

"Nah. What's he want with some swole-up woman anyway?" She laughed shortly. "Now, he wants some, he just barges on in."

I didn't say anything. I thought about the way, when I was pregnant with both Esau and Kate, Arnold and I had laughed our heads off in bed, trying to figure out what to do with my belly, which was somehow everywhere. I'd never felt so pretty in all my life.

"Now I just tell him if he wants another mouth to feed, go right ahead," she said. "That usually puts a damper on his business."

We laughed. We walked across the flooded parking lot at Frank's, the neon sign wavering in the thick rain. There weren't even raindrops. It was just water, pouring down.

We swung open the double doors and stepped into the crowded, steamy, smoky room, shaking our hair out. I saw Donna's eyes scan the room and her face light up like a little girl's. She turned toward the wall, hung my jacket and hers on hooks, and pushed her hair behind her ears.

She turned back to the room, tall and pretty and alive, now that all eyes were on us. She could have a few hours of her own now before she had to go home and play dead.

We threaded our way to the bar and took the stools vacated for us by a couple of men who tapped the brims of their wet hats. Frank poured us a couple of old-fashioneds and waved an irritable hand at my pocketbook. He whipped his cloth out of a back pocket. "Dripping on my nice clean bar," he muttered, wiping it off and grinning his upside-down grin.

I looked up at the Coca-Cola clock. It wasn't yet eight o'clock. Somebody put Johnny Cash on the jukebox. Jamie appeared, throwing his arms around my shoulders and Donna's, and said, "Game of pool?"

"All yours," I said, lifting my glass to Donna. I watched Jamie's hand hover near the small of her back as he cleared their path toward one of the two tables.

The thump and fall of the balls, the crack of the rack and the break, and Johnny Cash. The clatter of glasses and bottles, the rumble of voices, the barks of laughter and the shouts.

First time we went to the bar after Arnold died, the room went still. The few last voices were suddenly loud in the gathering silence and got shushed. I froze by the door and Donna shoved me forward, sticking close by my back as we made our way to the bar.

"Well, what in the hell's the matter with you fellas," Frank shouted, angrier than I'd ever seen him. For that matter, I'd never seen him angry. "Take your damn fool hats off. Act like you never seen a lady in your life."

Frank was such an odd one. He was a powerfully handsome man, that was the first thing you noticed. You couldn't help but notice. I, for one, had often found myself wanting to stare at him for longer than was right. He was tall, not as tall as Arnold, but tall enough, and built more solidly than Arnold had been at the end. Arnold had shrunk to half his size, and as I sat here now at the bar, watching Frank pour me a drink, I noticed the veins in his arms, and his habit of clenching his jaw; a little tic near his temple, pulsing, as if he had something he might just say, but then again, might keep to himself. He was a quiet man. Not a lot of words, just a few, carefully chosen, here and there. It was said he was an eccentric, and private, both strange things in this town where you knew everyone and everything about them, for better or for worse. He ran the bar but rarely drank. He listened to every man in town, all day, every day and late into the night. Everyone trusted him, almost; his privacy alone was suspicious. An upright sort of fellow, like a bookish old man trapped in the body of a youngish bartender. He reminded me of Esau.

I thought of our conversation at the beach: He knew all the stories. He was the repository of everyone's joy and boredom and grief.

What did he know about me?

He set my drink in front of me and smiled, his odd crooked smile lifting to the left. His fingernails were chewed down to the quick. His hands were rough. I watched him turn away to pour another drink, lifting his hand to smooth down his silvery hair.

Donna called me to the pool table. I grabbed my drink and, feeling a little giddy, went over. I dropped the dime, bent down to rack, lifted the triangle, looked up, and damned if I didn't see Jamie kiss Donna's ear.

I went to the wall to get a cue and chalked it. Over my shoulder, I said, "Somebody break."

I turned and Donna came over to my side. "We're shooting doubles. Us against Jamie and Hank," she said. I nodded and watched Hank break. I winced as two solids and a stripe went down.

Donna played well when she was nervous, even better after a few drinks. She ticked the clustered stripes off one by one into the lower corner pockets, walking around the table, chalking between each shot, leaning down. I glanced up at Jamie. It was hard to tell whether he was watching her or her shots. She got cocky and tried to bank an easy shot into the side, missed by a mile, and sank the cue.

"Damn!" she said. "You want anything?" I shook my head and she headed for the bar.

By the time Donna got back, we were down to a stripe, two solids, and the eight. She took a sip, set down her drink on the high table by the wall. She chalked. She took the stripe out easily. Then she leaned down over the lower corner, looked up at Jamie, and smiled. She steadied her cue. And shot the eight into the corner pocket by his crotch so hard he jumped.

"Oh, for God's sake!" I shouted. Hank and Jamie busted up. I went off to the bar to sulk and leaned there while Frank grinned and polished his bar.

He opened the register and pushed a quarter across the bar to me. "Put something pretty on the jukebox," he said. "If I hear another country song, I swear." He smiled briefly at me, and turned away. I wanted him to turn back and smile again. It did something to my stomach that I hadn't felt in years. I watched his back for a moment, broad in the shoulders and solid under his shirt.

I thought suddenly of Arnold, bent here at the bar, a double scotch glowing gold between his palms, a pack of cigarettes and matches just to his left. A little trinity, his hands folded around the glass as if in prayer. I thought of him calling out to Frank, talking to Frank, telling him things he didn't need to know. Telling him things that at this moment, watching his back, I didn't want him to know.

I slid off the bar stool, flushed.

I flipped through the records and played my favorites. I leaned back against the wall, ate the cherry in my drink, and wondered if I'd ever go dancing again. I looked around the crowded room. Who would I want to dance with? I wondered. Idly, my gaze shifted from Jamie, to Hank, to Kittie's husband, to Frank.

Good Lord, I thought.

It was my shot. I ran the table and put down my cue. "I'm done," I said. "Table's yours." I crossed the room to sit down in one of the booths. Donna followed me.

She was giddy, and she was drunk. "What's with you?"

"Nothing, thanks. Careful," I said, moving my drink out of her way. She put her chin in her hands and heaved a great sigh, smiling. "You having fun?" she asked.

"Sure."

"Oh, you're not either. What's the matter?" She turned and looked around the room. "All these nice fellows here, and you're being a stick-in-the-mud."

I snorted. She looked at me. "That supposed to mean something?"

"No."

"Well, *I'm* having fun."

"Honey, that's plain as day."

"'Scuse me?"

"You heard me."

She eyed me over her drink. "You got something to say, say it."

"I don't have a thing to say."

"You sure?"

I nodded.

"'Cause you look like you got something to say."

I shrugged.

"Something about Jamie, maybe."

I looked at her and put an ice cube in my mouth.

"Something about how maybe I should watch myself, maybe."

"Maybe so."

She nodded slowly, sat back in the booth, and ran her hand through her hair. "Maybe so," she agreed. "Maybe I just should."

But you won't, I thought.

She smiled, reached across the table, and took my chin in her hand. "Such a worrywart," she said. She smacked the table and stood up. "Come dance."

"I'm all right."

"Come *on*," she wheedled. "Or else I'll be out there dancing with myself, and how silly is that?"

Jamie and Hank showed up. "Ladies?" they said, holding their hands out. Donna dashed off to the dance floor. I stayed where I was.

Hank and I chatted while the night ran on. A few rounds later and it was time for me to be getting home.

Donna was gone.

I went into the ladies' room. She wasn't there. I stood at the back of the room, scanning it with my eyes. The crowd had thinned out. I sat down at the bar.

"They left." Frank's voice was low. He washed glasses in the sink below the bar. His eyes lifted for a second, then went down.

The last dancers came off the polished floor, grabbed their raincoats and hats off the wall, and called out their good-byes. By ones and twos, the rest of the tables cleared. Still I sat there, watching the Coca-Cola clock. It was after twelve.

"Want a cup of coffee?" Frank asked me.

I hesitated, then nodded, and he set a mug down. The last juke-box record clicked and went silent.

"Night, Frank. Claire." The wooden door swung shut.

I sipped my coffee, profoundly aware that I was alone with a man. The seconds on the clock ticked by as Frank came out from behind the bar with a broom. Suddenly, with no bar between us, I was conscious of how this would seem if anyone heard that I had lingered at the bar long after everyone had left. "Well," I said, standing up and heading for the door. "I guess that's that."

Frank turned his head. "Don't go," he said. "Here, just let me sweep up."

I stood there like a fool. "Well, all right."

While he swept, I put another dime in the jukebox and jumped back, startled, when the loud chords of the Beatles crashed into the quiet room. Frank laughed.

"She thinks I disapprove," I said, still staring at the jukebox, punching buttons aimlessly.

"You want more coffee?" he asked. "You didn't drive, did you?"

"No. Yes, I'd love more coffee."

He poured two cups and nodded toward a booth. "Have a sit," he said. He set a mug down in front of me and settled himself in. He stretched his head first one way and then the other, wincing. "Well," he said finally. "Do you?"

"What's that?"

"Do you disapprove?"

"Oh." I thought about it. He was forthright enough to make me squirm. I shouldn't have been discussing it with him one way or the other. It was just so easy to tell him what was on your mind. "Well, no," I said. "That's not it. I just worry."

He nodded. "I can see that."

"I mean, shit, excuse me, Frank. But she's married to Dale."

"That she is."

"And I hate him."

Frank looked at me. He took a sip. "He's not a happy man," he said. He chose his words slowly, as if selecting them was a process requiring care and concentration, and their combination a matter of extreme importance.

"I hate him something awful. I do. I wish I didn't. But there it is."

"There it is."

"So, hell no, I don't blame her. But I worry about what Dale's capable of."

"Tell you," Frank nodded. "I worry 'bout the same thing."

We sat there drinking for a minute and then he spoke. "Not a lot of times I think someone ought to just leave. Myself, I'm maybe old-fashioned that way. Not that I got any business, myself. But I figure, you get married and you make it work. But that one, I don't know. I don't think there'd be a way."

"It's killing her."

He looked at me. His jaw moved slightly. I could see the shadow of his beard coming in. His eyes had a hooded intensity that reminded me of a hawk.

"Living like that," I explained, looking away.

He nodded. "I know it is. It was the strangest thing, Claire. When I looked up tonight, saw them like that. You know." He laughed. "You can always see it coming. Tend bar, you might as well call yourself a fortune-teller, you can see things coming so far off. Anyways," he said, waving his words away, "I saw them like that, and I swear it made me happy. See her smile."

I studied my hands. "What's it like, Frank?" I said. "Keeping all these secrets to yourself."

He laughed. "Don't know. Everybody's got their tales." He shrugged. He squinted when he was thinking, and tilted his head back just a little, as if to read you.

"Why'd you and your wife split up?" I asked, and regretted it, and felt like a fool. He laughed at the look on my face and said, "That's all right. It was a long time ago."

"How long?"

He looked at the ceiling, thinking. "Twelve years." He looked back at me and shrugged. "Weren't married but five."

"You must've been just kids."

"That's the truth. I suppose that's why we split up. Didn't know my ass from my elbow, is what," he laughed. "She deserved better."

"Than what?"

"Than me. I wasn't but nineteen. What'd I know about how to treat a woman?"

"What do you know now?"

He smiled, surprised, his grin tilting his face to the side. My face burned and I excused myself to go to the bathroom. I sat on the toilet, holding my hands to my cheeks, trying to cool them off. What were you thinking? I thought. What on earth did you just say? I splashed water on my face and went back out.

"I tell you," I said hurriedly. "I don't know how it's got so late."

"Oh, it ain't that late," he said. "Don't leave yet." As I slid back into the booth, he said calmly, "I know a thing or two." We glanced at each other, and smiled, and suddenly laughed, embarrassed and relieved. I waved my hand in front of my face to cool it off and shook my head at him.

"You're a funny man," I said.

"I've heard that's so," he said, smiling, looking me over. Looking me over very carefully, the way a man looks a woman over, as if he's enjoying a good meal or a glass of wine.

It reminded me of the way a young man had stared at me in a New York club, arrogantly, from across the room, his white teeth shining in a private smile as he stood up to ask me to dance. The way a young man had pressed his hand into my back firmly, the first time I ever felt I could lean into someone else and let them lead, if only for a minute or two.

How wrong I was, I thought, and stared into my empty coffee cup.

"You must miss him something awful," Frank blurted, startling me. "He was a good man, Claire."

I stared at him. "I don't." The words fell out of my mouth, nakedly angry, and I didn't know what to do with them. I found myself trying to wipe them off the table. "I mean, I do, of course. Of course I do, he was my husband. But not like you're saying."

"I don't know what I'm saying, Claire." He looked mortified. "I'm sorry I said anything."

"It's all right," I said irritably. "Why does everyone apologize for talking around here? I do miss him and I don't. It gets easier. I've got my kids."

We drank our coffee.

"And he wasn't such a good man in the end," I said, shocking myself. I looked up at Frank. "Now was he."

He didn't look away. With his strange, extreme care, he said, "I can't say that he wasn't. And no, I can't rightly say that he was."

I got up to put another five songs on the jukebox. The Coca-Cola clock read 1:00. I decided I'd kill Donna when I got home. I'd wake her up no matter how drunk she was and wallop her a good one. It was her fault I was having this conversation.

I sat back down.

"Loved you something awful," Frank said. "Arnold did." He studied a point just northwest of my shoulder.

After a minute, I said, "For a while, sure. But that doesn't make it work."

He nodded. "Best not forget it, though. Not everybody has that."

I smiled. "That's true." I looked at him. "You ever been crazy in love?"

He laughed. "Lordy. Sure have, Claire. Terrible stuff, ain't it?" He turned his head to listen. "Great song." He looked at me. "Dance?"

"Now?" I sat there, stunned.

"Sure, now. Nobody to bump into."

We stood at the centre of the dance floor. He put his arms out and said, "Telling you, I got two left feet." I laughed and gingerly folded my hand over his, put my hand on his left shoulder. It was solid under my hand, I wanted to squeeze it, to feel it resist. I wanted to grapple with him, simply to feel his strength. Instead, I cupped my hand over his shoulder, nearer his neck than I probably had any business going, and rested the pad of my thumb on his skin.

We stared past each other and spun slowly in our stocking feet, as awkward as two kids in dancing class, around the floor.

The song ended. I started to pull away. His hand pressed so lightly into mine he could have just been leading, and he led me into the next song. Out of the corner of my eye, I studied the salt-and-pepper curl behind his ear. I could hear him breathe.

I can't do this, I thought. It's too soon.

I closed my eyes and breathed in his smell of smoke and soap and a faint tang of sweat.

I can't stop.

I don't know how long we danced. The last record dropped. I froze. Then I pulled away and headed for my raincoat. "I have to go," I called. "It's so late." I pulled my raincoat on and he ran after me into the parking lot, into the rain.

"Claire," he yelled.

"Good night!"

"Can I—"

I ran.

* * *

My front door was unlocked. I stepped in, shook myself off, and leaned back against the door.

I looked over the dark, dusty parlor that we never used, my eyes bumping at the edges of shadows of antiques and heirlooms, Arnold's and mine. We used to use this room, I thought. Arnold and I had company, and we used this room. The grandfather clock still ticks and gongs. I watched its brass bell swing from side to side in the dark, the only motion in the room. God knew how long it had been since I'd taken a dust rag to the piano, or how long it had been since anyone touched the keys.

I missed him.

I missed him such that it felt like a physical pain in the area below my ribs. I opened my mouth to accommodate it. I put my hand to it. A hollow, aching, piercing place. And I knew for the first time and with certainty that it would always be there a little, and I missed him, and I grasped the sides of my waist and bent over to wait out the mute hurt of this missing, and I wanted to say, very specifically, *Husband,* this is my husband, you are my husband, I am your wife.

But that was no longer technically true.

I went down the hall to my bedroom. I lay myself, carefully, face-down on the bed. And then I beat his pillow with my fist.

A week or so later, rain drumming on the roof, I woke up with a splitting headache and a row of trolls peering at me from the edge of the bed.

"What's wrong with you?" Kate asked.

"Are you sick?" Davey asked.

Esau stood there wringing his hands. "Are you sleeping all day?"

I rolled onto my stomach and pulled the cord that dropped the curtain to make the horrible light go away. I'd been drinking the night before.

"Do you have *any* idea what time it is?" Kate shrieked.

"Enough!" I said. "No more questions until I have some coffee."

"Do you—"

"No more!" I commanded. "I mean it." I pulled the pillow over my head and said, "Go away."

There was silence. I lifted the pillow and they were still standing there, staring at me. "Oh, for Chrissakes," I said, and swung my legs over the side of the bed.

"We want a soft-boiled egg," Kate said plaintively.

"All right," I said, steadying myself and following them into the kitchen. I poured myself a cup of cold coffee from the night before and gulped it down while the water came to a boil. I dropped three eggs in and the doorbell rang. "For pity's sake," I muttered. "Someone get the door," I called, hunting for bread.

"Mom!" came Kate's voice. "There's someone here to see you!"

"Who is it?"

There was a mumbling. I turned my head toward the sound of a man's voice.

"It's Frank!" she yelled. "Can he come in?"

I dashed down the hall, calling, "Tell him I'll be right out. Get him something to drink." I slammed my bedroom door and heard her say, "We have apple juice."

I jumped into the shower, scrubbing furiously. I smelled like a bar. Why didn't Frank smell like a bar? I wondered, washing my hair. It was full of tangles. I gave up, rinsed, and told myself to calm down. I stood naked in front of my closet. There was nothing to wear. It was hot and steamy and still raining. I yanked an old sundress out and tugged it over my head, remembering just in time to put on my underwear before I opened the bedroom door.

I tied my hair in a knot on my way down the hall. "Hi, Frank," I called. "I'm just about to put some coffee on."

"Mother," Esau said, pacing back and forth in the kitchen, rubbing his hands together. "I am feeling very anxious."

"Okay," I said, holding still and looking around wildly. "Sorry."

"It's all right. Why is he here?"

"Who, Frank?"

"Yes, Frank!" Esau said urgently, hopping from foot to foot. "What does he want?"

"I thought you liked Frank!"

"I do, but that is not the point at all!" He pounded his thighs twice for emphasis and hopped up onto the counter. He craned his neck around the corner, looking into the living room, then backed up against the wall as if he were in a police chase.

"I am only saying," he hissed, "I am only saying that this is out of order! He is out there playing cards with Kate and Davey!"

"He is?" I asked.

"Yes! Do we need to adjust the *routine,* is what I am asking." He pointed and flexed his feet over and over, put his arms above his head, and waved his hands in the air. "What I am asking," he said loudly, frustrated, "is do you have a crush on Frank, and if so, is he coming for breakfast very often?"

I dropped the can of Folgers and chased it across the kitchen. "Don't panic!" he said, hopping down and helping me clean up the grounds. "I'll make it myself. You have to go be the host. Also, the eggs are hard-boiled. You should probably start some new ones."

I grabbed him and kissed both his cheeks. "You are so, so wonderful," I said. He stared at me blankly. "Never mind," I said.

"Your dress is backward," he said. I looked down. "It's not that obvious, though," he said, so I took a deep breath and went into the living room.

Frank looked up from his hand of cards. He stood up and said, grinning, "Claire."

"Frank. Good morning." I fidgeted with the label of my dress.

"Mom," Kate said importantly. "It's afternoon."

"Right." I laughed.

"Sleep well?" Frank said, smiling.

"Don't even start," I said. "You hungry?"

"No, I ate, thanks. I was just—" He gestured. "I was just sitting down to play some cards."

I nodded. "I see."

As if to prove his point, he sat, picked up his hand, and started moving cards around. Esau came in with one cup of coffee, gave it to Frank, bowed regally, turned on his heel, and went back to get another cup.

I sat down on the couch next to Davey. "Where's my mom?" he asked, not sounding too worried. Sarah was asleep in my room.

"She's running some errands," I said.

"Where to?"

"Here and there. Had to get some shopping done," I said, wanting to kill her. "She'll be back soon enough."

That seemed to satisfy him. I drank my coffee and looked out the window at the rain. This, I thought, was very strange. I set my coffee cup down and went to cut oranges for breakfast.

Frank appeared at the doorway. I glanced up from the cutting board. "Hi there," I said.

"Hi there."

"Long time no see."

He laughed and leaned against the counter. "Donna didn't come back last night?"

"She did. She left again."

"She ain't at home."

I arranged the orange sections on a plate. "Is that so?"

"Dale came by the bar this morning."

I nodded. "Who's minding the bar?"

"Jackson's kid Pete fills in for me when he can. Gives me a little time off. I just stopped in this morning, see things were in order. Dale was there. That man is in a world of hurt."

I ran my hands under the water and dried them on my dress. I kept my face still. "I can't say I'm sorry to hear that."

"Well, it worries me."

I carried the oranges and a few plates out to the dining room. I came back in, crossed my arms, and leaned against the stove. He had ironed his shirt. A T-shirt, he had ironed a blue T-shirt. Maybe his jeans too. He smelled like Old Spice. His dark skin gleamed from a shower. Just having him in the house made me short of breath. The six or so feet between us were an intrusion, and I wished they'd go away, and I wished I'd stop noticing space every time he was around. It seemed I'd suddenly taken an excessive interest in the distance between here and him.

"He's on a bender and he's talking," Frank said, scowling down at his shirt and brushing at it as if there were crumbs. I wondered wildly if he had much chest hair, belly hair, and I turned bright red. I swore at myself and asked whatever powers that be to clean my head out with soap. But it was so strange to see him standing there where Arnold had stood, his broad back against the wall where Arnold had leaned, much like this, talking to me while I cooked. The phone on the wall to his right, the coffee cup on the end of the counter. The thick hands shoved into his pockets. All this, and a different man's face.

I felt ashamed to have him in the house and yet I could not have asked him to leave.

"Shut the whole bar up this morning," he said. "Had to ask him to leave. He didn't like that one bit."

"Talking. About Donna?"

He nodded. "Knows something's going on."

"How's he know that?"

Frank shrugged. "Doesn't much matter. I'm just saying."

"What?"

He winced and shoved his hands into his pockets. Clearly he didn't like this conversation. "Maybe she needs to come stay over here, don't you think? Figure things out before she tries going home again. He's not right, Claire. Not right."

I drank my coffee and refilled both our cups. "He's not threatening her," I said, and willed it so.

"Hell, you know he's just talking. Still." He looked intensely miserable. "You gotta know I don't like getting into people's business," he said.

"No, I know it." I looked out the back screen door. "Looks like it's starting to let up."

"Little bit," he said. He cleared his throat and I looked at him. "So I was going to say," he said, crossing one ankle over the other. "I was going to see if you might like to go on over to the supper club tonight. Have a bite, maybe dance." He stared at the floor, stunned.

I opened my mouth and nothing came out.

"I was gonna ask you last night, but, you know, you ran off so quick I didn't get a chance. I understand it's not polite, short notice—"

"Yes."

He looked up, surprised.

"I'd love to," I said.

The front door opened and I heard Donna go into the bedroom. She walked into the kitchen carrying a sleepy Sarah. "Well, hello there," she said to Frank.

"Afternoon."

She poured herself a cup of coffee and grabbed a chair. "I suppose you've disowned me."

"Don't be ridiculous."

She laughed. "Thank God."

"Honey, I think you should maybe stay here for a while."

She looked up at me like I was nuts. "Not that I wouldn't like to, Claire, but—"

"No buts."

She glanced at Frank. "Take it he knows." I nodded. "All right," she said. "Want to tell me what's going on?"

"Looks like your husband's got himself into a bit of a fit."

"What else is new?"

"Yeah, well, this time he's after you."

She set her coffee cup on the counter, crossed her legs, and looked at me.

"He came to the bar this morning, already drunk," Frank said. "Got himself kicked out, and that takes some doing."

"Was he on about me?" Donna said.

Frank scowled at the back door.

"Frank? He was on about me, wasn't he? What in the hell did he say?"

"Donna, I can't say I'm inclined to repeat it, except to say I think it's better if you don't go home right now. Let him drink himself out and sleep it off."

"Does he know?"

Neither Frank nor I spoke.

Donna sighed and flung an arm out aimlessly, as if she were sweeping everything off a table. "Well, shit. So he knows. Who gives a rat's ass. Had to happen sometime. Least now he's got a reason to leave."

"Donna," Frank said, raising his voice, "wake up. Man doesn't want to leave. He wants to kill you."

He cleared his throat and poured himself another cup of coffee.

Donna studied the floor. "He said that?"

"Yes he did. And a lot of other things too." Frank was quiet now, looking out the back door to where I kept my seedlings.

Donna looked at me. "Well, where in the hell are you gonna put me?"

I shrugged. "We've got plenty of space. Let's just tell the kids and leave it at that for now."

Frank pushed off the counter and turned. "How's about seven?" he said to me.

"All right," I said.

He tapped his hat and went to say good-bye to the kids.

"What's at seven?" Donna asked me.

"We're going to dinner."

"What?"

I shook my head. "Don't ask."

I sat at my dressing table in my underwear and a slip, putting on my makeup. Donna and all three kids had crowded onto the bed with a plate of cookies, to watch me. The baby lay on the floor, happily examining her toes.

"You're getting crumbs!" Davey shrieked at Kate, brushing them off onto the carpet.

"Well, excuse *me*," she said, indignant.

"Don't forget earrings," Donna said. "Scoot over," she said to Esau. "You're hogging."

"Sorry," he said. "Pass the cookies, please."

"Are you and Frank getting married?" Davey asked.

"They can't," Kate said. "She's already married."

"No she's not," Esau said. "She isn't, she isn't."

"Yes she is, stupid. She's married to Dad."

"Dad's dead. Dead Dad."

I looked up in the mirror and caught him thumping his thigh.

"I know *that*," Kate said.

"So she's a widow." Thump thump. "Black-widow spiders eat their mates." Thump. "Widows mostly mourn." Thump thump.

"Oh, that's really nice," Donna said. "That's enough about it from both of you."

"Apologies are offered," Esau said, his face furrowed. He stuffed a cookie in his mouth. I was worried about him. He hadn't let any of the three little ones out of his sight all day. He kept counting them. *One two three,* I'd heard him whisper, *one two three, all present and accounted for.*

"Esau, how are you?" I asked his image in the mirror. He glanced up, his cheeks bulging. "Are you all right if I'm gone for a few hours? Or not? You have to tell me the truth. Or I'll"—I didn't know what I'd do—"take your books for a week."

His eyes widened and he shook his head. "I'm okay. Really, super okay. Very much okay." He stuffed another cookie in his mouth. "Precisely how long will you be gone?"

"Three hours," I said. It seemed like a safe bet.

He looked at his watch, which I mightily regretted having gotten him, and said, "Ten P.M. That is your curfew. We'll still be up, so we'll know."

"All right, then. I won't be late."

Kate nibbled. I watched her in the mirror while I put on my blush. She looked confused.

"So are you not married?" she finally asked, worried.

I glanced at Donna. "I'll always be married to your dad, in a way."

"But you could get married again."

"I suppose I could."

"So are you and Frank getting married?"

I sighed. "No. Frank and I are having dinner. That's all."

"Dad," said the baby, sounding cheerful. We all looked at her. "Dad!" she said again, looking around, pleased with the attention.

Esau scrambled upright and grabbed her. She dangled, giggling. "Dadadadada!"

"She called me Dad! Did you hear her?" Esau crowed, and danced her around the room.

"Oh, Christ," Donna said. "That's rich."

"It's her first word!" Esau shrieked. "I'm calling Oma!" And he dashed out.

"For a wedding anyway she has to have a veil," Davey said disdainfully, pulling a pillowcase off a pillow and putting it on his head.

Donna flopped backward. "Claire, this is a loony bin."

"Yes it is," I said.

The doorbell rang and they all scrambled off the bed, Kate yelling, "Get dressed! Get dressed!" and slamming the door behind herself.

Okay, I thought, looking around. Okay. Okay. Here we go. Dress. I stood up and slid it out of its Norby's bag. We'd fussed around in my closet for an hour and finally settled on a blue not-really-silk number that, Donna said, *gave my ass a little oomph*. Out in the living room, I heard Donna offer Frank a drink, and had an unexpected jolt of panic as I heard him say, "Well, just a little splash, thanks."

I sat down with a thud on the vanity stool. I stared into the mirror. The vanity was the only piece of furniture I'd taken with me from my mother's house. It was old. Maybe valuable, who knew? It was mine, a piece of my memory, it was the way I'd always thought of her, sitting there fussing with her face, her hair, her treasures in a cloisonné box. I sat there, running my hands over the mahogany.

She and I stared at each other in the mirror.

What am I doing, I thought. It's too soon. There'll be talk.

They'll see us. We'll walk in; Frank will hold the door and take my wrap. They'll all look up.

And then?

I took off my wedding ring and opened the left-hand drawer. I put it in the cloisonné box with the other treasures. I reached for a bottle of perfume and decided against it. That was too much.

Somehow that settled everything, and I went out into the living room just in time to catch Frank knocking back a double. His eyes caught on me and tripped. He coughed.

"Hi, Frank," I said.

"Hello there."

"You're looking sharp." He did, in a seersucker summer suit, a little too short in the wrists.

"Don't look half bad yourself." Immediately he regretted his choice of words, and I could see him trying to figure out how to rearrange them or replace them with new ones, his face twisting up as if he were eating a lemon sour.

Donna looked from one of us to the other. She sat comfortably on the couch, under a heap of children. "Well, go already," she said, waving us toward the door. "Git."

"Yeah, git!" Kate said, braiding Donna's hair.

"All right, then," Frank said, setting his glass down. "If you're ready."

I bent down to kiss the kids. Esau stared straight ahead, Kate scowled. Davey, bless his heart, took my hand and kissed it. "Night," he said.

Frank held the car door open for me and bent down to fold in the edge of my dress before he closed it. We rode in silence down to the county road, and then he said, "Really, you do. Look lovely. I mean. Sure is a pretty-color dress."

"Thanks." I turned to look at him. "That's a good-looking tie."

He looked down at it as if he'd forgotten it was there. "Thanks," he said. Then he laughed. "I have to tell you, I had a hell of a time tying it."

"That so?"

"Ain't worn a tie in a while, that's for sure. Not much occasion."

"Well, it looks just fine."

"Good." He sounded relieved.

I giggled. "Well, now that we've got that sorted out."

He laughed. "Jesus. Act like a couple of teenagers."

"I know it."

"Out on a first date."

"Silly."

He cleared his throat and I looked out the window. In the late-summer dusk, the fields were a rich, fresh green from the rain and the barns looked like stains on the darkening sky.

"Pretty night," I said. He was two feet away. I could hear him breathe. In the closed car, I could smell him, his own clean scent mixed with aftershave and soap.

"Sure is," he said. The air between us hummed. I thought of the instant when Arnold had held out his hand to me, asking me that night in New York to dance: the few seconds that I looked at his thick hand and then took it, tentatively, and followed him onto the floor.

We passed the sign for Staples and the Elks Club came into sight on a hill at the edge of town. The parking lot was packed and you could already hear the music and a dull roar of voices from inside. Frank pulled into a spot and let the car run.

I stared straight ahead.

"Claire," he said.

For one frantic second, I thought he would kiss me. How so many kisses in my life had begun with that one word, my name. I turned my head slightly toward him and studied the dashboard, weirdly remembering the night I lost my virginity, and the dashboard light, and the boy saying my name, once, and then not knowing how to ask.

It was easier then. Everything's easier when you don't know.

"Claire," he said again, and leaned forward to set the odometer. His voice, it suddenly occurred to me, was beautiful, and I wanted to turn to him and tell him about the night I lost my virginity, my God, twenty years ago! and how suddenly I was realizing one day Kate would know, it would happen to Kate, and probably Esau too, and how could

I explain to them? How could I tell them anything? Protect them from anything? And I sat there, twisting my hands in my lap, finding to my dismay that my ring finger was *bony, shrunken,* while the others were a regular size, and I turned to Frank, wanting to tell him everything, wanting just to fill the crowded air with words.

He put his hands on the steering wheel as if he were practicing driving.

"Arnold and I were friends," he said. He shut his eyes briefly, as if bracing himself. I sat there. "And I have to tell you, I feel a little funny. I just—" He gestured. "You know. Don't want to be disrespectful."

"Frank," I said. I opened and shut the glove compartment. I wanted to say, He's dead. I wanted to say, I left long ago, and I am sorry and unspeakably sad, but I am alive. I am alive, and you are alive, and I am lonely and you are too, and I am not ready for this but there are two feet between us and we are only going to dance. And if we only dance one night, this will be all right.

I said, "You're not."

"It doesn't look good," he said firmly.

"Who's looking?" I knew perfectly well who was.

"Minute we walk in that door, the whole town will be. All I'm saying. That's all right. That's all right," he repeated, talking to either himself or the dash. "All I'm saying is, well, *Jesus,* Claire, this is difficult. I tell you, I feel like a grave robber. I feel like I'm stealing another man's wife." He looked out at the supper club, agonized. "Which is not to say I am making any assumptions, either."

I studied his profile from the corner of my eye.

"I think I am not technically another man's wife. Anymore," I said hesitantly.

"Still."

"I know," I said.

"Still, I swear to God, Claire, I feel like he's sitting here in the car between us. Just sitting here, I swear to God."

"I know."

He looked at me finally. I smiled. Before I knew I was going to do it, I smoothed out his eyebrow. He stared at me.

"And see," he said, shaking his head slowly, "that's just it. That is just it."

I nodded.

"Because the hell of it is, I can't do a damn thing about it now, anyway, now, can I? I can't stop it now anymore than I can jump in front of a damn train." He pounded the steering wheel once with the heel of his hand. "That is the *hell* of it, Claire." He looked at me. "So we'd best go in and have dinner."

At the wide red door of the supper club, he straightened his tie. "Ready?" he said.

"They're looking."

We were dancing.

"Of course they are. They're looking at you," Frank said.

"They might just as easily be looking at you. That *is* a particularly fine tie."

"Oh, yes. I'd forgotten. Maybe that's it, then. My tie."

"Is it late?"

"Don't think about it."

"What should I think about, then?" I'd had a bit of wine, it seemed.

"Me." He looked shocked at himself, put his cheek closer to mine, not terribly close, nothing obvious. Just enough that his ear was near my mouth.

"Pretty light on your feet," he said, as if he were complimenting my begonias. I giggled.

"For an old girl, I guess I'm not too bad," I said.

"Heh!" he scowled, disapproving. He drew his face back to look at me. And he put his rough hand out on my face and his thumb against the corner of my eye. "Not hardly," he said gruffly, and the Motley-Staples Big Band played us a Viennese waltz.

As ten approached, I said I had to get home. It was raining again. He held his coat over my head and we ran to the car. The tires whooshed through the water on the road, and it ran in sheets over the windshield, wipers slapping. I hummed.

"Whatcha singin'?" he asked.

I laughed. "Lullaby."

He smiled. "You got the luckiest kids in the world," he said. He pulled into the driveway and let the car idle.

"Damnation, she let them stay up," I said, looking at the living-room light, glowing through the needles of rain. We sat there for a moment. Then I said, "I should get in."

He was looking at me. I could see him from the corner of my eye. "Too soon to kiss you," he said.

I wanted desperately for him to kiss me. I nodded.

"Thought so. You're right, a'course." He was embarrassed.

I laughed. He scowled.

"Well, how about I call you, then."

"That'd be all right."

He got out of the car and came around to my side and we ran up to the front door. I opened it and knocked over Kate, Esau, Davey, and Donna.

"Did he kiss you?" Kate shrieked, then saw Frank. "Did you kiss her?" she shrieked again.

"That is *so gross.*" Davey stood there with his arms crossed, disgusted.

"Go," Donna yelled, shooing the kids, "scoot!" She followed them like a hen.

Esau popped back around the corner and whispered loudly, *"Invite him in!"*

I turned to Frank, only to find him leaning in the doorway, laughing. He straightened up.

"I have to go kill them now," I said, grimly.

He nodded. "Right. Good night, Claire."

"Thank you for a lovely evening," I called as he went down the steps. He lifted his arm to wave. I shut and locked the door, then leaned back against it. I listened to my blood pound in my ears awhile. It matched the ticking of the grandfather clock, shadowed in the dark room, its brass gong reflecting the light from the moon outside.

I walked through the house, turning off lights, and sat down in the living room, imagining that I could hear my children breathe.

This is too soon, I thought, shaking my head. Too soon.

The heat.

I'd never slept well. The heat made it harder. Northern heat is just as fierce as the cold. They're the same thing turned inside out. They are a pressing, changeless, mute and brutal thing. You endure them. That's what they're for. No matter how long you live in the north, each time the mercury plummets or soars past livable points— points where you can, say, breathe without freezing your lungs or drowning—you're shocked. Your face snaps to the side with the force of an invisible hand.

I fed Esau and Kate, and they wanted to watch television, but when I went in to join them after I did the dishes, they'd fallen asleep on the couch. I woke them and they stumbled to bed.

The rain let up and ushered in a waiting silence, a pause before the rain began again. I went outside.

Though it wasn't the beating heat of morning and high noon, or the wet, sucking heat of the later day, the night's heat was thick and damp and all-encompassing because there was no such thing as shade. The night and the heat became the same thing.

In the summer, when I was a girl in the south, I'd lie naked on top of the covers, all the windows open, and listen to the night. The trick was to arrange my limbs on all the quilt's coolest places. If you turned the pillow carefully, you could always find a cold spot. I wondered at the lack of shyness. Where does that go? I dressed for bed even now, with no one to see me. And the idea of sleeping without a blanket, without at least a sheet, was somehow threatening. It seemed so uncovered.

I laughed out loud.

I stepped off the porch and made my way carefully through the dark, wet garden, feeling the plants for dead leaves and plucking them off. I ran my thumb over the serrated edge of a rose leaf, and touched the tip of my finger to a new bud still encased in green. Esau would know what the name of that is, I thought. That green. He would have a word.

We had named it Kate's Rosebush Jane.

"Wouldn't you rather have a more . . . interesting name?" I'd asked.

She'd shaken her head firmly. "No. Kate's Rosebush Jane. That's her name," she said.

The girl did know her mind.

I picked two roses in bloom and went back inside. I put them in juice glasses with water and went first to Kate's door. She had made it only as far as the side of the bed and seemed to have flung herself down any which way when she got there. She was asleep on her belly, still dressed, her feet in their white sandals dangling off the edge. I set the rose on her nightstand, took her shoes off, and turned her. She muttered. I tiptoed out and closed the door.

Esau was asleep with his blankets folded in a flag fold at the foot of his bed. He'd learned it at State. It was of critical importance. Every morning, he unfolded them and remade his bed. Every night, he folded them back up. He never used them. If he was feeling jittery, he'd go out and get the afghan and roll himself up like a sausage and fall asleep on the floor of his closet. Tonight he was on the bed. Hands folded on his stomach. He was too still. I went over to his side and leaned down to listen to his breath.

His eyes snapped open. "Hello," he said, startling the hell out of me.

"Shh!" I was never really sure he slept.

"Why?" he whispered.

"It's night."

"What are you doing?"

"Bringing you a rose."

He turned his head on the pillow to look. "Thanks!" he hissed, pleased.

"You're welcome." I set it on his nightstand. "Go back to sleep."

"All right." He shut his eyes. "Love you!"

"Love you too."

Kate thumped the wall. "Some people are trying to sleep," she hollered.

"Sorry," we whispered loudly.

I shut the door and began to cross the room. And then my eye caught on the dark hollow at the other end of the house.

The hallway was the same as it always was, and my bedroom was the same. But tonight it was a hollow again, the way it had seemed when he'd first died.

I continued to the bar for a glass of wine. I went to stand in the hallway. I leaned against the wall and studied my bedroom doorway.

They're mine now, I said to it softly.

I took a sip.

Thank you, I said, feeling cordial. For them.

I turned my back on it and sat down in the living room. I looked at the chair. I did love you, I said. Terribly. All that time. It just didn't work.

I stood up and went out to the porch. The fingernail moon sent out an arc of bright-white haze. I drank my wine slowly and realized I wasn't quite finished talking. I turned and went back in.

Because you weren't you anymore. Because you left me here, with all of this, years before you left. That's why. I gestured with my glass. I might have left, I said. I might have left you. But you left them.

Then I had a little bit of a cry, and it didn't feel half bad.

I took a breath when I was done, and drank the last of my wine, and set the glass on the coffee table.

Good-bye.

I stood and went into the kitchen. In the junk drawer I found a hammer and a nail. I took down the large, framed photograph of Kate and Esau that hung in the front hall, walked into the bedroom, and turned on all the lights. I lay the photograph on the bed, went over to the wide, unnaturally white spot on the wall, steadied the nail, and started hammering.

At which of course Kate and Esau shot out of their rooms and across the house, awake for the first time all day.

"What are you doing?"

"It's night!"

"We're sleeping!"

"Why are you hanging a painting?"

"Let's put the map there," Esau said. I yanked out the nail. Kate ran to get the map off the fridge. "Get tape!" I called. Esau ran to get a level. He came back with a footstool, a mechanical pencil, and a tape measure, along with the level, and now we were having a production. For the next half hour we hung the map of the garden, and then we needed a snack.

Sleepily, we sat on the bed and studied our work, eating peanut-butter toast.

"I like it there," Kate said thoughtfully.

"It looks good," I agreed.

"Crooked," Esau fretted.

"Don't touch it," I warned.

"It's okay?"

"I think it's perfect."

"I don't have to be perfect."

"Nope," I said. "You don't." I stood up and put my hand out for their plates. "Bed!"

For the first time in seven months, I closed my bedroom door.

Since he died, I'd taken an extreme interest in my skin. My bathroom sink was cluttered with bottles and soaps and pots of creams. I told myself it was a waste not to use my discount at the store. Really, I just liked the way I smelled. I washed up, put on my nightgown, and lay down, throwing the covers off and pulling the sheet up to my waist.

Then I lit a cigarette and smoked it.

It was my bed. I could smoke in it if I liked. I finished the cigarette, reached up to turn out the light, and lay there listening to the thick northern night, the chirr of crickets pouring into my ears.

"Mom!" Kate called. I was in the basement doing laundry. Three days had passed since the date, and I had been ignoring the ringing phone as if I was afraid of bad news or bill collectors. "What?" I called up.

"Frank's here. Should I let him in?"

"Well, for heaven's sake, Katie! Yes!" The child had no manners. I didn't know what I'd done wrong. I clipped the last of the whites to the line, straightened my skirt, took a deep breath, and went upstairs.

I found Kate in the kitchen. She was wearing a red silk nightgown of mine, several strands of beads, and a pair of my shoes. She also had Frank's cap on her head. She was pouring him apple juice. She peered out from under the cap and said to me, "I told him to sit in the living room."

And there he was, discussing the day's goings-on with Davey, whose boots stuck out from under my green silk dress. Esau was reading the newspaper to the baby, who lay on her back with a bottle in her mouth, listening attentively.

It was a gorgeous day. Frank stood up when I came into the room, surrounded by the September sunshine that flooded in. Kate clopped in and handed Frank his juice. He thanked her graciously. I had a hard time looking at him and smiled at my feet.

"Frank wants to know if we can go for a drive," Kate said, climbing up next to Davey on the couch. "He says we can stop for lunch in Brainard. I said we had to discuss it."

Frank was looking pretty pleased with himself, in his yellow short-sleeved shirt and combed hair.

"So we're discussing it," Kate went on. "I think it would be okay."

"It's okay with me," Davey said.

"Esau? Do you want to go?" Kate asked.

Esau stood up and folded the newspaper carefully. He brought over the desk chair and sat down, studying Frank.

"I have concerns." He gnawed lightly on his wrist, then caught me looking at him and stopped. "Concerns," he repeated, nodding. "For example, will you have us home before dark?"

"Absolutely."

"Yes. All right. And how old are you?"

"Esau," I said. Frank laughed.

"Thirty-six," he said.

Esau narrowed his eyes. "That's how old our dad was. When he died."

Frank looked at him seriously. "I know. Your dad was a friend of mine."

Esau's eyebrows shot up. "I did not know that," he said.

"Yep," Frank said. "We knew each other since we were your age."

"Oh." This was a major development.

"You're sitting in his chair," Kate said. One of my shoes fell off her foot and she scrambled down to retrieve it. Frank looked down appreciatively.

"Am I?" he asked. "It's a heck of a chair, that's certain."

"It is a very fine chair," Esau agreed. "He liked it very much."

"Can't blame him. Fellow's got to have a chair."

"Do you have a chair?" Kate asked.

"That I do. I have a chair in my library."

"Is it a La-Z-Boy?" Kate asked.

"You have a library?" Esau breathed. He pulled his knees up to his chest.

"No, it's not a La-Z-Boy, I'm sorry to say, and yes, I have a library. You know, it's funny," Frank said to Esau, "your mother and I were just discussing my library a few days ago, when she was kind enough to join me for dinner at the Elk's Club."

"She was gone for exactly three hours," Esau said into his knees. His eyes were wide.

"Well, yes," Frank said. "She had a curfew, didn't she?"

Esau nodded and gnawed on his knee. "I want to go for a drive. A drive is fine. I'll wear the special coat. What about the library?" Esau asked, wiggling his toes.

I watched Frank blink. "Well. Your mother was just telling me you were running a little low on books, is all. That so?"

"Yes. I have read all the ones at school, and Miss Kipp says pretty soon we're going to have to call Detroit Lakes and get them to borrow us some more because I am done with science and almost done with history, except for the Second World War."

"What's your opinion of the Moors?"

Esau stared at him. "I have no opinion of the Moors. What are the Moors?"

"Hup! What's this? They didn't give you anything on the Moors?"

"No," Esau said, looking worried. "What are they?"

"Well, you see," Frank said. "That settles it. We're going to have to raid my library."

"Yes please. That would be fine. All right, yes. Oh. I have to go now," he said, and stood up and walked stiffly into his room.

"That just means he's happy," Kate said to Frank. "He'll be right back. Watch this!" she said, and hopped off the couch and yanked the La-Z-Boy handle with all her strength, flinging Frank backward in his seat. "Isn't that great?"

"That's fantastic!" Frank said, horizontal. Kate shrieked with glee.

She climbed in next to him. "Davey, come over here," she commanded. Obligingly, Davey gathered his skirt, stepped carefully in a pair of my pumps over to where Kate and Frank lay, and climbed up.

Esau ran back into the room with a piece of paper and a pen. "How do you spell 'Moors'?" he asked, sitting down and sticking his tongue out of the corner of his mouth.

"M-o-o-r-s." Frank, Kate, and Davey stared up at the ceiling.

"We don't like you yet," Kate said cheerfully. "Right, Davey?"

Davey lifted his head to look at her. "*You* don't like him. I like him fine."

"Esau doesn't like him, either," Kate said. Frank lay there with his hands folded on his stomach, listening to this discussion with a grin on his face.

"That is not entirely accurate," Esau said. "It is not that we don't like you, Frank."

"Well, thank you," Frank said.

"You're welcome. We simply have concerns."

"I see."

Kate said. "Are you going to steal her? Because you can't have her."

"No, ma'am," Frank said seriously. "She's not mine to steal."

Kate sat up. "Whose is she?" She turned around. "Mom, whose are you?"

"Yours, silly," I said.

"Oh." Her face lit up. "Esau, she's ours. I told you."

"No you didn't. I told you."

"Oh yeah." Kate hopped off the chair. "Well, let's go already!" she yelled.

The kids dashed off to change. Frank sat up and smiled at me.

"You look funny in that chair," I said.

"You want I should get out of it?"

"If you don't mind."

"Not a bit." He came over to the couch and put his right ankle on his left knee. "Where's Donna?" he asked.

"She went home." I looked at him.

"Getting her things?"

"I don't know. As of four o'clock this morning, she didn't know either, and that's the last I heard." I shook my head. "I expect she'll come and go awhile longer. Nowhere feels like home to her right now."

"Huh."

We sat there.

I can't do it, I thought.

He touched my knee lightly. I stared out at the yard.

"You there?" he asked quietly.

I thought for a minute. I felt the entire length of his body next to mine on the couch, his heat emanating like a small autumn sun.

"Not quite," I said. "Not yet."

I saw him nod slowly from the corner of my eye. I saw him turn his face toward me. I glanced over. He leaned in and kissed my temple so softly it hurt.

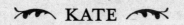 KATE

We had a plan to build a house. We would need a house, we figured, in case of unforeseen events such as Mom marrying Frank. And then we would have no parents. Because Dad was already dead.

Sometimes, I dreamed he was not.

Sometimes, I dreamed it was morning, and I came out of my room and sat down on the couch and he was there. In his chair. With his paper and his morning drink. I knew by then what it was, the booze, maybe I even knew it was what killed him. I can't remember when I realized that. What I do remember is that it was why he needed me; I saw the drink in his hand and knew he needed me to be in charge, so I sat down on the couch. It was always summer in my dream, with the warm late-morning light pouring into the room, all gold. And I didn't have school, in the dream, because it was summer, and so I nestled into the couch and pulled my feet up—I was still small in the dream, still six, though I had the dream for years—and put my chin on the armrest and gazed at my father. And he put down his paper and smiled. He said, "Well, Little Bit. What do you know?"

And I always laughed and shrugged, shy, and said, "Not much."

That was the end of the dream. I'd wake up and go out to the living room and sometimes curl up in his chair and look out the window at the dark.

Really it was fall, not summer, when we realized that we would need our own house. It was part of the backup plan, to be used in the event of an emergency, so Esau was staying up late drawing the blueprints on graph paper and showing them to us when we had our secret meetings after school. We were saving our allowances and also sometimes raiding the coffee can at Davey's house, under the sink, where Donna kept the mad money. The mad money was for extras anyway and they didn't need any extras, we decided. Also we raided Mom's stash, which was in her vanity, the heavy mahogany dresser where she sat putting on her makeup before a date with Frank. It had been her mother's and it would someday be mine, a day I worried about because I didn't want a vanity, I only wanted my mother, and if I got the vanity it meant she was gone. So I lay on the bed, watching her at her vanity, fixing her there in the mirror with my gaze. It's in the parlor, now, the garnet necklace in its secret drawer.

We found the secret drawer one afternoon that fall. My arm was halfway inside one drawer, feeling around for secret things, and my fingers fell on a little latch. I pushed it, then pulled it, and the bottom of the drawer slid back. We crowded our heads close to look, shoving for space. Esau announced, "I'm oldest. I get to look." Davey and I sat back on our heels while Esau reached in to pull out the contents of the drawer. Papers.

"Boring," I said.

He shook his head slowly, sitting on his knees and paging through the pile. "Money," he said. "They're bonds. And look at this." He held out a small square of paper to me.

It was Dad's death certificate.

"And this," Esau said. I took a folded sheaf of paper, looked at it, and said, "What is it?"

"Dad's life-insurance policy."

"What's that?"

"It's the money he left. He bought it in case he died."

"Is it a lot?"

Esau nodded, taking it back. "It's enough for our house. Plus some extra." He looked up. "We're rich," he said.

We stashed it with our other things, in a pale blue hatbox from Norby's, under Esau's bed.

Now we were safe. Protected, with a plan in the event of an emergency or unforeseen event.

We found out we needed a plan from Dale, who had been to Vietnam and lots of other foreign places in the service and who knew a lot about pretty much everything, we found out. Davey had said all along that his dad knew a lot of stuff, but we used to think he was mean, so we were afraid of him and didn't go to Davey's house almost ever. Turned out Dale wasn't mean at all, just a little funny in the head and also lonely. And since he was lonely, we sort of accidentally wound up visiting him, and he told us about the things he knew.

The first time we went it was definitely by accident. What I mean is, we went on purpose, but we didn't know he was there. And we were so startled when we figured it out that me and Davey sat on the back steps the entire time. Only Esau went down to see him. Dale pretty much lived in the basement, and Davey made Esau go say hi because we thought Dale's feelings might be hurt if we didn't. If we just walked in and then walked right back out without so much as a hello there. So as soon as Esau was downstairs, me and Davey hightailed it out to the steps. This was still back when we were scared of Dale. And they were down there talking for forever, so we got a little nervous and discussed between us should we go in and rescue Esau? When finally he came back out and shut the door behind him.

He leaned down to get his bike and looked at us. He said, "We have to get a plan."

So all that fall, since it turned out Dale was just lonely, we went to visit him. And he taught us all about knots and about how to use a bowie knife to skin a squirrel. And about how you should never shoot something you don't intend to eat, so unless you want squirrel stew, don't shoot a squirrel. I showed off my knots at school, no one made better knots. We were in second grade, me and Davey. Dale taught us about history and wars and how to tell if a thing was poison ivy or not. He went upstairs and brought down every single volume of the ency-clopedia so we could have it for our secret after-school meetings. He would lean forward, set his beer on the low table, and purse his lips around his cigarette. He'd open a volume. He started with A. And he would page through it until he found the important things. Then he'd stab the page with his skinny finger and say, "This here." And he'd lean back, take a big drag on his cigarette, and start talking, gesturing with his beer.

We learned everything in the world there was to know. To this day I remember what he taught us, waving his cigarette the way my father had, those eloquent scribbles of smoke. *Arlington. Battle of the Bulge. Chemical warfare. Destroyer,* also *Destroy.*

We would go in through the back door, and look to see if there were cookies—if Donna was staying at their house, she made cookies—and then Davey would lean down the stairwell and yell, "Dad? Are you here?"

And if Dale yelled, "Yep," we knew he was there.

After we were done, when it was time to go home or we'd get our butts busted for missing dinner, we'd shake his hand, me and Esau, and he'd kiss Davey's head.

Sometimes, he had spells. We would all be down there, sitting on the couch in a row. And Dale suddenly would stop talking and just stare straight ahead. Just sit there, not moving at all. We'd all get up, taking care not to jostle, and tiptoe up the stairs and out the door.

"He's here," Davey said, trotting back from the stairwell. "Get him cookies too."

I grabbed a couple extra. Esau went down first, then Davey. I went last because I was scared of the basement and wanted to be sure everything was all right before I went down. The basement was wet, and though I did not believe in monsters it was still a place where monsters, if they existed, would spend their time, especially wet monsters, who liked the dark. There were shadows in all the corners, thick, tall shadows that cloaked who-knew-what, and a room into which we were not allowed under pain of death to go. I had somehow linked this room in my mind to hell, and was under the impression that hell was in the back corner of Davey's basement, and Dale watched out at the gates of hell, sitting on the couch in his fatigues.

Besides which, you never really knew what would be going on inside Dale's head at a given time, so it was best to be cautious, I felt, on the stairs, and for that reason I dawdled on the way down until I heard him say, "Well, well, soldiers. What have we here?" In which case we knew he was not in a silence or a dark. Occasionally he would tell us to get the hell out, but not very often, and it was always worth a try because we figured there was no one to take care of him but us and we were up to the responsibility, especially Esau, who was in charge.

We filed across the room slowly, adjusting our eyes to the dark. From a small, high window came a thin, sharp stream of white light. It was almost winter, you could tell from the light. As fall went away, the light got cold.

"Well, well," said Dale, scooting over on the couch. "What have we here?"

"Us," said Davey.

"Us, sir," Esau corrected him. Since fall started, Esau had been getting weirder and weirder. He was busy all the time and referred to everyone as "sir."

"Us, sir," Davey said.

"Us, sir yourself," Dale said, and ruffled Davey's hair. I giggled. "How's by you, soldier?"

Davey shrugged, putting a cookie in his mouth and smiling around it. Spraying crumbs, he said, "We had pizza for lunch."

"Good man," Dale said, banging Davey on the back. He leaned forward and popped the top off a beer. "Katerina, did you bring cups?"

"Yes, sir," I said. "And cookies." I set them all down on the low table made from a huge old tree and sat down next to Davey. "We brought you extra because you're biggest. Sir."

Dale suddenly threw his head back and laughed his barking laugh. Sometimes he did that. Then he settled into his gravelly hack, pounded on his chest with his fist, turned his head to the side, and spat. "Heh," he said. "Heh." He shook his head, smiling as he poured a few sips of beer into my and Davey's cups. Esau got a whole beer. Dale got as many as he wanted, because they were his, after all.

We sat there peacefully with our beer and cookies, munching. Davey got the fuzz up his nose.

"Report!" Dale barked. "Esau first. Out of respect for the dead."

We all bowed our heads at the mention of Arnold. Dale had taught us not to cross ourselves, it was Catholic.

"First period!" Esau barked back. "Mathematics! Superior performance on Tuesday's test! It was an easy test, though," he said apologetically.

"No matter. A superior performance is always required regardless of duty." Dale stood up and walked to the back room of the basement, where we were not allowed to go. He came back and handed Esau a dull green cap. "Well done." He sat back down. "Proceed."

"Second period! Gym, sir," Esau said grimly.

"And?"

Suddenly light spilled down the stairs.

"Down the hatch!" Dale whispered, and the three of us tipped our beers back. "Turn in your supplies!" he hissed, and we passed our cups and Esau's bottle over. "All right! Move out! Into the back room! Follow me!" He stood up and, bent over at the waist, scuttled around the corner. We, bending over, followed suit.

The four of us stood breathing in the damp dark.

"Does she know you're here?" came Dale's hushed voice.

"Our bikes are out back," Esau whispered.

"Damn! Dammit. Next time, walk, soldiers! You got legs, last I looked."

"Sorry, sir," Esau said.

"S'all right. She's gonna have my hide. Davey, c'mere."

There was a thumping and something got knocked over with a crash.

"Jesus Christ, Davey! Watch where you're going! That was a gun, for Chrissakes!"

"I can't *see!*" Davey said plaintively.

"Whaddaya mean, you can't see?"

Donna's voice came down the stairs. "Hello? Dale? Are you down there? You better say no, I'll tell you right now."

Panicking, Davey yelled, "No!"

There was a terrible silence.

"Davey?" Donna called with frightening calm. "Is that you?"

"What do I say?" Davey whispered, frantic.

"Say yes, for God's sake! She don't think it's *me!*" Dale replied.

"Yes!" Davey called.

"What are you doing down there?" she called. We'd had a pact never to tell her or our mom where we went on our after-school expeditions.

"We're just talking!" Davey yelled, his voice shrill.

"We?" The stairs started to creak.

"Shit!" Dale said. "All right." He herded us into the tiny closet of a bathroom, shutting the door behind us. "Latch it!" he whispered. And he went out to meet his wife.

We stood crowded around the toilet, looking up at the pipes. The slats around the toilet pressed us in on four sides. Finally, Davey sat down on the toilet to make more room.

"What the hell's going on down here?" we heard Donna demand.

"Not a thing," Dale said, his voice flat. We heard the refrigerator door open and close, and the spit of a bottle top coming off. Then the thin metallic *ting* of the cap being tossed to the concrete floor. "Not that you trouble yourself to be around much to know." The couch's broken springs squealed under his weight.

We heard nothing for a moment. Then, Donna said, "Where are they?"

"Who's that?"

"Jesus Christ, you sonofabitch." She sounded calm, like they were just having a regular conversation. "Where in the fuck are the kids?"

"Watch your language, woman. Isn't fitting."

"Oh, go to hell, Dale. Just tell me where Davey and the others are and I'll let you sit here and drink your sorry self into a puddle, don't matter none to me what you do with your time. Ain't like you got a job to be at."

The springs squealed again, followed by a sound like a firecracker. Davey jumped and grabbed my hand.

Donna laughed.

"That's the best you can do?" she asked. "You gonna hit me for saying what I see? All right. I see one sorry motherfucker drinking himself to death when he's got two babies and a wife to take care of, that's what I see. I see some crazy motherfucker who can't get it up to—don't! Git off me!"

We burst out of the bathroom to find Dale wrestling Donna to the ground, the two of them grappling on the floor. "Dale, stop! The kids!" Donna yelled.

Dale turned his head and was on his feet in an instant, backing away from her, his palms flat out to her. He was red faced and his hair fell over his eyes. "No harm," he said, breathing hard and tossing his hair back like a restless horse. "No harm."

The three of us stood there and watched Donna get up off the floor. She stood with her hands on her hips, the left side of her face burning red.

"What're you doing here, anyway?" she asked.

Davey shouted, startling everyone, "I live here! He's my dad! I live here!"

Donna stared at him. Then she looked at Dale, though she was speaking to Davey. "No you don't. You pack yourself some things and be at Claire's in time for supper." Now she looked at Davey. "Don't you make me come get you. 'Cause I will." She looked back at Dale. "And you won't like that."

"Damn right," Dale mumbled. He sank down onto the couch and tipped his beer back.

He raised his beer to her retreating back as she went up the stairs.

He looked at us. His eyes were sad. He patted the couch next to him and we all piled on.

"Tell you one thing," he said, shaking his head. "We don't get along so good, but I sure did love your momma. Time was, I'll tell you." He put his arm on the back of the couch and petted Davey's head. "I sure did." He looked at Davey to see how he took this. "Easy to love a woman," he said. "Not so easy, getting her to love you. See how it is?"

Davey, glaring at his lap, finally nodded. I took his hand.

"Want a new beer?" Dale said, standing up and going to the fridge.

It was late fall. That day, it had snowed, fat flakes that clung to the grass and pavement when they touched down, then disappeared. At recess, we had chased them, grasping at them as if they were butterflies. When we came out of school, Esau was there at his usual post by the telephone pole, his face turned up to the sky, his tongue sticking out of his mouth.

"Hiya," I said as we approached, startling him. He stared down at us as if he was seeing us from a long way away.

"Almost winter," he said.

Davey and I stood there holding our books.

"Yeah, so?" I said.

Esau shrugged and turned away, starting down the sidewalk toward home. "Just saying," he said.

Mom and Frank were still going on dates. Esau and Davey and I had stepped up our plans accordingly. We figured if they were going to keep on dating like this, it could only lead to one thing. That night, Mom paced in circles in the living room.

"Mom, no offense, but you're making me a little anxious," Esau said, not looking up from his book. "Nothing serious, but a little and I wish you would sit down."

Mom sat down on the couch. "What time is it?" she asked.

Esau looked at his watch. "Five-oh-four."

"Oh, hell." Mom dropped her head onto the back of the couch.

"Perhaps you should have started getting ready a little later."

"Perhaps."

"Would you like to play Scrabble?"

"Sure," she said, surprising me.

"You know you'll lose," I said.

"I know," she said.

Esau set up the board. "Madam," he said. "Your Scrabble is served."

"Thank you," she said. He pulled out her chair at the table and scooted her in. I got up and went over to watch. He sat down across from her, bowed his head, and stuck his hand out for her to shake it. "Good gamesmanship," he explained. He passed her the bag of tiles. "*A*'s high."

She drew an *o*, he a *b*.

"Sorry," he said, took out his letters, looked at them for a second, and spelled out *decoded* before she'd even gotten her letters arranged. "Sorry," he said again.

"What for?" she asked.

"Seven-letter word. Fifty bonus points."

"Is that true?"

He looked at her, dumbfounded. Esau didn't lie, hardly ever. "Never mind," Mom said, and handed him the bag of tiles. Her letters spelled nothing.

"You have the *x*," he said. "You could spell *ox*."

"I don't want to waste it. How do you know I have the *x*?"

He shrugged. "It's not in the bag."

"You felt around for it?" He did that.

"Not exactly."

She spelled *ox*.

"What time is it?" she asked. He looked at his watch. "Aha!" he said, and leaped up. He went into the kitchen and came back with a glass of milk, two cookies, and his evening medicine. "Five-one-three."

"I want cookies," I said.

"Go get some," he replied, still watching his watch. I did, and when I came back, he said, "And now it is five-one-five," and tossed the pills back with a swallow of milk. He put a cookie in his mouth and spelled *boxite*, hitting a double-word score on his way by.

"Is there such a thing as *boxites*?" Mom asked. He shook his head.

Davey exploded into the house, with Donna behind him, Sarah bobbing on her hip. Davey climbed up on a chair at the table and looked at Mom.

"Are you going on a date?" he asked her.

"I guess so."

"What is a date?" I demanded, feeling left out.

"Kate!" Esau sighed. "I have explained this and explained this."

Mom looked at him. "You have?"

He shrugged, looking guilty.

"What did you tell her?" Mom asked.

"He told me Frank was trying to steal you," I piped up spitefully.

"You did not!" Mom said to him.

"No, I did *not*," he said, pounding the table. His tiles jumped off his rack and he replaced them, scowling. "I said he was going to *borrow* you some of the time now."

I pulled my feet onto the chair and sat on my knees. "He can't have you, you know." I reached over and picked up Mom's hand, studying her nail polish.

"He doesn't have me! He isn't going to have me!" Mom said, frustrated. We looked at her, baffled.

Davey, to make things better, recited, "Mrs. Schiller, you look very nice this evening. That is a lovely new dress. Is it new?" He'd confused himself, and furrowed his brow.

"Thanks, Davey," Mom said.

"You're welcome," he said, relieved.

"I don't think you look nice," I said nastily, and for some reason bit her thumb, hard. "At all." I turned her hand over and fit my forehead into her palm.

"Kate!" Esau shouted. "You are *not* helping."

We sat around the table, being miserable together.

Davey shifted in his chair so that he was sitting on his knees. "Tarnation," he said, stumped.

"I'll say," I mumbled into the table.

Esau got up and went into the kitchen. He came back with the baby and slumped in his chair, holding her.

"How long do you suppose you'll be gone?" he asked Mom.

"A couple of hours?" she said.

"How many hours exactly?"

"Three."

I lifted my head and sighed. She stretched her hand.

"And then you'll be back," Esau said.

"Of course I will. This is where I live. I live here with you."

Esau narrowed his eyes at her. "Things change," he said accusingly.

"What changes?"

"Everything!" I exploded, and stood up, and ran over to the couch and kicked it. I came and sat back down. "*Everything* just goes around changing all over the place. Right, Davey?"

Davey nodded. "Yep."

"Like for example we used to have a dad," Esau said flatly. "That changed."

"Yeah," I said. We glowered at her.

"Well, anyway," she said weakly. "I won't be gone but a few hours."

I snorted. "That's what they all say. Who said you could go, anyway?" I demanded. "I never said you could go. Esau never said. Davey never said. How come no one ever asks *us*?" I kicked her under the table.

She grabbed my foot and held on to it. "I said." She stared at me. "I said, because I am in charge."

That was a new idea. We let it sink in.

"But he can't keep you," I said. My chin started to quiver. "Okay?"

"Okay. Are we done with this?"

I nodded.

"Esau?"

"We will adjust our routine," he said to me. "It will be all right. He won't steal her. I told you."

I nodded again, slid off my chair, and slunk to the kitchen for more cookies. Davey followed me at a gallop. We got some and stood there eating them.

"Since when is she in charge?" I complained.

Davey stuck his hands in his pockets. "Since always, I guess."

I glared at him. "Whose side are you on, anyway?"

"Yours, stupid. I'm just saying."

"Well, don't. Now she's going to go marry Frank, I bet."

Davey shrugged. "Probably. But we have a plan. And plus, we could always stay with my dad."

I thought about that. "Okay," I said, and turned to go back in the living room. Then I turned back. "Are you going to go to the war?"

He looked at his feet. "Course I am."

"You can't."

"Who says?"

"I say!" I yelled, and stalked out of the kitchen.

"It's your go," Esau was saying.

Mom spelled *trees*.

"You shouldn't waste your *s*," Esau advised. She took it back. He spelled *equator*, and got a triple-word score and fifty bonus points.

Mom stared at the board. "What time is it?" she asked.

"Mother, you're obsessing," he said.

"Just tell me."

"Five-two-seven."

"Got ready a little early?" Donna asked, coming into the room.

"Shut up." Mom stared at her letters. "Should I have a drink?"

"No. Arrive sober. It's only polite."

"Donna, I think we should be giving Sarah carrots," Esau said. "She should be ready for vegetables and some cereals. I've been reading," he explained.

She looked at him. "Well all right, then," she said.

"All right." He nodded. "Mother, it's your go."

"I can't go."

"Of course you can. Want me to look?" he asked.

"No. I mean out. Tonight. I can't go."

"You're going," Donna said.

"You most certainly are," Esau agreed. "We have figured it out now. It will be fine. Right, Kate?"

I put my chin in my hands and said nothing. Mom spelled *hell*.

"Can't use it," Esau said.

"Why not?"

"Proper noun."

"It is not."

"What is it, then?"

"It's—a *curse*," she said, exasperated.

"Can't use those."

She dumped my letters on the board. He carefully took a look at them and spelled *holster*.

"I quit," she said.

He looked at his watch. "It's only five-three-six. Plus, I'm winning. You'll forfeit."

"I don't care."

"You are not showing very good gamesmanship," he said, tallying up the numbers. "You lose."

She stalked off to her room.

Esau looked at me and Davey. "It's five-five-one. Should I go tell her?"

"No," I snapped. "Let her be late."

"Mom," Esau said, running down the hall, pointing at his watch. He stopped at her door and looked in. "It is five-five-two."

We heard her ask, "Should I go?"

He stared at her blankly. "It will take you exactly five minutes to get there. Do you want to be late?"

She came out and kissed him on the top of his head. He tugged her sleeve twice, patted her stomach, and walked off down the hall.

Mom kissed Davey and me and left. We sat there, arranging letters on the Scrabble board.

"Esau's not getting weird, is he?" Davey asked.

I looked up sharply. "No."

Outside, at six o'clock, it was already pitch black.

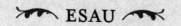

ESAU

When it happened, it was the beginning of winter. On the walk to school, the first snows hung heavy on the fir branches, falling off with their own weight. When it happened, there was never any light. We woke up when it was dark, and when we walked home from school it was already dusk, a purplish gray. It felt comforting, like a quilt of winter settling down around my shoulders, keeping me safe.

I was not sad. I had only just been feeling a little fragile, was all.

Just sort of like I was shatterable, and so it was better in my room with the door closed and I slept sometimes in the closet and got back in bed so I was there when Mom woke me up. Well, I didn't exactly sleep in the closet. I just stayed there, awake. But I took my things in with me, the things I kept in case of emergency, the blanket for heat, and the antifreeze, and the jumper cables, and a flashlight and also my notebook and charcoals and a book on Frank Lloyd Wright because I was designing a house.

Frank Lloyd Wright is a character, I am telling you. I liked his thinking. Clean, flat lines that don't mess with the shape of a place. No excess in Frank Lloyd's houses. No curves. A curve is not a real line. Well, sort of it is, but it looks like it could just go off by itself just about anywhere before you had the situation under control. So no curves in my Frank Lloyd Wright prairie house that I was designing for me and Kate and Davey when we had our money saved up. By the time we were on our own, which who knew when that could happen, we would be pretty well set and it was best to be prepared was our motto. And so we could build a house in the event of unexpected catastrophe such as Mom marrying Frank and Donna leaving Dale so that we had no parents.

So I was designing the house because for some reason neither Kate nor Davey could draw worth a damn. And anyway I was biggest so I got to decide what went where.

Which is all beside the point anyway because all I was saying was Frank Lloyd Wright has a house in the desert. We have never seen a desert and we don't know what it looks like except from *The Ten Commandments* with Charleton Heston on TV and we're pretty sure there are snakes. Frank Lloyd Wright also has a house in Wisconsin, which is right next door. And both these houses are like mazes. They keep a person safe, contained. And since Frank Lloyd Wright spent like years sleeping out in the desert just to get the feel of the place, it made sense that I spent time in my closet trying to capture for us the feel of *very safe.*

And anyway, once fall started like usual I was feeling kind of fragile. Because it always starts in fall and then it goes downhill from there. So I was saving up my medicines for in case of an emergency such as an episode, which was entirely possible. I was going pretty crazy feeling like my skin had come off in the bath or something, and now all my nerves were on the outside of me, getting brushed up against and bumped and jangled all the time and I started to get that feeling again that everything could get at me, with its hands, that things were going to get me and maybe eat me, it was that scary. Like it always is. But what I had learned in State was this, to go to a safe place and 1. CONTAIN yourself, 2. DISTRACT yourself, to 3. CALM the fear. CDC. It was easy to remember. It was like STOP DROP ROLL. SDR. Easy. Under my desk, into the closet as need be. Also useful in the event of an earthquake or nuclear fallout.

Which meant that despite the fact I was all nerves and jangling and despite the fact that I was all crashing and cymbals inside my head, and the thing had started again where it felt like there wasn't much of a wall between *me* and a thing *outside of me,* such that for example we would be sitting at dinner and gradually all the sounds would move from *outside* to *inside my head* like the forks and knives grinding on china would get lodged in my left ear (cochleal area) and the clock behind me would move *into my skull and keep ticking,* at the base of my skull, and just sit back there ticking, over and over, ticking and ticking, and Kate to my right drinking water in big gulps as if she were sitting on my shoulder gulping loud on purpose just to drive me crazy, which she wasn't, and the light fixture with its one flame-shaped bulb that flickered just a little came *into my right eyeball* and flickered there, making it impossible to see out of that eye and also I had to press the heel of my hand into it to make it stay a little stiller, and then the talking, talking, talking, all of them at once and the baby crying and I would put my hands over my ears and scream and Mom would right away hustle me to my room to wrap up in the quilt and have a little song and rock while we sat on the bed.

My mom is really good at being a mom, especially since my dad died. I bet she was sort of bored before she had kids. She cracks up when I say this and I like to make her laugh. I am pretty good at making people laugh and I figure even if I don't get the joke, they did, so they can have it.

Anyway it didn't happen very often and I learned at State it's just sensory overload. I pictured it in my head like blinking red neon lights, SENSORY OVERLOAD, and a big loud horn sounding in my head and the fireman's bell. At State, Staff said that was a pretty cool thing, that I had that kind of forewarning and could get to shelter quickly.

So when I was hoarding my medicines unfortunately it turned out to lead to sensory overload. And to feeling like I was a raw nerve. I drew a picture like that and hid it. A picture of me covered with my nervous system. It is pretty good.

The nervous system is the most amazing thing possibly ever. The human body is a giant walking electrical storm. So if you have ever seen an electrical storm on the plains, like I have, well, it is something else let me tell you. It is a thing to make you afraid of God. And that is what it is like inside the human body *all the time*. Basically we're made of lightning. A very complicated, very precise map of electrical sites that cast lightning bolts at each other and they light up and cast them somewhere else. Spine to brain to foot. Amazing. And what is even more amazing is that this whole system and also parts of the organs can keep right on functioning with or without any effort on your part, *even in a coma or after we are dead for example,* though very briefly. That would be enough to make me not want to be the mortician because suddenly this dead body kicks you. Or lifts its hand. Like it has something to say. That would freak me out for sure and you have to have a strong stomach to be the mortician. Also there is something very weird about putting a *tag* on a *dead toe*. Kate and Davey both say it's no different than a live toe and so I guess I am the only one who thinks that.

The picture took me *two weeks*. I worked on it at night. I taped it to the wall and drew it standing up, to perfect scale so it was exactly the size of me, so I would have *a sense of me* and also of just how intricate the nervous system really was. I did the spinal column first and then the head. There are a lot of nerves. It is hard to draw fast enough to keep up, but it is very exciting work so you are very motivated and don't want to go to sleep so it is important not to take your medicines which make you sleep. Also the excitement is sort of like a race where you can't stop. Which sometimes scares me but I always forget that part and only remember the progress. Like when I was simultaneously drawing the electrical system of me and the blueprint for the house. I would go back and forth and back and forth because when you are doing your best work it is important not to lose your momentum, important not to let a thought slip, and thoughts are slippery things, they can get away if you don't get them down on paper *right away* so it is important to have a lot of paper around just in case. And my brain would go *click* and it was time to work on the body and then it would be some hours later and my brain would go *click* and it would be time to work on the blueprint. And back and forth like this and I have to say I am pretty impressed with how I kept up with my brain, which was pretty busy. There was a lot of lightning. The brain was superhard. So were the hands. Turns out there are tons and tons of nerves in the hands, also in the tongue. And so but what I was thinking as I was doing the brain, which looks like a road map (and actually I drew it from several angles so you could really get a good look at the frontal and posterior lobes), was that the medicines were *messing with my nerves*. Of course they were, that was their whole point. They were *interfering with the system*. And I have to say I just couldn't see how that was a good thing at all, though I did not like the episodes any better than anybody else but I was figuring out a way to have the *very productive part* without the *crazy thing that always happens, which I hate.*

But so I didn't know how the electrical impulses looked was the problem. I didn't know what directions the medicine sent them. I could not accurately assess their activity or record their whereabouts. I could not keep a log. So I decided that in the interest of accuracy I would, for a length of time later to be determined, stop taking my medicines. Plus which, since pretty soon Davey and Kate and me were probably moving into our new house, it was best to be prepared was our motto, and you have to have a contingency plan like Dale said so we saved up the medicine for in case.

I don't really remember the episode. And anyway it was a minor episode so I didn't have to go back to State, about which I guess I was pretty much relieved though State is awfully nice and safe what with the Staff and the locks. In general I like locks. Mom won't let me have a lock on my door because then she can't get in, which she is not okay with, she says. I can see how she would feel that way but I would still like a lock. As of before the episode, she was considering letting me have padlocks that she knew the combination for so she could get in in the event of an emergency, but now she won't ever, I can already tell. And we can't have our new house until we are like *grown-ups*.

I don't really know why I had the episode and everything else went all to hell, it kind of happened all at once. And I wish it had all not started in the first place because now Mom is always watching. It wasn't even that good an episode insofar as I did not get that much, comparatively speaking, done. Two drawings is *completely nothing* for an episode whereas usually I get sometimes hundreds. And as for numbers, well, this episode was a complete *zilch*. Turns out all the equations I did are wrong now that I look at them, like *so wrong* I can't imagine what I was thinking when I did them. It all seems like a million years ago since what happened yesterday.

But to explain that you have to know what happened before that so I will go back.

It was around three o'clock in the morning when I opened my door slowly and tiptoed across the dark house to the dark kitchen for a glass of water. I nearly tripped over Mom, who had come for the same thing.

"Good evening," I said, reaching over the side of the sink.

"Well, hello there. Can't sleep?"

"I could. I prefer not to. I am busy."

"What are you busy with?"

"I am designing a house."

"Is that so?"

We stood there in the dark, drinking our water. She poured another glass. "You want to show me your design?" she asked.

"It isn't finished," I said. "When it's finished, I'll show you." I was quiet for a second. "You can come to my room, though."

We felt our way through the living room to my door. We moved some papers aside and sat down on my bed with our feet sticking off. My desk lamp was on. I looked around and realized with some nervousness that it might look a little funny, the state of affairs in my room. The desk and floor were covered with books. Sheets and bits of paper covered the books and the carpet and bed. My handwriting which is pretty much a tight scribble covered the paper, every inch of every page filled. I had written first horizontally, and then turned the paper and written across it again, so that it looked like cross-stitch. I turned my pen in fast cartwheels over my fingers. It was a trick I had learned at State, for use when I was for example feeling superbusy, to relieve stress.

"They're running out of books for me again," I said sadly. "I have already gotten all the way through science and I am approximately three quarters of the way through history. All I have left is the Second World War." I stared at my desk, glum.

"Is that as far as history goes?" Mom asked.

"At the library," I said, rolling my eyes at her. Sometimes I wondered if she ever paid any attention to the facts at all. Then again, she was pretty smart, and she knew more than me, anyway, about the state of affairs in general. "Not really. But Miss Kipp at the library says history is always being written."

"That's true."

"She says it is a dark chapter in history. Right now."

Mom nodded. "She's right."

"She made me promise not to tell anyone she said that. In case they thought she was unpatriotic." I looked up at Mom, worried that I had broken Miss Kipp's trust. I loved Miss Kipp with all my heart and self.

"I see." Mom smiled.

"I don't think she's unpatriotic," I said.

"No."

Relieved, I turned around on the bed so that I faced the wall. I picked at the edge of my wallpaper, which was coming off nicely. I had made a huge hole in it, almost the length from the pillow to the foot of my bed. It kept my hands busy. I started working on the area above my pillow. "So I am keeping a record of events," I said. "As they occur."

"Is that what all this is?" She gestured out at the room. Which I had to admit to an outsider might look a little messy, though it was not really messy at all.

"Obviously. So much is happening all the time." I turned my face to look at her. "It is an enormous undertaking." Suddenly the weight of it, the fact of it, overwhelmed me and made me cold.

She studied my face. "Lovebug, have you been taking your medicine?"

"Of course." I scowled and looked back at my wallpaper hole. I worried my thumb under a blue corner, got hold of it, and ripped. "You give it to me, don't you?" I asked reproachfully.

"But do you take it?" she asked, getting worried. "Have you been hiding it?"

"Has Frank kissed you?" I suddenly wanted to know. I had been dying to know. It made all the difference, it was the *central question this minute.*

"Esau, answer me right now!"

"No I have not been hiding it!" I shrieked. Kate pounded the wall and I pounded back twice, which meant *shut up!*

"You have! Haven't you?"

That was when it happened. I launched myself off the bed and across the room and started beating my head on the wall.

What happens is you see yourself from *outside* when it happens. You watch yourself for example pressed to the wall like it is something you want to be inside, flailing in your Spiderman pajamas, and you watch your head beat on it like a hammer.

Then you watch her, though in real life you would not be able to see her (she is *behind* you) fly off the bed toward you, her arms reaching to pull you back.

She yanked me backward, I wriggled like mad and she pulled me to the floor, I shrieked, "Has he? Has he? Has he kissed you?"

She held my wrists behind my back with one hand and rubbed my temples with the other, which calmed me a little bit, sort of. I wanted my dad. I screwed my eyes up tight and pictured my dad.

"No," she said. "Of course not."

I wanted my dad to run in and grab me and wrap me up in the quilt that Great-grandmother Katerina had made so that I would be safe. But my dad was dead. If my dad wasn't dead, he would call the doctor and I would tell him everything. If he wasn't dead, he would tell Frank to go *straight* to hell, whether or not he kissed my mom. If he wasn't dead, for that matter, Frank who I liked but wanted to go away wouldn't be coming over all the time in the first place.

I desperately did not want to go back to State. Even though it was safe. If I went back to State who knew how long they would keep me and what all could happen when I was in there. Last time for example my dad died. And he had said to hang in there and I was going to hang in.

I turned my face to the side. "I'm ready to get up now," I said.

"I don't think so."

"I will not bang my head if you let me up."

"Are you sure?"

"Very sure. I don't want to bang my head."

"You did a minute ago."

"I know. It was a bad choice."

"What choice would you make now?"

I studied one of the papers near my nose. "I would like to go in the closet."

At State they encouraged me to remember that closets were for clothes, not people, but that in emergencies it might be necessary.

"Is this an emergency?" she asked. "Have we run out of other options?"

"Has Frank kissed you?"

"No."

"You're lying."

"I'm not. Do you need to go in the closet, or could we wrap you in the afghan?"

"Closet."

She let me up and I walked meekly to the closet, swung open the door, and sat down, tucking my legs up and wrapping my arms around them.

"You can come over here," I said. "And talk to me."

She sat down with her back against the foot of the bed. We faced each other below a row of ironed shirts. I liked to iron.

"Kiddo, you've got to tell me," she said. "I think you've been hiding your medicine. And not taking it. And that's why you're up all night. And that's why there's all this paper, with all this scribbling on it—"

"It is not scribbling!" I shouted, and whacked the closet wall with the back of my hand. I put my knuckles to my mouth and sucked on them. "There are important, very important things there," I said through my fingers. "They are encoded. They are for me. Me, not anybody else. I am working out a system. That is why it is encoded."

"I apologize," she said. She sat there with her bare feet sticking out from under her nightgown. "You know what?" she said.

"What."

"We're a hell of a pair," she said.

"Yes." I nodded, feeling miserable.

"You've been hiding your medicine."

I tipped over and lay on my side, still facing her, my arms wrapped around my legs.

"I have been saving it," I said quietly, "for emergencies."

She nodded. "How long have you been saving it?"

I shrugged. "Two weeks."

"You have quite a bit saved up, then."

I nodded.

"Did you think you would run out?"

I shrugged. "I just thought it would be good to be prepared."

"For what?"

I poked the floor and recited, "Best to be prepared. Never want to be caught with your pants around your ankles. Never want to wonder where your next meal's coming from. Gotta plan for the contingencies." I sat up. "This is only a test. In the event of a real emergency, we will broadcast a high, sharp tone. Watch this," I said, and dove under my bed. I hauled out a folded gray wool blanket, the first-aid kit, a gallon of water, a tangled set of jumper cables, four moldy oranges, a jug of antifreeze, and a twenty-pound bag of rock salt. I sat back on my heels and walked along like a crab, putting them in order. Then I walked, crablike, into the closet.

"We're saving money too," I said, pleased with the pile of my things.

"Who is this we?" she asked, looking in wonder at the pile. It was everything from the back of her car. The things you were supposed to have with you if you got stranded in the snow. So you wouldn't freeze to death. It happened.

"Kate and me. Obviously." I rolled my eyes.

"So you were saving these things. And your medicine. Where's that?" she asked casually.

I shook my head firmly. "Gotta keep it in a warm, dry place. Says so on the bottle. Can't risk it. Gotta keep it safe. It's the backup plan."

Her head snapped toward me.

"Not what I meant," I said, putting my head in my hands. "Not to *off* me!" I pounded my thigh, frustrated. "I have no such plan of attack." I sighed. "Not to, I promise. Merely in the likely event of an episode."

"But that's why you have episodes!" she nearly yelled. I scooted backward in the closet and glowered at her. She looked like she wanted to shake me. "You have episodes when you don't take your medicine, remember? That's what it's for. You get dark, Esau, you get like this, confused, and you hate it!"

I stared at her.

"You don't remember it, do you?" she asked, as if realizing it for the first time.

I shook my head and turned so I lay on my back with my neck up one wall of the closet and my feet on the other.

"You just remember the good part. Where you have lots of ideas."

I nodded. "I get the answers."

"You record the events."

"Exactly." I smiled and slapped the carpet, pleased.

She sat plotting.

"Will you be all right if I get up and go to the bathroom for a minute?"

"You're not going to the bathroom," I said calmly. "You're going to call the doctor."

"Do you mind if I call the doctor?"

"I have no need of a doctor." I turned my head and gazed at her, my eyes low lidded, like a snake's.

We sat there, trapped.

"Kate!" Mom finally yelled.

"Pete's sake! What?" I heard her shout through the wall.

"Get in here!"

I heard her fall out of bed and open her bedroom door. She appeared, her quilt wrapped around her shoulders. She blinked and took in the situation.

"Are you in a dark?" she asked me.

"No," I said. "Definitely not."

"Go get Donna," Mom said.

"What's wrong with you, then?" Kate asked me. "What are you doing in the closet?"

"Kate!" Mom said. "Go get Donna right now."

"I am in the opposite of a dark," I explained.

"Oh." She crinkled her nose at me. "Are you seeing pictures?"

I folded in half and put my head to my knees. She said to Mom, "Betcha he's seeing pictures. He sees pictures, you know." She turned and trailed down the hall to get Donna.

Mom looked at me. "Are you seeing pictures?" she asked.

"They're mine."

"I know. I'm just asking."

"That isn't your business, madam." I chewed the cuffs of my pajamas.

I heard Donna's feet slapping down the hall. She came in and saw me and put her hands on her hips. "How many days has he been up?" she demanded. They looked at me.

"Four," I mumbled, peeking out between my knees.

"Jesus Christ," she breathed, winded. "Claire, who's your doctor? Christ almighty," she said, looking around my room.

"Parker. Tell him it's an episode."

"Not an episode," I shouted into my knees.

Kate stepped gingerly across the floor, moving papers out of the way with her toes. "Can I come in there too?" she asked. I scooted over to make room for her. She sat with her back against the wall and looked at her feet. She patted my knee. "You want I should go get the emergency medicine?"

Davey wandered into the room, shoved paper and books off my bed, climbed in, and promptly fell asleep. Davey could sleep through anything.

"What?" Mom said. "You've been hiding it for him?"

Kate looked guilty. She screwed her mouth up and said, "He asked me to and I said I would and it's none of your business anyway so never mind." She crossed her arms.

"It's her business now," I said. "You can tell her."

"Why?" Kate asked.

"'Cause she already found out."

"How?"

"How should I know? She found out, is all. Nothing to be done. Might as well tell her the whole thing."

Kate looked at me skeptically, then said to Mom, "We hid his medicines."

"So I hear."

"We wanted them in case of contingencies. In case of an episode. This is an episode, isn't it?" she asked me.

"No."

"It is, isn't it?" she asked Mom. Mom nodded. Kate's eyes widened. She whispered loudly, "I'll go get the emergency medicines," hopped up, and ran out of the room.

A while passed while me and Mom had a staring contest.

"Will you take your medicines now?" Mom said.

"Negative."

"Why not?"

"I do not presently need them."

"Yes you do."

"Nevertheless I will wait for the doctor's orders."

She sighed. We waited. The hands of the Mickey Mouse clock made their way around. After a while, Donna and Doc Parker walked in, looking exhausted. Doc Parker nodded to my mom, set his bag down on the floor, loosened his tie, and crouched in front of the closet. "How's it going in there, young man?"

I sat cross-legged, facing the corner of the closet, my back as stiff as a Zen monk's.

"All right if I join you?" the doctor asked me. He untied his polished oxblood shoes, stepped out of them, lined them up neatly, and crowded his long limbs into the closet. He looked like Alice in Wonderland, trapped in there, three times the size of everything else, including me. I leaned back into Doc Parker's shoulder and sighed.

"Looks like we're in a bit of a fix, then," the doctor said.

"He's been saving his pills," Mom began, but the doctor waved a hand at her.

"Esau, buddy, we're going to play twenty questions. Ready?"

"Yes."

"Know where you are?"

"Closet."

"Ten points. Remember what you ate for dinner?"

I did not.

"Skip it. Doesn't matter anyway. Remember the last time you got some sleep?"

"Tuesday."

The doctor studied his hands. He had large, heavy hands, which were good when a person needed to be picked up and set on the examining table, also when a person needed to be rolled up in a blanket. I was glad he was here. "Quite a while, then, hup?"

"No. No. I have been busy with the project."

"Who's the president, my friend?"

"JFK. The project of creating a system. My system of contingency plans."

"Afraid the president's Nixon, Esau."

"Oh," I said, and reconsidered. "I don't like him. He's weasly."

Doc Parker laughed. "Man's entitled to his opinion, anyway, that's sure. Now, I know you hate this one, but what year've we got going on here?"

I punched the wall and the doctor grabbed my wrist on the rebound. He held my hand firmly.

"What sort of project you working on?" he asked casually, picking up a blackened sheet of paper, covered with my tight, intersecting script, and holding it far out in front of him. He peered down his nose and turned it in several directions.

"I am encoding the answers."

Doc Parker brought the paper close to his face. "Know what that looks like to me?" he said.

"What." I smiled.

"Looks like the periodical table, is what it looks like to me."

I shrieked, pleased to have been found out.

"Well, buddy, I'm afraid you gotta go to sleep sometime, and now's as good a time as any. Don't you think?"

I nodded, glum.

Doc Parker reached for his bag.

"I don't want a shot," I whimpered.

"Aw, you know it's just a little bite," the doctor said, rolling his sleeves up and taking out a small vial. He turned it slowly upside down, watching the clear liquid turn opaque. "And ain't no other way to get you to sleep just now, do you think? Think you're wound pretty tight, wouldn't you say?"

"Yes. Fairly tight. Are you going to send me to State?" I stopped breathing and watched him draw the medicine up into the barrel of the syringe.

"Course not, kiddo. Few days, you'll be right as rain. Wanna pull that pajama top off?" he asked. "Ladies, if you don't mind stepping out," he said to Mom, Donna, and Kate.

They filed out of the room and I pulled my Spiderman pajama top off.

"Want to get in bed first?" the doctor asked.

I nodded. He got up out of the closet and waited for me to get in bed.

"Want I should roll you up?" he asked. "Might sleep a little easier, do you think?"

"Yes please."

He rolled me in the quilt so I was in a cocoon to sleep.

"Arm," he said. I wriggled my arm out.

"Night, kiddo," he said. "Sleep tight."

He laid his hand on my forehead and I felt the sting and then I was falling backward into sleep.

I slept most of the day and nodded off during dinner with a bite of hamburger in my mouth. Kate and Davey were elaborately quiet. I knew from before that everyone would be quiet for a few days while I slept. I curled up next to Mom on the couch and we watched TV. Just when I felt my head falling forward again, I jerked awake and said, "Is Frank going to kiss you?" I gazed straight ahead at the television set.

Mom pulled some lint out of my hair. "I don't know. Not if you don't want him to."

"Do you want him to?"

Kate and Davey looked up from their matchbox cars, curious.

Carefully, like she was tiptoeing, Mom said, "I don't like this line of conversation."

I nodded. "Oh." I kept looking at the TV. "Well, do you? Want him to kiss you?"

"I don't know."

"You can tell us."

"I don't want to."

"Oh." I thought that over. "I guess you don't have to."

We watched *The Tonight Show*. Kate and Davey laughed along with the laugh track, like they were singing the chorus to a song.

"I might not be a scientist-inventor," I said, tucking my hands between my knees and folding my legs onto the couch. "I might be an architect-librarian."

"That's a fine idea."

"I think so too. Do you want to know my logic? This is my logic," I said. "First, I could design the library just exactly to how I want it and then it would be mine. If I had a whole library, I could know everything about everything and not just everything about a few things. And I could organize the books. And I like to do that. And by the time I had read all of the books, there would be more books to read."

"It's true."

"I like Frank. But he can't have you."

Mom was quiet for a minute. Then she said, "He doesn't have me."

"But he is around now."

Kate and Davey ran their matchbox cars back and forth over the same patch of carpet, listening.

"More than he was before, which was not at all, so statistically speaking he is around more, by definition," I prompted.

"If you put it that way."

"So we will have to adjust our routine."

She looked at me. "I guess, a little."

"A lot. A very large lot. Did you know that if a butterfly dies it affects the entire ecosystem of a rain forest in South America?"

"No."

I nodded. "Systems are fragile." I turned my face up to her. "Systems are simultaneously very strong and very fragile." I turned back to the television, satisfied. "That is my favorite paradox," I said.

 CLAIRE

A few weeks after Esau's episode, on a cold December morning, the phone woke me up. I slammed my hand around on the nightstand trying to find it with my eyes closed and only succeeded in dropping it on Donna's head where she lay in her nest on the floor.

"Jesus Christ," she yelled, and picked up the phone. "'Lo!"

The phone came flying up onto the bed. "It's for you," she mumbled. "Tell them to go away."

Donna and the kids had been staying with us for a week, in the wake of another fight. This time, she swore she wasn't going back.

I put the phone next to my ear and shifted in the sheets. "Hello," I said.

"Morning," said Frank. My eyes snapped open.

"Morning," I said, not wanting to move in case he could hear the sheets and then picture me in bed. Somehow that was very important.

"You said I could call."

"I did." I had. I had not expected him to call while I was in my nightgown.

"So I'm calling." I would've sworn I could hear him regret it.

"Who the hell *is* it?" Donna asked.

"What are you doing tonight?" he asked.

"Um. No plans, really."

"I'd like to make you dinner. If you're free. If you'd like."

This called for a pause. This was an invitation to his home. This was a whole new level of something. "You cook?" I finally said.

"Is that Frank?" Donna asked. "What the *hell* time is it?"

"I do cook," Frank said. "I cook pretty well, I guess. You wouldn't starve, at any rate."

"Hang on a sec," I said, and put the phone under a pillow. I leaned over the side of the bed. Donna was lying there with her hands behind her head, wide awake. She smiled.

"It's Frank," I said. "He wants to know if I can come over for dinner tonight."

"Are you serious? To his *house*?"

"Yes! What should I tell him?"

"Well, shit!" She sat up and crossed her legs. "What are you going to wear?"

"I don't know! Should I even go?"

She thought about it. "Well, what the hell. Why not. But what do we do with the kids?"

I stared at her.

"I was going to see Jamie," she said, wincing.

"Please don't tell me that."

"Well—"

"Please tell me you're joking."

"We can drop the kids with your folks."

"No we cannot! They are *our kids*! Oh, I can't even *tell you* how pissed I am at you right now." I flopped back onto the bed and put the phone to my ear. We would drop them at Oma and Opa's. They'd be delighted.

"Frank?"

"Right here."

"Sorry. What time should I come by?"

"Oh!" It seemed he hadn't thought that far. "Six? Seven?"

"Six."

"Okay. Great."

"Want me to bring anything?"

"No no no no. I've got it all under control. Good. All right then. See you at six."

He hung up. I put the phone down and leaned over the edge of the bed.

"What am I doing?" I asked Donna.

"Going on a date."

"Going on a date to his *house*. That's something different." I paused. "More to the point, what are *you* doing?"

She wrinkled her nose in thought. "I need coffee to answer that." She got up and went out to the kitchen.

I lay in bed staring out the upside-down window. What to wear, what to wear, what to wear.

She came back in, handed me a cup of coffee, and settled herself at the foot of the bed. "Figured it out," she said.

"What's that?"

"Leaving him."

We drank our coffee.

"Okay," I said, nodding. "Honey, don't go see Jamie tonight."

She didn't say anything.

"Don't," I repeated.

She was looking out the window. "Sleeting," she said. "Gonna be icy." She looked at me. "I have to," she said.

"Goddamn, but you are stubborn."

She grinned. "I know."

"Stubborn and stupid," I said, getting out of bed.

I dropped the kids at Oma and Opa's and drove back into town. Now Oma would feed them sugar enough to choke a horse, and bring them home at midnight when they were asleep.

I was mortified by Opa's little wink.

Then I sat in front of Frank's house, fixing my hair in the rearview mirror and talking myself out of the car.

I liked him. I did. I must have. I liked him enough to be sitting like a teenage girl in my car, fixing my hair and fussing with my plastic pearls. You didn't just go to a man's house for dinner for a casual date. You were agreeing to something, by going to his house, you were not preventing inevitable things such as talk, or possibly kissing. I was agreeing to these things. Though he was quiet, and patient, and not what I was used to, foreign, and at the same time becoming all too familiar, uncomfortably familiar, as if on purpose, and he tended bar and had unruly eyebrows, and probably there were numerous other things I did not know about him yet but would not like, nevertheless, I liked him. He felt comfortable to me. Like I could lean into him for a while and rest.

I opened the car door and smoothed down my skirt.

He must have known I was out there, because I had only lifted my hand to knock when he flung the door open and said, "Come in! Sit down! I'm just finishing up," and he ushered me into the kitchen.

I had never seen a kitchen so clean. Not just-cleaned-this-afternoon clean. Empty clean. Bachelor clean. On the counter, in a row, were a silver toaster and silver tins for flour, coffee, sugar, and salt. They gleamed, and were possibly only there to fill space. There was no basket of browning fruit, no onion skins, no piles of mail. Just a little row of Schilling's spices to the left of the stove, all caps neatly on. No dishes in the sink. All four burners burbled. It smelled wonderful.

"Just a little something," he said, lifting a lid and stirring. He wiped his hands on the towel that dangled from the waistband of his jeans. "What can I get you? Red wine? White? Or I stopped by Y-Knot and got a little of your favorite," he crowed, and produced a bottle of Black Label from the cupboard above the fridge.

"Frank!" I said. "This is too much!"

"My house. I can do what I like." He dropped an ice cube into a glass and poured a splash over it, cracking the ice. He handed it to me.

He didn't let go of the glass. I looked at him. "Welcome," he said, and leaned in to kiss my cheek.

I knew something like this would happen. I had been kissed. I had been there less than five minutes and already I had been kissed for the first time in a year.

He flushed and turned back to the stove, humming.

I found myself dipping my tongue into the scotch, staring at his broad back.

For the first time in a year. I had not been kissed by a man, even on the cheek, since my husband died. Who was no longer my husband, because he had died. Who had died, thus flinging open the door that led to being kissed on the cheek by a man, in that man's kitchen, in that man's home, in which there was likely a bed.

"Make yourself comfortable," he said, waving a wooden spoon. "Have a look around." Gratefully, I broke my too intent stare at his back.

There was music playing in another room, and the kitchen table was set. Two brand-new candles sat unlit in their wooden holders. He'd used napkin rings. Where on earth, I thought, did this man come up with napkin rings?

Through the kitchen doorway there was a dining room he'd turned into a little study, with a desk in the corner facing out onto his lawn. I peered through the screen. Mulch covered a vegetable garden for winter, and his fence was overgrown with ivy that flickered in the heavy sleet that was turning to snow.

It had not snowed since a lifetime before, when Arnold was my husband and absentmindedly kissed my cheek. I would lean over his game of solitaire on my way to bed. He would glance up, not even with his eyes, just with his face, and kiss my cheek. Then he would go back to his game.

I had missed this nightly ritual for so long I had forgotten when I had forgotten to miss it.

I looked away from the window.

Through a wide arch, the living room had a set of red velvet furniture, antique, the kind my mother would have killed for. He'd painted the room a darker red, and it was lit by low yellow lamps with stained-glass shades. He'd set out an ashtray, though he didn't smoke. The candy dish was full. And there were flowers, dusty pink roses, in a vase. In the corner, a phonograph spun. On the mantel, a Bible, the kind in which you record the family tree: gilt edged, enormous, in an ebony stand. I walked over to it. It was open to the Psalms.

I pictured him standing there at five to six, looking around the room, looking for a flower out of place, a picture hung wrong.

I glanced up the wide, curved staircase. A light illuminated a hat rack in the corner at the top of the stairs, with his caps and hats. They were the only sign anyone really lived here at all.

And yet the house was filled with him. He emanated quietly from the kitchen. I could feel him listening to my steps.

The kiss on my cheek had in truth been quite close to my mouth.

He joined me in the hallway. "Go on up," he said.

"Oh, that's all right."

"No, really. I want to show you."

I looked at him and started up the stairs. "Here," he said, taking my elbow and guiding me into a room. "Look."

He left his hand on my arm longer than was necessary as I took in the room.

Bookshelves lined the walls from floor to ceiling, books stacked two and three deep, laid on their sides atop each other. In the corner, there was a fat leather armchair with a stained-glass window above it, bookshelves built into the wall above that. The lamp above the chair cast colors from the stained glass in patterns over the wood floor.

I thought of the stained-glass window in the church. When Arnold had died and I had looked away from his coffin and through the glass window that shot jewel colors over Kate's face as if she were a harlequin doll.

I was in Frank's church.

"I was thinking," he said, striding across the room, "maybe Esau could find a thing or two he'd like in here." He pulled a book off the shelf to show me, then set his drink down on a towering stack of books, put on a pair of reading glasses that had sat on the arm of the chair, and tilted his head to the side, pulling books out and handing them to me faster than I could keep up.

I studied his profile in the lamplight, the glasses perched on the tip of his broad nose. I was overwhelmed by the sheer number of books, the knowledge they implied, the fact that I was here in the room to which he clearly retreated each day. His refuge. I felt I ought to close my eyes to the nakedness to which he had stripped himself down. All these months, waiting patiently for me, never forcing me to look. But constantly letting me know that I could.

I wanted to look. I wanted to show him a refuge of my own. I wanted to tell him my secrets, whatever they were. I opened my mouth to speak but did not know what to say.

I watched his wide brown hands cradle a heavy book as you would an infant's head. He studied the page, perhaps having forgotten I was there.

"How many books—do you have?" I finally asked, feeling stupid.

"Three thousand and change." He shrugged, closing the book and setting it on a shelf. "I collect them. I thought Esau might like it."

"He'll think he's died and gone to heaven." To my relief, the moment passed.

Frank laughed. We stood there for a minute. "I collect buttons too," he said, and cleared his throat. "But I don't enjoy that nearly as much."

I laughed.

He looked at me, smiling. "What?"

"You just look so pleased with yourself." I went over to the book-case and pulled out a volume. I paged through it. "Never figured you for a reader," I said lightly, trying to release some strange tension that had crept into the room.

"No, I don't suppose."

"Why's that?" I looked at him.

He shrugged and wrinkled his brow. "Well, don't suppose you fig-ured me for much of anything a'tall."

I smiled at the book. "That's not true."

"Huh."

"It's not."

"Probably had me figured for some illiterate," he said. It was hard to tell when he was joking. "City girl like you? Backwoods bartender, that's all I was."

I laughed. "So what do you know? Tell me something you know." I shut the book.

He pushed his hands into his pockets, thinking. "I know my Shakespeare pretty good."

"Oh yeah?" I laughed. "Tell me some."

He raised his eyebrows. "Is this a quiz?"

"Yes." I was flirting. I'm flirting, I thought, alarmed.

"'Be not afeared,'" he intoned abruptly. "'The isle is full of noises, sounds and sweet airs that give delight and hurt not. Sometimes a thousand twangling instruments will hum about mine ears; and sometimes voices that, if I then had waked after long sleep will make me sleep again; and then, in dreaming, the clouds methought would open and show riches ready to drop upon me, that, when I waked, I cried to dream again.'"

I stared at him. I wanted him to keep talking. He smiled. I took a swallow of my drink. It made my face burn. "That was pretty," I said.

"And I know a few other things too."

"Yeah?" I smiled into my drink.

"Yeah." Now we were definitely flirting.

"Is that your big secret?" I asked, looking up. "That you're not really a bartender, you're a secret book reader and a, a *button* collector? Hiding away up here in your room?"

He shook his head. "Nope," he said, smiling. "That's not it."

"What is it?"

"Time to eat," he announced, and turned down the hall. "Come on."

He lit the candles, pushed my chair in to the table, and set out an incredible spread. "It's not fancy," he said, "but it should taste pretty good."

The room seemed to wrap in around us as we ate and talked. We danced around the fact that we were in his home, at his table, the fact that we had, for months, been meeting up and pulling apart, each time with a little more to say, a little more ease, a little more laughter at each other's oddities. And each time a little more frightened by what came tumbling out of our mouths, unbidden but unstoppable, like a stream.

I watched him lean his elbows on the table as he ate, fork in his left hand, knife in his right, the way men up north always ate. I watched his forelock fall over his forehead, and his habit of tossing it back like a restless horse. I watched the corners of his mouth tilt up in his crooked smile and I realized I had been watching them for so long I had come to anticipate them, had come to know just an instant before he raised his hand to lift his glass that he would do so, just an instant before he tilted back his head and stared down his nose at me that he was about to laugh, and I craved it.

Somehow I had grown used to him. And yet there was still so much I kept clutched to my chest, my things, my life, my children, my home, my secrets, my wounds. I wondered where, in the jumble of this, Frank fit. Because it was plain that he did.

He stood up and brought me a brownie with ice cream. "You want coffee?"

I watched him pour it and slide into his chair.

"Frank," I asked, turning my mug in slow circles, "how much did you know?"

He furrowed his brow. He lifted his mug and took a swallow. "About Arnold?" he said. I nodded. "I guess this had to come up, didn't it?" He sighed and leaned back in his chair, looking over my shoulder at the dark window. "It did, you're right. All right. I'll tell you, but on one condition."

"What's that?"

"I don't want you to pay a bit of mind to what I think. Ain't no one in the world knows what goes on inside a couple's house, and no one should, so what I think, well, it doesn't matter a damn bit. That's important. I think you want to know, so out of respect to you I'm gonna tell you. But out of respect to Arnold, I want you to remember him well."

I sat there. Finally, I said, "Thank you."

"I knew Arnold better than I should've." He shook his head slightly, as if trying to dislodge a memory from his brain. "I thought he was a good man. When we were kids, I worshiped him. I really did. He was the smartest and the fastest and the best looking, but I'll tell you, even then. Even then he had something. Some kind of dark streak, I guess. He could get mean. For years, I thought it was because of Rose, you know." He looked at me and I nodded. He shook his head. "Wasn't. He loved her, but that wasn't it. In high school was when we started drifting apart. It got so I couldn't keep the two separate, the good and the bad of him. One night, he was drunk, he hit his girl." Frank shook his head and pressed his finger into crumbs on the table. "That was about it for me."

I watched the look on his face. So many memories, I thought, all stored up in this man. So many secrets and stories. I wanted to listen and I didn't. I wanted him not to have to carry this himself, I was suddenly overwhelmed with a desire to reach across the table and touch his face, as if that would magically lift away the things he knew. I wanted us to say it, the thing that mattered, to stop circling around the story that pushed us apart.

And yet, if we did stop, what would happen? Would we be flung together, broken by the impact of two lonely people who were fragile enough without the force of something like love?

He smiled at me. I smiled into my coffee. I liked the laugh lines by his eyes.

Frank went on. "When he left, I don't think anyone figured him for one who'd come back. He always said he was getting the hell out of town when he graduated, and he did. Gone for a few years, but then here he was again. With you." He smiled at me, took a swallow of coffee, and then crinkled his eyes as if something behind me would tell him what to say. It didn't. He looked at me. "And he was still the same fellow, on the surface, I guess, but still, something had changed."

He sat silently for a while. "He got desperate," he said. He looked at me. "The man just got so, so sad."

I nodded. "He did." I pictured Arnold with his deck of cards. Shuffling them seven times for luck, for better odds.

"Do you know why?"

I sat there for a minute. "I want to say I don't. That he was sick, somehow. But if I'm honest, I think it was because of us." That hurt. "Because of me."

Frank smoothed the napkin on his lap. Quietly, he said, "Not my place to say it, Claire. But you're wrong." He looked up.

"I'd love to believe you."

"Do. Believe me."

I sat there. I took a sip of coffee. "You know why?"

He shook his head. "No. But I know he loved you, and the kids, like nothing else. You were what he had."

"That's not enough." I sounded bitter. I hadn't meant to.

"Well, that's not enough, Claire," he said angrily, as if something inside him had snapped. Suddenly we weren't circling this, not anymore. We'd walked right into it. "Not enough for anybody, is it? I'll tell you something." He leaned forward, his elbows on the table. "I stood there behind that bar for years, listening to that man tell me what a worthless wreck he was, drowning him in booze myself. And you know, after he'd been sitting there saying the same *goddamn thing* for long enough, I started to believe him. I did. I stood there, and *I* poured his drinks, and I watched him start to believe his own sob story, and I started to believe it myself, and I got a little goddamn tired of it. Because you know what? You know what? It's all fine and good, you love your wife and kids. All well and good, sure. But then what the hell're you doing drinking yourself to death in a bar in the middle of the goddamn day? Why in the hell aren't you at work? Doing a good day's work like a decent man? What the hell're you doing telling the *bartender* how much you love your wife and kids? 'Stead of going home and telling them yourself? Or at least *acting* like it. Claire, I pour a lot of drinks and I listen to a lot of stories, hell, I know the kids around town, and the wives, better'n half the men who own 'em, like they're *my* kids, *my* families, that's my life. That's what I do. But I'll say one thing, and that man did *not* go shoot hisself because of you, no thank you. He did it because he crawled into a bottle, and I know he loved you, as well he should, but he was a *selfish sonofabitch and that is the end of it.*"

He straightened up. He wiped his mouth with his napkin. "Excuse me," he said formally, and stood, clearing our plates, taking them to the sink and turning the tap on full blast.

I sat there with my coffee cup halfway to my mouth. I noticed it and took a sip. When he was done with the dishes, Frank slid in across from me.

"I apologize," he said, smoothing his hair with nervous, damp hands.

"No need."

"I let my mouth run. I'm sorry. No excuse."

"Frank." I looked at him and shook my head. "No need. Really."

He smiled. "All right," he said, and took a breath as if he'd been needing one.

The truth of what he'd said hung between us. He looked left, I looked right.

"Let's take our coffee to the living room," he said quietly. It was an invitation. To whatever came next.

I accepted.

I sank into the sofa and took my shoes off, looking out the window at the now thick snow. He crouched down to light the logs in the fireplace and sat down at the other end of the sofa.

"Winter's finally here," I said, my face turned away from his, toward the rush of flames in the stone fireplace. I listened to the crackle of dried apple wood. I did not know how to do this. I waited for him to tell me or show me. I wanted him to lean close so that I could smell the salt on his neck. There were perhaps three, four feet between us. Too many, pushing against us, into the corners of the couch. And yet I would have sworn that I could feel his heat.

He watched the fire. "I love winter. Keeps you mindful of your place in the world. Keeps you still."

I nodded.

"Ought to go for a drive. Out to the north shore, maybe."

I looked at him. He studiously ate a mint. "I'd like that," I said.

"All right," he nodded. "We'll do that."

We. We will have to adjust our routine. I looked out the window, down the block toward Main Street. I pictured the little light above my front steps, flickering in the shadow of falling snow. My children's beds, waiting for small bodies to warm them like tiny fires.

"Claire," he said thoughtfully.

"What's that?" I said, turning back.

"Your dress is beautiful." He articulated this as if it was a new vocabulary word he was trying out.

He stirred around in the candy dish, looking for, it seemed, the green butter mints.

"It's new," I blurted.

"That so."

I nodded. "Bought it today," I said, wishing to God I'd shut up.

"Oh?"

"Well," I said, feeling very short of breath, "Donna bought it for me. It was a present. I bought her a ring she liked. It was only paste, but she liked it so much."

"You stay in town?"

"Staples," I breathed, then set my coffee down on a coaster and stood up. "We had lunch at Betty's," I called, going out of the room. "Excuse me," I said, and hurried up the stairs. I opened a door, thinking it was the bathroom, and gasped to find myself staring into his bedroom. I shut the door. Then opened it again. I peered in. Antique dresser, four-poster bed, tightly made. Bed stand, piled with books, an old cedar chest that contained God knows what and was stacked feet high with old magazines.

I took one long step in and stood still. I lifted my hand, hesitated, and then lay it on the bed, lightly, the way you touch the forehead of a sleeping child.

The hush of snow stilled the room into a kind of sleep.

I reached for a green flannel shirt that hung from the four-poster. I raised it to my face. Old Spice and his smell.

I wanted to know what his pillow would feel like under my head. Whether he slept with his mouth open, whether he slept on his back or his side. I wanted details, I wanted to know the precise place where he would rest his hand in the curve of my waist while he slept. I wanted to watch him sleep. I wanted to guard him while he slept, be the body that he reached for in his dreams. I wanted to be the thing he knew, the thing as close as breath.

He sat downstairs, waiting for me. I could feel the pull of him from here.

I breathed in his shirt for a while, then hung it back on the post. I smoothed my hand over a pillow, and shut the door on my way out.

I washed my hands for a very long time. My cheeks were splotched with red. I decided I couldn't stay up there all night and went back downstairs.

"So," I said, rounding the corner. I sat down.

"Claire."

"So she's leaving him."

He started laughing. I picked up my coffee cup, which was empty, and looked around the room. "It's not very funny," I said.

"No, of course it's not," he said. "You are."

"I am not."

"All right, then." He kept laughing. I turned to give him a piece of my mind.

He leaned over and took my head in his hands and found my mouth and kissed me. Then he pulled back.

It was much too brief. I couldn't remember what it felt like. I needed him to do it again so I could be sure he had done it in the first place. I realized I was sitting there staring over his shoulder with my mouth open. I looked at him. His eyes were brown, like chocolate.

He went over to a stand in the corner on which sat the decanters of booze. He poured two tiny, crystal glasses full, and set one down in front of me. He looked around the room.

I picked up my drink. "You're trying to get me drunk," I said, filling air, killing time, wishing he'd do it again.

"Doing no such thing," he said, firmly. He set his drink on the table. "Here," he said, and tucked his hands under himself on the seat. "I'll be a gentleman. Keep my hands to myself."

I looked at him. Morbidly serious, he gazed back.

"Scout's honor. Come here." He tipped his head. "C'mere. Just once."

I laughed. I took a breath and leaned toward him. I pulled back. "I can't."

"Sure you can," he said, getting desperate. "You just did it, a minute ago."

"Surprise attack."

"Okay, so this time you've got fair warning." After a moment, he added thoughtfully, "Though you're a ways away. You might want to get closer."

"Frank," I warned.

"I'm just saying. What if you tip over? Trying to get here from there?"

I laughed, set my drink down, braced myself, and came face-to-face with his mouth. I found myself studying his lips. The dark opening behind them. His soft breath on the side of my face.

"Claire," he whispered, and when he said my name, the tip of his tongue touched the whites of his teeth.

"What?"

"Kiss me."

Curious, I did.

And then we kissed like people starved. Clumsy, unfamiliar, young. He bit my lower lip. I leaned closer, and then I crawled across the couch. I wanted to climb into his mouth, all give. I fumbled for his hands. I wanted him to hold me. Hard. I wanted his hands on me. I felt his mouth smile under mine, and he kept his hands where they were. "No," he mumbled into my mouth. "I promised."

"Never mind."

"I *promised.*" He caught my throat with his teeth, gently, just the right muscle, and I twisted my head. He kissed my throat, my collarbone, I crawled onto his lap, he kissed his way back up to my ear.

"I'll stop," I threatened.

"No you won't."

"Arrogant!"

He wrapped his hands around my waist and laid me down on the couch, brought his hands to the side of my face, reached up to turn off the lamp above my head so there wasn't a glare in my eyes. Then he kissed me for a very long time.

At a certain point, I caught his wrist in my hand and smiled into his mouth.

I had forgotten about the sad, mysterious end of a kiss—how both mouths know, somehow, to soften and pull apart. That delicate sphere of warm breath passed back and forth before speech edges in.

"Time to go," I whispered.

He rested his forehead on mine for a second, then sat up. I straightened myself and looked at his face, shadowed in the dark living room.

"Thank you," I said. "For dinner."

He switched on the lamp and grinned at his feet. "Sure," he said. He smoothed his hair.

"I'm sorry I have to go," I said. "I told the kids I'd tuck them in by midnight."

"You'll be early. How're they with all this?"

I looked at my hands, trying to decide how to answer him. "What is this?"

"I don't know. Do you?"

"No. I want a word." I laughed. "Esau would have a word." I stood and went to stand in front of the fire. I smoothed down my skirt. "This is something, isn't it?" I asked, my back turned to him.

Carefully, he said, "It is for me."

I opened my mouth and nothing came out.

"Is it for you?" he asked. My silence filled the room. I should turn around, I thought. I need to turn around and face him when I say this, whatever I'm going to say.

I turned. "I want to say no."

"Then say no." For the first time, I heard an edge of bitterness to his voice. It stung.

"They're upset," I burst out, turning to face him. "The kids. They're upset. They're scared."

"I bet they are."

We studied each other.

"So am I," I said. I felt myself pleading with him for something. He gazed steadily back at me, giving nothing away, fixing nothing. I wanted to hit him. I wanted to kiss him again. I wanted him to drag me upstairs to bed and be done with it.

"Want a drink?" he asked, going past me to the decanters. I watched him pour two.

"Frank, I can't do this." It just came out. There it was. It was true the instant I said it, and it was a lie, and I didn't care, I just wanted the waiting to be done.

He showed no response. Just handed me my drink and walked past me again to the couch. He sat down. "Why's that?" he asked.

I looked around the room. "Because it's too soon."

"For who? You?"

"It's just too soon."

"Is it too soon for you?"

"I guess it is," I said.

He nodded and drank. "Yep. Well, that's bullshit."

That knocked me back. "I beg your pardon?"

"You heard me." He glared at me and shot his drink down his throat. I tried a different approach.

"The kids—"

"Ain't about the kids. This is about you." He rubbed the bridge of his nose.

"You gonna let me get a word in edgewise?"

"Kids are all right, Claire. Me, I'm all right. Ain't comfortable, but I'm all right. I can do this. That leaves you."

"Yes it does. And I can't do this."

"Tell me why, and I'll leave it alone."

"I don't have to tell you why."

He set his glass down on the table and put his hands behind his head, peering down his nose at me. "You come over, spend an evening in my home, spend time with me"—his mouth opened as if he had no words to describe what had happened, and he gestured, baffled, at the couch—"so as not to tell me why?" He leaned forward, looking straight at me. "You expect to finally, *finally* let me near you, near enough to *taste you*"—I turned away, he was doing this on purpose—"near enough to hold you like I've been dying to for all this time, and then you say, 'Can't do this,' and expect me to just show you the damn door? Are you out of your mind? I don't *want* to show you the door. I want you to stay here. I want it more than anything." He stood up and walked over to where I stood. I turned away from him and we went in a slow circle, his mouth near my ear, just behind me, chasing me with his words. "I want you in my life, Claire. I want you in the morning and at night and I want to hear your voice and watch you raise your kids, goddammit, Claire, *I want you in my life*! I want you to let go of whatever goddamn thing you carry around with you that keeps you all closed off from me because I *want to get inside there*!"

"You can't!" I shouted, spinning around to face him.

"I could," he snapped, "if you'd so much as let me." We glared at each other.

"You just want to pick a fight," he said slowly, realizing it. "So you don't have to think anymore about it, or feel guilty anymore about it, or torn or upset or anything a'tall about it. You just want it to be easy."

I looked at the dying fire and took a swallow of my drink.

Frank turned to face the window. "So if you're going to pick a fight, go on and do it, then. I'm not stopping you."

"You're arrogant," I said.

"All right, I'm arrogant."

"You're weak," I said, furious. "Your kindness, your incessant *kindness,* you make me sick with how *kind* you are. Act like a goddamn saint," I spat. I poured myself another shot of whiskey, face flaming. I turned to face his back. "You come around my house, act like those are *your* children. They're mine. *Mine.* Telling me what to do. Telling Donna what to do. It isn't your place, none of it. Telling me about my husband, who he was." I heard my voice rising. "What do you know, who he was? What do you know about it? He was sick, is all, and he tried his best, and who in the hell are you to even *think* you have a right to talk about him? Spit on his grave? You're right, you are a grave robber. How long you been thinking about another man's wife? How long you been waiting for Arnold to die?" I found myself crying and wiped my nose on my sleeve.

"Not waiting for him to die," Frank said quietly, looking out into the night. "Never wanted him to die." He turned his head slightly toward me. "Couldn't help that I loved you."

That stopped me. He'd said it. I was overwhelmed with a rush of fury and damn near pitched my glass at his head.

"Do you know how much I loved him?" I shouted, my head trembling. "Do you know that there is a *hole* in my *life* where he *was*? And you've got the *gall* to try and step in and fill it?"

He shook his head and looked at the floor. "I'm not trying to fill it."

"Well, you can't. You can't fill it. It's mine. You can't fill it and you can't make it go away and it will *always be there.*"

We stood there in silence. Perhaps ten feet apart. I took a sip of my drink.

"Always," I repeated, staring at the fireplace.

"'Spect that's true," Frank said, turning around. "You hang on to it hard enough."

I threw what was left of my drink in his face.

"Well, I appreciate that, Claire. I do. We done here?"

"No," I said, surprising myself.

He yanked his shirttail out of his pants and wiped his face. Finally, he said, "Are you waiting for me to agree with you? Say, 'Oh, I know it must be hard. It must be just awful, your husband goes and shoots his head off, leaves you all alone.' 'Cause I'm afraid that's beyond me. Damnation, woman. Of course it's hard. Life is hard. This is hard. Doesn't mean I pity you."

"I don't want your pity!" I shouted, turning to get another drink.

"Hell you don't! Siddown," he snapped, taking my glass and setting it on the end table next to him. "Sit down," he repeated. "I wanna see if you can have a goddamn conversation without a drink in your hand."

"*Fuck* off."

He stared steadily at me. "Jesus, you know what? You're greedy as hell. You are one greedy woman. You want a word for what this is. You want pity. You want promises. And you are sitting there telling me you ain't gonna stick around to find out what this is because that is just too damn hard. Hell, Claire, you know what this is. This is love. That's all I can give you. That's all I've got. And you don't want no part of it." He stared at me.

"You think I've got something else you need," he said, shaking his head. "Well, let me tell you, I don't." He laughed shortly and turned away, pacing across the room. "Arnold is dead and you think I know why. You think I can clear that up for you, maybe make it a little easier. Maybe tell you it wasn't you. Is that why you're here?" he shouted, turning back to me. His face was flushed. "It is. You don't want nothing about me. You want something for *you*. You want me to tell you why, long as it ain't your fault." He shook his head. "All right, Claire, I don't know. I don't know. I don't know why a man takes his own life. I do not have the faintest goddamn idea. How you'd get that blind and sad. How you do that to the people around you. I don't know. Maybe it was you. Maybe it wasn't. I just watched it happen, and wasn't a goddamn thing I could do."

I sat there, thinking.

"Claire," he said, suddenly calm. He shook his head and slumped into a chair. "Dammit, you know, you're sitting here and what the hell am I supposed to do. I ain't got what you want. I don't pity you. I got more respect for you than that. I'm no better or wiser than anyone else, get that damn fool idea out your *damn* fool head. I got no better idea than you how to do this."

He put his head in his hands and rubbed his hair. His elbows on his knees, he stared straight ahead and said, "Well, we got two choices."

I waited.

"Either you come upstairs, or you go home."

I sat stunned. "Now?"

"Yeah, I think so. 'Cause if you're going home, I can't keep looking at you."

I panicked. Finally I said, "I don't think I'm ready to go home yet."

"You sure?"

I nodded.

He stood up and offered me his hand.

And I followed him into the next part of my life, peeking over his wide shoulder at the closed door at the top of the stairs.

Later, when I had heard the unfamiliar, terrifying, beautiful sounds. His, and stranger still, mine.

When he had undressed me, whispering, as if I were a book he was reading aloud, alone. Later, at the window, I cried.

It woke him. I heard him wake up. His breathing hesitated, then began, shorter, the breath of children or men who are pretending to be asleep. He held too still. I wiped my nose on the sleeve of his green shirt. I was wearing it. It smelled like him.

He let me cry.

It snowed.

When he was sure I was done, I heard the sheets shift. He came to stand behind me. He gathered my hair off my shoulders and wrapped his arms around my waist.

"I like your shirt," he said.

I laughed damply and wiped my nose again.

"There's nothing I can say right now," he said. It was a question. I shook my head.

"Want to come to bed?"

I took his hands and held them to myself. I turned and put my face in his chest. He was sweaty and salty and I listened to his heart. I took off the shirt and climbed into bed.

His eyes glittered in the dark. "Why buttons?" I asked.

"I don't know," he said, very seriously. I laughed.

"I love your laugh," he said.

"Tell me more Shakespeare."

He laughed and rolled onto his elbows, looking down at me. "'Indeed,'" he said, his voice tilting into its strange song, "'the top of admiration, worth what's dearest in the world!'" He tucked my hair behind my ear. "'Full many a lady I have eyed with best regard, and many a time th' harmony of their tongues hath into bondage brought my too diligent ear. For several virtues have I liked several women; never any with so full soul but some defect in her did quarrel with the noblest grace she owed, and put it to the foil. But you, so perfect and so peerless, are created of every creature's best.'"

I laughed.

"What, you don't like it?" he asked, flopping down.

"You just look so funny talking like that," I giggled.

"It's old," he said, grumpy. I hit him with a pillow. He rolled over and put his head on my stomach.

"What's it mean?" I asked.

"It means," he said, running his hand down my hip, "that you have the most delicious thighs." He pulled the sheets over his head. I shrieked, scrambling and laughing, but he held me down, and eventually I wasn't laughing anymore.

He did know a thing or two.

The room exploded and I crashed back into the bed. I yanked the sheet off his head and found him cheerfully lying with his chin in his hands, shamelessly staring.

"Well, get out of there already," I yelled. Slowly, he crawled up me, smiling.

"What," I said, suspicious. He just smiled. "What?" I demanded.

And he entered me, hard, and I said Oh, and arched.

* * *

"Claire."

"Umm."

He was pressed into my back. "I have to tell you something."

I smiled. "Mm-hmm." I pushed further back into him.

His mouth in my hair, he said gruffly, "You're in love with me. Nothing you can do about it. Might as well stay."

I reached behind myself and felt around for his hand. I pulled it up to rest between my breasts. "Okay," I said. Then I fell into a half sleep where nothing made sense, really, and I no longer cared.

A phone rang. I woke with a start, terrified that something had happened to Esau. Frank handed it to me.

"Mother?"

"Sweetie, are you all right? What's wrong?"

"It is past your curfew," Esau said severely. "You are a half hour late."

"I'm sorry. I'll be right home." I smiled, hugely relieved.

"It's all right. We aren't home anyway. We went out," he said.

"What?" I nearly screamed. "You went out where? Where are you? Where's Donna?" Frank flew out of bed and pulled on his jeans.

"How am I supposed to know where Donna is? That man came by to get us. Dale. He let us all ride in the truck."

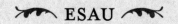 ESAU

It's not like it was anything very complicated.

The first time we went over to Dale's, we had been playing explorers in the marshland with the high reeds after school and we got hungry, so we stopped at Davey's house because it was closer. This was back in the fall, a couple of months before Donna and Davey and Sarah came for good, I remember because there wasn't snow yet, only frost. So we leaned our bikes on the back stoop and went up and Davey jiggled the lock and we went in.

And then I have to say I immediately regretted it because the house stunk. It smelled like a rotten old man. And I should have turned us around and sent us straight out the door once I had the bad feeling because I was biggest and in charge, sort of. But I didn't.

All the yellow-and-white-checked curtains in the yellow daisy kitchen were drawn and the refrigerator door was open, blowing cold air. But that was probably also why it stunk so bad, because there was rotting stuff in the fridge, Kate and Davey looked.

"It's a dead steak," she said flatly, her butt sticking out. "It's got blue."

"It's gray," Davey added. He turned around and asked me, "Do you think it's got maggots?"

"Might," I said, standing there.

"What should we do with it? How do we make it not stink?" Kate asked, picking it up and slapping it with her hands. "Phew!" she shouted, and dropped it in the sink and turned the tap on full blast.

I thought for a minute. "Dump Ajax on it. That might work."

Davey put his thumbs through his belt loops and looked around the kitchen. "Dark," he said thoughtfully.

"Well, are there cookies or not?" Kate demanded, standing on a footstool and scrubbing her entire arms with Ajax. "Because if there aren't any, we're leaving as soon as I'm done. This place gives me the sads."

Davey nodded. "It's a sad house," he said, dragging a chair away from the table and over to the cupboards. He opened one and a box of cereal fell out and spilled all over the floor. I chewed off my thumbnail and looked at it. I pressed it with my other thumb to stop the bleeding. I really wanted to leave.

"Davey!" Kate said, exasperated. "You are such a klutz!"

"Ten-four." Davey stared down at the shallow sea of Cheerios.

"Well, git down and clean it up! What am I, your maid? Sheesh!" She slapped her hands on her blue jeans to get them dry.

Davey climbed carefully down from the chair and went over to the stairwell to get the broom.

He came back and stared at us with his big eyes. "My dad's down there," he said.

I looked at the stairwell. The house looked like nobody'd set foot in it for weeks.

"What do you mean, he's down there?" Kate said, after a startled pause.

"I mean he's down there, Kate! That's what I mean!" he said, raising his voice.

"We should go," I said. "We should probably go right now."

"We have to say hi," Davey said, scowling at the floor. He jammed his fists into the pockets of his tiny Levi's. "He might feel bad if we don't."

"What for?" Kate nearly shouted. "If he wanted to say hi, he would've come up already. He can hear us perfectly fine. If he's down there, let him stay down there! I'm going," she said, and stalked toward the door, where she stopped. Davey didn't move and Kate wouldn't go anywhere without him.

Davey looked up at me, stubborn. "Go down and tell him we're here," he said. "So he can come up and say hi if he wants."

"Why should I do it?" I asked, chewing a hangnail. "He's your dad."

"Because you're biggest and in charge. Just go," Davey said loudly.

I turned and stalked over to the stairwell.

The narrow stairs were built of raw wood, the walls lined with shelves of cleaning stuff and tape and batteries and cellophane and tinfoil. The stairway seemed to narrow at the bottom, like a cone, with a small black hole at the base.

I took hold of the handrail and squeaked down the stairs. At the bottom, I stood still, gazing at the beam of light from the tiny ground-level window, waiting for my eyes to adjust. It smelled damp down here, a little like soil. Softly, the pipes clanged.

"A visitor," said a voice. The voice coughed. "Well, come in, then."

I took a few steps forward and the smoke from his cigarette came into view. It sat perched at the edge of an ashtray amid a crowd of beer bottles and a pile of girlie magazines. Gradually, in a shadow, I could make out Davey's dad, sitting on a sagging sofa with his knees apart and a beer planted at his crotch.

"Esau, isn't it?" he said. I nodded. He hadn't shaved in ages and his face looked like it was covered with gray mold. He was skinny, his chest and cheeks caved in. His army fatigues hung on his body like a scarecrow's clothes. "Well, how's by you, then? Come over and set awhile," he said, patting the cushion next to him.

"All right," I said, edging closer and gingerly sinking on the edge of the couch. I stared at the magazines. No matter how hard I tried, I could not stop looking. Dale laughed, reached across me, and opened one. I gasped. A girl stared back at me, naked as a jaybird, smiling, her rump in the air.

"Go on and look," Dale said. "Ain't nothing wrong." He lifted his beer to his mouth and drained it, then launched himself up with a grunt and went over to a round-edged old fridge, pale green. He set a beer in front of me and sat down.

I stared at it, then back at the magazine. I picked it up for a closer look.

"Been well?" he asked.

"Yessir."

"Glad to hear it. Looking forward to school?"

"Yessir."

He nodded. "So as to the whereabouts of my wife," he said, squinting up at the sun through the window. He looked at me. I took a sip of beer and turned the page to find another, completely different, naked girl, this one with small, tight breasts that I wanted to chew on, but not so's it would hurt. Just a little.

"She's staying with us," I breathed.

Dale nodded. "I figured as much. Any idea she's planning to come back? Or is she just about done with me?"

I looked at him and shook my head. "I don't know," I said. Something behind me dripped. I took a couple swallows of beer.

He nodded, narrowing his eyes at me thoughtfully. "That's the thing. Man's got to have a contingency plan. Got to be prepared for emergencies. That's one thing you learn in the service, I'll tell you. Got to have a plan."

I nodded. My head was starting to feel a little wobbly.

"I'll tell you, in the service, you're trained for this sort of thing. When you're up against an enemy that moves at night, a sneaky enemy that don't play by any rules, you got to be prepared or you're dead."

I nodded and put the magazine back on the low table so I would stop looking at it. I leaned back against the cushions and pulled my knees up, facing him. I was fascinated by his face. I wanted to draw him.

He shook his head. "You're dead, is what," he repeated. "You got to look at the contingencies. You don't, you're liable to step on a land-mine, get snuck up on from behind, all sorts of things you ought to have thought of, and ain't no one to blame but yourself." He shook his head. "So you got to have the things you need. Like, say, it don't matter none she's gone," he said, looking at me, "'cause I been stockpiling the things I need, food and suchlike. Ammunition." He waved an arm at the basement. "I got a roof over my head, dry clothes on my back, plenty to eat, drink," he lifted his beer, "and what in the hell do I care? Want to see something special?" he asked suddenly, and set his beer on the low table. He stood up and lifted the worn blue cushion on which he'd sat, exposing more girlie magazines, some papers, and a gun. He fished out a piece of paper softened with handling and folding, pushed the cushion in again, and sat back down.

We sat peering at the paper in the dark. It was some kind of official form. "'Honorable discharge,'" he said, pointing to the words. "'Dale Olav Knutson,'" he said, pointing. "That's me. Look at this." His shaky finger rested on the words "Purple Heart." Then it skittered across the page to another box. "Expert marksman," and then "VKC: 118."

He leaned back, holding it out in front of him. "You know what that means?" he asked. I shook my head, sleepy. He pointed at the letter *C*. "Count," he said. Then he pointed at the letter *V*. "Verified." His finger stopped at *K.* "Kill," he said. He dropped his hand.

He looked at me. "Hundred and eighteen bodies. Hundred and eighteen perfect shots." He laid the page in his lap and gazed up at the window. "I get their faces. Nights." He waved a hand in front of his face. "I see their faces. Even though I never rightly saw them in the light."

He stared straight ahead awhile, his angular profile outlined by the thin light. Then he turned his face to me. "On t'other hand, it takes some doing, that's for damn sure. Didn't earn the Purple Heart by standing around doing nothing. Got a little shrapnel, sure, but that's not what the Purple Heart's about. Not just any motherfucker gets his leg blown off can get a Purple Heart. You got to earn it," he said, nodding. I drank the rest of my beer. "Did it by studying strategy. Plans of attack. Learning them so's I knew them better than the sound of the blood in my own ears. And one thing that's certain is a man's got to have a contingency plan. In the event of unforeseen ambush or trap." He rested his hands on his knees, stood up, and came back with two beers. I held mine to my forehead. I was dizzy and hot.

"Your father," he said. "He was good about that. Had a plan, and used it only when it was time. You don't best be wasting your reserves on just anything. You wait until the time is right, until it's called for. Then you can act in good conscience." He looked at me. "Your father was a brave man. You best know that."

I nodded.

"No matter what folks say. A man's life is his to do with as he likes, as he sees fit."

I nodded again. He turned away, satisfied that I understood. "Ain't nobody can say for a man when enough's enough. That's a line between him and God, and when it gets crossed, ain't nobody can fairly judge how he chooses to act. Your mama doing all right?" he asked suddenly.

I nodded once again. "She's a lady," Dale said. "She is an upstanding woman." He looked out the window. "What do you think, then?" He turned his watery eyes toward me. "I ought to kill her, or divorce her? There's satisfaction in one," he went on, not waiting for me to answer, "but then you got your consequence. You got to look ahead to the outcome. Got to plan for the contingency. Be prepared for what's around the corner, that's best. So you got to weigh," he said, lifting his bottle and his empty hand, "that satisfaction against what comes of it. You got to consider the lesser option, for your own sake, long term."

He paused, as if he were considering it right then. "What you got to do is kill them in your mind," he said, tapping his temple and dropping his hand. He fell silent for a moment. "That way when you kill them they're already dead."

He gazed up at the light. I felt like I was intruding, and looked at the small, tight breasts of the girl in the magazine. After a while, I looked over at him, slid off the couch slowly, and creaked back up the stairs.

I found Kate and Davey sitting outside on the top step, side by side, next to a bed of frostbitten marigolds. I looked down at them.

"We need a plan," I said. "In the case of unforeseen events."

The night Mom had dinner at Frank's, night before last, it was wet and super cold and the slushy snow had been coming down hard all day. Over at Oma and Opa's we built a snow fort in the yard and afterward we had hot chocolate with marshmallows. We all slept in the car on the way home.

That night, I dreamed someone was banging a drum by my head. I woke up and realized it was Kate and Davey, pounding on the wall. I sat up. "What?" I yelled.

The pounding stopped. I heard their door open and they ran down the hall. My door opened and there they stood in their matching flannel nightgowns. They said, at once, "There's a noise."

I sat stiffly holding my sheets to my chest. "What kind of noise? Like a raccoon?"

Kate shook her head. "Like a someone in the house."

The three of us stared at each other, thinking.

"It's probably Mom or Donna," I said. "Did you look in the kitchen?"

Kate stamped her foot. "We already went and checked their room. They're gone, both of them. Gone. This is the emergency. You have to go look and see what it is."

I slid out of bed, put on my shoes, and lifted the baby out of her cradle. She shifted comfortably in my arms and drooled. "All right," I said. "But you're coming with me."

They each grabbed hold of my pajama bottoms and jogged alongside as I went down the hall.

We stopped when we saw him. Dale was sitting at the table. Just sitting there. After a while, he slowly looked up.

He didn't look right. He looked crazy.

"Where's your mother?" he asked Davey.

Davey shook his head and hid behind my leg. I started counting backward by elevens.

"Speak up, boy!" Dale shouted, banging the table and standing up. His chair hit the wall behind him. "Where in the hell is your mother?"

Davey started to cry and that made Kate start to cry, so I said, "Sir, she went for a walk with my mom." I shifted the baby to my other hip and tugged on Davey's ear so he'd shut up.

"Hell she did!" he shouted. Kate and Davey cried harder. My left eye started to twitch. The baby slept on. Dale seemed to calm down and he looked at them distractedly. "All right, then. Get in the truck. Go on." He waved in the direction of the door. "All of you. Go get in the truck."

He sounded tired. We filed out the door and he lifted us into the back of the giant pickup truck that was full of snow and bags of salt. He slammed the door and got in on the other side and reversed with a grinding of gears. We all huddled up with me in the middle and hung on to the sides as we zipped backward out of the driveway and tore around the corner and went straight on Main for a while, whipped right at Ash Street, and slammed to a stop in front of Davey's house. Dale pulled us all out, one after another, and herded us into the kitchen.

Kate and Davey were covered with snot and snow and we were all soaking wet and Kate had the hiccups. "You two," Dale said, picking up first Davey, then Kate, and putting them in kitchen chairs, "Stay put. You move, I'll kill you. You set there till your brother says get up. Gimme that child," he said to me, taking Sarah and stuffing her into her high chair. She fell asleep with her head on its table. "You," he said, turning to me. "Come with me." And he started down the stairs.

I followed him into the darkest part of the basement, where we weren't usually allowed to go. He turned on the light, exposing a plywood worktable piled high with army gear. He reeked of alcohol, something stronger than beer. He was tapping each item, taking inventory of the table's contents: water bottle, bowie knife, flak jacket, rope. A row of just-cleaned guns gleamed, their ammo belts laid alongside.

First, he put on the mud-brown helmet. Then the cargo pants and the flak jacket, and then he leaned down and stuck the bowie knife into his sock. "Here we go," he said to me, strapping two belts of ammo around his waist. "It's time to engage the contingency plan. Events necessitate a shift in strategic maneuver." He clipped his water bottle to his pants and stepped into a pair of combat boots, leaning down to lace them up with violent jerks. He stuffed a revolver into his belt, grabbed the coil of rope, and picked up a rifle. He paced past me, around the central heater and water pipes, to the dark centre of the basement where the drain dripped with melted snow. He picked up a chair. The low table was cleaned off, only the empty ashtray left.

"Set up the sentries," he said, stepping onto the chair and throwing the rope over a pipe. "One at the back door, one at the top of the stairs. Give them both a gun and take one for yourself. They're loaded, so don't shoot each other, for Chrissakes. Use only in the event of an emergency. You'll know what to do," he said, tying a slipknot in the rope. "You're a smart kid, you'll make a fine soldier. This is your first mission. Go on and put them in position."

I went and got the guns. This is my first mission, I thought. I am Lieutenant Esau Elton Schiller and I have a duty to do. It is not mine to say right or wrong. I answer to my superiors. I wrapped an ammo belt around my waist and headed up the stairs with my arms full of guns. My duty is toward my country, I thought. The people who serve it are held in highest regard. I am entrusted with the rights and privileges of my fine rank, and held to its responsibilities. Rounding the corner, I found Kate and Davey huddled together on one chair. When they saw the guns, Kate's face went white.

"You have to be sentries," I said.

After a minute, Davey said, "What're sentries?"

"You have to stand guard at your post. One at the back door, one at the top of the stairs. Kate, you're at the door. Davey, you get the stairs. Take the baby into the living room."

Davey picked her up and staggered off with her. A second later, he returned. Kate said, "Who are we shooting?"

"I don't know yet," I said. "It's not ours to judge." The clock ticked in the frontal area of my skull. Toward the back, the drain dripped. In my inner ear was the sound of rope rubbing against rope, and a chair scooting loudly on concrete.

"What are we guarding against?" Davey asked, and approached me slowly, eying the guns.

"Intrusion," I said. "Surprise attack."

He nodded and gingerly lifted the smallest gun from the top of the pile. Holding it like you would a pair of scissors, by the handle, facing the ground, he backed toward the stairwell and pressed himself to the kitchen wall.

Kate jumped off the chair, came forward, and put out her arms. She sank under the weight of the gun. She sat down on the floor with her back to the door. I said, "Point it at the stove." She set the gun on the linoleum and carefully turned it so it faced the stove.

I was left with only one gun, the biggest of the three. I held it the way my father had shown me when I was six: across my midsection, right hand wrapped over the hilt, left hand wrapped under the barrel, for maximum safety and speed. "All right," I said. "Stay still. Stay there till I come up. Davey, take your hand off the trigger. Just hold it by the handle. Okay. I'm going down."

Holding the gun tense and just away from my body, I marched down the stairs.

Dale was standing on the chair with his neck in the rope's loop. Peering out at me from under his helmet, he said, "We're good to go?"

I nodded.

"Ten-four," he said, and pushed his shoulders back. "Get me a gun."

I went around to the table and came back with a snub-nosed revolver.

"Perfect," he said, looking at it, pleased. "You are a smart son of a bitch, you know that? You've done well." He looked down at me and smiled.

"Thank you, sir," I said.

He saluted me. I saluted him in return.

"Soldier, turn around to face the stairs," he said. I did, and closed my eyes.

I decided I would not turn around.

No, I thought. A soldier does not shirk his duty in the field. A soldier has a responsibility to account for all members of his platoon, and to report the dead.

The reverb of the shot was ringing off the concrete walls and spiraling into my ears like a screw. The sound of the shot itself had lodged at the top of my spine. The wooden chair had cracked against the floor.

I decided it would not be necessary to turn around.

"Sir," I said. I counted to one hundred, then said, "Sir," again.

One dead.

I marched forward and came to the bottom of the stairs. "Attention!" I called. "Lay down your weapons! That is an order!"

"Is it safe?" Davey called down. His small body was outlined against the kitchen light and he held his gun straight at me. Right hand on the trigger, left hand over the barrel. The most accurate hold, a marksman's hold.

"Pretty much," I called up. He clicked the safety on the gun and laid it down. "Stay put, Kate!" he commanded, and thumped out of sight. I came up the stairs.

Kate wouldn't let go of her gun. Davey tried to take it from her but she yelled at him. He tried coming up from behind her, but she bit his ear. Finally he looked up at me.

I shrugged and slumped down in a chair at the kitchen table. "Let her have it if she wants it," I said. "She's probably scared."

"I'm not scared," she said calmly, the gun on her lap. "I just want to hold it."

"Put on the safety," I said, "and you can hold it."

"Okay," she said. "Where's the safety?"

Davey showed her the safety. She clicked it and settled back against the door.

We sat there awhile. I wiped my forehead with the cuff of my pajama sleeve. It was hot.

"Is my dad dead?" Davey asked.

I nodded. "One man down."

Davey sank down next to Kate. She lay her head on his shoulder, patted his knee, and put her hand back on the gun. Then Davey gently lifted her head, stood up, crossed the kitchen, and opened the cupboard beneath the sink. He crawled in. Kate, looking torn, laid down the gun and followed him in. They sat quietly, their four bare feet sticking out.

Through the window it was still deep dark. I looked at the clock. It was only one in the morning. There were hours and hours till day.

I stood up and went over to the phone by the fridge. I dialed Frank's number, which I had memorized in the event of an emergency such as this. Behind me, Davey started to cry with maybe sadness or tiredness or relief.

EPILOGUE: KATE

Let me begin again.

Far north, in the centre of winter, I am leaning in the bedroom doorway. The flowers, dead in a vase on a table in the corner of the room. The music box, lid ajar but not singing. A pack of old matches, one dead match. The clothes by the side of the bed, still holding their shape: the sock wearing an invisible foot. The jeans wearing a woman's hips, curved, as if she lay on her side on the floor. The sweater's arm flung up in a gesture, as if in sleep.

The sound of my hands, dry and whispering to each other, keeps some sort of time.

A man is sleeping. Facedown, his shoulders a separate shade of white from the sheets, a shade separated by shadow, lines like a charcoal drawing.

Here in the deep north a man is sleeping. From the doorway, I watch the way moonlight slides down the curve of his lower back, giving it a gleam, seashell smooth, that sunlight would never allow. He sleeps. I can feel the heat of his body from here.

I go down the hall, the floor cold against my feet. I press my fingertips to their doors as I go by: Peter, curled in a knot at the foot of his bed; David, snoring, one socked foot dangling out from under the covers; Sophie, belly down in her crib. I hold still, willing my heart to hush so I can hear their breath. Under Esau's door, a fan of light on the floor: I pause, and hear a shuffle of papers, muttering. He does his best work at night.

I hurry down the stairs to the kitchen, shifting from foot to foot, waiting for water to boil. I watch the winter moon on the white row of roofs, and the way the moonlight avoids the darker hollows of the bare black trees.

We have an easy life. We have our family, and coffee and the children and the paper. We have quilts. Downstairs, the grandfather clock tells four.

Soon it will be five. At five, it is almost day. I can make coffee and wait for the paper. And wait for him to come down, bleary-eyed, smiling, kissing me, Morning, good morning, I'll say.

You cannot live with the past cluttering up the house. You cannot waste your love. You must love what is left, and has the will to live.

The past ends, in my mind, the night that Davey's father died. After that, we became what we are. People need their broken places, their secrets and stories. Once you have these things, you can go on. Then they either kill you or they don't.

That night, Mom and Donna and Frank all showed up at once, and when we told them what had happened, there was crying and yelling and it was loud and confusing. Frank went downstairs and came back up. Then Donna bent over and let out a wail like an animal and he grabbed her by the shoulders and led her into the front room. I heard her say, "How am I supposed to do laundry now? How can I go down there?" and start crying again.

Davey and I sat silently in the cupboard with the cleaning supplies.

Davey shifted and sighed. "Now both our dads are dead," he said flatly.

I scratched my nose. It was true.

"Should we get out of the cupboard now?" I said finally.

He considered this.

"In the morning we could make a snow grave," he said, somewhat cheered.

"Okay," I said. "We could get Esau to bury us."

They came and dragged us out of the snow graves the next morning, though. We spent the next day floating through the house like small phantoms, trying not to disturb Donna, who sat rocking, rocking in her chair, holding baby Sarah on her lap, staring straight ahead and silently crying. My mother murmured on the phone. We had cereal for dinner, and Davey fell asleep with his head on the table. Frank carried him upstairs and put him in bed. I crawled in next to him.

"Shove over," I whispered, and grabbed a pillow. He looked at me, blinking.

He sighed. "He's in heaven, probably," he said.

"Yeah."

He nodded and rolled over with his back to me. I threw my arm over his side so he'd know I was there for sure.

Down the hall, his mother cried, and the floor creaked under her feet.

I woke early the next morning. Over Davey's shoulder, I watched the sun rise, all red and orange.

Let me try again and then I swear I will begin.

Memory is a story. It is a story from a long time ago. It is a movie one recalls having seen. It is seen in frames and images, out of sequence, disorderly, without reason or plot.

And now this. The shocking tumble of children who are somehow my own. Esau, his papers, his orderly walk to the library and back. The strangely elegant dream of his days. My mother and Frank, their shoveled front steps, the fragile invention of their life. The calendar, the clock, the graveyard, the pastor, the grocer, the town to which we are chained. The man whose heavy sleep gives this all a centre, who has mass and holds down the bed.

I am always afraid that he will step just slightly to the side. That the crucial joint will slip and the floors fall askew, leaving me skidding, sliding backward, arms reaching out for the toppling walls.

But he won't. He can't. He was there. We put up the storm windows and brace the house for cold.

Our house is very clean and everything matches. He is untidy and easy in his bulk, and throws his coat on the sofa, and swings the children in the air. He holds my waist when he kisses me hello, I hang up the coat, trailing behind him, picking up the pieces of paper and mail he drops as he goes, the scarves, the hat and gloves, the tangle of words he tosses over his shoulder like a pinch of salt, scattering all over the floor. I pick these things up and put them in their place.

This is how I love him. I love him. He knows this as well as he knows the beat of his own heart, without question or notice or need. This is how he loves me. This is as it should be.

I sip my tea and start up the creaking stairs, my limbs cracking with cold. He shifts in bed, turns onto his back. A thin wind spins helixes of sharp snow from the eaves.

Soft as a sigh in sleep, the centre of winter implodes.

Sometimes, when I crawl into bed with him, I confuse my breath for his breath. He flings his arm over my side, as he's always done, since we were small.

"Dave," I whisper.

He smiles. "Hmm."

Now I will begin.

My name is Kate.

P.S.

Ideas,
interviews
& features ...

Author Biography

School
"Nature is more powerful than education; time will develop anything" Benjamin Disraeli

Marya Hornbacher's education followed an excessively intricate course. She bobbed up in college at only sixteen. There, at the University of Minnesota, she majored in philosophy and almost certainly vexed her peers with garish exhibitions of early development. She transferred to American University (Washington, D.C.) on a Presidential Scholarship and once again laid siege to the philosophical realm. She then transferred back to U of M on yet another scholarship, plunged into the English program, and received a veritable bouquet of awards. After student-teaching for two years, she pardoned herself from her studies – or, as she calls it, "dropped out."

She resurfaced at the New College of California, aged twenty-three, and not only finished her BA in philosophy but picked up an MA in poetics and held down an assistant professorship in the English department. The end of her studies marked no small cause for celebration. "I wore," she says, "an excellent dress to my graduation party, got insanely drunk, and my mother broke all my china in a fit of pique."

Work
"The only thing I was fit for was to be a writer, and this notion rested solely on my suspicion that I would never be fit for real work, and that writing didn't require any" Russell Baker

Marya Hornbacher's job experience is by her own admission "limited." She did not, for instance, put in time as either a flag-waver on a road crew (as did novelist Louise Erdrich) or a mannequin-dresser for a department store (as did novelist Russell Banks). She did, though, work at a popular hamburger establishment. "I started working at McDonald's (illegally) when I was fourteen. I was almost a manager when I quit to take my first job as a reporter; I was especially good at fries. My only negative experience there was when some jerk threw a bacon-egg-and-cheese biscuit at me because it 'looked funny.'"

During college she wrote an academic book, worked full-time as a reporter/editor, harvested more awards, and wrote *Wasted*, a memoir about her struggle to overcome bulimia and anorexia. "I decided to write the book because there was a gaping hole in the literature on eating disorders. I felt strongly that much of what had been written about them was romanticized and glamorized (that 'oh these mysterious girls' attitude, unbalanced by the gory, physical reality of a fatal disease – an attitude which only feeds our fanatical worshipping of the anorexic iconography around us)."

Also during this time, she was married and divorced and otherwise preoccupied with geographical reassignments of herself – twelve moves in all. (She now lives in Minneapolis.)

Following the above jobs – as newspaper reporter and as managing editor of a small wire service in D.C. – she served a magazine ▶

6 My only negative experience there was when some jerk threw a bacon-egg-and-cheese biscuit at me. 9

Author Biography *(continued)*

◀ internship writing features, including "a long piece on window treatments, though I can't remember why." ("Washington," she wrote in the *Guardian*, "was very exciting. I remember it vaguely for the most part, because I was dying.") In 1993, she won the White Award for best feature story of the year.

Next came a long writing period. "I supported myself by working at a totally dysfunctional Baskin-Robbins, Kinko's, and Bruegger's. I lived on pistachio ice cream and salt bagels, and stole all my writing paper from the Kinko's gig." It was during this time that she began to publish stories and poetry.

In 1998, *Wasted* hit the shelves and struck the critics with wonder. "Hornbacher," said the *New York Times Book Review*, "describes [eating disorders] with a stark candor that captures both their pain and underlying purposes ... She is wise beyond her years."

The author had yet to finish school. She went on a long book and lecture tour, after which she began to teach English and to write her novel. "I messed around with *The Centre of Winter* for an absurdly long time. At some point I developed, edited, and wrote for an arts section in a magazine, which required me to work in an office; I am not good at working in an office, so I resigned and continued writing. Finally I finished the novel and sent it off, and then it came out and so forth, and now I am working on a new novel, research for a new nonfiction book, and a bunch of articles for various magazines." She is "vaguely" at work upon a book of poetry, too.

❝ I lived on pistachio ice cream and salt bagels, and stole all my writing paper from the Kinko's gig. ❞

She has lectured on writing and culture at many universities, including Yale, Columbia, Vassar, and Bennington. In 2004, she was honored with a Yale Morse Fellowship.

Play (or Travel)

"Travel is the most private of pleasures. There is no greater bore than the travel bore. We do not in the least want to hear what he has seen in Hong-Kong" Vita Sackville-West

Marya Hornbacher now and then slips away from her routines of literary production and volunteerism (at homeless shelters). Such occasions afford the opportunity to travel between Minneapolis and St. Paul; sometimes she betakes herself to places more distant still. Favorite journeys include many trips to London and the surrounding countryside, to St. Lucia, and Portugal. The Netherlands she has survived: "Amsterdam was neat, though everyone was incredibly tall and I almost fell into a canal." When possible, she visits New York, the Oregon Coast, and Mexico. She is unimpeachably Minnesotan, plucky and robust: "I've done a lot of long-distance hiking, and my favorite hike so far covered a lot of the Sonoran Desert. I love to travel, and it is a good thing my job is portable or I would never get anything done." ∎

❝ She is unimpeachably Minnesotan, plucky and robust. ❞

My Love Song to the North

I WAS BORN IN California, where wild birds of paradise grew untended next to the house, wisteria wound over the roofs and down the sides of narrow, colorful houses, the hills rose up and slid down, and the bay sent clouds of low-slung fog through the hard city streets. California is Eden for a child, and I loved it. But Minnesota is home.

The thousands of lakes sprawling and sparkling a brilliant blue, the dense foliage and subtropical wet heat of summer, the wildflowers of the prairie, the long wide ribbons of road that amble through fields of corn – and the winters, the thick sheaves of snow that slip from the roofs of farmhouses and city homes, sifting to the ground, where they slide into the slopes of snow that lean against the house, the bitter hard cold that presses against your chest and takes your breath, and the red-brick and cobblestone heritage of an old river city, the small towns and diners, the thick accent, the hallowed tradition of coffee and pie, and the rich history of a hard immigrant life: this is the place where my grandparents lived, where my German-Russian great-grandparents found themselves after a long voyage from Odessa, Ukraine, where I grew up and fell in love with the landscape and rhythm of seasons, where I am able to settle into an old house and sit, in winter, in front of my fireplace and write in the season's stillness and peace. I have moved away countless times, and yet I return and return. This place reaches into my heart and holds it tight. I couldn't leave if I tried.

> 6 The small towns and diners, the thick accent, the hallowed tradition of coffee and pie, and the rich history of a hard immigrant life … 9

The Centre of Winter is my love song to the north. I came here as a child and spent summers in my grandparents' house, running barefoot down the beach and waking to the smell of homemade yeasty cinnamon rolls rising in the kitchen. The characters of Oma and Opa, Kate and Esau's grandparents, who struggle through the loss of their children and protect Kate, Claire, and Esau from the force of their grief in the wake of Arnold's death, wise and warm people who rest their bones in a tiny northern town, are based on my own grandparents, Ben (Barnard) and Ellen Hornbacher, who played bridge and drank and loved each other there, and whose arms were wide and welcoming. Our enormous family gathered on holidays and shouted and laughed till the uncles fell asleep and snored in the chairs. I remember sitting in the kitchen with my beloved cousins Christie and Brian in my silly red snowsuit on Christmas Eve, all of us wild and impatient for the presents we'd open after midnight church, waiting in hopes of snacks from the feast my grandmother prepared.

The characters that populate this book are based on my years of listening, in diners and bars, at weddings and funerals, to the farmers, the hard-drinking men, the stoic women who loved fiercely and with food. Donna, Frank, Dale, Claire, and the children live in a difficult world that is regulated by the seasons, the dark months of winter and the beauty of summer, fall, and spring. This is a place of powerful feelings, difficult struggles with the forces of nature, tight ▶

> ❝ The characters are based on my years of listening to the farmers, the hard-drinking men, the stoic women who loved fiercely and with food. ❞

My Love Song to the North *(continued)*

◀ families who love each other deeply and shout over each other to be heard.

I'm a solitary sort of person, and I find myself most at home where I can hide in the house and walk in the mountains and forests that cluster at the edges of vast Lake Superior. In winter, I wake while it is still dark, wrap myself in blankets, and sit down to write each morning. One hibernates in winter, scuttling from place to place, huddled against the cold. In spring, I watch through the windows of my room as a green-gray rain slushes down, melts the snow, and summons the season's early flowers from the ground. In summer, my windows are wide and the sun plays over my hands as I write, the geese honking loudly as they fly by. I walk down by the lake each day, breathing in the smell of new grass and water and the warm summer breeze. In fall, outside my window, the trees spread out their brilliant red and orange and pink and yellow leaves, all showy and proud. The smell of wood smoke in the dusky evenings drifts through the yards, piercing the cool night air.

I have always lived in the city, and I make my home in Minneapolis, but the tight-knit, hard-living small towns have warmth and a closeness that comforts me. Motley, Minnesota, is a real town, and in writing *The Centre of Winter*, I drove out of the city and up County Road 10, past roadside farmers' markets and through the low rises and falls of the farmland, to visit the town. Frank's Bar, where Arnold drank in solitude, where Claire paid his bills, and where she later danced slow with Frank as she was beginning to come alive again after Arnold's death, is

❛ Motley, Minnesota, is a real town; Frank's Bar, where Arnold drank in solitude, is actually called the Hi-Top Bar. ❜

actually called the Hi-Top Bar, across the narrow Main Street from the old houses that cluster along the neighborhood's neat rows. Nimrod, where Oma and Opa live, is an actual town as well – you turn right off County Road 10 and travel nineteen miles east and you'll find yourself on the brief flicker of Main Street. If you blink, you'll miss it. I set the book there because I've driven through it every summer and winter, on my way to Detroit Lakes, since I was very small. Growing up, my cousins and I would bounce on our seats, shrieking, "Motley Motley! Motley Motley!" and collapsing in giggles as we drove past Y-Knot liquors and on toward the town of Staples, where we always stopped for lunch at the now long-gone Cardinal Café, where the pie was homemade and gizzards were on the menu, along with every food imaginable – deep fried.

A lot of writers make their home here, and I'm convinced it's the perfect place to write. I, too, live by the seasons, and I love the window that looks out on the landscape where I live. *The Centre of Winter* deals with the pain, joy, and daily life of the place I live, a place where the ghosts of the Iron Range linger, where people have come from many countries to make their way, where kids bundle up in snowsuits and leap into the snow and lie on their backs and make snow angels and run inside again at night and sleep the deepest kind of dreamless sleep ■

> ❝ *The Centre of Winter* deals with the pain, joy, and daily life of the place I live. ❞

Marya Hornbacher's Favorite Novels

Beloved
Toni Morrison
Perhaps the most powerful, brilliant book I have ever read, this story changed my life, gave me a glimpse into the horror of slavery and its terrible impact upon the people who suffered under it, and presented me with a staggering interpretation of legend and a kind of writing I had never read before. This is one of the most important books ever written, probably the best of the twentieth century.

One Hundred Years of Solitude
Gabriel García Márquez
This epic sweeps through time and tells the tale of the mythical town of Macondo through the lives of the many members of the Buendía family. Love affairs, the entanglement of family and history, magical myth, and breathtaking prose all mark this famous work by the master storyteller.

The Sun Also Rises
Ernest Hemingway
One of the major novels of the twentieth century and perhaps even further back, this is Hemingway at his peak. The spare, incisive prose and the beautifully drawn story are gruffly tender, painful, and a classic example of the delicate power of pared-down language and great plot.

The Great Gatsby
F. Scott Fitzgerald
I reread this one at least once a year.

> ❛ *Beloved* is one of the most important books ever written, probably the best of the twentieth century. ❜

Fitzgerald's astonishing insight into early-twentieth-century American culture, into the lives of the wealthy, empty, and longing characters, into youth and folly, should be required reading for anyone who wants to understand the strange evolution of this country.

Ulysses
James Joyce
A day in the life of a deeply weird man, this epic moves into the mind of one Leopold Bloom. By turns hilarious, purple-prosed, oppressively interior, and moving, this is one of the outstanding books of the modern period.

Mrs. Dalloway
Virginia Woolf
Written around the same time as *Ulysses* — oddly, Joyce and Woolf hated each other's work — Woolf's version of a day in the life of a woman living in tightly circumscribed circumstances in London society, perched stiffly at the edge of her life, as she prepares for a party, is one of the most piercing, accurate explorations of the quiet madness of a stifled soul.

The Handmaid's Tale
Margaret Atwood
Another classic, this terrifying, beautifully written book is a futuristic story that is haunting in its plausibility. An argument against the tightening grip of a society where women and their bodies are under siege, ▶

> ❛ *Mrs. Dalloway* is one of the most piercing, accurate explorations of the quiet madness of a stifled soul. ❜

Favorite Novels *(continued)*

◀ this is an absolutely crucial book to this culture.

Anna Karenina
Leo Tolstoy
A novel of a man and a woman both trapped in the restrictive roles imposed by society, this is one of the greatest books ever written. A sweeping criticism of society, Tolstoy's classic manages to weave an intricate story of two people who break free of social demands and begin new lives at the edges of their worlds.

> ❝ *The Amazing Adventures of Kavalier & Clay* is easily one of my favorite contemporary novels. ❞

The Beet Queen
Louise Erdrich
A family epic that takes place in the Native American communities in North Dakota, this is the twisting, passionate story of the entangled lives lived over a forty-year period. Generations of the family travel through years of miracles, love affairs, feuds, family mayhem, cultural leaders and small towns, and the entire range of human experience.

The Amazing Adventures of Kavalier & Clay
Michael Chabon
Easily one of my favorite contemporary novels, this modern epic sweeps through the landscape of mid-twentieth-century Middle America. From comics to lifelong friendship to love and sex to music to the very heart of the century, the two title characters inhabit the precarious structures of the American dream, coming out the worse for wear but inextricably bound by friendship and time. ■

Have You Read?

Wasted

Precociously intelligent, imaginative, energetic, and ambitious, Marya Hornbacher grew up in a comfortable middle-class American home. At the age of five, she returned home from ballet class one day, put on an enormous sweater, curled up on her bed, and cried – because she thought she was fat. By age nine she was secretly bulimic, throwing up at home after school, while watching *Brady Bunch* reruns on television and munching Fritos. She added anorexia to her repertoire a few years later and took great pride in her ability to starve.

Her story gathers intensity with each passing year. By the time she is in college and working for a wire news service in Washington, D.C., she is in the grip of a bout of anorexia so horrifying that it will forever put to rest the romance of wasting away. Down to fifty-two pounds and counting, Marya becomes a battlefield: her powerful death instinct at war with the will to live.

Why would a talented young girl go through the looking glass and step into a netherworld where up is down, food is greed, and death is honor? Why enter into a love affair with hunger, drugs, sex, and death? Marya sustained both anorexia and bulimia through five lengthy hospitalizations, endless therapy, the loss of family, friends, jobs, and, ultimately, any sense of what it means to be "normal." In this vivid, emotionally wrenching memoir, she recreates the experience and illuminates the tangle of personal, family ▶

Have You Read? *(continued)*

◀ and cultural causes underlying eating disorders.

"A scary but tentatively triumphant memoir ... Told with grace, sharp humor, and candor." *San Francisco Chronicle*